"THIS IS A MAGICAL COUNTRY. MAYBE IT CURES HEARTACHE."

Others' Child looked up at Night Hawk, startled.

"I have been thinking about Elder Brother and the dead girl baby and the way things were between us before they died," he said.

Others' Child's eyes filled with tears. "Nothing cures heartache," she said tightly, but she put her hand in his.

"I told Sea Otter we would stay a moon," Night Hawk said.

Now her eyes widened. She held out her arms and closed them around his ribs tightly, cutting off his breath.

"I will learn their talk," she said, "and how to cook the snail things and make acorn meal, and I will believe you about the fish that is bigger than a buffalo, and you will not be sorry."

"It's only for a moon," he said.

She smiled at him, rapturous. Anything could happen in a moon.

D1042914

Other Avon Books in
THE DEER DANCERS *Series by*
Amanda Cockrell

THE DEER DANCERS, BOOK ONE:
DAUGHTER OF THE SKY

THE DEER DANCERS, BOOK TWO:
WIND CALLER'S CHILDREN

THE DEER DANCERS

BOOK THREE
The Long Walk

AMANDA COCKRELL

AVON BOOKS ◆ NEW YORK

THE DEER DANCERS, BOOK THREE: THE LONG WALK is an original publication of Avon Books. This work has never before appeared in book form. This work is a novel. Any similarity to actual persons or events is purely coincidental.

AVON BOOKS
A division of
The Hearst Corporation
1350 Avenue of the Americas
New York, New York 10019

For Tony

Introduction

Stories move. They travel, seemingly of their own accord. In our days, they advance swiftly, translated around the world in an electronic blink. But step back. If you lived five thousand years ago among the Kindred of the Rio Grande Valley, where New Mexico is now, news would journey more slowly, but then, too, your world would be compacted. From your summer hunting grounds to the shores of the Endless Water (where our Pacific Ocean laps the California coast) would be a migration of several years, undertaken only by the boldest.

Distance, like time, is a sinew to be stretched and released, and none of our measurements may be true. Permanence lies deeper in the heart, in the first tales told when the people first began to know that they were human and could look for their own truth and make things with it. Mythology holds things that we have always known, because it is of our blood still, the collective story of the human race. Tales out of Africa, out of

China, out of Europe and the Americas may vibrate on the same note.

Walk backwards against the current of Time. Let it lap around your ankles until the barriers between all our modern worlds grow transparent, and anyone may appear. Then you will find Grandmother Spider weaving Time's circular sleeve, and Coyote poking his gray nose through, and Great Condor cleaning up the mess. In our day, we have made them abstract nouns, the stuff of metaphor. We have clothed them with technology to keep them tame, but they do not always obey. In dreamtime they will still come leaping, howling, scuttling into reality, insistently telling their stories, remaking themselves again. And our new stories, which we fling across the world in an electronic heartbeat, are only ripples of those old ones. We are all the children of the First Ones, and Coyote, dancing on the stars, is our uncle.

Prologue

The snow on the winter wind is thin and powdery and dusts Coyote's coat as he scurries along the riverbank. His yellow eyes cut through it like lighted windows. Above him, in the dwellings that the cliff people have built into living rock, Old Grandmother watches him. She is bundled in three blankets, and her eyes are as cloudy as the snow, but she can see him anyway because she knows he is there. He looks up at her, teeth grinning, and she smiles back, toothless. They understand each other.

Coyote is part of the storm in the way that he is part of every wild thing. He is unreliable and untidy, his jokes are crude, and his sexual appetite is insatiable. He is like an uncle, fascinating in his sheer awfulness, who you wish would not visit you. He is Life, which, of course, contains Death. The old woman knows all this because she is aged and ageless, the repository of her people's knowledge, old enough to remember things that

3

happened before she was born, and perhaps things that have not happened yet.

The chieftain of the cliff people peers out the window set in the mud walls of the room. "What are you watching, Old Grandmother?" The riverbank is far below, lost in the swirling snow.

"I am waiting for your people to give me proper respect," the old woman says with asperity. She turns away from the window and settles her two long, thin gray braids over her shoulders, and her fingers across her belly. The fire in the fire pit is smoky but warm, and the chieftain's wife has brought her a hot drink of willow tea for her bones. She allows herself to be mollified.

The cliff people gather around her now, russet-skinned men and women and bundled children, climbing down the ladder through the entrance from the chamber above, settling themselves in the fire's warmth.

The old woman rubs her hands slowly, making the blood flow, pulling out the bones of her story, thinking about Coyote hungry on the riverbank. Winter is the time of death. Firelight tales keep away fear and substitute for full bellies, but they are also the way that the cliff people's children learn how it was in the beginning, so that they may be proper people in the world.

A young man, Old Grandmother's grandson, is beating a clay drum softly at her feet, cross-legged on the mud floor. "There are lands beyond ours," Old Grandmother says, and lets the drumbeats carry her listeners like footsteps through the snow and over the top of Red Rock Mountain until they can see the distance for themselves. "Once, long ago, when people were not at all as we are today, and did not know many things, a man and woman went there and saw wonders.

"These people had only just learned to plant maize and make music on the flute, so you can see that they were very new people, and the world was very young.

"A man had come from the south, a man that Coyote sent, and he brought the people maize and the bone flute. After a while they killed him for it, because he was really a god and they were afraid of him. But before that, he had married a woman of the Yellow Grass People, and his children took the music and the seed to all of the human people, and one of them became Maize Girl, and one of them became Flute Boy, and so that was as it should have been.

"But the third child was a different child, and no one knew what to do with her. She came from a stranger people to begin with. Like her mother, she saw how to make pictures, which was also new and magical then, and to call the game with its own image. But they said that Coyote had been her father, and they may have been right. Grandmother Spider wove her first into the Yellow Grass People, and then into the Squash Band of the Kindred, the stranger people, but each time she ran away. Now she was trying to run away from the man she ran away with. . . .

" 'This is not good.' Grandmother Spider hissed at the places where her web was torn, and knotted them up angrily, swinging her great silver-gray bottom back and forth over the rents. She was very old and powerful even then, and to this day she does not approve of disobedience.

" 'You are wasting your time,' was what Coyote said. 'That one is not likely to do as she is told. She wants something.'

" 'Well, what does she want?' Grandmother Spider said, exasperated. 'She has a man, and babies, and enough to eat, and work to do, and magic, which is all that any human person ought to want.'

" 'For one thing,' Coyote said, grinning, all his teeth showing, 'she wants to know what keeps happening to her babies.'

" 'That is life,' Grandmother Spider said. She finished her mending and hung on the edge of her web, waiting to see what flew into it. 'Look at how many eggs I lay. You can't keep them all.'

" 'She blames me,' Coyote said. He looked cunningly rueful and scratched his ear.

" 'She is foolish,' Spider said, 'even though she is

right.' The earth would be covered like an anthill with human people if none of them died. Coyote keeps the balance, because that is what he is there for.

" 'Everything gets eaten eventually,' Coyote said about that. 'Even I do.'

"As everyone knows, when Coyote dies, he comes back up like the grass in spring, bragging just as loudly and looking for someone to ask him to dinner. Coyote wants, too, just like the third child, the woman whose name was Others' Child because there were no people to whom she belonged. Others' Child wanted, even if she didn't know what it was that she wanted yet. Spider could see that she was going to make trouble with that, because there is nothing as likely to cause misfortune as getting what you want, and you don't have to know what that is to call it. If the sister of Maize Girl and Flute Boy kept running away, it would spread like a disease until everyone was going back and forth where they didn't belong, tilting the Universe with their weight, and then there would be no order in the world. Spider said so, feet dancing angrily on her web, looking down through the stars to which she had anchored it, to the earth below, looking for the woman who was upsetting everything.

"Coyote grinned. He scratched a flea in his dusty yellow-gray coat and did a little dance of his own. Spider could see the pattern in her web, but not the deeper, roiling chaos behind. It was only Coyote who could look on that unafraid and see that without disorder, everything would stop. Without the fly blundering in, the volcano erupting, the rising tide, there would be no change. And then there would be no life, no art, and we would not be able to make beauty."

The cliff people lean forward, poised on the edge of that beautiful and terrible brink, to hear how it was that these things came into the world. . . .

I

Two-Legged

The caves where the Kindred spent the winter were high in the red sandstone mountains. Up there the low sun warmed the rocks for a few hours, and the piñon pines made fat, oily nuts when the ground was covered with snow. Every year, when the browse began to die, the deer moved up the slopes after the nuts, and the Kindred followed the deer.

That was when Night Hawk the Trader and his wife would come home, if they were not wintering elsewhere among monsters and False People—this according to the old Grandmothers of the Kindred, who knew that all that was real and true fell within the borders of the Kindred's hunting grounds and the bloodlines of the Kindred. Night Hawk's wife had been born to the Kindred, but then she had been lost to the Trespassers in the south, and anyone could see what had come of that. She was not called Others' Child by both peoples for nothing. As for Night Hawk, that one had been footloose since a hawk had flown across his mother's path when she carried him. The Grandmothers told each other this with emphatic nods and gestures, toothless lips compressed.

Winter was the slow time, the digging-in time, like rabbits into burrows. The women made clothes from the hides tanned in summer and fall, the Three Old Men talked to the gods about the Sun, and the other men gossiped, and hunted if the weather was good. When the weather was *not* good, which was as often as not, the Kindred lived on stories told around the fire pit to quiet rumbling stomachs. In winter no one was ever really alone, not even if he was dying. The caves were smoky and cramped, and your neighbors knew all your business, and you theirs.

Now it was the third moon after Turn-of-the-Year, and the mountains were wet with melting slush, which made the faint new green of the aspens look like leaves of ice. Night Hawk was sharpening his spears and mending his pack and his dogs' travois, and whenever he looked up from that, his eyes went over the horizon.

In winter, the Kindred could see south down the red mountains to the high blue peaks beyond, with the river valley in between, and farther yet the black desert, leavings of a time when fire had come out of the earth and melted the stone. Everyone knew that country—they hunted over it. But behind them to the north lay the high desert and the land where the dead lived under their lake. In the east, the buffalo hunters lived on the plains, and the tall grass went on for miles. And beyond the high mountains to the west lay the coast, where the Endless Water lapped at the shore and the people ate strange, spined fish. The Grandmothers didn't know about any of those last, nor did they wish to be told.

Others' Child was making yucca rope, twisting the fibers on her thigh, rolling them expertly against her deer-hide leggings with one flat palm. They always seemed to need more rope by year's end, and rope making was not something to be done in one evening, on the trail. The late winter air had a bite to it, and the wind had picked up, whipping the cold damp off the melting snow and flinging it at them like a wet hide, puffing up the smoke from the hearth in gray clouds. She coughed, and her eyes streamed. The Grandmothers flapped their hands in front of their faces. When they peered through the smoke at her, they looked like the wrinkled masks that the Three Old Men put on to tell the future.

"It is going to be another boy." Old Woman Many Grandsons poked a finger at Others' Child's thickening waist. "I can tell. You should stay here until it comes. Otherwise it will be unlucky, like the last one."

For a fleeting moment, Others' Child yearned to stay. Then she saw the other old grannies watching her with tooth-sucking disapproval, and her own sister, Maize Came, bouncing her fat son and daughter on her knee, and rebelled. "The last one was not unlucky," she said. Little Brother was sitting by the fire pit, fanning the smoke away from his mother and her visitors with a deer-hide fan. She knew they were talking about Elder Brother, who was dead now (a quick stab in her heart when she thought of him) or the one she had lost on the trail halfway through her term. But really they had come to tell her what she ought to be doing. That was never what she *was* doing, according to the grannies. Others' Child had grown up with the Trespassers, and so she was tainted and forever suspect.

"Unlucky is finding death in your trail," Grandmother Snake said.

"Coyote will get it like the last one," Grandmother Watcher said.

Others' Child put her hand on her belly. It was too soon to feel the new one moving, but she willed it to give her some sign, something to counter the Grandmothers and their vociferous disapproval of all that she did. They didn't cluck their tongues at Night Hawk, her husband, she had noted. He was male, of course; his wanderings didn't tie knots in the rituals the Kindred had devised for themselves. There was a proper way to do everything, from making snowshoes to boiling soap, and Others' Child's ways were all wrong, primarily because she wasn't penitent, did not regret sufficiently the years she had been separated from the Kindred.

"They mean well," Maize Came said when the Grandmothers had been fed with mush and dried meat and had consented to go on their way again. Maize Came smoothed back the sleek bands of her black hair from her round, beautiful face, and smiled affectionately at Others' Child.

"They are stupid," Others' Child said. "That is not the same as meaning well."

"How can you talk like that about your own people!" Maize Came was shocked. Since she had married, Maize Came had grown very orderly.

"*Your* people," Others' Child said. "They are your people." Which was ironic, because Others' Child had been born to the Kindred, and Maize Came to the Yellow Grass People, which was the true name for the Trespassers. But Maize Came had brought the great gift, the maize. She was holy now, whereas Others' Child was only willful. Others' Child fingered the angular bump in her nose, and the abrupt jut of her chin. It didn't matter what she looked like; she wasn't theirs.

"You think everyone is stupid," Maize Came said astutely, "when they don't agree with you."

"No one has to agree with me," Others' Child muttered. She wrapped her fingers around the yucca rope she had been plaiting and jerked vengefully on it, straightening out the kinked coils. She wished she could straighten out her life that easily, just shake it and give it a good yank. "I only wish they would stop telling me how I should do things, and what I have not done that I ought to do, and how my husband will hardly stay with his people over winter now—as if that was my fault."

"That one had a wandering foot when you met him," Maize Came said placidly, with the contentment of a woman whose own husband was important in the councils of the tribe. "They are only vexed because they said that no one would marry you, when you came back to them and weren't biddable, and then he did."

"Well, that is stupid," Others' Child said stubbornly. "They didn't want him to marry one of *their* women and take her foot-on-trail. Me, they could spare."

Maize Came giggled. "Well, you don't listen to them. Why should they love you? They are old. All they have to enjoy is making people listen to them. One day you will be like that."

All women were, Others' Child thought. It was the only power they had. "I will not," she said defiantly. She would make trouble instead. The Grandmothers could wait and see.

Others' Child thought resentfully of ways to make trouble all the next day while she sewed a deer-hide shirt for Night Hawk. The bone needle drew the sinew in and out through precisely punched holes—no one could say that Others' Child could not make fine clothes. She would decorate this shirt with turkey feathers, she thought, a row of them all along the bottom. She had a hoarded sack of them. Maybe she would put some on Little Brother's new shirt, too, and listen to the Grannies squawk about that: *She spoils that child, it will come to no good end. It's because the other one died, of course. She grew too fond of it, and an evil spirit heard her. You should never praise your children. That one praised her children.*

Others' Child knew that she wasn't the only mother to have had a child die of a fever, much less to miscarry one. But it seemed to her that too much of her life had been loss, and she had grown fiercely resentful. Of what or whom, she was less certain.

Her mother among the Yellow Grass People had died when they had killed her husband, Others' Child's foster father—just faded away like smoke thinning in the air, until she was gone. Maize Came, Others' Child's sister, was settled among the Kindred. She was holy, and they approved of her. Mocking Bird, her brother, had gone back to the Yellow Grass People and was chief of the hunters there. He had even made his peace with old Cat Ears, who had killed their father. Even Others' Child's birth mother from the Kindred, Leaf Fall, had given up trying to make her be the way she should, and now she mothered Maize Came instead. Others' Child made a face. She loved Maize Came, but it was hard not to resent her complacency. Why did everyone know their place, like geese homing in the winter, except for Others' Child?

Her fingers were numb, and she blew on them to warm them. The air had turned cold again overnight, and the wind was blowing a storm in. She lifted her face to the gray-white sky hanging like goose down above the cliffs. *It will snow,* she thought, even though it was late in the year for it. She put her sewing down and went to find Little Brother. Snow changed the landscape. A child who remembered only one winter here might become lost, confused by the reflected similarity of sky and earth. In such a storm he might wander upward and be taken by the clouds.

She found him by Maize Came's fire, playing with his cousins, his body bundled in his old deer-hide shirt and too-small leggings lined with coyote fur, his breath a frosty white cloud in front of his face. The cousins had a puppy in the cave with them and rolled on the pine-needle floor with it, shrieking.

Maize Came squinted at Others' Child's shadow in the cave mouth. "It will be fine tracking weather when this clears," she said. "That man of yours came looking for mine, and they've gone to talk to Deer Old Man about where the deer are bedding."

Others' Child thought hungrily of fresh meat. The store of dried venison was nearly gone, and early this moon the Kindred had eaten the last of the deer they had killed at midwinter and buried in the frozen ground. All the men would hunt as soon as the snow stopped. The deer were wary in winter, and they moved often, looking for browse and piñon nuts. Hoofprints in the frozen earth were hard to read, but snow made visible all the hidden trails, wrote the secrets of the deer across the ground.

That night the Kindred huddled in their caves, encapsulated in the falling snow, grateful for its insulation and protection from the harsh, raw wind. The red glow of their fires leaked past the hide curtains and splashed the white ground. Night Hawk slept restlessly, thrashing against Others' Child and Brother, stirring the blankets into unwieldy mounds. Others' Child snatched the blankets back, found one of his dogs snoring beside her instead of her husband, and burrowed against it for warmth.

Night Hawk left before daylight with Maize Came's husband, Wing Foot, and the other men. When the dogs went with him, Others' Child came fully awake, solitary in the cold, Little Brother buried in the mound of blankets. Others' Child flung herself off the bed and poked up the fire. Only an undutiful wife slept while her husband went hunting, unfed. She wondered if he had tried to wake her. These days she slept deeply, all her energy put to growing the baby inside her.

Others' Child looked out the cave mouth, pulling back the hanging hide that curtained it. The world was smooth and white, the trees capped with it. Not a deep snow, this late in the season, and perfect for tracking. The men's feet crisscrossed the camp, dogs' paws pattering beside them, ghost hunters and ghost dogs in the morning sun, only their footprints visible.

Others' Child made maize cake on a flat stone in the fire. Brother, only recently weaned, woke and butted against her breast.

"No, you are big now." Others' Child pushed him away and gave him a piece of hot cake and a drink of water from the skin that hung from a peg driven deep into a cleft of the cave wall. She patted her thickening waist. "I'll have another to feed soon enough."

Little Brother pouted. She wasn't sure he understood. At two, in his world, people came and went mysteriously, their traffic an enigma to him. She wasn't even sure he understood what had happened to Elder Brother, only that now there was no one to play with. He clung to his young cousins lest they somehow vanish, too.

At nightfall, the men came back with a deer slung from carrying poles, laughing and pleased with themselves. It was a winter deer, thin as old bones, its hide mottled with bald patches and scars.

"Yah hah, it probably fell down dead of fright when it saw you," Others' Child said, laughing.

Night Hawk ruffled her hair. "I had to kill it three times. It was so thin my spear went through without hitting anything."

"If the wife of Night Hawk doesn't like our deer, she needn't eat any of it," Wing Foot said huffily, so Others' Child stopped laughing to placate him. One couldn't joke with Wing Foot the way she did with Night Hawk, she had learned. To Wing Foot everything was important.

"It is a fine deer, and the men are very wonderful to catch it," she said dutifully. She caught Night Hawk's mouth twitching and looked away from him so she wouldn't laugh.

Night Hawk went away arm in arm with Wing Foot while the women skinned the deer. The hunters ringed the communal fire on the edge of the dance ground and danced their thanks to the gods for the meat, their voices rising and falling in the still air, their footsteps silent in the soft snow. When they were finished, they sat down on hides around the fire and warmed their hands and told jokes and lies. Others' Child could hear their voices and pick out Night Hawk's from the rest, as soft and melodious as his flute. He was happy here in the company of these men, she thought. He had become a man in the same year as Wing Foot, and he had the respect of the Three Old Men who were chieftains over the Squash Band of the Kindred. What more did he want?

She hacked at the deer with her skinning knife, her fingers numb again.

"You'll spoil the hide," Old Woman Many Grandsons said, breathing the smell of onions and bad teeth on Others' Child's neck. "That is not the way to do it."

"Old Woman should stand closer to the hide," Others' Child said crossly. "So she can see that it is bad already. And maybe she will give me lessons." She held up her skinning knife with one hand while she tugged at the loose edge of the hide with the other.

Old Woman Many Grandsons stalked away muttering,

and Others' Child grinned. She could find as tart a tongue as they had. And it didn't matter. When the snow melted she and her family would be gone. Whether she was ready to go or not wouldn't matter, either.

If Spider had asked Others' Child, when she first went to sleep in Night Hawk's cave, what she wanted, Others' Child would have said just this: not to have to listen to the Grandmothers. Nor to the elders of the Yellow Grass People, who had raised her and then killed her father with rocks because they thought he was a god who had given them magic and then taken it away from them. She would have said, "I will go foot-on-trail with my husband," and meant it—even though she had done that already with her brother and sister for three turns of the year, between the Yellow Grass People and their coming to the Kindred. With a husband it would be different—with a man who made her skin ache when she looked at him. But now the ground was harder than it had been, and one of her knees hurt when she climbed.

Others' Child snuck a look at Night Hawk while Little Brother paddled in the stream at her feet. She saw how even the curve of his back was familiar to her now—she would have known him by that one line, bent over his snare, the vertebrae making little knots in his russet skin. She could close her eyes, too, feel the bones under his flesh, and know him. It was only the country behind him that changed, yanking her out of one place into the next.

Just now he was silhouetted against towering peaks of gray rock, as angular as his bones and capped with snow. There were still teeth in the air, and she thought they should still be with the Kindred in their winter caves. But this year Night Hawk had been ready to leave them early. Budding like the willow tree, Others' Child thought, with a green urge to be gone.

He looked up from his snare, his cropped hair hanging in his eyes, and beckoned to Little Brother. Brother hopped up and padded through the reeds to him, his mother forgotten.

"This is how it is done," Night Hawk said, and Brother watched solemnly as he knotted the line.

"Duck?" Brother said hopefully and watched the sky.

"Ducks. And then maybe we will have green feathers to take to the people at the Endless Water."

"Yah bah," Others' Child said to the turtle shell she was cleaning in the stream. "This many years ago you were going to show me the Endless Water." She held up five fingers to Night Hawk's back. "So far I have seen strangers' villages and too much empty country." She sighed, because at first she had loved that. It was easy to remember, but not to bring back the joy of it.

There were things that the other women of her people had never seen, that Others' Child had walked up to and touched—tall, needlelike spires of rock towering above her, raised fingertips of stone. Bones half buried in a riverbank, that once had been a cat longer than twice her height, with fangs the length of her forearm. She had seen its skull, and the ribs protruding from the clay, and her heart had hammered in her own ribs for an hour afterward.

All that had been before the babies had begun to come. Before Elder Brother and Little Brother and the one she had lost. Before this new one in her belly had left her slow and waddling again. Before she had found that she couldn't go like Bitch and have them by the trail and raise them rough and leave them to fend for themselves in a year.

Night Hawk came up through the reeds with Little Brother on his shoulders. "I have a mind that we'll trade with the buffalo hunters this season," he said. "There has been rain, and the grass will be tall. They will have hides to trade for that greenstone we brought from the south last year."

Others' Child scratched the outline of a duck in the mud on the riverbank for good luck in the snares, and stood up stiffly. The dogs' gray heads popped from the grass beside her, out of their trampled-down nest. Thief and Gray Daughter were Bitch's pups, and three parts coyote, product of one of her expeditions into the hills, her last litter before she died. Too many deaths, and all of them badly scabbed over, even a coyote-dog's.

They walked up the twilit riverbank to their camp. Others' Child could hear the coyotes in the hills begin their hunting song, wild yips that reverberated down the canyons and coalesced into an undulating howl, reaching up to the thin buffalo horns of the moon. The two at her heels ignored them. The other pups had scattered to the wild, but Thief and Gray Daughter stayed; Others' Child wasn't sure why.

Night Hawk had built a spring house, a journey hut of newly leafed branches, beside the river. He was good about that since the babies came. They didn't sleep in trees anymore, or in strange caves where Rattlesnake might be living. Every night he cut fresh brush for a shelter while Others' Child made fire with the fire drill if the slow-burner they carried in a buffalo horn had gone out. She knew that life had been simpler when he had been alone on the trail, but each year when they wintered with the Kindred, he never suggested leaving her. She wouldn't have stayed. Now she thought that there were other people besides the Kindred.

"The buffalo hunters live well," Others' Child said as she poked at the hot ash in the fire pit to see if the fish she had wrapped in leaves and buried there was done.

"They do," Night Hawk said. He sat down by the fire and stretched his legs. "Meat all year. I would get fat and lazy. Imagine not hunting but once a moon."

"They run them off a cliff," Others' Child said. That always killed more than the hunters could eat. It struck her as wasteful, and she shook her head disapprovingly, forgetting that she was trying to entice him, lure him toward life among the buffalo hunters.

"It is something to see," Night Hawk said. "I saw it once. They are like thunder come alive. Once they start there is no stopping them. I saw a man caught up with them and killed. They found him at the bottom."

Others' Child tried to imagine that, to feel herself lifted on the great furry backs, rolled among the thundering hooves, flung, surprised, outward into empty air. To drop in an instant of wonder as if you were Hawk, and then to smash. She shuddered. It seemed too easy for that to happen. Elder Brother had gone that way, lifted on the fever to some place she couldn't reach. And then he had dropped suddenly, clean out of life. Others' Child's eyes filled with tears, and she poked angrily at the fish.

Night Hawk watched her, puzzled by the sudden shift. The child didn't occur to him. It had been nearly a year.

A tear splashed into the coals and spat back up at him. "What is it?" he said. Maybe it was the new baby. Pregnancy made women odd, there was no denying that. He supposed it would make him odd, carrying someone else around inside himself.

"Maybe if we had been with the buffalo hunters, I could have saved him," Others' Child said mournfully.

"No, you couldn't," Night Hawk said, figuring things out. He had loved the child, too. Elder Brother had been his firstborn, but he knew Death when he saw it. Elder Brother had gone Away because Death had held out something that he wanted, like a shiny stone. That was all there was to it.

"There are healers among the buffalo hunters," Others' Child said. "I am not a healer, that is plain." She wrapped her arms around herself and rocked back and forth while Little Brother stared at her.

"It wouldn't have made a difference," Night Hawk said, exasperated. "It wouldn't have mattered if you had had a healer."

' "It would not have all been *me*!" Others' Child said. "And what about this one?" She pointed at Little Brother, who was pounding a stick on the rocks by the fire pit. "Who is going to raise him?"

"We are," Night Hawk said. What had happened? She had been happy to be a hawk with him, and now she was a thornbush, trying to put down a taproot.

"Indeed?" Others' Child glared at him. It had become easy to fight over this. They were neither of them malleable people, and now they seemed to have hardened in just a few moments into their respective shells, like turtles. "And who will help me with them? Where are the aunts and grannies who watched *you* when you were small?"

"You don't like the Grannies. You are rude to them."

"Other Grannies. There must be some place for us to be." She patted her belly. "How will they grow up, knowing no proper people, no proper way to be? Who will they marry?"

"I don't know." Night Hawk smiled and bent over, nose to nose with Little Brother. "Who will you marry when you are old enough?" His hawk-nosed profile was sculpted by the firelight, and his eyes gleamed red.

"You have not thought about it, have you, Most Scornful?" Others' Child said.

Night Hawk sat back on his heels. "No," he said. "Things happen that we don't arrange for. Hush and think about those things, and don't talk to me like Rattlesnake. I am your husband."

"I am afraid," Others' Child said. She spread out her hands so that he could see she had no courage hidden in them.

Night Hawk came around to her side of the fire and put his arms around her. He rocked her the way she had rocked herself, silently, back and forth, his breath warm in her ear. After a while he could feel the stiffness loosen in her arms, flow away down them like water. She leaned against him limply. Little Brother crawled into her lap and stuck his thumb in his mouth.

"It will be all right," Night Hawk said in her ear.

"How will it be all right?" she answered wistfully. "Foot-on-trail with a lapful of babies?"

"Cuddle up with this one," Night Hawk said, "and I will take the fish out of the fire before he is charcoal." And what husband of the Kindred would touch a cook fire? But Night Hawk had cooked his own meat long before she came down his trail.

Others' Child curled on the bed of grass he had cut for them and watched him, bewildered. When he brought her the fish in a turtle shell, she ate it, digging her fingers into the hot flesh hungrily, picking out the bones. Brother opened his mouth like a magpie's baby, and she fed him pieces she had cleaned the bones from.

Night Hawk opened his pack for the flute, which he had learned to play from Mocking Bird, who was Maize Came's twin. That had been before the Kindred had driven Mocking Bird off again, back to the Yellow Grass People. Night Hawk put it to his lips and made it sing a little bouncy song that Brother would go to sleep by. The world outside the brush hut was settling into twilight. The curved moon hung in a pink and turquoise sky, and a nightjar boomed over the valley beyond the clump of cottonwoods. Brother was a sticky bundle curled in the hollow of her knees and belly. Thief sat by the hut door, looking out at the twilight, and Gray Daughter turned around three times by the fire and flopped down in the dirt. Others' Child closed her eyes.

Thief stood up, stretching, nose to paws, his back bent into a concave line, his black-tipped tail erect. He yawned, his teeth white as the cat's bones in the twilight, jagged snow mountains upside down in the pink and turquoise sky.

He cocked an eye at Others' Child, and she could see that he was smaller than he had been, and his gray nose longer. The ruff across his chest was matted, and there were feathers clinging to it. He licked his muzzle. . . .

"Many thanks for the fine duck," he said to her. He nosed among the ashes in the fire pit, too. Night Hawk didn't seem to notice him.

"That is my husband's snare," Others' Child said indignantly.

"That is why I knew you would want to give me the duck," Coyote said. "After all the fine things I have done for you."

"Ha!" Others' Child said. "What have you done for me?" She knew it wasn't wise to insult Coyote, but you could argue with him. Coyote liked to see who could get the better of whom.

Coyote scratched vigorously behind one ear before he answered her. He was thinking. "I found you a husband,'' he said. He lolled his tongue out. ''I will take him away again if you want me to.''

''No!''

''You don't like him; you want to go live in a warren with rabbits. Why don't you give him to me?'' He looked at her sideways, a yellow gaze that set the hair up on the back of her neck.

''I am very happy with my husband,'' Others' Child said. She looked at Night Hawk, playing the flute. Was it her imagination, or did he look paler, as if she could look through him? ''Go away.''

''If you were happy with him, I wouldn't be here.''

''I am happy.'' She looked at Night Hawk, terrified that he would somehow hear, that thinking about him would pull him into the dream with her. Dreamtime was as real as waking time, and sometimes more dangerous. It was dangerous to fall into another person's dream. You were like the buffalo falling off the cliff with no way to stop yourself.

''Do you want my advice?'' Coyote said.

''No. Go away.''

''There is a great deal of dissatisfaction with you in certain quarters.'' Coyote grinned. She could see the iridescent green feather that clung to his nose. ''Spider was saying so only the other day.''

''Tell Grandmother Spider that I am sorry if I have offended her,'' Others' Child said carefully. Coyote was capricious, but he forgot to be angry with you when the next thing distracted him. Spider never forgot.

''You are disturbing harmony,'' Coyote said. ''There is no balance because you are trying to want four things at once. It is mixing everything up. Just last night, a mouse spoke back to me, and Bat came out in daylight and flew into a rock.''

''You should have known I couldn't go foot-on-trail with babies,'' Others' Child said. ''You and Spider didn't tell me that.''

''Oho, are we supposed to tell the puma to eat rabbits?''

''My baby died.''

"If nobody died, the world would be filled up with people, bumbling about on top of each other like a gourd full of fishing worms. We have death to keep you from bumping into each other."

"He hadn't got started yet."

"Did we promise you a certain number of years? This woman is specially exempt from death? Different from all the other people?"

"You didn't say my babies would die," Others' Child said stubbornly. "My mother and my father both died. That should be enough for you, Hungry."

"Thank you, I believe I will." Coyote nosed in the ashes again, found the remains of the fish, and ate it.

"That is my breakfast." She started to say, "Also, it has bones in it," but she supposed a bone in his throat wouldn't hurt him.

"You are most kind." Coyote looked thoughtful for a moment, gagged, and coughed up a fish bone. He wrapped his tail around his toes, chatty. "It's Two-Legged's fault that everyone is different and can't get along," he said. "Personally, I've always liked human people—they are the only ones who ever go mad for no reason. All the same, it was a human person wanting what she couldn't have that separated the human people from the animals. Naturally after that the humans started quarreling with each other, too."

"She," Others' Child said resentfully. "Why do your stories always make things some woman's fault?"

"Did I say fault?" Coyote said. "Doing, maybe. Women make things happen. They give birth to chance the way they do to babies."

"And what did this one give birth to?" Others' Child asked suspiciously. She put a hand on her belly.

The story started as a puff of smoke that came up out of the fire looking around for someplace to tell itself. Or maybe it came from Coyote's mouth. Others' Child couldn't be sure.

"Well, her name was Bear Woman," Coyote said.

* * *

Bear Woman was very pretty, and not at all suspicious, not like women are now. She went berry-picking by herself one day, and the Sun saw her.

The Sun thinks a lot of himself, but he's an old disgrace, and he can't let earth-surface girls alone. Mother Earth has never been able to keep him from sticking it in whatever takes his fancy, and a long time ago she decided just to let him have his way, so now there are always three or four of his children trying to climb up the sky and look for him.

Sun saw Bear Woman picking berries by a pond, and he went right over to her, dressed up in a girl's hide skirt and talking in a high voice. Bear Woman didn't seem to notice what was sticking out from under his skirt.

"How about a swim?" Sun said, tossing his hair. "Isn't it hot?"

Bear Woman thought that it was hot, too, so she said all right, and put her berry basket down on the bank. She took off her own skirt, and Sun nearly fell in the water craning his neck to watch her. Steam came up in clouds from the mud he was standing on.

Bear Woman waded in and turned around to see what was taking him so long. The pond was cool and mostly hidden under a bank of alder boughs. Her breasts floated on the surface like plums.

That was enough for Sun. He threw himself into the water, snatching his skirt off, and Bear Woman had just time to shriek at what was under it before the pond disappeared in a cloud of steam.

Bear Woman fought with him, but Sun goes where he wants to, and pretty soon he had gone into her. At evening, of course, he left, and Bear Woman didn't know what to do. She couldn't follow him over the mountains and kill him, which was what she wanted to do—not everyone thinks this sort of thing is an honor. And even if she caught him, it wouldn't be a good idea to kill the Sun, because then where would we get light? Bear Woman was so angry and tired that she just lay down in the ferns by the berry thicket and cried.

Mother Earth heard her and went to see what was going on, and when she found out that Sun hadn't even asked this girl first, she was very angry.

"I will make women more suspicious," she said, in a voice that didn't bode well for anybody. And then she told Bear Woman that she could fix it so that Sun would never bother her again, if that was what Bear Woman really wanted.

"I don't ever want anything to do with another man again," Bear Woman said.

"You may be being hasty," Mother Earth said.

"I know what I want," Bear Woman said angrily. She brushed at the purple bruises on her skin as if she could rub them away.

"Very well," Mother Earth said.

Bear Woman's face grew very round, and her nose got longer and so did her teeth. Her brown arms grew furry, and she found that she had very satisfactory claws at the ends of them. Then her shoulders broadened, and she could feel heavy muscles rippling along her flanks. When she stood up, she saw that she would tower over the men of her people.

"Go and look in the water," Mother Earth said.

Bear Woman went and looked. She swiped the water with her long, curved claws. The water rippled away with her marks in it. She swung her heavy head to look at Mother Earth. "It is good," she said. Let some man come and try to rape her now, she thought.

"What is done cannot be undone," Mother Earth said.

"I don't wish it undone," Bear Woman said. "I and my children will own the forest, and all men will be afraid of us."

And so it was. But she had been a human person before she was a bear person, and human people have this way of changing what they want. After a number of years had gone by, what Bear Woman wanted was a human man. There were plenty of bear men, but she didn't care. She still thought that she would cut the Sun's ears off if she ever caught him, but when she saw a human man near the pond where the Sun had first raped her, she fell in love with him, despite everything she had told Mother Earth.

This human man was named Fisher, and he was very beautiful. He was tall and muscular, with skin the color of dark honey and hair like an obsidian waterfall. Bear Woman wanted him, but when she told Mother Earth that she did, Mother Earth shook her head, and said, "Oh, dear, I warned you."

"I want him," Bear Woman said stubbornly. And she got him, too, but she had to sneak up on him and hold him down with one paw and tell him that she wouldn't hurt him, before he would believe her. After that Fisher fell in love with Bear Woman, because he was not the kind of man to whom beauty is most important. And they got married, but the fact that his wife could hold him down with one paw anytime she felt like it must have made him uneasy.

Fisher and Bear Woman lived together very happily, a little away from his people—she did make them uneasy. In the winter she didn't sleep like the other bears, but softened the deer hides from the autumn hunting, chewing on the tough skin so that he could sew it with his delicate five-fingered hands. In summer she climbed the bee trees and brought him hives of sweet honey. The angry bees clung to her fur and she would sit in the pond to drown them before she went home to her husband.

They lived very happily this way until Bear Woman took it into her head next to want a child.

"I don't know if that can be done," Fisher said dubiously. They had heard of animal people with human mates, of course, heard of it being done, but they had never seen it. And it might be an easy thing to get wrong.

Bear Woman was determined. She wanted a child. And so she made all sorts of magics, composed mostly of wanting, which is always dangerous. And one evening when her husband came home from hunting, she had a baby to show him.

Fisher didn't say anything at first. He just looked at

the baby in its woven cradle and then at Bear Woman's beaming face. Then he turned around to the cave mouth and pulled on his hair, screaming.

"Well, what is the matter?" Bear Woman said.

"The matter? Are you blind? It is a monster!"

"It's not," Bear Woman said. She hugged the cradle closer to her furry chest.

Fisher gave her a long look that made it clear he was thinking about things, and Bear Woman gave him back a look that said she wasn't going to change her mind. They roasted the meat he had brought back and went to bed without saying anything else to each other. Bear Woman put the cradle over on her side of the bed, away from Fisher.

When her husband was asleep, she pulled the blankets away from the baby and looked at him again.

All mothers are blind to the faults of their children, but even Bear Woman had to admit that there was something odd about this baby. He didn't look like a bear at all, or like a human person. He had claws, but not like hers. His were short and curved and sharp as needles. Where his nose ought to have been was something that might have been another claw. Bear Woman looked at that nose for a long time, trying to see it as anything else, but she finally had to admit to herself that it was a beak. And his body definitely had feathers. There was no getting around it. This baby wasn't a bear and it wasn't a human, or any combination of the two. It was an owl.

Whatever magics she had made obviously hadn't been done right, but no one was going to say that any child of hers was a monster. He was a perfectly good owl. But she knew that if she didn't do something quickly, Fisher was going to kill the child when he woke up. She had seen it in his eyes and his thoughtful expression last night.

So Bear Woman got up in the cold before the Sun rose (because she wouldn't be surprised if this was somehow something left over from him), and she took the baby into the pine woods, deep into the darkness

*where no animals ever went, where Mother Owl, the old
feathered cat of the pines, lives in her nest at the top of
the tallest tree.*

*Bear Woman climbed the tree and put the owl baby
in Mother Owl's nest before Mother Owl came home
from hunting. Then she went sorrowfully home again,
but she never forgot about her baby, because no mother
ever does.*

*Meantime, Owl Boy grew up as an owl person, learn-
ing to see in the dark and to fall silently on his prey like
swift-feathered death. He slept in the day and grew
larger and larger, too big for Mother Owl's nest. He
began to hunt with her for his little brothers and sisters,
bringing rabbits and birds back up into the dark
branches of the pines, caught on his claws. He lived as
the owl people live, and he should have been content.*

*But it is the two-legged blood that breeds discontent.
On some nights he could see the fires of his father's
people, far away across the valley, and once when he
went to investigate he saw them dancing around the fires
and singing. He went back and told Mother Owl about
it.*

*"Stay away from them," Mother Owl said. "They are
daylight people and we are night people, and they will
do you an evil."*

"I know them, I think," Owl Boy said discontentedly.

*"You don't want to know them," Mother Owl said,
and she closed her round yellow eyes just as the sun
came over the ridge.*

*The spears of light pained Owl Boy, and he closed
his own eyes, but when the sun had gone away again,
he left his mother's home in the pine woods and flew
through the moonlight to a place that smelled of people.
It was an old hunting camp, abandoned now, but it sang
to Owl Boy, sang to his blood under the owl feathers.*

*In the camp he found an old bone comb with many
teeth missing, and a tattered basket with a hole in it.*

*"If you go to the south," the comb said, "you will
find your mother's people."*

"If you go to the north," the basket said, *"you will find your father's people."*

"Well, which way should I go?" Owl Boy asked.

"Which way do you dream to go?" the comb asked him.

"I don't know. I dream to go home."

"That is a mistake," the comb said. *"These are two-legged human people, and they will kill you."*

"I have claws," Owl Boy said. *"Nothing can kill me."*

"Foolish," the basket said. *"Your own can always kill you. Anyway you are no match for two-legged people. They will kill you as surely as the sun is going to come over that mountain in the morning."*

"I want to go and look at them," Owl Boy said stubbornly. *"They are mine."*

He slept that day in the abandoned camp, and at twilight he found an old deerskin robe, almost tattered to bits, and put it on. Then he flew to the camp of his father's people.

When he got there, they were having a feast, and a dance on the dance ground. They were all singing, a song Owl Boy didn't know but a song that talked to his blood the way that the comb and the basket in the camp had. He stood on the edge of the dance ground yearning. The dancers flew by, and he longed to be a part of it, to take his place with these people who acted as if the world was made for them.

Owl Boy wrapped his tattered robe around him tighter and hobbled out onto the dance ground, awkward on his feet. He tried to dance, to step like the human people, but the spurs on his feet tripped him up and he fell, still awkwardly holding his robe around him with his wings. The human people laughed. They pointed at him and chortled, and not one of them tried to help him up.

Owl Boy went hot and then cold with fury and shame. These were his blood, but they wouldn't let him be one of them. He flung the robe off, wings beating the dance ground. He lifted over the crowd of dancers and snatched a child from a woman's lap.

Wings beating higher, Owl Boy rose above the shouting two-leggeds on the ground, into the moon-washed sky. The two-legged people had scorned him. Now he would scorn them and be their enemy. Burning with anger, he flew into the forest with the child in his talons, and in the top of a blue spruce he killed it with his claws and ate it.

Sated now, Owl Boy closed his yellow owl eyes and slept as the furious sun came up over the mountains.

Owl Boy was still sleeping when the hunters came looking for him and found him sleeping in the spruce. The father of the stolen child threw a spear and pierced him through one wing. Owl Boy fell from the tree, howling in pain, and the light stabbed his eyes. The hunters converged on him, their spears ready, while he cried for Mother Owl, who was already asleep and too far away to hear.

It was Bear Woman, his real mother, who heard him, and came bounding from the forest, swatting the hunters away with her huge paws. The men scattered and ran, and Bear Woman pulled the spear from his wing.

"Why were you among human people?" she asked him with tears running down her furry nose.

"I wanted to be one," Owl Boy said bitterly. "But they laughed at me."

Bear Woman looked at the child bones underneath the spruce tree and thought that now they would do something worse than laugh at him. "You have to go away from here." She licked Owl Boy's wounded wing and nudged him, but he wouldn't fly.

He stumbled and floundered, eyes squeezed shut against the sun, and Bear Woman wondered again if Sun really was his father, if this was her punishment for running away from him and telling on him to Mother Earth. "You have to fly," she said, nudging Owl Boy again with her great paw.

"I can't. I am broken. You might as well kill me!"

Bear Woman ran for the pine forest where she had taken him as a baby, and woke up Mother Owl. "Our son is hurt and you have to come and get him."

Mother Owl opened a gold eye. "I will come when it gets dark," she said. "If he does not live till then it will be his punishment for not listening to me when I told him about the two-leggeds."

But she did come that night to the spruce tree where Bear Woman was standing guard against the two-legged hunters and Owl Boy was sobbing in a heap of feathers amid the child bones.

"Tchah! You are foolish," Mother Owl said. But she taught him, none too gently, how to fly with a wounded wing, and took him back off to the pine forest with her. Neither of them once looked back at Bear Woman standing on her hind legs to watch the two of them melt into moonlight and pine shadows.

After that the owl child became all owl and kept to the dark forest, and forgot that he had ever had human blood or wanted to be one of them.

Now the two-legged people say that Owl Boy deserved what happened to him, that he had his chance to be friendly with them and lost it. And that is why when you see an owl, it means death. But to hear the owl side of it, it was the human people who were cruel, and he never ate any child, it was only an old rat person stealing scraps in the midden. Owl Boy had only wanted to dance with them and not be laughed at.

I expect both are true. Both sides of a thing generally are. But it all came of a two-legged, Bear Woman, who wanted to be something she wasn't, and then wanted to be what she had been again, and then wanted to be something else entirely, until the Universe was mixed up, and all sorts of things happened. None of the animals or the two-leggeds have trusted each other since. The two-leggeds go on eating animal people, but to this day they make a great fuss if an animal person eats them.

II

Owl Eyes

In the morning, Coyote was gone, as he always was; and waking, Others' Child was never sure whether he had been there or not. The fish was gone, too, but Thief had ashes on his nose, and he wasn't named Thief for nothing. Others' Child sighed and went down to the snares by the stream. There were feathers on the ground, and a pair of duck feet, sad and flat-looking, tangled in the snarled lines.

"I will wait by the snare with rocks next time," Others' Child said to the stony hillside above the stream. Nothing answered her, and she shrugged uneasily. When a spirit came to you in dreamtime, it was important, but dreams were often ambiguous, keeping meaning just out of reach. All Coyote had told her was what she knew already, that life was chancy. The duck had found that out, too.

"Something got your snare," she said to Night Hawk. Night Hawk prodded Gray Daughter with his toe.

"Lazy. I will tie you by the snares if you don't keep better watch."

Gray Daughter looked at him balefully. She knew what had come in the night, Others' Child thought, but she wasn't saying. Others' Child wasn't sure she could say, either. She looked at Night Hawk, who seemed untroubled by dreams or untoward visits from spirit people or even the urge to find a resting place, and sighed. She made the sigh loud enough for him to hear.

It didn't do any good. For two moons they tramped through a countryside that changed like the shifting terrain of a dream, from red rock bluffs and canyons striped yellow and brown and blue-black like birds' wings, to dry washes tangled with old, tumbled stone and alive with the sudden buzz of snakes, and then finally through a flat river valley choked with reeds. The water flowed sluggishly there, as if it, too, was reluctant to go any farther, and a white heron stood on one foot in it with a still-wriggling fish in its beak. When it saw them, it rose in a sudden flapping of wings, legs trailing like a wasp's, and sailed up over the cottonwoods into the sky. Others' Child wondered what it would be like to lift that easily from the ground instead of tramp across it.

Beyond the river they came to the camp of the Buffalo Hunters, where the tall grass grew. The grass seemed to go on forever to the east, like a flat lake of green and yellow, whispering in its rippled stalks. The Buffalo Hunters lived in skin shelters on the prairie and lived easily, Others' Child thought. She spoke a little of their language, but Night Hawk spoke it fluently, and she watched with envy the women that he bartered with— fat, comfortable women with babies on their hips and baskets balanced on their heads, held lightly with one hand. They pressed around him, prodding with their fingers at chunks of red dyestone, turquoise beads, and deer-bone flutes, shell fishhooks that had come from a man who had got them in the west. They spread their own wares out for Night Hawk to inspect—soft buffalo robes with the curly fur brushed and shiny. *I am lucky*

if we stay in one place long enough to tan a deer hide,
Others' Child thought.

She put her hand on her belly and arched her back,
trying to take the ache out of it. The shaman saw her
and solemnly pressed his fingers on her backbone and
belly. He wore a horned headdress that looked like a
low moon riding on his brow, but he had a kind, wrinkled face and thick, tufty brows like an old badger.

"I had another baby," Others' Child said to him on
impulse. "He died of a fever. How could I have saved
him?"

The shaman shook his ponderous head, horns swinging against the red sky. "The sickness has to be sucked
out," he said. "It was in there in his skin."

"Could I do this?"

The shaman shook his head sorrowfully. "No."

The chief's woman came up and took Others' Child
by the arm, tugging her toward the fire pits, where meat
was roasting, a whole carcass. Little Brother padded after them, following the smell.

"This would be a fine place to live," Others' Child
said at night, when she lay down with Night Hawk, their
bellies full of meat and mouths greasy, in the hide shelter
that the Buffalo Hunters had given them.

"Oh, most certainly, Puts Down a Taproot," Night
Hawk said. He looked at her scornfully. "I could listen
to old men tell lies around the fire, with their buffalo
growing bigger every tale, until I die of boredom and
disbelief."

"Men tell lies like that everywhere," Others' Child
said. "And it isn't only their buffalo that get bigger with
the telling, Always Wanting Something. These are no
different. They are a good people. We would be welcome here."

"Heart, they are no different from the Kindred."
Night Hawk rolled over and closed his eyes, head pil-
lowed on his arm.

They were no different from the Kindred, Others'
Child thought, but they had a shaman who could suck
out sickness. The conviction that that would have been

enough to save Elder Brother lingered, tangled in her mind with the dream of Owl Boy. She looked at the smooth hide walls and imagined staying here inside them, wearing them like a turtle shell. She imagined that she belonged to these comfortable people.

In the morning they moved on, the buffalo hides lashed to the dogs' travois.

That summer Others' Child found each camp a fine place to stop and stay. For a few nights, Night Hawk would be content to drink cactus liquor with the men and throw knuckle bones beside the fire, and her hopes would rise, and then always he was itchy-foot, ready to move on. She and Little Brother trailed after him through the heat between the camps of the Buffalo Hunters, trading obsidian spearpoints and turquoise and southern greenstone for hides and meat. Others' Child grew bigger-bellied.

At midsummer they watched a hunt run down the ponderous wild-eyed buffalo, four or five hunters hidden under buffalo robes, driving the herd into a frantic stampede until they toppled over the cliff, thundering hooves pawing air.

Others' Child clutched Little Brother to her with both arms and felt the pounding in the ground like an earthquake rumbling along some hidden fault line. The buffalo flew by, a dark sea of woolly hides and curved horns, heads bent low, their humped backs like mountains moving. Where did buffalo spirits go when they died? she wondered. So many spirits lifting up from the broken bodies beneath the cliff. Were they angry that the humans killed so many of them and could not eat them all? If you were dead, did it matter if your death had served a purpose? Others' Child had been taught that it did. Did the buffalo know that? What if they turned in their anger and trampled the camp, stamping the two-leggeds' children into the grass and dust? What if they decided to eat people, like the flesh-eating antelope who had been killed by the Hero Twins when the world was young? Could they do that?

"You worry too much," Night Hawk said when she asked him, watching the hunters' women skinning the great beasts and cutting the meat from the humps. "It is the baby, I expect."

"It is not. It is only that I think about things."

"So do I," Night Hawk said. "But I don't worry about being eaten by buffalo."

"I'm not. I am just *thinking*." She looked at him, exasperated. There was no way to explain the feeling that somehow the wild had reached out and snatched her child because she had no home and was vulnerable.

"Here is a fine place," she said again, the night they came to a camp of the Buffalo Leap People, who were in some ways related to the Yellow Grass People as well as to the Buffalo Hunters. The camp had good water, and a little stand of cultivated maize, and beyond it was a thicket of berries and wild sweet plums, easy to pick. "What is wrong with this place?"

"Nothing, if I want to turn to stone like the buffalo cliffs," Night Hawk said. "I have seen this place. I have seen these people. Now I want to see new people."

"Yah, always new people!"

"Otherwise I would be a crazy person," Night Hawk said. "Running around in my skin under the moon, yipping like Coyote. I cannot live with one people for more than a winter. That is long enough to feel my guts stiffen like an old hide. And you, too. By winter's end you are insulting the Grannies and causing talk because you aren't biddable."

"That is the Kindred. There are other people to live with."

"Then we will go south this winter and see some of them," Night Hawk suggested. "In the south a man can keep moving. They don't shut themselves up in caves that smell like an old bear and sit in each other's smelly laps all winter."

"I don't want to see them!" Others' Child said. "I want to belong to them."

"Well, why? You don't even know them. We'll keep

foot-on-trail through the winter and see the Endless Water. I know you want to see that. You said so.''

Did she? She had once. "I want to go home," she said now.

"Then we will winter with the Kindred," Night Hawk said with elaborate patience.

"Not to the Kindred!"

Night Hawk rolled himself in his new buffalo robe and turned his back to her, but snuggling up, backside to backside, so she would know he wasn't angry. There was no use arguing with someone who couldn't think reasonably about things. They would go to see the Endless Water and trade with the men of the coast. If they turned south now, they would be able to travel all winter and not worry about the baby being born in bad weather. Warmth, that was what babies needed. It would be better for Little Brother, too. And there would be something new to see, to distract Others' Child from her restlessness. All in all, it seemed a good plan. Night Hawk had been as far as the coast only once. Without doubt there were many more things to see there than he had seen. He reached behind him and patted Others' Child on the backside, to tell her that things would be all right.

It was almost the autumn equinox when the baby got ready to come. Night Hawk kept track of these matters with a tally stick that the Three Old Men of the Kindred had given him, so that no matter where he wandered he would know what part of the year it was. The Grannies had decided that the equinox was the right time for the baby, and Others' Child had counted on her fingers and said that for once they knew something. Maybe it would make it magical.

But there was nothing magical about the country they had come to, unless sheer ugliness was magic, and it might be. Others' Child thought that she had never seen a land so ugly, not even the desolate black badlands that lay south of where the Yellow Grass People lived. Here was nothing but dry sandstone and strange trees like old men with beards, and if the flesh-eating antelope monster still lived anywhere, it was here. They ate dried meat and meal and drank stale water from skins tied to the dogs' travois.

The pains that began to grind across Others' Child's belly seemed to come from the hot sand, as if her body was drawing them up out of the barren landscape. She walked stiffly, knowing from experience that the longer she kept moving the better. Little Brother saw her taut face and tugged at her skirt, so she took his hand. Night Hawk was ahead of them.

All that broke the monotony of the landscape were occasional outcroppings of rock and the vagaries of the trail. All of this trail was old, Night Hawk had said, older even than the Kindred or the People Who Lived at the Coast. As old maybe as the time when human and animal people had all come Up From Below. In places it was worn knee-deep in the soft stone.

The sky overhead darkened, and Others' Child looked around them anxiously. In the desert, storms came with furious speed, boiling up over distant mountains and thundering their way across the land like the buffalo, roaring with great open mouths.

Night Hawk looked back at Little Brother and Others' Child when their shadows disappeared, and pointed his arm to a stone that loomed ahead of them, rising from the valley floor like a fish's back. "Hurry along. We may be able to keep dry. I remember that, I think. It is called Old Woman Holding a Hide."

Others' Child put her hand to her belly and gritted her teeth. She hurried after him, with Little Brother trotting beside her. Little Brother was tired, and he whimpered as he tried to keep up. She picked him up and swung him onto the dogs' travois, among the bundled hides.

The air turned black, and a flash of lightning crackled through it. The rain began falling, a cold, wind-driven drizzle and then a downpour that plastered their hair to their faces and turned the trail to mud. The pains came back again with it. Others' Child held out her hands toward Night Hawk's back. "Wait!" she howled at him.

He turned around, peering at her through the rain, a hand shielding his eyes. She clutched her belly. Night Hawk began to splash his way back toward her.

Others' Child stumbled on the rain-slick trail and Night Hawk grabbed her hand, his pack swinging wildly from its strap.

"The baby is coming," she said between her teeth. Little Brother climbed down from the travois and clung to her legs.

"We're almost there." Night Hawk steadied her as a pain doubled her over. "Get back in with the hides," he said to Little Brother. "I don't want to lose you in the rain."

The dogs tucked their heads down and pulled, bumping the travois along through the mud. Others' Child stumbled after them. As they neared the rock outcrop, she could see that it was really two rocks and that the trail ran between them, under the shelter of the Old Woman's Hide, a hanging ledge of stone. She wondered if there would be any fire left in the slow-burner of shredded tinder they had lit this morning.

The pains seemed now like a cold hand that gripped her belly. If she were warm, maybe they would stop, she thought. The Grannies all said that a woman never remembered from baby to baby how bad the last one had been. Otherwise she would never let her husband put another one in her. But this child seemed to be trying to rip her belly out and crawl through the torn flesh. She howled and doubled over again. The rain beat on her back and poured down her nose.

When the pain stopped, she ran for the stone ledge, with Night Hawk and the dogs splashing after her. Under the outcrop there was not quite a cave, a hollow place in the stone that was still dry. Others' Child huddled on the ground, and a lizard skittered out from under her hand into a crack in the rock. The pains started again, and she curled into a ball.

Night Hawk was pulling hides from the travois. He had set Little Brother in a corner of the shelter and told him to stay there. Little Brother watched wide-eyed as

Night Hawk piled three hides on top of each other and prodded Others' Child onto them.

"They will get spoiled," she said between gasps. "It will spoil them."

Night Hawk looked at her as if the dogs might make more sense if they started talking. "I will make you something to drink. What should I make you?"

"Laurel tea," Others' Child said. She whimpered, trying not to yell. It was not dignified to yell, and it might make the gods think you didn't want the baby. She wrapped her arms around her belly, trying to hold the baby, tell it to be patient, not to fight with her. Little Brother looked at her from his corner with round owl eyes.

Night Hawk made a fire—she noticed it first when she smelled the smoke from the tinder he had taken from his pack, and she wondered hazily if the tinder had still been burning or if he had used the fire drill. She wasn't sure how long it had been. It didn't seem worthwhile to lift her head to see. He must have put some of the hoarded wood he had lashed to the travois on it, because after a while he brought her laurel tea in a turtle shell, and she drank it. She felt as if she were moving in and out of a red and black fog. She could almost see the pain when it came, burning like the coals, a red mist like a rain of blood that picked her up and twisted her like something wringing a duck's neck. And then when the pain receded, exhaustion took her and pulled her down into a dark place that was like sinking in black water, arms and legs like stone, too heavy to move.

There were eyes in the darkness, she thought, or maybe it was stars, if the rain had stopped. It was hard to see. The eyes looked at her with a yellow stare. The pain came again like a knife, and she clenched her hands in the curly buffalo hair, twisting her fingers in it. The hide felt like something alive, as if it might get up any moment and bear her away on its back, lumbering into the rain.

"Drink this." Night Hawk was holding a bowl to her mouth. Others' Child swallowed. Thief and Gray

Daughter sat side by side under the rock ledge, or maybe it was only one of them. It was hard to tell. "Go away," she said to the gray form that seemed to coalesce from their paired hides. It winked out, and the dogs looked at her curiously. Little Brother was crying in the corner.

Another pain gripped her, and Others' Child gagged, trying to vomit the baby up maybe, since it wouldn't come out the other way. She could feel the buffalo robe wet and slick under her. She leaned her head back and fell into the black water again, warm black water, holding up her stone legs and arms. She could feel Night Hawk pulling at her legs, but it didn't matter; she was too tired to move them.

The red mist sliced through the black one again, like a splash of blood falling out of the air. Others' Child screamed and flung her arms wide. Night Hawk pushed her back down. His face popped out of the mist at her suddenly, like a moon coming up, a red-brown moon, burning with the firelight, dark eyes wide and intent. His mouth opened, but he made no sound.

Others' Child lay back as the pains stopped, or maybe she had only gone away from them somewhere else. She couldn't be sure. She saw the eyes again, owl eyes, she thought now, but she was pretty sure she wasn't dead. Then teeth snapped at the owl eyes and they went away, and other eyes were watching her above a long gray nose.

"Pah! That tastes bad," Coyote said.

"What does?"

"Whatever was watching you. Like old eggs that haven't hatched."

Others' Child shivered. Maybe she was dead. "Am I dead?" she asked him.

"Do you want to be?"

"No!" If she wasn't, would the pains start again? "I don't know." She whimpered it to herself. She couldn't see past the mist, couldn't see Night Hawk and the baby.

Coyote sneezed and blew a hole in the mist, and Others' Child could see Gray Daughter through it. "I could put you in her," Coyote suggested. "You could come with me."

Others' Child thought about that, felt herself changing as Bear Woman had. Thick fur warmed her cold legs as she slid into Gray Daughter like putting on new leggings. She saw that Coyote was watching her dress.

She tossed her head at him and felt his yellow eyes on her as she wriggled into her new skin. He was hairy but not unhandsome, with a thick shock of gray hair and a broad chest. His long tongue hung out over white teeth. He danced a few steps in the dark mist.

Others' Child imitated him, new nails clicking on the stone, and felt the ground light under her feet. Coyote leaped upward, and she followed him. She could see that they were on the star road. Below them, Old Woman Holding a Hide was very small, with the thin wisp of Night Hawk's smoke drifting up from her. Others' Child could smell Coyote's musky scent on the cold wet air and feel his warm breath on her neck.

They trotted past the stars that hung like balls of ice where Coyote had thrown them long ago. He stood on his hind legs, rolling blue-white spheres around the sky.

"You can't change them!" Others' Child protested.

"Why not?" Coyote trundled past her, trailing cold sparks.

"How will human people find their way at night?" What would Night Hawk and her babies do? How would any of them go home? She shivered, and her new gray fur skin loosened a little.

Coyote looked surprised, his ears straight up. "You'd better make up your mind."

"Make it up about what?"

"About whether you're a human person or not. It isn't as easy to change about as it used to be."

"I didn't ask to change about," Others' Child said indignantly.

Coyote leered at her. "You looked to me like you did. You hopped in that hide fast enough."

Others' Child looked uncomfortable. "Well, maybe I made a mistake."

Coyote stood with his paws on a star. The musky scent was overpowering. She could see his penis jutting out, bright red.

"I have a husband," she said. She drooped her tail, a little ashamed of herself.

"You'll split the laces on that hide," Coyote said, "if you try to keep a conscience in there with you."

Others' Child could feel it tearing as he spoke. She started to protest, but the fur was parting down her chest and belly. Then she fell through the stars like the hunted buffalo. She and Gray Daughter soared for an instant and then plummeted, landing together on the bed of hides under the Old Woman's outcrop. Gray Daughter got up and stalked over to the fire as if nothing had happened, but Others' Child saw the yellow glimmer of her eyes. Then Gray Daughter curled up, black-tipped tail over her nose, and her eyes closed. Others' Child could see through the mist now, she noticed.

She could feel her arms and legs heavy as stone again, lying in the wet muck on the buffalo robe. Her stomach cramped when she moved.

Night Hawk bent over her. His face was smeared with blood and dirt, and she thought he had been crying.

"Where's the baby?" she demanded.

Night Hawk shook his head. "She isn't here. She wouldn't come here at all."

Others' Child tried to sit up. "Where's my *baby*?"

Night Hawk wiped a smeared hand across his eyes. "Wherever they go. She left before she came out."

Little Brother was snuffling beside the fire. He crept up and into the hollow of Night Hawk's chest where Night Hawk bent over Others' Child. He buried his face under Night Hawk's arm.

Others' Child began to howl. She beat her fists on the buffalo robes. "Dirty coyote, you didn't tell me!" She glared malevolently into the darkness and rain.

Frightened, Little Brother crawled deeper under Night Hawk's arm.

Others' Child grabbed Night Hawk by the neck. "I want to see my baby! Where have you put her?"

Night Hawk shook his head. "No."

"I want to *see* her!" She couldn't bear to think of the baby out there in the cold rain.

"I put her in the earth," Night Hawk said. "I couldn't burn her in this rain."

"Already?" Others' Child's fingers dug into his neck. *"Already?"*

"It has been three days," Night Hawk said. He hung his head. "I thought you were going to die, too."

"No. I . . ." Others' Child's head began to swim.

"Lie down. I made some broth for you to drink. And sage tea. The Grannies always say it stops the milk."

Others' Child put her hands to her breasts. They were hard and they hurt. She began to whimper, and the milk trickled from them through her fingers. "How could you leave her in the rain?"

"She isn't here," Night Hawk said. "She wasn't ever here. I did the best I could. The hole kept filling up with water. It rained, and then it stopped and then it rained again, and you wouldn't wake up." He closed his eyes. The hands that rested on the buffalo robes trembled with fatigue. After a moment he stood, setting Little Brother aside, and got a bowl full of broth and another of bitter tea that would make the milk dry up.

Others' Child drank them silently, one after the other. "She would not have died if we had been with the Buffalo Hunters," she said angrily when she was finished. She shoved the bowls at Night Hawk.

"Babies die everywhere," Night Hawk said gently. "Babies die among the Buffalo Hunters and among the Kindred and among the Trespassers. This baby just didn't want to come to us."

"Not here in the rain in an ugly land on a trail that goes nowhere!" Others' Child spat at him. "With no shaman to make a good magic for her."

Night Hawk's lips compressed, and he looked out into the rain. "I have seen babies die with three shamans making magics to bring them back," he said. "Babies die when they want to."

"She didn't want to die!" Others' Child collapsed

back onto the bed, sobbing, curled in a ball, knees to her chin. "She wanted to be with us, I know she did."

Little Brother started to howl.

"Hush, you are scaring him."

"She wanted to come to us." Others' Child hiccuped. "She tried, but there was too much rain, and it was dark and cold, and you left her alone out there in it!"

Night Hawk cradled Little Brother silently, letting her weep.

Finally, Others' Child struggled up until she was sitting, her legs out in front of her, hands braced on the sticky blood-soaked hides. Her tangled hair hung around her face like a thornbush. Dark eyes caught the faint gleam of light from the dying fire, like reflections of the rain. Dark brows drew together above them, and her chin jutted out at Night Hawk. "This is your fault!" she hissed at him.

Night Hawk winced. "It wouldn't have made a difference where we were."

"And do you know that? Are you a midwife? Are you a shaman? Are you a soft man in a woman's dress that you know all about women and babies?"

"I know enough," he said. "Heart, it would not have mattered."

"Yah! He says it wouldn't have mattered!" Others' Child stared at him angrily, determined to force admission of fault from him. It must be somebody's fault. This was what had been watching her, what Coyote had snapped at. It was Owl Boy come for her baby, and Night Hawk had let him in.

Night Hawk shook his head silently. He brought her more tea and more broth and got clean hides and spread them out and helped her lie down on them. She didn't speak to him because he wouldn't admit it was his fault. He put the dirty hides outside the shelter in the rain that was still falling, to let it wash them.

"It's hardly let up," he said over his shoulder. "Three days and only a few hours of sun. All the washes are flooded. It's like Sky God emptied his water basket all at once."

She didn't answer him, face deliberately turned away. She envisioned the baby, her first girl baby, floating on the muddy swirl, her small body battered against the rocks. Others' Child saw the thin wraith of the baby's spirit moving through the rain. It drifted behind her eyelids, borne on the cold wind. Little Brother let out a howl as if he could see it too, and finally she reached out an arm for him and drew him close.

III

Great Condor

In another day the rain stopped, and Others' Child's tears stopped with it, leaving her dry-eyed and stiff, like stones walking. Her bleeding stopped, too, and her milk dried up, as if all the liquid in her body were being sucked back into dry rock like the rain into the sandy bottoms of the washes. She didn't die, as Night Hawk still feared, but she walked slowly, as if it hurt just to exist. When she had rested three days, they loaded their water-soaked belongings on the dogs' travois and into their packs, Night Hawk talking gently to her of this and that, Others' Child in stony silence.

Little Brother followed Night Hawk and Others' Child, wrapped in his own silence but never far from one or the other of them, a small brown hand clinging to clothes or skin, fingers clenched tight as a burr. He asked only once where the baby had gone, and Night Hawk showed him the grave, a muddy depression in the ground where the loose dirt had sunk down. There were vultures in the sky and a coyote's tracks nearby, so

Night Hawk piled rocks on it before they left, while Others' Child sat beside the travois and refused to look. She had wanted to see her baby, not turned mud with her baby under it.

Night Hawk put his hand on her shoulder and kissed the top of her head when he came back, but she ignored it. She picked up her pack and slung the strap over her shoulder and a second one around her forehead. She set her face to the west and started walking. *I won't look back,* she thought, *or I might stay here.*

The trail went west from the Old Woman into a desert already pale green from the rain. Tiny leaves uncurled like cupped hands under their feet, and the ugly land was suddenly beautiful. Others' Child resented that, as if it was the life that it had sucked out of her baby that was making the land green.

Night Hawk knew which of the plants that grew here were edible, and he showed them to Others' Child, coaxing her with fresh greens. She cooked whatever he brought her, throwing it all together into a cooking basket. Sometimes she didn't bother to check it until everything was mush, and then she ate stoically, as if the slimy, gelatinous mass was his fault. She talked to him only when necessary. When it was not necessary, she didn't, clutching her silence to her the way she clutched Little Brother.

"You'll squeeze the breath out of him," Night Hawk said, when she sat at night with Little Brother on her lap, arms wrapped tightly around his middle as if something might come from the air to take him.

"Do not be telling me how to take care of my babies, Itchy Foot," she said venomously.

Little Brother squirmed. He enjoyed the cuddling, but there was something in his mother's fierce possessiveness now that made him restless.

"You will spoil like meat left in the sun," Night Hawk said, "if you don't stop hating me."

"I don't hate you," Others' Child said furiously. "I only want you to say you are wrong."

"Well, I won't, because I'm not. If you don't stop trying to find someone to blame for the way life is, you will tie your belly in a knot, and not even a dozen shamans will be able to untie it."

She balled her hands into fists. "Liar! If we had been with the Buffalo Leap People, she wouldn't have died."

"How do you know that?"

She drummed her fists on his thigh until he grabbed her by the wrists. "I know it!"

Night Hawk pushed her hands away from him. "Yah, and who told you?" he asked with disgust. He got up and went outside the brush-and-hide shelter he had built. Tomorrow he would hunt, he thought. He doubted he'd kill anything except burrow dogs and maybe a snake in this country, but it would get him away from Others' Child. Maybe fresh meat would appease her. There wasn't anything else to try. Others' Child's anger left Night Hawk bewildered. She seemed to harden as she got well until she wore her anger in a casing of chitin like the insect people, and nothing could touch her.

Since she had been well enough to couple with him, she had refused to, and made much of her refusal, turning her back on him and putting Little Brother between them. It was like traveling with a hornet that hummed just beyond his face, elaborate in its disinterest but poised and venomous.

It did not occur to him that if he had said he was at fault when he was certain he was not, she would have been mollified. If it had, he would not have done it. Her assumption that he didn't mind about the baby stung him. Now that he was certain she was not going to die, he could afford his own anger.

They moved on slowly; there was no particular moon that mattered. Even in winter the weather this far south would be mild. A moon after the rain, the desert began to burn with flowers, red and orange and yellow, the flowers of amazement that sleep in the sand until there is rain. Then they burst out quickly at any time of year, putting all their effort into making seed before the water in the soil is gone. Then the new seed sleeps and waits for the next rain.

These desert flowers were an ephemeral thing, brief and giddy as butterflies, and they knotted Night Hawk's throat with their beauty. He knelt in a carpet of pale yellow blossoms barely taller than his toes, bent and peered into the cup of each bloom. The centers were dark and furred like bumblebees.

"Ha!" Little Brother raced toward him, through a thicket of red clover as tall as his shoulders. "Flowers!" He threw a handful into the air and watched it rain down. He danced on the fallen petals.

A worm humped its way across Night Hawk's finger, bunching up like a piece of rope and then straightening. "Watch," he said, and Little Brother flattened himself in the yellow flowers beside him, squinting his eyes at it.

"Worm," he said. "Eat it?"

Night Hawk inspected it. "I don't think so. You can try, but I think that one will taste bad."

Little Brother nodded sagely. Some things tasted very bad indeed. He got up and wandered off to pick more clover. Night Hawk followed him, in case Rattlesnake was sunning himself there. Others' Child was in the journey hut, he supposed.

"Let's pick Mother these flowers," he said on impulse. Young clover was good with other greens, and she would like the redness of the blossoms. Maybe she would put them in her hair.

Little Brother grabbed a handful, and Night Hawk showed him how to break the stems at the ground instead of pulling the flower heads off them. A long-legged runner bird skittered through the clover, saw them, and swerved abruptly. It paused, cocked a yellow eye at them, ducked its head, and dashed away again.

"He eat the worm," Little Brother said with interest.

"Did you want it?" Night Hawk inquired.

Little Brother shook his head. "No."

It had been this way when it was just himself and Others' Child and Elder Brother, Night Hawk remem-

bered. As soon as that first baby had learned to walk,
he had begun to discover the world, and it seemed to
Night Hawk now that there had been flowers everywhere
then, too.

Sometimes Night Hawk thought that when you died,
you didn't go to the Skeleton House at all, you just
started over again. After all, time stretched like Grandmother Spider's web; if it didn't, shamans wouldn't be
able to see the future. And if that were true, then whatever you did in life should be done honorably, he decided, because you would have to do it again forever.
He wondered what Others' Child would think of that
notion, and whether it would comfort her. He didn't
know if it was true, but if playing with babies in the
flowers came to him again and again, he wouldn't mind.
He scooped up Little Brother and their bundle of red
clover and took them back to the journey hut.

Others' Child was mending his best shirt with a bone
needle. She took the clover, then flung it suddenly away
from her with a howl of pain as if there had been a bee
in it. But there wasn't any bee. Night Hawk picked it
up and knew for certain that even if life did not keep
turning around, memory did. The clover had had Elder
Brother and their dead daughter in it, humming at the
heart of the blossoms.

They traveled through the winter and the next spring
and summer, while Little Brother got bigger and nobody
was very happy, not even Little Brother. But gradually
the sharp edges of anger faded like the angles of old
stone because it was impossible to keep resentment
fierce when you lived every day with its target and
yearned for things as they had been.

Gradually Others' Child began to talk of the state of
the buffalo hides they still had bundled on the travois,
and the red and blue feathers for which they had traded
a hide to the people who lived in the southwest. When
Night Hawk pierced the end of a red one and gave it to
her to wear in her hair, she asked irritably who would
see her and put it back in the skin bag with the rest. But

in the next village she bargained fiercely for a pouch of obsidian spearpoints and a spotted catskin that had come from the south.

"His name is Jaguar," she said of the catskin. "Father told me about him." Her eyes flicked to the horizon with fleeting curiosity, and for a moment the shell around her seemed to crack.

Night Hawk inspected the size of the hide, impressed. He had heard of Jaguar and seen a skin a time or two, but he was not going to tell her that. Let her instruct him. "I do not want to meet him," he said, "but that was fine bargaining, Tight Fist."

They moved west again until they came to a great river on the edge of another desert.

"It is bigger than Water Old Man," Others' Child said of the river, goggling. She smiled at him, and Night Hawk felt pleased, as if he had made it up. Slowly she had begun to slip the hard shell until he thought hopefully that he might see her step out of its stiff, translucent outline and turn to him one morning, arms outstretched.

But the shell grew thicker again after they crossed the river into the new desert. They walked at night, panting in the shade of the hide journey hut in the day.

"What kind of place is hot in the *winter*?" Others' Child demanded. She sucked a warm, stale mouthful from a waterskin and gave a sip to Brother.

She saw Night Hawk watching them carefully. He had the water calculated with a tally stick, rationed for each of them and the dogs. They supplemented it with the sour, wet pulp of basket cactus, and zigzagged their way across the sand each night, aiming for the squat shapes of cactus spotted by daylight, Night Hawk with one eye on the stars. They didn't always find a cactus, either. Sometimes there was nothing but the flat expanse of sand, empty and hot as the air.

"Who would live here?" Others' Child wanted to know.

"No one does."

When at last they saw a hillside humping up from the horizon and then the dark green shapes of scrub brush

dotting it, she felt as if she had escaped the jaws of some
fearsome animal, its hot breath still in her hair. *We will
have to go back across this*, she thought, seized with
sudden horror. *No.*

The hills were not like those they knew. These were
rounded and tawny-furred like a puma, dotted first with
scrub and then with the contorted arms of live oaks.
They visited no people yet, because Night Hawk had
decided they wouldn't until he had shown her what they
had come to see. He felt perversely that if the People
Who Lived at the Coast showed it to her, they would
get the credit.

The ocean came abruptly, because he didn't warn her,
and also because he had forgotten exactly how far it was
himself. They could hear a sound that he said was the
water—a dull roar like the sound when Others' Child
cupped her hand over her ear—and smell a sharp salt
smell, but all they could see were the brown hills. Then
they came over a ridge and saw that the tawny grass that
flowed down its side had changed into thick yellow and
green tufts and then vanished altogether in pale sand that
bounced the blazing sun back from each grain and hurt
their eyes. Beyond the sand was water, gray-blue with
the sun rippling in dazzling patterns on its surface. There
were islands on the horizon. Beyond them, the gray-blue
water went on forever at the same time that it rolled
toward the shore. It roared endlessly, broke in white
foam on the sand, retreated, and rolled toward them
again.

Web-footed birds screamed and soared over the water,
picking among the kelp on the sand. Others' Child ran
down the slope, and they vanished in the air, *awk*ing and
circling her. They landed on the water out beyond the
breakers. She picked up a piece of kelp and peered at
its bulbous stems and strange, finny leaves, while the
wind tangled her hair around her head.

Night Hawk and Brother slithered down the slope behind her with the dogs and the travois. The dogs rushed
at the roaring water and barked at it.

"No, you fools!" Night Hawk laughed, dancing in

the surf, dragging them back. "You'll get everything wet!" He untied the travois from their harness. "Don't drink it, either," he said, but they had already lapped at it curiously and retreated.

Others' Child tasted the surf on her fingertips. It was cold and salty as blood or tears. She stared at it in surprise. It seemed to her suddenly that this might be what people were made of, a cold, vast womb of water where the world had been born.

What would it be like to belong to the Endless Water? she wondered. She saw the web-footed birds out beyond the surf, bobbing on the blue surface, and wondered if it would be like that.

Others' Child stared at the horizon, straight as a spear shaft with the islands bumping up out of it. If you could fly like the web-footed birds, would you go on forever above this water, or was there something on the other side? It didn't seem to flow like a river. It looked more as if it were trying to get out, climbing up on the land. She could see by the marks on the sand that sometimes the water came higher. There was more kelp stranded there, and empty shells. Others' Child dug in the sand with her toe, and water rose up in the hole. The surf deposited something that looked like a large pale bug at her feet. She jumped back as it burrowed into the wet sand, all its legs scrabbling itself down.

Night Hawk stood beside her. "There are fish in the deep water," he said, "and things with shells, like big snails, in the shallows and under the sand. This is where the People Who Live at the Coast come for their food."

"Could you eat that?" Others' Child pointed where the bug thing had dug itself into the sand.

"Probably," Night Hawk said.

"Where are the people who live here?" she asked him.

"They are here." Night Hawk glanced at the hills. "They know we are here." He caught the dogs by their harness as they raced by, still barking at the waves. "We will go to them now. We are nearly out of water, and you can't drink this. If Fool and Foolish don't stop barking at it, they will have a thirst that will make them sorry."

"I am thirsty," Brother said, and they realized he had been dipping cupped hands in the surf. They set him in the travois and followed what Others' Child could see, now that she looked for it, was a trail up the coast, angling inland where the low hills flattened out into a rocky riverbed full of tumbled stones. The water in the center of the channel was shallow and brackish.

They were only partway up it when a man met them, trotting purposefully along the bank. He stopped and waited, and it was clear that they were not a surprise to him.

Night Hawk lifted one hand in greeting and said something in a language that Others' Child couldn't understand. In their wanderings, she had learned the tongues of several other peoples, but this one was incomprehensible.

"The trader from where the sun comes up," the man said, laughing. He wore a short hide breechclout and a shell ring through a hole in one earlobe. His heavy hair was cropped off below his shoulders and tied out of his face with a thong.

"My son has been trying to drink the ocean," Night Hawk said.

The man handed a waterskin to Brother, who sucked on it greedily.

Night Hawk fished for the man's name and pulled it out of old memories. "Sea Otter." This one had been a boy then, the son of an important man, Night Hawk thought he remembered. "This is my wife, Others' Child," he said. In the coast people's language it came out Strangers' Daughter. It was the closest he could get.

Sea Otter smiled at her. He had an oval face, more rounded and less beaky than Night Hawk's, that lifted easily in a smile. He put his hands together in what Others' Child thought was a gesture of respect, and she smiled back at him, gravely, as if she were out of practice.

"Ho, you have got a family since we saw you last," Sea Otter said to Night Hawk.

"And you?"

"Not yet. But my sister, Foam, is married. Do you remember her? She married a man from the Knifenose Fish Clan, and now she wants to come home again. She is making a great deal of trouble." He waved Night Hawk and Others' Child up the trail, chatting as they went. "On behalf of my Channel Clan, I make you welcome. I think those dogs are mostly coyote. You have grown very bold. Or your bitch did." Sea Otter laughed. "I always said you were crazy"—he smacked the side of his head for emphasis—"not to stay home and be comfortable, and now I know it. Why do you drag this poor woman with you?"

"So I'll be comfortable," Night Hawk said, grinning, relishing momentary safety. If Others' Child had understood him, she'd have cuffed his ears.

Sea Otter's Channel Clan lived in a village of domed houses made from willow poles thatched with reeds. It sat on the edge of a creek that fed into the riverbed they had been following. Just beyond the village the land dropped sharply toward the sea, so the Channel Clan had a fine view of whoever might be coming. They were waiting in a bunch for Night Hawk's family and its escort.

Others' Child studied them covertly, because staring was rude. Even now in winter there was no snow, and in the foothills away from the Endless Water the wind had stopped blowing. The Channel Clan wore only short breechclouts like Sea Otter's, and many necklaces and bracelets and ear ornaments of shell. The finer of them clattered when they walked. Fat, well-fed children clustered around Brother, and one of them handed him a piece of the flat cake she had been chewing on.

"Ha! Little Sister likes your boy," Sea Otter said. "Time to arrange a marriage."

The Channel Clan laughed at that, and the chieftain and the shaman came forward to make the welcome of-

ficial. The chieftain was very grand, a bear of a man
with a tame eagle clinging to a hide strap on one arm.
The shaman was thin, with a lizard's elongated boniness
and a wild mane of hair like a bird's nest. He clapped
Night Hawk on the back and roared a greeting, jumping
up and down. A tall woman just behind the chieftain
wore the proprietary air that Others' Child was used to
seeing in wives, but her manner lacked the expected def-
erence. She was big-breasted and as broad-shouldered as
the chieftain, with a knot of eagle feathers in her black
hair.

The other women crowded around the travois, too
well mannered to open the bundles on it, but too curious
to stay away. They poked at them gently, hoping one
might perhaps spill open by accident. Their voices were
musical and reminded Others' Child of her brother's
flute. *I could learn this language,* she thought. It seemed
almost as if she knew some of the words already. The
women smiled and patted Brother with admiration, holding their hands above the ground to indicate their great
astonishment at his size. He grinned back proudly.

When Night Hawk had finished his conversation, he
came back to Others' Child and said, "There will be a
feast tonight, to honor us. Coast people are hospitable,
and they like to eat. Also, they are giving us a house to
stay in that belongs to Sea Otter's family."

"To stay in?"

"While we are here." Night Hawk began pulling bundles off the travois. "First we will show them what
we've brought. They'll look, and then start bringing us
things they want to trade in the morning. These people
like to think about things for a while."

Sea Otter helped them unpack. "My father is First
Fisherman," he said, "and also he is Great Condor in
the dances, so he is very important, and we have several
houses. We will give you a good one."

"That," said the woman who had been with the chieftain, pointing at the spotted jaguar skin. "I will trade
you something for that." She stroked it and held it to
her bosom to see the effect.

"I thought they liked to think about things," Others' Child chuckled after Night Hawk translated. She saw that they could get a good price for it.

"This is Cannot Be Told, sister of Abalone Catcher, the chief," Night Hawk explained. "She does what she wants to."

Others' Child thought that was an admirable trait. She smiled at Cannot Be Told. Cannot Be Told smiled back.

Others' Child watched the Channel Clan curiously through the afternoon, while Night Hawk displayed their wares and told stories (some almost true) of his adventures. He translated their comments for her in asides that left her somewhat more puzzled than before. These people seemed unlike the Kindred or the Yellow Grass People to Others' Child. They had no summer or winter camps, for one thing. They always lived on the edge of the sea since there was always food there. Big-eared deer lived in the hills, Night Hawk said, but the hunters never chased them very far. There were other things to eat. And what place was better than the one they had?

"You have seen many things. But no place better than here, eh?" Sea Otter slapped Night Hawk on the back. "Why don't you stay?" Night Hawk didn't translate that.

As darkness fell, Others' Child could see the glow from the fire pits along the cliff. Little Brother ran shrieking with a gaggle of the Channel Clan's children, flitting like a bat in the dusk. They swooped past the fire pits and snatched something out of a basket while the women scolded them. A big fish was baking in a pit lined with seaweed and sand—three men had come up the trail from the sea with it, a bigger fish than any she had ever seen, a magical, monster fish. The people caught the fish with nets and spears from boats that you could sit in on the water, Night Hawk said. In another pit, blue and green flames leaped up from salt-soaked driftwood where the women were roasting meat on sticks. Cakes like the one the little girl had given Brother bubbled on hot flat stones, and the air was heady with salt and meat smells.

Sea Otter broke off a piece of hot cake, tossing it from hand to hand, and brought it to her. It tasted a little like nuts.

"That's acorn meal," Night Hawk said.

"Acorns are nasty." Others' Child looked disbelieving.

"They wash the meal with water, two, three, I don't know how many times. It takes the bitter taste out."

Others' Child nibbled the cake again, and the chieftain's sister stopped whatever errand she was bent on and nodded approvingly. She said something that sounded pleasant and strode on purposefully toward the fire pits.

"She offered to teach you to grind acorns," Night Hawk said.

"She acts like . . . one of the Grannies," Others' Child said, searching for comparison. In her experience only old women or magical women had power.

"She is the chieftain's family. Among these people, the chief is always the old chief's son, so the family is powerful."

"What if he doesn't have a son?"

"Then maybe his brother's or his sister's son. If the new chief is a baby, the baby's mother is chief until he's grown. If there isn't anyone, then the chief's sister can be chief until the tribe votes for a new one."

Others' Child's eyes followed Cannot Be Told. "No wonder she walks like that."

"She is promised to a man whose mother was the old shaman, so they will be very powerful. And Abalone Catcher has no sons."

"Oho," Others' Child said. She thought about all that. Women could be shamans here. But only men were allowed to hunt and catch fish, although women could dig clams, the things that Night Hawk said were like snails. And only men could drink the sacred drink, which was made of something Night Hawk said was poison, although maybe she hadn't heard him right. Who would drink poison? All this news seemed very baffling, like a story passed through three messengers that had got garbled on the way. She wished she could speak their language.

The women began raking the sand away from the buried shell things in the pit. They scooped them out with bone spoons and tipped them into baskets. The thing that Night Hawk handed Others' Child had a rough black shell that was opalescent on the inside, like a cloudy sky with the sun behind it. The meat was hot and hard to chew, like gristle, but it tasted of the ocean. She swallowed it and felt as if she were swallowing the Endless Water, and as if there was magic in that.

Brother whipped past her in a cloud of children again. He skidded to a halt and grinned. "There are children here," he announced.

"There are always children in a village," Night Hawk said.

"These children are better children," Brother said. "They like me." He darted off again.

Others' Child laughed. "It will be good for him to have playmates, awhile." She poked with curious fingers at the steaming piles of things in shells, ready to try something else. There was the other kind of snail thing that Night Hawk said was a clam, and something else whose name she forgot. The big fish had dark, rich meat that crumbled in her fingers. The meat on sticks was seal, they told her, and she shook her head because she had never seen one. Sea Otter tried to imitate one for her—who could come from so distant a place that they had never seen a seal? The Channel Clan roared when he got down on his stomach and swung his elbows, barking.

There were fresh greens (in winter!) and dried berries, and a baked bulb called soaproot, which Night Hawk said you could also use for washing your hair, or coating tool handles, or poisoning fish, but he couldn't have translated that right, either. Others' Child poked at it dubiously, but everyone else was eating it, so she took a bite.

"Very good for you!" The shaman slapped her on the back. "Makes babies!"

Everything was carried in baskets sealed with a thick, gluey tar that was better than anything found where the Kindred lived. There were pools of it in places that you had to watch out for, they said.

"I've seen all kinds of things go *bloop* down in that tar. And they don't come up." Sea Otter's father shook his head. "But it is fine stuff. No matter what is broken, you can stick it back with tar."

"Oh, she has seen better things than tar pits," another woman said. She eyed Others' Child enviously, and Night Hawk translated. "All the places she has seen, big mountains and the cat longer than two men—"

"That was bones," Others' Child said. "Did you tell them it was a live cat?"

"Of course not," Night Hawk said, but she thought he had.

"That must be very wonderful," the woman said. "To come home and tell everyone all about it." She laughed. "Maybe I will leave my old husband and go with you."

Everyone else howled with laughter again. "Ho, Laurel Tree, you would be homesick the first night out. You would hear a nightjar and come running home saying the Rolling Head was after you!"

"Maybe," Laurel Tree said, abashed. She gave them a haughty look. "But it would be a fine thing to do, all the same."

And what if she could trade Laurel Tree the chance, Others' Child thought, in exchange for Laurel Tree's house of willow poles and Laurel Tree's husband, who very likely did not always have to be moving? What then? She ate another snail thing and thought about it, rolling the taste of the sea in her mouth.

Later, curled in Night Hawk's arms in the willow-pole house that Sea Otter's family had lent them, it was easier to imagine staying here forever with Night Hawk, her husband suddenly and wonderfully tamed by miraculous fish and snail things, by enough to eat, living with a people so rich they didn't need to be suspicious. Dozing in the morning while the first light seeped through the reed thatch, she was still imagining how it would be, snuggled down in fur blankets and half asleep. Sometimes Night Hawk seemed to be talking to her about it all, and sometimes he was still a lump curled beside her, with Brother wedged between them, and the dogs on their feet.

Then there were feet running through the dream, and angry voices outside the house, and she sat up groggily. Night Hawk was up before her, crouched naked by the door, his fingers around his spear. Others' Child grabbed Brother protectively, but as Night Hawk listened, he laid the spear down again. He slid back into bed and grinned.

"What is it?"

"Family matters. That is Sea Otter's sister out there." He cocked an ear. "Her husband is a boring old turtle," he informed Others' Child.

"That is what she says?"

"And she is going to live at home again." An angry bellow shook the willow poles. "And her father does not wish to give back her bride-price."

Others' Child climbed out of bed. She crept to the doorway and peeped out. It was bad manners to listen to another family's business, but she couldn't help but hear, so she might as well see, too. And anyway, she couldn't understand the shouting.

Sea Otter's father, Condor Dancer, jerked the door flap open, and Others' Child shrieked and wrapped the blanket around herself.

"Come out and tell my daughter she is disobedient and a fool!" he roared, apparently seeking reinforcements.

Others' Child looked at him uncomprehendingly while Night Hawk pulled his breechclout on.

Condor Dancer stalked back to his daughter, still shouting. The daughter, Foam, put her hands on her hips and shouted back, rising on her toes to level her nose with his. Sea Otter's sister was wiry and graceful, with a stubborn, jutting jaw that just now was covered with bramble scratches. She stamped her foot while her mother fluttered around her, wringing her hands.

"These people buy their wives, and they're stricter than our people," Night Hawk said in Others' Child's ear.

Others' Child couldn't imagine anyone stricter than the Kindred.

"If the bride-price isn't paid, the children aren't even considered real children. But if she wants to leave him, her family has to give back the bride-price. I think it was a lot."

"No one made you marry him!" Condor Dancer shouted.

"Oh, we wouldn't do that!" Her mother, whose name was Blue Butterfly, wrung her hands. "You know you said you wanted him."

"I made a mistake." Foam folded her arms.

"What's wrong with him?" Sea Otter demanded, exasperated. "This is the second time you have come home."

"He is old," Foam said.

"He is the same age as me. And he is the Octopus Dancer."

"He snores, and he wants to tell me about the fish he caught."

"A wife should listen to her husband."

Foam stuck her chin out at him.

The other three glared at her.

"Bah! I want my breakfast," Condor Dancer said suddenly.

Blue Butterfly scurried into their willow-pole house and popped her head out a moment later to say to Foam, "If you are here, you come and help me."

Others' Child laced up her hide skirt before any more excitement happened. "Will they let her stay?" she asked Night Hawk. "How far did she come? Will her husband come after her?" It all seemed very interesting, like hearing a story and watching it happen at the same time.

"The Knifenose Fish Clan live up the coast. I think chasing her is probably beneath her husband's dignity. He will send a messenger and demand his wife or his bride-price back. This is the second time she has run away.''

Others' Child clucked her tongue. The bride-price must be a big one to make such a fuss. Among the Yellow Grass People a deer hide was enough, and easy to give back. It came of having more than you needed, she supposed. She thought wistfully of the snail things and wondered if she could have them for breakfast.

Brother crawled out of the bed and butted his head against her leg. She took him by the hand and went out to see what the Channel Clan did all day.

There were four or five outside waiting to bargain for Night Hawk's trade goods. Or maybe to see what Foam's brother and her parents would do now—everyone was speculating freely when the trader came out of his house, and they turned to him to demand his opinion. Night Hawk shrugged his shoulders.

''Why should this man care what Condor Dancer's daughter does?'' Cannot Be Told said repressively. ''I want to trade with him for his spotted catskin. Be quiet and don't bother him.''

No one paid any attention to that. Others' Child sat down on a log, wriggling her bare toes in the soft dirt while the foxtail grass tickled her knees, and listened to them argue. She tried to make out the few words that Night Hawk had taught her. She wanted to be able to speak to these people, ask them things. Brother was communicating with mysterious competence with a small girl who wore a string of shells around her neck.

''Maybe there will be a war,'' someone said.

Night Hawk cocked his head toward the speaker.

''You can't have a war unless someone won't pay compensation,'' another man retorted.

''Well, Condor Dancer won't give back all those abalone.''

''*That* would start a war. Haw!''

''Of course he can't *now*. Other abalone.''

''The Shell Men haven't said he has to, yet,'' a woman said.

"They will, and then when he doesn't, we can raid the Knifenose Fish Clan."

"No, they get to raid us first. Because Condor Dancer won't give back the bride-price."

"Well, *then* we can raid them."

Night Hawk smacked his forehead. He turned to Others' Child. "These people are crazy," he said over his shoulder. "They play war like a game, with rules. And someone to tell them when they can fight." He snorted. "When someone gets killed, then they stop."

"That sounds very civilized," Others' Child said.

Night Hawk rolled his eyes. "Civilized" was a notion that Others' Child's mother had had. It meant not killing people. The Kindred were a tenacious tribe, and they fought *real* wars. Night Hawk gave a derisive hoot of laughter, but Others' Child held her ground.

"They are civilized," she said again firmly. "Their rituals are for things that make sense."

Night Hawk chuckled and held up the catskin for Cannot Be Told to admire. She seemed uninterested in Condor Dancer's troubles. "Jaguar is a very fierce cat," Night Hawk said to her. "He nearly skinned me before I could skin him." He extended his forearm, laced with a jagged white scar.

Others' Child sucked in her breath indignantly. That scar was from an old knife fight. It was another thing they did not agree on—whether it was all right to lie when they traded for things.

Night Hawk saw her expression and laughed. Cannot Be Told didn't believe him anyway—the scar was too old. "This is ritual, too," he said to Others' Child.

Others' Child sniffed. "You should be careful what you say," she informed him darkly. Any sane person believed in magic. You could call it up without meaning to, too, and maybe Jaguar would come with it.

Night Hawk ignored her after that, the way his wife ordinarily ignored the gods when it seemed practical to her to do so—as if they were a band of unnecessary and argumentative relatives. In her present mood she found significance in the fact that the sun came up in the morning.

He extended the catskin to Cannot Be Told and let her feel it some more. "It is very powerful," he assured her. "It would be very dangerous for anyone not in the chieftain's family to wear it."

"Spots," Sea Otter said to Others' Child. He pointed to Cannot Be Told in the jaguar skin.

"Spots," Others' Child said, wondering what it meant. Arrogant, maybe.

"No spots." Sea Otter smacked his palm on his own plain hide cape. Night Hawk translated.

Oh. Now there were eight words she knew, including "dance."

It was the winter solstice, and the Channel Clan were going to make their Condor Dance, and Sea Otter was going to explain it. Others' Child and Night Hawk sat on the edge of the dance ground, waiting. It was a mystery, Night Hawk said, like the Deer Dance of their own people. Condor helped turn the sun around.

Others' Child had seen a condor once above their trail, soaring over the warm brown hills, its wingspan as long as two men's height. Condor was a scavenger, but he owned a mystical dignity that Buzzard didn't possess. Great Condor kept the world clean, the Channel Clan said. A chill mist had come up with the dusk, and Others' Child wriggled farther under her blanket of coyote skins. Her eyes peered over the rim of yellow-gray fur.

"Condor Dancer," Sea Otter said, and she caught her breath. A great dark bird had come out on the Channel Clan's dance ground, wings dipping ponderously from side to side. He was taller than a man, and his outstretched wings swept over the heads of the watchers. Two other dancers accompanied him, rattling bracelets of shell beads around their ankles, their heads crowned with feathered topknots like birds' crests. They made a sound like a thin whistle, but Great Condor was silent. He stepped to the rhythm of shell rattles, swaying, his beak an implacable curve.

His wing lifted and blotted out the moon that rode like a fat white shell over the ocean. His head turned, and Others' Child thought he was looking at her, and burrowed into her coyote skins. When she peeked out, she thought that no one else dared to move, either. Even Cannot Be Told sat upright in her jaguar skin, hands shaking shell rattles, eyes on the dark dancer.

Foam watched him warily, despite knowing that it was her father under the dark-feathered head and moon-curved beak. He paused for a moment in front of Foam, then passed on, dancing solemnly, one heavy foot after the other, marking the ground. Foam edged away, so that he would look at someone else if he came past again.

The bird creatures followed, shaking their topknots and chanting now, something that Others' Child couldn't understand. The other Channel people were chanting, too, and she heard Night Hawk's voice among them.

The salt wind whispered around them, ruffling the foxtail grass and making the blue-green flames in the sacred fire dance. The moon watched them like a white eye. Afterward the boys who were becoming men would drink the sacred drink and see visions, but Others' Child thought that she had seen magic enough.

IV

Picture Magic

A storm came in the night, lashing a cold rain around the willow houses and turning the sea gray and spiteful, battering against the sand and rocks on the shore. Others' Child thought that maybe the dance had been done wrong, and Great Condor was angry, but no one seemed to be frightened. When it cleared, leaving the sky still clouded but with the faint sheen of an abalone shell coming through the gray, the Channel Clan went down to the shore with baskets to see what the waves had washed up. A storm was a gift in these parts, it seemed.

The channel in the riverbed had widened, and it was brown with mud washed from the dry hills. The air was dank, and Others' Child shivered in her furs, but it was still hard to believe it was winter. The Channel Clan scrambled down the rocky trail and pawed among the wrack along the sand—driftwood and shells and stranded fish.

"Sometimes there is a whale," said Tern, a short woman with a round moon-face. She stood in front of

Others' Child, holding her hands wide to indicate the immense size of this bounty.

"A big fish," Night Hawk translated. "Bigger than a buffalo."

Others' Child eyed him skeptically.

"Knifenose Fish drives him ashore," Tern said. She pounced on a pronged piece of driftwood, like a deer's horns, and put it in her basket.

"Why?" Night Hawk asked her.

Tern's eyes widened. "Because Whale is useful. Knifenose Fish chases him onto shore and leaves him there." She put her wrist to her nose, forefinger pointed outward like a spear. "We make a dance to him, too."

Sea Otter had come up even with them, a pack on his back. "Maybe I should pray to Knifenose Fish to chase my sister home to her husband." He clapped Night Hawk on the back. "Don't leave while I am gone, friend."

Night Hawk saw Foam standing beyond them, arms folded, mouth in a furious pout. "How are you going to make her go?" He envisioned Sea Otter carrying her, wriggling like a snake.

"Father said she is to go." Sea Otter shrugged. "So she goes."

Night Hawk thought that some of Foam's wrath stemmed from being afraid to argue with that. If Condor Dancer sent her back to her husband, she would go. Then she would probably run away again.

"How long a journey?"

Sea Otter spread two fingers. "So many days. To go and come back. Maybe. If I don't have to carry her."

Night Hawk laughed. "We will be here. My wife likes your people. We will stay a moon." He had decided that suddenly. He felt expansive, generous. It would be fine to loll about in a willow-pole house for a while and eat fish.

Tern had gone on down the beach, leaving behind her wet footprints that filled with water. Night Hawk saw Others' Child staring at them.

"The sea is under the land here, too," he said to her.

"A magical country. Maybe it cures heartache."

She looked up at him, startled.

Little Brother had stopped to peer earnestly at his own footprints, and Night Hawk said, "I have been thinking about Elder Brother and the dead girl baby and the way things were between us before they died."

Others' Child was still looking up at him, and her eyes filled with tears. "Nothing cures heartache," she said tightly, but she put her hand in his and stood up.

"I told Sea Otter we would stay a moon," Night Hawk said.

Now her eyes widened. They were the color of wet, dark berries after a rain, and two little moons glowed in them. She held out her arms as if she were soaking up the mist that hung in the air, and her hair gleamed like the slick wet leaves of the kelp. Her arms closed around his ribs, tightly, cutting off his breath.

"I will learn their talk," she said, "and how to cook the snail things and make acorn meal, and I will believe you about the fish that is bigger than a buffalo, and you won't be sorry."

"It's only for a moon," he said.

She smiled at him, rapturous. Anything could happen in a moon. She raced after Tern, her footprints giddy in the sand. Little Brother watched her, perplexed, fist full of wet sand. Night Hawk scooped him up and put him on his shoulders. They saw Others' Child pointing at things, and Tern telling her words.

"Boat," Tern said.

Others' Child ran her fingers along it, feeling the magic in the reed sides. In this she could float on the Endless Water. She picked up an oar. "Paddle," she said, remembering that word, too. New words hung in the air of the past half-moon like rainbows.

Tern pushed the end of the canoe into the surf. Others' Child followed her, wading out into the cold water, hands guiding the bobbing boat until Tern said to climb in. They did, and the canoe rocked under them. Tern grabbed a paddle and dipped it into the water. The canoe righted, its nose swinging toward the mysterious islands on the horizon.

Around them other canoes put into the surf. Night Hawk was in the chieftain's with Abalone Catcher and the shaman, whose name was Old Tidepool. Little Brother was on the mainland with an old granny of the Channel Clan; only nursing babies and children old enough to paddle had come in the canoes. The sun flashed on the blue water, and Others' Child felt the canoe move on the swells the way she imagined the birds must move in the air, or the fish people underwater. In the bottom were baskets of acorn flour and two soft deer hides, the possessions of Tern and her sister. The Channel Clan traded such things with the people on the islands and got shell beads for them. In the men's canoes were spearpoints and dried deer meat, but the flour and hides belonged to the women.

That people lived on those islands seemed magical in itself to Others' Child. The islands floated beyond the edge of the world, gateway to the place where the coast people's spirits went when they died. Tern had told her how the Shell Clan on the islands could see spirits passing in the dark on their way over the water, trailing blue light. If someone had died of a disease, you could see the disease rolling like a ball of fire beside him, Tern said. Sometimes if the Shell Clan shouted, the spirit might turn back, and the one it belonged to might not die. But sometimes it kept on, and then they would hear a bang like a stone dropping when the opening into the Otherworld closed behind the spirit.

Because they lived so close to the Otherworld, the Shell Clan's wisdom was respected. They were the arbiters in disputes between one village and another. If Condor Dancer asked them whether he should give Foam's bride-price back to her husband, they would tell him, Tern said. But he wasn't ready to ask.

"Maybe this time she will stay and behave herself." Tern chuckled. "One time, Sea Otter took her back and she was back here before him. Condor Dancer was *very* mad."

"What is wrong with her husband?" Others' Child wanted to know.

Tern lifted her shoulders. "I don't know. I think he just annoys her, like an itch. When she sees him, it makes her grit her teeth. People like that should not be married to each other." She considered. "My husband is old and fat, but he makes me smile when I see him. That is right."

Others' Child thought about Night Hawk. She could see him in the chieftain's canoe, looking into the wind, his short-cropped hair standing up around his head, his teeth whiter than the sun in his dark face. He was restless already. She could feel it. He wanted to be like the canoe, or the islands, launched on the Endless Water. A gull swirled above them, shrieking, and for a moment she expected him to lift like it on the wind, arms spread.

"My husband only wants to leave places," she murmured. She dipped a finger into the bright water and drew a picture of Gull in water on the inside of the canoe—wings spread so that he would fly away before he took Night Hawk into the air with him.

"That is very wonderful," Tern said, wide-eyed. She looked at the other canoes dotting the water in the channel and thought what a great thing she had to tell them about the new woman. "Is it magic?"

One of Gull's children lit on the side of the canoe, squawked, and flew off again.

Others' Child laughed. "Sometimes." Surely the magic was in the place. It didn't matter that Night Hawk wanted to leave. Great Condor would change his mind if she asked him properly.

Others' Child's knees were beginning to cramp from kneeling in the canoe bottom, and her arms ached from paddling—it was hard to dip the paddle cleanly into the water the way Tern was doing. The paddle was unwieldy and would flip away from her to lose itself in the sea, or lift suddenly and hit her on the chin. But she could see the islands drawing close now, rising from the long breakers, their backs furred with green bushes. The magic that flowed over the shining surface of the water, sparkling with every wave, seemed to enfold the boat, suspending it like a bubble in the air.

Tern looked over her shoulder and nodded approval at Others' Child. "You will grow the right muscles when you have paddled some more. We are nearly there."

Others' Child laughed. "Maybe I will stay there. My knees have turned to stone." The paddle felt as if it were made of stone, too, wanting to sink in the water and never rise. But the waves lifted it, pushed it back at her, while the gulls wheeled over her head.

"There will be a big time tonight," Tern said. "With stories and food. We won't load the boats till morning." Her dark eyes gleamed. It was always exciting to go to the islands of the Shell Clan, and most of her village had kin there.

Tern ran the canoe onto the sand in shallow surf, and Others' Child lurched forward and hit her nose on the paddle. They dragged the boat up on the beach, where the Shell Clan were waiting for them. Tern's sister, Bone, had climbed out of her own canoe and was jabbering (too fast for Others' Child to follow) with a woman of the Shell Clan, who Tern said was a third sister.

Others' Child felt like the gulls suddenly, like feathers in the air, now that she had let go of the paddle. Untethered, she thought the wind might lift her, or she might dance down the beach, dancing out some prayer she had only just thought of.

Tern caught her by the hand. "The men will all talk about the weather and lie about fish they caught. The women's fire is where things will be interesting." She pulled Others' Child along.

The Shell women were digging a pit to bake mussels, and Tern elbowed her way into the thick of the work and began laying seaweed leaves flat in the bottom.

"This is Strangers' Daughter, who came with her husband from where the sun gets up in the morning," Tern announced. "She can make gulls come out of her fingers." She nudged Others' Child. "Show them."

Others' Child smoothed the sand by the fire pit cautiously. When you made things just to show off, the gods might think you were too pleased with yourself. She scratched a gull into the sand, its wings tucked back and its head cocked curiously at them. It was hard not to preen before the round O of Bone's mouth.

The third sister, Waxing Moon, made gull noises and clapped her hands in delight. "Awk! Scree!" She danced on the sand.

The women stopped work and pushed around her, trying to see.

"Make a dog."

"Make a bug."

"Make the ocean."

"I can't make the ocean," Others' Child said, laughing.

"Make another bird. Make Great Condor!"

"No, don't," someone else said quickly. "Foolish,"she added under her breath.

Others' Child shook her head solemnly in agreement with that. "Things come sometimes when you make them this way. It calls to them. I do not think you whistle for Great Condor as you do for a dog."

They nodded at each other, understanding.

"Can you make a whale?" Bone wanted to know.

"Not until I have seen one," Others' Child said. "I have to see him first."

"He is big," Tern suggested.

"So is a mountain," Others' Child said.

"I know!" Waxing Moon edged closer to Others' Child. "Can you make a baby? Can you make it come to me?" Despite her name, she was as narrow in the waist as a straw.

Others' Child thought about it. She had never done that. She scratched with her fingernail in the wet sand, wishing she could call the baby to herself instead. But it was Waxing Moon who had asked for it, and anyway she didn't want just any baby, she wanted her own ones back. If she had wanted a new baby, she knew how to do it.

She began to draw a person in the sand, short-bodied and big-headed. Carefully she gave it two eyes and a mouth and nose and two ears, the right number of fingers and toes.

"A boy," Waxing Moon said.

Others' Child added that. She felt vaguely apprehensive, but the women were urging her on. Waxing Moon had been married for three turns of the sun and never had a baby. Her husband was impatient and talked of another wife.

"Another wife could do work," an old woman said. "You should let him have her."

"No more wives," Waxing Moon said. "That is *my* man."

"You will think different when your bones are as old as mine. I would find *my* husband a new young wife, but no girl would have him." The old woman chuckled and clucked her tongue between ragged teeth. "He is too ugly."

"I will not think different when a new wife has babies and my place by the fire," Waxing Moon said.

Others' Child drew circles around the baby in the sand, trying to enclose it in Waxing Moon's womb.

"Babies are easy to get," a plump girl said. "You must be doing something wrong."

"I am not." Waxing Moon stiffened, but she was watching the sand baby covetously.

"Then the gods are angry with you." The plump girl looked superior. "*I* have three babies already."

"Yah, and none of them your husband's," Waxing Moon snarled.

Plump Girl grabbed her by the hair. "You take that back!"

"I could get babies, too, if I slept with snakes." Waxing Moon dug her fingernails into Plump Girl's wrist.

"My husband doesn't need a second wife!" Plump Girl yanked at Waxing Moon's hair, and Waxing Moon sank her teeth into her shoulder.

Others' Child put her arms over her drawing in the sand. Bone and Tern watched with interest but didn't interfere. It was not their village. Waxing Moon and Plump Girl were rolling on the edge of the fire pit when the wife of the Shell Clan's chieftain bustled up and kicked them both hard with a bony foot.

"Spiteful cats! Behave yourselves in front of guests!" She bent down and yanked them upright by their hair. Plump Girl spat at Waxing Moon, and the chieftain's wife backhanded her across the face.

"You get babies so easy!" Waxing Moon said. "The next ones will come in a litter, like dogs. With dogs' heads!"

Plump Girl crossed the fingers of one hand at her, middle finger over forefinger, and hissed.

"Go and be ashamed of yourselves!" the chieftain's wife thundered, and they backed away from each other, lips stuck out.

The chieftain's wife looked at Others' Child's baby in the sand. "The shaman from the mainland is very welcome among us," she said softly and made a gesture of respect at Others' Child. "We are sorry our women are bad-mannered."

"I am not a shaman," Others' Child said.

No one looked as if they believed that.

"You have made a great new magic," the chieftain's wife said.

Cannot Be Told nodded in agreement. She looked pleased and proprietary. After all, the stranger woman was visiting in *her* village, not the Shell Clan's, who made themselves so important, living next to the spirit world. It made them flighty, if you asked Cannot Be Told. Look at the two who had been rolling on the ground in front of guests.

Others' Child smiled and said gently, "It is my only magic."

"I will show it to my husband." The chieftain's wife looked important.

"And why should men have it?" Cannot Be Told demanded. "They will only want her to make things for themselves. Things they don't need," she added. "Second wives and bigger cocks."

Others' Child snorted with amusement. She was almost certain she had heard right. "I never made one of those, either. They are too easy to find as it is now," she said, and the other women whooped with laughter.

"Think if they could make more," Tern chortled, "they would want two of them!"

"They would make them bigger and bigger. They would walk like this!" A Channel woman staggered bowlegged along the sand, and the other women howled.

A group of men looked over at them from their own fire, and the women laughed louder, burying their faces in their hands.

Others' Child patted the baby down into the sand, enclosing it before someone stepped on it. Then she scooped up the sand and gave it to Waxing Moon, who had edged back toward the group, one wary eye on the chieftain's wife.

"I never made a baby before. I don't know if it will work."

"It will work," Waxing Moon said. She took the sand and went away with it.

The other women had gone back to making their fire pit, the laughter bubbling over their heads like salt spray. The men looked at them once more, haughtily, and turned back to their own fire.

"What is your woman saying to our women?" the Shell chieftain asked Night Hawk suspiciously.

Night Hawk spread his hands with a half-smile. "She hardly knows the language yet." He knew better than to ask the women what they had been laughing at. They had been laughing at the men. He could tell that. He thought the chieftain could, too, and disapproved.

Abalone Catcher, the Channel Clan's chieftain, saw Night Hawk's silent grin. The Channel Clan were less careful of their dignity than the Shell Men. He edged closer to the fire while the eagle on his arm ruffled its feathers. "Maybe Condor Dancer should ask the Shell men what his daughter is laughing at," Abalone Catcher suggested slyly, elbowing Condor Dancer.

"Hoo! Condor Dancer's daughter is laughing at her husband," Old Tidepool, the shaman, said. "Anyone can tell that."

Condor Dancer glowered at him.

"Does Condor Dancer of the Channel Clan wish the Shell Men to tell him what he should do?" the chieftain of the Shell Men inquired.

"No," Condor Dancer said. He hadn't wanted the subject brought up at all.

"The Shell Men will arbitrate," the chieftain said, as if Condor Dancer had said yes. "That is why we live on the edge of the Otherworld."

"Not yet," Old Tidepool said, seeing Condor Dancer begin to fume. He chortled. "But soon."

"Maybe the daughter of Condor Dancer will stay where she belongs this time," Abalone Catcher said.

A fresh burst of laughter came from the women's fire. One of them was walking bowlegged down the sand again, waggling an imaginary penis at the others.

Abalone Catcher wisely ignored her. "If she does not," he said, "the Knifenose Fish Clan will very likely come to the Shell Men, so we need not trouble ourselves with it now."

"I sent her back," Condor Dancer grumbled. He pointed at Sea Otter, who had taken her. "What more do they want?"

"That she stay, maybe," Abalone Catcher said, chuckling. He turned to Night Hawk again. "That family's women were always stubborn."

"What will happen if she won't stay and her father won't give back the bride-price?" Night Hawk wanted to know.

"Then they will raid us and take something," Abalone Catcher said. "And then we will raid them. Maybe someone will be killed. When everyone has retrieved his honor, we will ask the Shell Men to settle it, and they will say who has to pay recompense."

Night Hawk shook his head. These people made no sense. War was war, not a game.

Abalone Catcher gripped his side, fingers splayed over

his belly, above his breechclout. He grunted, and Old Tidepool looked at him with lifted bushy eyebrows. "Go away," he told Old Tidepool. "It is nothing."

"If it is nothing, I will suck the nothing out for you," Old Tidepool said.

Abalone Catcher glared at him, his teeth gritted. The eagle opened its beak and rattled its wings.

"When we go home," Old Tidepool said.

Abalone Catcher nodded his head, his shell bead top-knot clicking. "You sucked it out for me before," he said irritably. "Why does it come back? And why does it come back to shame me in front of the Shell Men?"

"Only the demon in your belly knows that," Old Tidepool said. "I will ask him."

"It is not a large demon," Abalone Catcher said to Night Hawk, who had watched them uneasily. "Old Tidepool drives him out for me." He looked up at the Shell Men to make sure they had not noticed. The eagle stepped from side to side on his arm. Its eye was round and gold like the sun that was going down over the island's western edge.

"It is a great responsibility to be chieftain," Night Hawk murmured. It would give him pains in his belly, too.

"I do not have a son yet," Abalone Catcher said. "I have buried one wife already, and no sons. Maybe it is the demon."

"It is possible," Old Tidepool said. "In the summer, at the Trade Moon, I will look for an amulet for you. Something with power, from another place."

"That is bound to cure the chieftain," Night Hawk said to be polite. He had seen pains in the belly before and sometimes, when they were not from too much back-fat washed down with cactus juice, they did not go away no matter how many dead spiders and small stones the shaman sucked out of them with his sucking tube. "What is the Trade Moon?" he asked, because the other was not a good thought to dwell on.

"It is in the summer," Abalone Catcher said. "When we and the Knifenose Fish Clan and the Abalone Clan and the Split Rock Clan from inland and the Shell Clan and all the others of us meet to trade things with one another.''

"What if you are at war with the Knifenose Fish Clan?''

"That does not matter," Abalone Catcher said, surprised. "Trade Moon is more important. We get shell beads and fishhooks from the islands to trade for acorns from the inland people and many marriages are made and everyone gets very drunk. That is more important than war.''

Night Hawk smiled. "I must get things to trade at Trade Moon. I can see that."

"It is foolish to wander about the way you do," Abalone Catcher told him. "You only have to go to Trade Moon, and then you will not have to live in the wild places.''

"My wife has told me this. With respect, you do not need to tell me, too.''

"I only tell you because you may not know what a fine place this is to live," Abalone Catcher said. "There are many fine girls for your son to marry, and food all the time. What else is there to want?''

"To see things," Night Hawk said.

"There is plenty to see. I will show you a whale.''

Night Hawk gave up. He lay on his back in the sand and looked at the stars winking into the sky while the Shell Men and the Channel Men talked about fish. He had wanted to see the Endless Water again, even a whale. But now that he had seen it, what was the point in seeing it some more?

There were trails through the stars. Night Hawk could see them like milky swaths of light across the sky, and wondered where he would go if he could set his foot on the start of one. Up past the Great Bear, perhaps, until he could talk with the Moon in her white house and ask her why things were the way they were. He narrowed his eyes until he could see the Moon's face on her white disk, like a piece of abalone shell in the sky. Maybe abalone shells were pieces of the Moon that had fallen off. What made him wander? And what made the dogs, who were three parts coyote, make their home with human people? What made you do a thing that was not what your kind should do? He would like to ask the Moon that.

Old Aunt, who had tried to mother him for years with little success, said that his own mother had startled a feeding hawk, and it had flown in her face when she was carrying him. That had given him a traveling foot. It was Hawk's doing, Old Aunt said. It irritated Night Hawk to think that the way he was might be determined by something other than himself. *It is not Hawk,* he thought irritably, *it is me.*

After a while the mussels roasting in the women's fire pit were cooked, and the men went to where the women were. Night Hawk sat next to Others' Child, and they ate mussels out of hot shells, wiping dripping chins with their fingers. He could see lines in the sand where she had been making things for the women.

Old Tidepool stared at the lines, his head cocked like a bird's to one side and then the other. He scratched his nest of hair and stamped one foot. He bent over to peer more closely, hands on gnarled knees. "Har! That is a deer! Anyone could see that." He straightened and squatted down again in front of Others' Child. "Very powerful. You will teach me how to make these marks."

"Not everyone can do it," Others' Child said doubtfully. She didn't want to insult him. But when she had tried to teach Night Hawk, he had made horrible squiggles that looked like spiders.

"I can do it," Old Tidepool assured her.

Cannot Be Told stopped beside them, balancing a basket of hot shells on her head. "Ha. I told you the men would want it for themselves."

"The chieftain's sister is powerful already," Old Tidepool informed her. "She does not need magic."

"The shaman is jealous because he does not have woman magic." Cannot Be Told stuck her chin out at him. Her heavy breasts seemed to stick out, too, defiantly in his face.

Others' Child giggled, and put her hand over her mouth.

"The chieftain's sister will be married soon and have a husband to find her other things to do," Old Tidepool remarked.

Cannot Be Told departed with a switch of her hips.

"A woman of sufficient power already," Old Tidepool said. He looked at Others' Child thoughtfully, assessing her. "Tomorrow's tomorrow, you may teach me to make things in the ground."

The day after tomorrow's tomorrow, when they had come home from the Shell Clan's island, Sea Otter dragged a huge carcass across the hillock where Others' Child's willow-pole house sat. "This is Knifenose Fish," he said, panting. "We caught him today. He was hard work, but he is very good to eat."

Wide-eyed, Others' Child stared at the carcass. Knifenose Fish was bigger than Sea Otter and had a long blade sticking out from his snout. No wonder he was sacred. Anything that strange-looking would have to be.

"Old Tidepool says, now that you have seen him, will you please make his image in the dirt, so that Old Tidepool can learn to do it, too?"

Others' Child sighed. Old Tidepool so far had tried to make a quail, a deer, and a regular fish. They staggered drunkenly along a patch of soft dirt that Others' Child had smoothed out for him. She wasn't sure what might come out of them if she left them there.

"How do you catch a fish so big?" She started to draw Knifenose Fish in the dirt, practicing the sweep of his tail, so that he could swim to the fishermen's boats.

"With nets." Sea Otter rubbed his shins where the rope fibers had scraped them. His dark skin was dusted with a white sheen of salt. "Will you make something for me?"

"I will tell you what I have told the others. I will make it, but things do not always come when I call them. And sometimes you call things you didn't mean to. I wish you would tell that to Old Tidepool."

Sea Otter chuckled.

"What do you want me to make?"

He grinned and sat down beside her. "A woman."

"What?"

"I do not have a wife yet."

"There are many women among the Channel Clan," Others' Child pointed out.

"I am related to most of them."

"The Shell Clan, then. Or the Split Rock Clan. The Knifenose Fish Clan if they are not angry with you."

"My sister hasn't come home again yet," Sea Otter said. "So far. And those women do not interest me. I have seen them."

"What is wrong with them?" Others' Child asked him, annoyed. Men seemed to her to have too many requirements.

Sea Otter thought. "They are all alike," he said. He looked at Others' Child's aquiline nose and the angular planes of her face, as if interested in her strangeness. "Make me a woman who is different."

She drew Sea Otter his woman and Old Tidepool his fish. When the men came to her again the next morning and asked her for a deer, she made that, too. They were going inland to hunt the big-eared deer that browsed in the chaparral this time of year. Winter and early spring were the rainy times, Night Hawk said. Since they had come to the Channel Clan's village, Others' Child had watched the hills turn green overnight, like the desert after a rain, furring themselves over softly with young grass. By the Trade Moon they would be brown again, and the deer would go higher up the foothills.

Since the trip to the islands, the Channel Clan had treated her as an honored woman, with status aside from that gained by being Night Hawk the Trader's wife. It was a new position to Others' Child, and she got up every morning and put it on like a new skin. As the days went by, and the Channel Clan came to ask her for a good catch, or a rainy day, or a new patch of soaproot, she began to feel herself settling in like a dog on a hearth. Like a dog, she turned her belly to the fire and basked in the warmth of belonging.

When the boats came back full of fish, the fishermen brought her the biggest one, and even Old Tidepool gave her respect because making the magic lines in the earth was proving harder than it had looked. When the hunters came home without a deer, she expected blame for that, but Sea Otter said they had found the trail of a mountain cat instead, and nothing could call a deer past cat scent. No doubt they would find the deer she had called for them the next time.

There were plenty of other things to eat. Others' Child was greedy for the snail things, for which she was slowly learning the true names. And Knifenose Fish was as good a meal as Sea Otter had said he was. The men put on fish disguises and danced a dance to him after they ate him so he would know they were appreciative.

The Fish Dance didn't put Others' Child's heart in her throat the way the Condor Dance did, even though she knew how he could drive Whale onto shore. Try as she might, she couldn't feel that she was talking to a fish. But Great Condor was another matter. She could sense him hovering in the air when she went out across the hills with Little Brother to look for soaproot and camas bulbs. He was like a hide stretched over them, watchful and curious, wondering what she was doing here, she thought. Sometimes she saw his shiny eye come out of the clouds.

She was still afraid to draw him, but silently he began to show her things that she could draw.

These new drawings had no pattern that Night Hawk could see, and he began to watch his wife uneasily.

"They are not real things," Others' Child said, exasperated, when he asked her again what she had made.

"They must be something."

"They are something."

"Then they must be real."

"No. They are not real like a fish, or a spoon. They are something I see in here." Others' Child put two fingers to her forehead. She wiped out a pattern of wavy lines and redrew them.

Night Hawk couldn't see the difference. He shook his head. "You sound like these fish men when they have drunk poison. They don't make any sense, either." They had both seen the initiates at the solstice retching and reeling over the dance ground.

"It isn't poison," said Others' Child, who had been learning things. "It gives them visions." She remembered the faces, eyes blank, staring at things no one else could see. She had wanted to see those things, too.

"It makes them sick when they drink it. That is poison."

"Well, I have not drunk anything."

"Do you really talk to Great Condor?" Night Hawk demanded. "That is what Old Tidepool said when they caught all the fish."

Others' Child stopped and thought. "No, I don't think so." She wasn't at all sure he could get past Coyote. "The fish bring themselves."

"Old Tidepool says Condor will talk to me, too, if I listen," Night Hawk informed her sardonically. "He is crazy, I think, from drinking poison."

Others' Child shrugged. "Maybe Condor has a different way of talking. It might be that." She spread her hand over the lines in the earth. "These are things that I want. I don't know why they look like this."

"What are?" Night Hawk glared at parallel lines of dots. They might be the sun's rays. Or rain. They might be lines of dots.

"These." She looked at them dubiously. "I see them when I dream. I don't know what they are, either."

"Are they magic?" Night Hawk was used to the idea that his wife had magic in her fingers. He wasn't used to thinking of it running around loose.

"I don't know." Above the dots she drew something that might be a sweep of wings.

Night Hawk looked overhead, without meaning to. A dark rustling seem to hover over them for a moment and then dissolve in the sun. The sun was bright, reflected off the water that lay beyond the ridge.

Others' Child sat cross-legged, studying her composition.

It made Night Hawk queasy. All those lines of dots rolled like breakers in the water. He began to feel as if the ground were swelling under him. He had been sick in the canoe going across to the islands. Others' Child had not.

"When this moon is over, we will go inland," he announced. "And north. We will come back for the Trade Moon," he added magnanimously.

Others' Child looked up. "Maybe I will wait for you here," she said, as if it had just occurred to her. Her shadow fell across the soft earth she had been scratching in, so that the shadow enfolded the dots and waves and they were carved across her chest. Her slim russet legs bent like the tangled branches of the live oaks that dotted the rolling hills beyond them. She swayed a little in the evening breeze, and the shell beads in her hair rubbed against each other, muttering like leaves. Night Hawk thought that if he tried to pick her up, she would have roots that went deep through the new grass and the damp earth into the rock below.

"I do not wish you to wait for me here," he said flatly.

"You would have left me with the Kindred if I had asked."

"You did not wish to be left with the Kindred."

"That is why you were willing to," Others' Child said astutely.

Night Hawk sighed. He sat down next to her and put his hand on her knee. His long fingers splayed across it like the starfish Tern had shown Others' Child at low tide. She lifted one finger. It clung like the starfish's feet.

"You are my wife," Night Hawk said, as if that settled that.

V

How They Parted

Others' Child didn't say anything more about staying with the Channel Clan while Night Hawk went north. She merely waited until a moon had gone by and then announced that she was not going with him. The whole village could hear the battle, and despite its being conducted in the language of the Kindred, it provided the Channel Clan with more excitement than they had seen since the Condor Dance when the old shaman, who was dead now, had actually turned into a condor and flown into a tree. (Abalone Catcher's father had seen this himself.) They ringed the combatants interestedly, offering suggestions, now largely comprehensible, to Others' Child.

Night Hawk planted his feet wide apart the way he did when he was going to be stubborn about something. "You are my wife. You can't stay here without me."

"You can stay here, too," Others' Child said reasonably.

"I can't stay here. I am a trader. How can I be a trader in one village?"

"Then don't be a trader anymore. I don't care." She smiled at him, wheedling. "You could learn to fish."

Night Hawk scratched his head. "Why would I want to do that?"

Others' Child folded her arms. "I have found out what the pictures I have been making are. They are this place."

"Did you dream that?" Night Hawk demanded.

"No. I just know."

"If you didn't dream it, you don't know."

"I know. The lines are the sea here, and the hills, and the way I fit into them. I have found a place to belong here."

"Ha," Night Hawk said.

She jutted her chin out at him. The salt breeze came up from the coast. She could taste it in the air. She thought that it had tasted her that way, too, and decided it wanted her. "I want to *be* someplace."

"Yah—Taproot." Night Hawk looked disgusted.

"Yah—Itchy Foot," she spat back at him. "This is my place now. I have a place."

"You should all stay with us now," Abalone Catcher said, although no one had asked him.

"This man is crazy," Tern's sister Bone informed her husband, Sand Owl.

"All foreign people are crazy," Sand Owl said. "The woman, too. She wants to tell her husband what to do." He could tell that just from her voice.

"Maybe because she knows more!" Bone snapped. "Her head not being full of feathers and fish bones."

"Yah, I tried to give you what you wanted," Night Hawk snarled at Others' Child. "I stayed a moon here, because you blamed me for things that were not my fault, and I thought maybe it would sweeten you. And now you are wanting more! Always more. That is like women."

"I want to be here," Others' Child said. Her lip trembled.

Little Brother poked his head out of the willow-pole house where she had told him to wait. "I want to stay, too," he announced.

"Am I told what to do by women and babies?" Night Hawk shouted at them.

Little Brother buried his face in his hands.

"Now you have frightened him," Others' Child said.

Night Hawk glared around him at the interested faces. "Go away!" he shouted at them. They didn't move. Several sat down cross-legged on the grass for a better view.

"Little Brother and I will be glad if you will stay with us," Others' Child said, as gently as she could manage. She wanted to throw rocks at him.

Night Hawk looked as if he knew it. "Don't play peacemaker with me, Most Imperious. You began this."

"Then put rocks up your backside," Others' Child said obligingly.

"He should beat her," one of the Channel men commented to Tern's husband, Old Seal Barking.

"The way you beat your wife?" Old Seal Barking chortled. "Har, I saw the lump she gave you!"

"He should stay here," Tern said. "Imagine dragging your children all over the desert to get eaten by monsters."

"Go away!" Night Hawk roared at them. They backed up a pace or two.

"You should do something about this," Cannot Be Told said to Abalone Catcher.

"She is not my wife. And they do not belong to my village. I can't even understand what they are saying."

"Anyone could understand. That's what they are fighting about, about going away or not," Cannot Be Told said.

"Then it will solve itself. Either they will stay and be of my village, in which case they won't be fighting. Or they will go, in which case it won't be my affair."

Old Tidepool came out with his rattles and a bunch

of feathers tied to the end of a pole. He waved them at Night Hawk and Others' Child.

"See?" Cannot Be Told said. "I said it was important."

"Maybe you could stay just a little," Others' Child said to Night Hawk.

"I have an itch between my shoulders already," Night Hawk said, "from sleeping in that house. It makes me feel like the sky is closing up around me."

"How could the sky close up around you?"

"I didn't say it was. But maybe it does, for all I know. It happens when I am in caves and houses too long." He looked upward dubiously, as if he could see the blue sheets of the air folding themselves inward on him. Old Tidepool shook feathers at him, and Night Hawk crossed his fingers back at him.

"Yah," Others' Child said disgustedly. "If we mattered to you, you would stay."

"If I mattered to you, you would come."

"I belong here now. I have a place to belong. They won't throw *my* bones in a dry wash for the coyotes to eat!"

"No, they will just rot here. Before you are even dead," he added. He gave such a malevolent look to Old Tidepool that the shaman retreated. Night Hawk stalked into the willow-pole house and began stuffing gear in his pack. "And don't think I will leave you the dogs," he said over his shoulder.

Thief and Gray Daughter lay, noses on paws, watching him. When he dragged the travois out of the house, they lifted their ears.

Others' Child sat with her back to the door, looking off toward the ridge that hid the sea. She looked right through the Channel Clan ringing her. After a while, when nothing else was said, they began to drift off.

Little Brother buried his face in her arm. "Is Father going away?" he said quietly.

"Yes. Do you want to go, too?"

Little Brother shook his head, bumping it back and

forth in the crook of her arm. After a while he heard
some children playing by the stream, and got up and
padded after them. *Nothing is real to children*, Others'
Child thought. *They don't know the things that can happen.*

There was silence all around her now in the still afternoon. The sun warmed her bare knees, and a bee
hummed in some red clover just by the door of the willow house. Above them a condor rode on the thermals,
its shadow sweeping over her. *Why don't you tell me
what to do?* she asked it in her head, but it only soared
on, smaller and smaller in the distance as she watched.

She could hear Night Hawk packing his gear, angrily,
as if it were threatening to leave him, too. A pain in her
chest nearly doubled her over. She got up and went into
the willow house.

Night Hawk looked up. He didn't say anything. They
stared at each other. The sun came through the reed
thatch in dappled bars and spots, like leaves on the floor.
Their bed was still there, a soft deer hide and an otter-
skin blanket spread over thick, whispering grass.

Others' Child licked her lips. She couldn't find anything to say that wouldn't start them screaming at each
other again. She didn't think Night Hawk could, either.
He had stopped packing and was looking around the
house as if to see if he had forgotten something. His
expression when he looked at her was puzzled and sad.

"You don't have to go tonight," she said carefully.

"No. I wasn't going to. In the morning." He bit the
inside of his mouth to stop tears. Maybe he could make
her feel differently about it in the morning. He came
close enough to put his fingers on her cheeks.

Maybe he will see it differently in the morning, she
thought. She touched him carefully, hands on his ribs,
and felt his heart thumping under them. He put one hand
on her breast. She leaned into it, anger translated into
wanting by who knew what unwieldy magic.

He pulled at her hide skirt, and she slid down onto
the bed under him, kicking it off into the jumble of his
possessions on the floor. *This will make the difference,*

she thought triumphantly. *Now he will stay and we will never fight anymore.* She rolled under him, pulling him into her, laying claim.

Night Hawk pressed his mouth over his wife's, trying to grasp her, hold her to him, like trying to catch fog. Slowly she solidified under him, became his old wife, the wife he had had babies with and travels, the wife he knew how to talk to. *Now she will come with me*, he thought. *Ha-ha! Now she will change her mind.* Relief flooded through him, stronger than desire. He let his breath out slowly.

In the morning she woke to find him packing her things as well as his.

"Liar! What are you doing?"

Night Hawk looked at her, baffled.

"You said you weren't going to leave!"

"I said we weren't going to be apart. Because you were coming with me."

She sat up, throwing off the furs. "I never said that. You were going to stay."

"I never said that. I said I didn't want to go away without you."

"That is the same thing."

He considered. "No," he said finally.

"Yah! Get out! Go!" She flung the words at him and then snatched the pack from his hands. "And give me back my water basket and my needles!"

Night Hawk shoved them at her. His mouth made a tight line, like a hide someone had sewn up.

Others' Child scrambled out the door, not caring that she had no clothes on. She pulled at the laces that tied Night Hawk's bundles to the travois. "And my grinding stone and my sling, and half the food is mine!" She scattered her reclaimed possessions on the ground, digging deeper. When she was satisfied, she gathered them in her arms and marched back to the house. The villagers noted with interest that she had a pale spot, like a small white stone, on her right buttock. Her tangled black hair stood out around her as if a storm was coming.

Night Hawk kicked the plundered travois. He pushed everything back under the top hide, tied it raggedly, and stuck his fingers between his teeth, whistling for the dogs.

Others' Child sat in her willow-pole house until it was dark. Someone was feeding Brother, she assumed; there was always a spare mouthful for a child who wandered by a cook fire. As Night Hawk was leaving, Brother had woken up and cried for a little while. Then he had gone out to play. Others' Child thought that he had decided for himself that his father would be back.

"Yah," she said, "at the Trade Moon. Maybe." Night Hawk had salved his pride by shouting at her that he would be back for her then, but she knew she wasn't going to go with him then, either. There was too much here to hold her, the things she hadn't been able to make him see—the round shapes of the houses that suffocated him but to her were like the sky dome overhead, comforting and enclosed; the voice of the Endless Water murmuring beyond the ridge, the breakers always rolling inward; the place by the fire where she could see herself woven into the Channel Clan like a strand in a basket, entwined by the flames, taken up, taken in. Her place by the fire was always a good place, near the chieftain's sister, because of her picture magic.

I am here, she thought, testing that idea, patting the hard-packed earth under her crossed legs, feeling a tiny stone in it bite into her ankle. It was just uncomfortable enough to be real. Others' Child grinned suddenly to herself. She got up and began poking kindling into the embers of that morning's fire. There was dinner to cook for herself and Little Brother, and then there was soap to make, and they both needed new sandals, and maybe she would take her basket of yucca leaves down to the fire and listen to Old Tidepool tell stories while she combed them out. There were so many things to do, pleasant things, while time rolled away from her like the brown, mouse-furred hills; time to belong and live at home. Night Hawk could have the wild lands.

Others' Child stood up and walked down to the village fire pit with her basket of yucca leaves. Sea Otter made room for her, and mostly the rest had the manners not to stare. Also it was dark, which helped. Brother saw her and came scooting from a hunt that he and two small boys were conducting with sticks for spears and their imagination for deer. He plopped himself in Others' Child's lap.

"Father went away. He doesn't like houses," he informed Sea Otter.

Sea Otter nodded gravely. "Your father is a fine man. However, it is true he does not like houses."

"He took our dogs," Brother said wistfully.

"There are more dogs," Others' Child answered, embarrassed.

"You are the first woman I have known who left her husband by staying in one place," Sea Otter commented to Others' Child.

"*He* left," Others' Child said firmly.

"Ah." Sea Otter smiled, bemused. "Perhaps you could teach my sister to do it that way. She always wants to be moving. First she wanted to move to the Knifenose Fish Clan, now she wants to move home. I don't understand all this wanting to move." He waved an arm at the fire and the glowing faces around it, inhaled the smell of cooking fish and the sharp, briny tang of kelp. "Where is better than here?"

Others' Child chuckled. "Don't you ever go anywhere?"

"Certainly," Sea Otter said. "I go to the islands, and I go fishing. I go to see my sister—har! More often I take her to see her husband! When it is Trade Moon, I go there."

"Oh, many places," Others' Child said with a grin. She combed the yucca leaves between her fingers with a bone pin.

"And is it different, where you have come from?"

"We have to move in winter. Up the mountain. Otherwise there is no food."

"That does not sound like a good place to live at all.

Here is much better." Sea Otter reached across her and picked a piece of dark fish off the hot stone where the Channel Clan had cut it open. He picked the bones out carefully and held it to her mouth.

"Here there is very good food," Others' Child agreed, smiling through the mouthful of fish. She watched him pick bones from a piece and hand it to Brother. For a moment Night Hawk was almost beside her, and she ached for him from her throat down to her belly. *Well, he is not here,* she thought angrily. *He won't come home, so let him go someplace else.*

"I don't understand looking for other places when you have a good one," Sea Otter said to Brother. "You could get killed that way. There are too many ways to get killed without looking for more. Remember that when you grow up."

Brother seemed interested by that idea. "Tell me some," he said.

Sea Otter looked as if he wished he hadn't brought it up. Talking about ways to get killed was bad luck. "I'll tell you about the Rolling Head."

"What is the Rolling Head?"

"Oooh, he has never heard of the Rolling Head!" Laurel Tree said, mock-serious. "You must tell him immediately, in case he should meet it."

"Be quiet, Sea Otter's going to tell the Rolling Head story," someone said. The murmur of conversation died down, and two more little boys scooted up to Sea Otter. Brother climbed down off Others' Child's lap and sat next to him. A small girl, finding the lap empty, climbed into it.

Old Tidepool beamed. Rolling Head was a children's story, beneath his dignity. All the children liked Sea Otter. Old Tidepool composed himself to listen like a child. That was good for a man.

Once sometime there was a man who was a fine hunter. He had to be because he had a very big appetite. His people called him Growling Bear because his stomach always rumbled.

Growling Bear ate deer and he ate elk and he ate seals and he ate turkeys and grouse. He ate tuna and he even ate whale, at one meal. One day he decided to go hunting, and his wife made him a journey cake out of acorn meal, and gave him a sack full of camas bulbs and baked soaproot, and another bag of dried deer meat.

She thought that was probably enough to last him till lunch, but Growling Bear ate it all before he was out of their camp, and then he came back and asked her for more.

"If you keep on eating like that, something terrible will happen to you," his wife said, frowning.

"I am hungry," Growling Bear said. "Listen."

His wife put her ear to his stomach. "Of course you are empty, because you have eaten so much that now your stomach is as big as Whale, and nothing could possibly fill it. You will have to learn some self-control."

"Hmmph!" said Growling Bear. And he went away without any more food because there wasn't any more in the house. He had eaten it all.

After a while he came to a bank where he knew his wife dug camas, and he rooted around in it with the end of his spear and found a few bulbs. He popped those in his mouth and went on, but he wasn't full. "I will kill a deer," he thought, "and eat it, and then I will feel better. Then I will have enough strength to run down Elk, and maybe a few more deer for the way home."

So he killed a deer and skinned it and ate it, all of it, every bit, from the liver to the marrowbones, without even thinking about how his wife had warned him. While Growling Bear sat belching and picking the gristle out of his teeth, he thought about how good the deer had tasted. One meal always made him want his next one.

Now this was what worried his wife, but Growling Bear wasn't the kind of man to let his wife tell him anything. He already knew everything, and mostly what he knew now was that he was hungry. So he went on through the woods, tracking Elk and thinking that maybe *he would eat the first one himself, and then he could catch another.*

Now Elk is an animal who knows his worth. He knows he is big enough and powerful enough to feed a whole village, so he was angry with Growling Bear for being so greedy. And when Elk is angry, he does not let you catch him. He bellows in the forest and laughs at you.

Growling Bear chased Elk through the woods and through the tule reeds, up one hill and down another, and Elk just went on ahead, laughing at him. Elk did not appear to get tired, but Growling Bear got tired. He was so big and his stomach was so hard to carry around.

Finally, Elk started uphill again, and Growling Bear stopped and looked up the hill, which to him looked higher than the mountains where the snows are, since he had to carry his stomach up it.

"Hoo!" he said. "That is a high hill. And I am HUNGRY!" He was so angry that he stabbed his spear into the ground by his foot in a temper. And because he was angry, and that is not a good way to be when you have a spear in your hand, the spear went through his little toe, and he hopped and howled until you could have heard him on the islands or even across the water where the dead live. His people heard him in their village and were very much frightened by his roaring. His wife recognized his voice and knew that something terrible had happened.

Growling Bear hopped up and down on one foot, howling and trying to get hold of his little toe, until he fell down under a live oak tree in all the prickly leaves. He rolled around in them, not even noticing the prickles, and stuck his little toe in his mouth, because it hurt very much indeed.

And no, I do not know how a man that big could put his little toe in his mouth, so do not ask me. Maybe he had lost some of his stomach with all the hard climbing. But he did stick it in his mouth and suck on it because it hurt so, and that was the beginning of the terrible thing.

Growling Bear's toe was bleeding hard, and the blood tasted so good (remember how very hungry he was) that he kept on sucking. He sucked all the blood out of his toe, and then he took a bite out of the toe itself. That tasted fine, so he took another bite. His stomach began to growl louder, and he bit off the rest of his toes. After that he started in on his feet and his ankles and up his shin bones.

When he had eaten his shin bones, he ate his fingers, and his hands and his wrists, crunching all the little bones, making a dreadful noise. His wife heard it back at their village and said, "He doesn't listen to me. I told him."

Elk watched him from the trees. Elk watched him eat his arms and his shoulders and his liver and his heart, and all his ribs right up to his neck. And then, because this was in some way Elk's doing, Elk went to Growling Bear's village to warn them.

The wife saw Elk standing in the sunset just beyond the houses, and she threw her water basket over her head and screamed.

"He will come from the north," Elk said, and left.

"Get your weapons," the chief said, because now they could hear a rolling and a rumbling in the distance, coming toward them from the north.

So all the people got their weapons and went north to wait for Growling Bear. After a while they saw him coming, just a big head rolling along, much bigger than it had been, because it had all the rest of him inside it. His mouth was as wide as the river, and his teeth were like pine trees.

Growling Bear scooped up the chief and threw him in his mouth. (Well, I believe he may have grown some new hands out of his ears.)

The people pointed their spears at him, but his mouth was so big that he just crunched them up, spears and all. Now Growling Bear's head bounced and rolled down the hillside into the village and bounced all around the houses while the people ran screaming in every direction the way ants do when you dig up their hill. He threw them all in his mouth anyway except for his wife, who was hiding flat in the fire pit, covered with ashes.

When the head had eaten everyone in the village except his wife, he went roaring and rolling on to the next village up the coast, and he ate them, too, and then he bounced across the river to the west and threw all of those people in his mouth. And it went on like that until Growling Bear's head had eaten every single person he could see, even when he climbed up to the northern edge of the sky and looked all around. So then he remembered his wife and remembered that he had not eaten her yet.

Growling Bear went bouncing and rolling back toward his home village and started chasing his wife. She wanted very much to stop and say, I told you so, but there wasn't time. She ran and ran as fast as her legs would take her, and still the head rumbled behind her. Finally, just when she was getting out of breath, she came to a wide river, too wide for the head to bounce across. There was a thin bridge of ropes across it, and she started out on that.

She could hear her husband's head growling and bouncing behind her, but she didn't dare stop to look over her shoulder. Finally she got to the other side, just as the head reached the middle of the river. She bent down with her skinning knife and cut the end of the bridge, and the head fell in the river. A pike jumped up and swallowed it, and she got away.

The pike kept the head in its stomach, but every so often it spits it out again for a while, and then the head goes rolling around the hills again. And that is why you should never go off in the hills away from your mother, because it is still very hungry and always will be.

Sea Otter grinned, opening his jaws wide to show white teeth. He closed them with a snap in front of Little Brother's face, and Brother said, "I am not afraid of a head!" But he looked over his shoulder anyway, into the mysterious night where, as everyone knew, anything might be.

"Tomorrow," Others' Child said to Sea Otter, "I will tell *you* about the antelope that eats human flesh. I have heard that it comes into these parts sometimes." She grinned back at him. She suspected he had just thought it up about the new hands growing out of the head's ears.

"Tomorrow we are going to see my sister," Sea Otter said, "who is making her husband crazy enough to bite off his own foot. He sends us messages about it. You may come, too. She might listen to another woman."

Others' Child doubted that, since Foam wouldn't listen to her own mother, but she wanted to see the Knifenose Fish Clan's village. And she liked the idea of herself as a woman of some wisdom, a woman to be listened to, who might talk sense into people's sisters.

They dragged their canoes from the surf at the Knifenose Fish Clan's village at dusk, with a pack full of presents for Foam's husband, whose name was Not in a Hurry. The presents were for him because Foam had been so disobedient. Condor Dancer was still hoping to keep it a matter between families, with no need for the Shell Men to put their noses in and make pronouncements. Others' Child suspected he would end up giving Not in a Hurry many good presents and then have to give his bride-price back, too.

They spent the night in the village, in a house belonging to Not in a Hurry. In the morning they sat around Not in a Hurry's fire, Not in a Hurry in the best place. Blue Butterfly and Condor Dancer sat on one side of him, and Sea Otter and Others' Child on the other. Foam sat across from her husband, where she was supposed to be ashamed, and listened to her parents and Not in a Hurry discussing her. She folded her lips tight and made no retort. It would have been bad manners to say anything, since she was supposed to pretend she couldn't hear, but Others' Child thought Foam would burst if they kept it up for too long. There was a twitch in her jaw.

"I have built your daughter a new house," Not in a

Hurry said to Condor Dancer. He was a big, solid man with the air of one who thinks long about everything before he does it. "It took me much time and cost me five shell necklaces to the Split Rock Clan, who live where the best willow trees grow."

"It is a very nice house," Blue Butterfly said, looking around. It was big, with fine mats on the floor and a well-made smoke hole. The fire hardly smoked at all.

"She doesn't stay in it," Not in a Hurry said. "And she does not listen respectfully when I talk."

"What do you talk to her about?" Condor Dancer inquired, glowering at his daughter.

"Proper things. Things that she should know. How my mother grinds her acorn flour fine. How to smoke a hide the best way."

"Those are important things," Condor Dancer agreed.

Blue Butterfly looked irritated. She had taught Foam how to grind acorn flour perfectly well herself.

"I tell her exciting things also, about the fish we caught and how long we fought with him."

"That is proper."

"She does not listen."

Blue Butterfly gave her daughter a severe look. It did not matter if her husband told her things she did not need to know. She should listen to him anyway, and then do as she wished. That was how it was done. Blue Butterfly could not say so in front of Foam's husband, but everyone knew it. Foam knew it, too.

Foam's eyes slid speculatively to Others' Child.

"This woman is a shaman who has come to us from far away to the east," Blue Butterfly said. "She knows that a wife should stay at home, and thinks you are most disobedient."

"She has stayed at home even though her husband would not," Condor Dancer said. "That is how well behaved she is."

Others' Child thought it over. It was the first time she had been called well behaved. No doubt these things depended on who was talking, but it was fine to be held up as an example of virtue. "Home is important," she said, looking at her hands, properly modest. She knew Night Hawk would laugh at her if he heard her mouthing proprieties so she said defiantly, half to him, "I have seen this in my dreams since I have come here. The dreams that I make with my hands when I am awake." She took a cold stone from the edge of the hearth and scratched a round house in the floor to show them.

Not in a Hurry peered at it with his head cocked sideways.

"She makes marks in the earth that are like the things we see with our eyes," Blue Butterfly said. "She will make one to keep Foam at home."

"This maybe," Others' Child said, and drew a ring around the house. She didn't think it would hold Foam.

"This woman is very powerful," Sea Otter said proudly.

Foam tossed her thick black hair out of her face with the kind of gesture that was calculated to say *You are stupid* without saying it.

Condor Dancer and Blue Butterfly stood up. "Our daughter will stay with you now."

Foam slitted her eyes at them, but she didn't say anything. Others' Child could see her thoughts like a black cloud over her head, thinking themselves in the air. Sea Otter touched Others' Child's elbow, and she stood up, too. Foam stayed where she was. If she was not supposed to hear them, then she could not see them, either, and did not need to be respectful.

"My sister is very willful," Sea Otter said to Others' Child as they walked back down the trail to the shore.

"All women are willful," she said with a smile. "We would not survive living with men otherwise." She felt happy, though. The sun was like a bright disk of shell in the sky, and the air was warm on her arms. A cloud of birds circled in the blue air, going nowhere, dancing with the wind.

"*My* wife will have fish to eat in the morning and clams at night and many deer hides to dress in, and she will not need to be willful," Sea Otter said. "Also I will not tell her boring stories."

"Oh," said Others' Child.

She helped Sea Otter drag the canoe into the surf. The water rushed around her ankles, cold even though spring had come. The sea never got warm, Sea Otter said. She climbed in, expertly now, without tipping the canoe, and picked up her paddle. Tern had been right. There were new muscles in her arms, and the paddle no longer tried to hit her in the chin. She began to dip it into the water in rhythm to Sea Otter's stroke. The sun dried her wet legs and warmed her bare back.

The Knifenose Fish Clan lived on the edge of a little bay, and as they put out from shore, Others' Child saw a real sea otter, floating on his back in the swells, pounding an abalone on a rock that he held balanced on his chest. She giggled and pointed.

Sea Otter laughed and wrinkled up his nose at her, twitching imaginary whiskers. "When I was little, I used to swim out past the surf and float on my back so I could look at the sky. That is why I am called Sea Otter."

"What did you see in the sky?" she asked him curiously.

"Clouds. Birds."

"Great Condor?"

"No. I am Sea Otter because I do not need magical visions. I am content to look at the clouds." He dipped his paddle neatly, expertly, into the water.

Night Hawk had never been content to look at the clouds, Others' Child thought. He had wanted to go to them. He would go anywhere if you showed him a road to it.

"Look!" Sea Otter said.

Farther out Others' Child saw graceful shapes curving out of the ocean, gray-blue above and white below. They were big, bigger than the boat, and they surfaced and dived with a joyous abandon like birds.

"Oh, what are they?"

"Dolphins." Sea Otter angled the canoe a little toward shore as they came closer. "They like to play with human people sometimes. They are curious. Also, they are very good to eat, but they are smart and know there are not enough of us to spear them now.''

Others' Child leaned over the edge of the canoe, her paddle wavering. They were wonderful, magical. She longed to fling herself over the side and join them, frolic in the cold salt water, dive and rise, blowing streams of bubbles. An eye looked right at her as a blunt-nosed face surfaced just beyond the canoe. The dolphin's back bowed, and it disappeared with a flip of its tail. She leaned farther over, wondering if she could touch one.

''Don't do that,'' Sea Otter said. Condor Dancer and Blue Butterfly were paddling toward shore.

A dolphin rose from the water almost under her hand, offering its bowed back. She leaned toward it, yearning to leap through the water with it, cool and alive in the mysterious sea.

''No!'' Sea Otter said, but she had already fallen, tumbling from the canoe, sending it end-up in the water. Sea Otter's paddle flew into the air and came down hard on her arm. The salt waves caught her and rolled her under the capsized boat. Something soft and slick bumped her from below, sending her upward, mouth full of salt water.

Others' Child flailed in the water. It was cold, like falling through the ice into a winter river. She tried to catch the edge of the boat, but it was out of reach, and her arm hurt. The cold sea pulled her down again. Was she going to drown in it, she thought, panicked, because she had tried to touch the fish? One of them bumped her with its head, pushing her up again, but another tumbled her down with an unseeing flip of its tail. They swarmed around her, curious eyes inspecting her, prodding her with their noses.

The sky overhead was bright blue, brighter than the glare of the water, and when she came up, her eyes hurt with the glare and the salt. A stinging fog danced between her and the boat. She could see a dark shape that might be Sea Otter, trying to right the canoe, holding one paddle in the other hand.

A wave spilled over her face, filling her nose again, and no matter how she flailed her arms and legs, she couldn't stay on top of the water. Then something grabbed her by the hair and another hand by one foot. The next thing she knew, she was being tumbled over the side of the canoe.

The canoe was half full of water. Others' Child rolled over spluttering and saw the dripping face of Condor Dancer rising up over the edge. Sea Otter surfaced on the other side. They climbed in gingerly.

"Hoo!" Condor Dancer said. "We will have to teach you how to swim."

Others' Child gagged and spit up water.

Sea Otter pounded her on the back. "I think there is more ocean in you than out there."

"I wanted to touch the fish," she said contritely.

"They can tip a canoe," Sea Otter said.

Others' Child saw that Blue Butterfly had paddled her canoe away from the dolphins and sat waiting there, dipping her paddle lightly to keep it in place.

"I am sorry."

"I will teach you to swim," Sea Otter said. "You are too adventurous for a woman."

Others' Child remembered curious snouts prodding her in the ribs, the slickness of their bodies. She folded her hands in her lap, well behaved. "Very well."

Sea Otter and his father paddled the canoe until it was next to Condor Dancer's, and Condor Dancer slipped over the side. He climbed into his own boat, shaking himself like a wet dog, and Blue Butterfly looked worriedly at Others' Child.

"We should stop and light a fire. She will take a chill."

"I am all right." Others' Child spit up more water.

"We will stop when the sun is high," Condor Dancer said. "This is not a good beach." The distant shore was rocky, with steep bluffs lurching upward above it. He shook his head. "It is a good thing we kept the food with us. It does not swim, either."

Others' Child ducked her head and began to paddle, embarrassed. Her arm hurt. After a while, Sea Otter looked over his shoulder. "I will teach you to swim tomorrow. It was not your fault."

"Your father thinks I am a fool," she said.

"Foolhardy. Also, the chieftain would be very angry if we had drowned you."

Others' Child sniffled. The salt water made her nose sting. "Will you teach Little Brother to swim, too?"

Sea Otter looked over his shoulder, a smile lighting his face. "I will teach him to swim, and to fish, and to dance the men's dances." He turned back before Others' Child could wonder what that would mean.

The ache in her wrist deepened, but she kept paddling. It was her fault they had turned over. She was not going to whine and make Sea Otter paddle the canoe himself. And she knew he would if she asked him. By the time they stopped, when the sun was overhead, her wrist was swollen and black and blue. Blue Butterfly clucked over it and went foraging for leaves to make a compress, but Others' Child insisted that it was not sore.

In an odd way the ache was something she wanted to keep. It tethered her to the moment, to the adventure in the water and the strange sleek fish who had skin instead of scales. And to Condor Dancer and Blue Butterfly and Sea Otter. To belonging. When they had eaten, she climbed back into the canoe behind Sea Otter, balancing surefooted in the bottom, the paddle across her knees. She trailed her wrist in the water, letting the cold take the ache away. They would get home at dusk, and already she could see how it would be, the moon hanging over the dark water, leaving its silver tail in the sea; the lights on the hillside inland where the people would be kindling their cook fires; the smell of sage mixed with salt and the grass that was already beginning to burn dry; and Sea Otter's broad back to follow up the trail from the sea.

VI

If You Make My Likeness,
I Will Come

Others' Child was swimming. She raised her head above
the swell, spitting water, but she was not falling through
it anymore. She curved her arms over her head, first one
and then the other, pulling the water backwards, herself
forward. That was how Sea Otter had explained it to
her.

Sea Otter swam beside her. When the water suddenly
stopped supporting her, he put a hand under her stomach.

She clung to him, gagging. "What happened? I was
lying on the water the way you said, and then it pulled
me under."

"It is very treacherous," he said solemnly. "Also,
you have only been swimming one day. You decided
you knew too much, I think."

Others' Child hung her head. She paddled in the water

with her feet to keep from sinking again. "I am bad that way." She could feel his arm under her elbow, holding her up.

He snorted with laughter. His black hair was plastered down on his head and splayed over his shoulders like seaweed. "It is like trying to teach Little Brother. He wants to learn all at once, too. It is easy to see whose child he is."

She spit more water and looked at Brother on the beach, waiting impatiently for his turn with Bone and her children. He had a little driftwood spear that Sea Otter had carved for him, and he flung it over and over into the wet sand, piercing a flat piece of kelp until it was ragged. In a few more months he might have forgotten his father, Others' Child thought with a quick stab of pain under her breastbone. She ignored it. It was from swallowing seawater. She began to swim again, toward shore now. Sea Otter hardly had to hold her up. She liked it that when they came to the beach, he hardly looked at Bone or any of the other women who were gathering kelp. He picked up Little Brother and swung him onto his wet shoulders, not minding the sand on Little Brother's backside.

"You should marry Sea Otter," Tern said to Others' Child.

Bone said, "He is a catch."

The women were grinding acorns, sitting cross-legged on a flat stone above the creek. The stone was pitted with hollows, wide enough for seven or eight to grind flour at once.

Others' Child looked at her hands, which had stopped abruptly in their rotation. Her acorns lay in the bottom of a hollow worn deep in the stone, and she peered in at them a long time as if she thought a bug had fallen in. "I have a husband," she said finally, as if she had considered their idea some time ago and reluctantly discarded it.

"Are you waiting for that other one to change his mind and come back?" Tern asked. She thumped a cy-

lindrical grinding stone on her acorns, pounding them
flat. She rotated it in the hole, leaning her weight on it.
"Because he looked chancy to me."

"You should decide he is dead." Bone nodded to
herself. "He probably is."

"Men like that never change their minds. I had one
like that," Old Seagull said flatly. She touched two fingers to her gray hair as if to indicate its source.

"Besides, if you are going to stay here, you will have
to marry," Tern said. "Otherwise the men will be fighting over you, which is not good."

Others' Child bit her lip, catching it between her dog
teeth and chewing it while she thought. She had known
this. Women were not allowed to stay unmarried unless
they were warrior women who acted like men (and she
had never actually seen one of those) or they were old
and ugly. No one would force her, of course, but there
would be pressure, and if she didn't marry, she wouldn't
stay welcome here. It was the same way among the Yellow Grass People or the Kindred. It seemed that men
were not able to leave a woman alone if she belonged
to no one. Some other man had to own her to keep them
away.

She sighed, quietly so as not to offend these women
who had made her welcome. Sea Otter didn't make her
skin tingle the way Night Hawk did, but he brought her
oysters, and he was good to Little Brother. And he was
restful. Being with Sea Otter was like sitting, well fed,
by a fire. Night Hawk wasn't restful. Night Hawk was
a tiring man. It tired her out just to think about walking
from here across the desert with him again.

"Blue Butterfly likes you," Tern said. "That is important."

"Never marry a man whose mother doesn't like
you," Bone said. She nodded again.

"He is a good fisherman," Seagull said. "Just like
his name."

Others' Child thought about what Sea Otter had said
about lying in the water looking at clouds, but she decided they wouldn't understand that part. Who could

watch clouds when there was work to be done? Women weren't raised to understand things like that. Not here; not anywhere. She wasn't sure how it had come to her. She thought that maybe Coyote had given it to her; it would be like him, to give her something useless that would make her uncomfortable among ordinary women.

I will show him I do not thank him, she thought. *I will belong here.* She could love Sea Otter, she thought. She could love his mother and father, too, as befitted a good daughter-in-law. But mostly she could love the belonging, the being part of a whole, like a hive of bees, safe inside that warm hum. Let Little Brother grow up here and learn the men's dances from Sea Otter. When he was grown, he wouldn't want to wander.

She held the grinding stone with both hands, leaning her body over it, grinding its round flat end into the acorns, slowly turning them to flour. When they were ground fine, she would make a hole in sand and line it with leaves. Then she would put the flour on top of the leaves and pour water through it the way Tern had taught her, and slowly the water would leach the acorn bitterness away. It took four or five washings sometimes.

Others' Child saw herself as the acorn flour, the Channel Clan pouring over her like water. When they had gone clear through her, she would lose the acrid taste of grief that she had kept under her skin for so long.

The women came back from the grinding rock at dusk, dragging meal in skin bags over their shoulders.

"Grinding is hard work," Sea Otter said appreciatively, noticing Others' Child's bag. He had a bundled hide under one arm, and she thought he had been waiting for her.

"It is like grinding maize," Others' Child said so that he would know she was not completely uneducated. These people had looked at the maize in Night Hawk's pack with polite disinterest. Why go to the trouble of planting something when acorns already grew on trees? She put her sack down and walked along with Sea Otter, rubbing her aching wrists. She could feel the Channel

Clan's attention following her, a benevolent scrutiny observing their courtship and her education in their ways. Blue Butterfly opened Others' Child's flour sack and rubbed the meal between her fingers before Others' Child was even out of sight.

"In the fall," Sea Otter said, as they passed the edge of the village, "we will go with the Knifenose Fish Clan and the Split Rock Clan to pick acorns in the oak groves. All of us but the Shell Clan. The rest of us take acorns to them and get shells."

Or advice, Others' Child thought. When the Shell Clan arbitrated a dispute, you had to do what they said. "Why do they know so much?" she asked.

Sea Otter took her arm and helped her solicitously over a jumble of rough stones beside the river. He spread out the hide on a broad, egg-shaped rock that balanced itself above the stream, around a bend from the village. There was a pool below it where Others' Child could hear the faint plop of frogs.

"The Shell Clan never leave their islands," Sea Otter said. "Sometimes they will come at the Trade Moon, but mostly they are dreamy and stay out on the water, watching the sun go down, or the moon float, I suppose. It comes of living so near the Gateway of the Dead, I think. When you talk to one of them, he looks as if he will float away."

Others' Child drew her knees up under her chin. The moon was caught in the sky just now, pinned through the stars like a fishhook so that its light was thin. "What did you ask them about me?" she murmured. With the Channel Clan's fires hidden around the bend in the stream, Others' Child could see only the faint gleam of Sea Otter's eyes and teeth. The rest of him was a warm shadow beside her, like breath.

He laid his arm across her back, fingers cupping her shoulder. She could feel the individual warmth of each, five small points of heat like stones from the fire pit. "I didn't need to ask them," he said into her ear, his breath like another warm hand. "I told you I wanted a woman who was different from Channel people, and you made her for me. Do you remember?''

In her mind, Others' Child saw the woman she had drawn in the dirt. She thought it had her face now. ''I remember.''

''I will teach Little Brother, and we will have more children, and when my father is dead I will be Condor Dancer after him,'' Sea Otter said.

Others' Child nodded. With Night Hawk, they had not planned things out first; they had just gotten into his bed together, and things had happened afterward the way you would expect them to, like a handful of rocks flung downhill. This way was obviously better.

She could feel Sea Otter's hand on her breast and his other hand between her knees. Now that he had told her how things would be, she could see that he wanted to do this, too. She lay back on the rock and watched his shoulder blot out the moon and his mouth fit down over hers.

They spent all night on the rock, on the hide blanket. Now that she had finally decided to do that again with a man, Others' Child was startled at how much she wanted to do it over and over while the moon stitched its way through the sky and the pale sun came up. She thought Sea Otter was surprised, too. In the morning her backside ached, and she was ravenous with hunger. She thought the rock might have their imprint left on its surface, but when Sea Otter picked up the hide, it was still just flat brown sandstone, sun-washed and blank. Sea Otter had a broad grin as he walked her back to the village.

Blue Butterfly was putting kindling into the cook fire when they came home. She gave them only a cursory look, but her lips curved up in approval.

Condor Dancer came out of his house while Others' Child and Sea Otter were gobbling cold acorn cake from yesterday. He scratched and stretched. He laced his fingers together, cracking his knuckles, his expression satisfied. ''Go wake up my grandson,'' he said. ''I will take him fishing. Har! And tell your sister that one of you knows how to please an old man who has no grand-children.''

So that seemed to be that. She was married to Sea Otter, and Little Brother had a grandfather to take him fishing. Old Tidepool came, wearing a headdress that had straw points sticking out from it like the sun's rays, and shook acorn flour over them to make a blessing, and Sea Otter moved his spears and fishing poles into Oth-ers' Child's house.

When he emerged again, the men slapped him on the back, and they all went off to the shore to fish, taking Little Brother with them. Others' Child looked around her, thinking there must be more to it than that. What about a bride-price, which had caused so much trouble for Foam? But to whom would he pay it? Night Hawk? That idea left her sardonically amused.

Blue Butterfly sat down in Others' Child's doorway. She had a pot of soaproot and was pounding it to mush. ''My old husband is walking around with his chest stuck out. You would think he was the one who had just mar-ried. So I will wash my hair and smell good tonight while he still feels this way.'' Her wrinkled face spread in a broad grin, showing a row of sand-worn teeth.

There was sand in everything these people ate, sand in the leached meal. Others' Child could feel it between her molars. She wriggled her tongue into the hollow of one. ''I am happy if my husband's mother is happy,'' she said politely, wondering if she was, now that Sea Otter had gone and the day seemed a little flat after the promise of last night.

''With Foam away, I have wanted another woman for company. It is lonely with only men. They don't know anything. They don't talk about what women do.''

Others' Child chuckled. ''I wonder what they do talk about, when they are alone.''

''They tell lies, I think,'' Blue Butterfly said. ''I lis-tened once, to my old husband and his friends. It was very wicked of me and served me right that I heard no good.''

Others' Child waited to see if she would tell her what she did hear.

Blue Butterfly snorted indignantly. "He said, the old coyote, that he would take another wife because one was not enough for him! And then they all compared how long theirs was and told lies about that. Anyone could see."

Others' Child giggled, liking this woman now. "I am sure he didn't mean it, not about another wife. It was only wanting to look important."

"I know that," Blue Butterfly said tolerantly. "And anyway, Abalone Catcher would not let him have two wives when Abalone Catcher only had one and she died last year. Abalone Catcher would have to marry twice first."

"Will he?" Others' Child asked. "Once, anyway? He has no children."

"No, his wife didn't make babies. Even the shaman didn't know why. Maybe that was what she died of."

Others' Child had never thought of dying of *not* doing something.

"But I will have grandchildren now," Blue Butterfly said placidly.

Others' Child knew that she was counting Little Brother among them. Children were precious. There were too many ways for babies to die. If you had a son, it didn't matter that another man had once been his father. "Foam will have babies," she said. She made it almost a question, not quite. Now that she was married to Sea Otter, she supposed she could ask things that would not have been her business yesterday.

"Foam will have to make them out of acorn meal," Blue Butterfly said acidly, "since she won't let her husband put it in her." She sighed into her soaproot.

"Maybe Condor Dancer will let her come home."

Blue Butterfly sighed again. "She will come home anyway."

Others' Child envisioned Foam traveling pack-on-back by herself, a day's walk. She had complained of the distance and the blisters on her feet, never mind that no one had asked her to come. Others' Child had walked days, moons, years down trails she would just as soon have let alone. Maybe it seemed different to Foam.

"Life is short," Foam had said grimly the last time she walked home. "I don't want to look at him every morning until I die."

"And who do you think you might want to look at instead?" Condor Dancer had thundered. "Bear? Knife-nose Fish?"

"I don't know," Foam had said. "Somebody else."

Others' Child waited for Sea Otter to come home, the somebody else she had found, the man rooted to a place. When he did, he had a string of bright silver fish, like living water.

Brother had one, too. He waddled under its weight. Blue Butterfly and Others' Child cooked them all in a basket with oysters and seaweed, boiling the salty water with hot stones. The fishhook moon rose over the ridge, and a mockingbird burbled and squawked its message to a female of its kind somewhere in the manzanita scrub. Brother went to sleep with his face in Others' Child's lap and his feet in Sea Otter's.

When the spring warmed into summer, the air dried, and the grass turned the same furry golden brown that Others' Child remembered from the time she had first come. It felt like an animal to her, something warm and sleepy, a full cat stretched in the sun. It might be something to be afraid of, she decided, if it woke up. Sea Otter said there were earthquakes here. But no one else worried, so it was easy not to, to fill her days with grinding meal and hunting for manzanita berries.

When the weather grew dry, the men burned off the hillsides. It was carefully controlled, a quick flame unleashed through tinder-dry grass so as not to harm the trees. The burn would leave a layer of ash over everything, a dark blanket to nourish the clover and bulbs that would sprout under it. All the same, it didn't pay to be careless. Others' Child watched the men, marveling— running along the dry hillside, flaming torches in their hands, swifter than the fire. Sea Otter came home ashy and gray at night, with cinders in his hair, and plunged into the stream to wash.

"Hoo! That nearly had us," he said, his singed voice spluttering through the water. "Abalone Catcher fell and couldn't get up. He has a pain in his belly that he doesn't talk about. Sand Owl and I pulled him away."

"Is he all right?"

"He doesn't say." Sea Otter splashed out of the stream and grabbed Others' Child by the waist. He buried his wet face in her shoulder. "I am just glad to be home. Let's go and make another baby."

Others' Child was glad enough to try, but so far no baby had come. *It isn't as if I don't know how,* she thought.

Later, Blue Butterfly said not to worry about it—how many times had she been pregnant with her first husband?

Too many, Others' Child thought, but she smiled and shook her head and said, four times in five years—one had miscarried. (Blue Butterfly knew all about the two who had died.)

"All right, then," said Blue Butterfly. "It is bound to happen again."

But for some reason Others' Child had thought that it would happen right away, a new child with a new husband. It would make it real, make it feel less as if she had made a six-day marriage at a Gathering and Night Hawk would be at home waiting for her. She thought about drawing herself a baby in the earth the way she had done for Waxing Moon, about asking Old Tidepool about it. *I will if it doesn't happen soon,* she thought.

Inland, the air was now as hot as a cook fire, with hot dry winds that blew up from the south. At midsummer the Channel Clan spent most of their time on the shore between the cold ocean and the hot inland wind. They built journey huts to live in and fished sometimes for almost a moon at a time. When they made fires at night, the driftwood that washed up onto the sand burned blue and green with the salt.

Others' Child began to draw secret children in the sand, but she didn't ask Old Tidepool. Old Tidepool spent most of his time with Abalone Catcher and Abalone Catcher's pain. Ever since the fire the chieftain had looked gray and old like the powdered ash, and he was a young man. Cannot Be Told spoke for him sometimes at Council meetings now when they met with the Knifenose Fish Clan.

At the end of summer, the whole village packed its belongings and went to the Trade Moon, four days' travel, and Abalone Catcher had to be carried part of the way. For the first part of the walk, he leaned on Old Tidepool and Fisher Skunk, who was going to marry Cannot Be Told as soon as he had finished paying her bride-price. But two days out, Old Tidepool shouted at him until he lay down on a travois and let dogs pull him, the trade goods from the travois piled around him as if he were an egg in a nest. The tame eagle clung to the travois and screamed at them.

All of it made the Channel Clan afraid. When a young man grew old-looking, it was a dangerous magic.

"It isn't good," Sand Owl said under his breath so many times that Bone finally shouted at him and refused to walk with him anymore.

"As if saying what we all can see wasn't going to make things worse," she muttered to Others' Child. "You are lucky to have a husband with sense."

Others' Child saw Bone eye Sea Otter wistfully over her shoulder and wondered how many women had wanted to marry him before she had come along; also whether he had heard Bone. It was hard to tell because Sea Otter had a canoe over his head; he marched along steadily like a boat that had grown feet. No one made such good boats as the Channel Clan. Others' Child thought she saw the feet do a little dance in answer to Bone's flattery.

She chuckled. It felt good to be walking along beside him carrying her tightly woven baskets—nothing the

Channel women made was any finer than the baskets of
the Yellow Grass People—with several to spare to trade
for thick black tar and maybe a catskin from the mountains, where the fur would grow thick. And maybe there
might be a spray of eagle feathers for her hair. Sea Otter
was sure to get a good price for his canoe. Others' Child
felt smug and happy, wanting to show off her fine husband to Night Hawk, who might be there. And at the
same time whatever wind was blowing from her felt
reckless, and she wondered what might happen when she
saw him. Her feet ran over the trail as weightless as
sunlight, and Little Brother had to trot to keep up with
her.

The Channel Clan and the Knifenose Fish Clan and
the Split Rock Clan all camped next to one another at
the bottom of an inland valley scooped out of the hills
like a round bowl. Spread out from them were all the
other clans of coast people—Manzanita and Tarpool and
Hot Springs and even a few of the Shell Men. The Trade
Moon was always the last full moon of summer, and its
light was so white and bright you could see colors by
it. On the first night Others' Child thought the moon
looked bigger than she had ever seen it, hanging over
the whispering foxtail grass and the old oaks, with coyotes yipping in the foothills all around them.

Yah, you can't hunt us, she thought. *We are too many.*
But she moved restlessly among the camps as if the
moon or the sound were luring her on. She hadn't seen
Night Hawk. Surely he would be among the Manzanita
or the Hot Springs Clans; he had talked of them, of old
acquaintances in their bands.

Others' Child picked her way past the Channel camp.
Brother was in their journey hut of grass and downed
oak limbs, asleep for the night, and Sea Otter was talking
with the Sun Dancer of the Abalone Clan, who was his
mother's brother. Others' Child felt like the tide, lured
farther and farther onto some odd shore by the fat weight
of the moon.

There were fires burning all around the valley, hun-

dreds of them, like red stars. She walked past them unnoticed, hearing snatches of talk like puffs of smoke:

"Three elk, you couldn't see their feet in the fog—"

"The year the old shaman died—"

"A bad wet year. All the fruit rotted—"

"Fish as thick as berries in the water—"

"Told her to tell that to a bigger fool—"

She wandered past a camp that seemed to be some
more of the Manzanita Clan—Others' Child wasn't sure
of all the clans yet—and a gray shape lunged out of the
shadows at her. She stepped back, wondering at a coyote
foolish enough to get this close to men, and saw that it
was Gray Daughter.

Others' Child sat down suddenly in the foxtail grass,
her arms around Gray Daughter's neck while Gray
Daughter leaned on her. "Yah, you are a crawling dog,"
she said, laughing at her. "Your mother would be
ashamed."

Gray Daughter lay down with her paws and nose in
Others' Child's lap.

"And where is your brother, who has more dignity
than to fawn on people?" Others' Child asked, but she
was laughing. She rubbed Gray Daughter behind the
ears.

"Here," Night Hawk said, and she saw him and Thief
standing together in the moonlight under the knotted
limbs of an oak. The little branches made crosshatched
patterns on his face, so she couldn't see him properly.

Others' Child stopped rubbing Gray Daughter. She
looked at Night Hawk and sat very still, waiting for
whatever he was going to do. She didn't know what she
wanted him to do.

Thief came out of the shadows and stuck his nose up
to hers, maybe a handspan away. His yellow eyes were
the baleful color of the hot springs whose water smelled
like rotten eggs. Others' Child inclined her head toward
him, and he sniffed her suspiciously. She thought he was
angry with her for leaving them. She scratched his ruff
and felt him relax a little, loosening the taut muscles
clothing his angry bones.

"The dogs remember you," Night Hawk said. He leaned against the tree now, arms folded, keeping his distance.

She could hear wanting in his voice. She smiled down at Gray Daughter's head in her lap and said, "Thief is angry." She went on scratching his ruff.

"And I am not?"

"I don't know." She looked up, trying to see him through the shadows. She couldn't, but she could feel the moonlight full on her own face like water. It wasn't fair. "Are you?"

"I was angry when I left," he said. He sounded non-committal now. The wanting was gone.

"But you left." Baffled disappointment enveloped her.

"And you stayed."

She wondered how long they were going to stay there repeating the obvious. Nothing was right. Even the air felt askew, as if it had solidified and been bent somehow, or she had bumped into it. It was sitting between her and Night Hawk. "I had to," she said quietly.

"What?"

"I *had* to! If you would come away from that tree you could hear me."

"I hear you now." His voice was rueful.

"How long have you stayed with the Manzanita Clan?" she asked him.

Night Hawk shrugged. She saw his shoulders move as if they were trying to lift the shadows off them. The shadows settled back like Abalone Catcher's tame eagle.

"I heard you have taken another husband," he said.

Others' Child looked down again. She wasn't sure what she had wanted to happen, but this wasn't it. "Little Brother needs a father," she whispered.

"He has a father." Night Hawk had heard that well enough.

"Not here. Not in the village. Not anywhere that we are." Others' Child glared at him, stung by his indifference. What had she thought would happen? That she would spend the night with him and then go back to Sea Otter?

"Why did you want another husband?" Night Hawk said. He shrugged again. "Lately you didn't even want to do it with me."

"Of course *any* woman would rather do it with you," she snarled. *He* had left *her*. He didn't even miss her. She didn't think he even wanted her; he was just angry about Sea Otter.

"Most of them do," he said. He sank down against his tree trunk until he was squatting. The moonlight caught his face out in the open. His mouth twisted.

"Then you won't miss me."

"I miss you," he said.

"Enough to come back and stay?"

"No."

She wrapped an arm around Thief's ruff, caressing him, not Night Hawk. "I have another husband anyway," she said to him.

Night Hawk nodded. "Maybe he won't like you looking for me."

He wouldn't. "I wasn't looking for you."

"You were looking for something." Suddenly his mouth curled in a half-smile.

"What makes you think it was you?"

"How many husbands do you have?"

"One. And I wasn't looking for you." She wanted to cry. Nothing was right.

"Oh."

"You could have looked for *me*!"

He tilted his face, half-smiling again. "The dogs found you."

"Why did you want to find me if you don't want to come back?"

"How can I come back? You have another husband."

"Yah! I hate you!" She jumped up, flinging Gray Daughter out of her lap. She flung the words at him like the handful of rocks that had been their life together. "You don't want to come back, you only want me to be unhappy because you won't. Yah, who wants you?"

Night Hawk flinched. "Who wants *you*?" he snapped. He stood up, glaring back. He looked as if he was going to reach for her, and she wasn't sure what she would do if he did.

"You used to!" she snarled.

He folded his arms behind his back, as if he wanted to keep a grip on them, as if they might take hold of her against his wishes, and if they did her skin would burn him or stick him with quills. He rocked on his heels. "Maybe it was more grief to me than it was worth."

"Yah, nothing is ever *your* fault!" Others' Child turned on her heel, her eyes stinging.

"I want to see Brother!" Night Hawk shouted after her.

"You left him! You left *us*!" She plunged through the foxtail grass.

"I am here now!" he shouted back. "I will be here tomorrow, too."

She felt the low cat's-back ridge that ran through the valley pressing against the soles of her feet as she crossed the bony spurs of its spine. She thought she heard it stir, as if their quarrel had woken it up, but it was only a meadow vole quivering in the long grass. She stumbled through the trees, skirting the strangers' fires, and a dark shape dropped through them in front of her. Others' Child shrieked, cowering like the vole, her heart pounding. It was too big for an owl. She blinked and it became clearer, an ungainly form with hunched back and dark folded wings. It opened its beak at her and blurred into the shadows as if she should follow it. She put her hand over her mouth and ran the other way.

Sea Otter was asleep when she got to their camp, with Little Brother curled in the fold of his body. Others' Child slid under the blanket with them, heart racing. Too much was alive in the night: the ground, the gnarled trees, and whatever had dropped out of their branches.

She woke with the full moon in her eyes, its bright whiteness pouring through the door. It illuminated the yellow of the dry grass stems that thatched the journey hut and the pale green lichens on the oak branches. The dead leaves whispered above her head. When Others' Child looked around, Sea Otter and Little Brother had disappeared, the journey hut had gotten bigger, and she could see that it was really a grove of trees. Above her a dark shape was perched on a limb, the dots of the fires in the distance outlining the hunch of its wings.

"You are a very disturbing element," Great Condor said. His voice was heavy and hollow, as if he were speaking from the mouth of a deep cave.

Others' Child stared at him wide-eyed, her fingers splayed out like the tree branches, as if she could push him away.

"If you make my likeness, I will come, you know."

"I didn't want you to come," Others' Child said. "With respect."

"You have been talking to me anyway," Great Condor said gravely. "Everything you do in this world talks to me. I am the end of every dance."

"Yah bah, old Feather Broom," said a voice, and the pinpoints of fires coalesced into a pair of yellow eyes. Coyote sat down under Condor's tree and looked up at him.

"I'll be the end of your dance, too," Condor said.

Coyote lifted his leg on the trunk of Condor's tree while Others' Child watched him, terrified, wishing he would go away. "Not till the End Time," Coyote said. "And even so, it will all start again."

"It won't be any different, though," Condor said lugubriously. "All to do over again, that's all."

Coyote pulled a ball out of the air. It glowed like abalone shells. He bounced it on the ground and stretched it until it was all strings and Others' Child could see herself and her mother and father and Night Hawk, Maize Came and Mocking Bird and even old Cat Ears, who had wanted to marry her mother once, and an old shaman named Looks Back who had been dead for years, all running up and down along the strings. He rolled it together and stretched it again, and she could see Foam and Brother and her dead babies and Abalone

Catcher. He stretched it once more, and they were all mixed up together.

"It's never the same," Coyote said. He tossed the ball back and forth, pulling different pieces out of it.

"It's all the same to me," the hollow voice said from above them.

"You mean everything tastes the same," Coyote said. "I wouldn't do it, your job."

"I try to keep the world tidy," Condor said. "Someone has to."

"Is that what you're telling little Make a Picture here?" Coyote jerked his gray snout at Others' Child. "She's one of the untidy ones. You won't stop it."

"She's here," Condor said. He hunched his heavy shoulders in a cape of dark feathers. "She's made a nice nest."

"Wait till you see what the eggs hatch," Coyote said.

"Oh, does she belong to you?"

"I thought so."

They both looked at Others' Child.

"The Channel Clan think she is theirs now," Condor said.

"I told you not to do that," Coyote said to Others' Child.

"You didn't." She felt stubborn. She was very afraid of Great Condor, and Coyote was making it worse, insulting him. "Anyway, what eggs?"

"Waxing Moon is pregnant," Coyote said. He sat down and curled his tail around his paws. She thought she could see little glints of light in it, as if he had brushed it through a cloud of stars.

Others' Child eyed him uneasily. If picture magic had made a baby for Waxing Moon, why hadn't it made one for her? She wanted to ask them, but she was afraid.

"You have to be still to hatch things," Condor said, as if he knew what she was thinking.

"Oh, no you don't," Coyote said. "It depends what you want to hatch."

"If you're a cuckoo, you don't have to hatch it," Others' Child said crossly. If Waxing Moon was pregnant, she felt rather like a cuckoo herself, putting her egg in Waxing Moon's nest. Was that what Coyote had meant? She felt irritated that they couldn't agree on what she ought to do.

Condor dipped his curved neck down, and his cape of feathers spread out around it. His eyes were small and red, like coals. "A messy bird, the cuckoo," he said. "And ill thought out."

Others' Child wished she hadn't been flippant. The red eyes looked right through her; she could feel him assessing her bones, her secret cuckoo self hidden under layers of muscles and fat, concealed with old scars and betrayed by the white spot on her backside. When she was dead, only the bones would be left. Condor would clean up the rest, skin and scars and birthmark. *I'm not dead yet,* she thought, and she edged uneasily away from him.

"Yah," Coyote said in disgust. "Don't you think about anything but keeping the place clean? You're like an old woman."

"If it weren't for me, the world would be a disgrace," Condor said disapprovingly. "You make more of yourselves as fast as you can. Someone has to clean up." He looked at Coyote. "Litters," he said with distaste. "My wife only lays one egg a year."

"And your children are ugly," said Coyote.

"Hush!" Others' Child hissed at him. "You are making everything worse."

"If there isn't any mess," Coyote said, "nothing will change. Old Feather Broom knows that. That's why he wants to sweep you up."

Others' Child didn't like the idea of being swept up by Condor, but she didn't trust Coyote, either. She edged away from the two of them while they argued.

"Change gives me indigestion," Condor said.

"You would still be a winged lizard with no feathers if we didn't have change," Coyote said.

"That took a long time," Condor said.

Coyote bounced his ball on the ground and began to pull strings out of it again, silver and golden, glimmering like threads of water with the sun on them. Others' Child backed farther away as Coyote bounced the threads around the oak tree and she could see little people fall out.

Coyote grinned as the ball flipped over his head. He pointed at Others' Child. "This one will make some of it happen. You can't keep her in your nest to sit on your egg."

Great Condor bent his head farther down until he was beak to snout with Coyote. Coyote's ears were pricked forward, his muzzle lifted above his teeth so that they showed in a cheerful white row along his jaw. Condor's bald red head loomed above him. A mist surrounded them now so that they floated in the air, the stars winking like white sparks behind them. Everything else was dark. Others' Child couldn't see the woods.

"I keep everyone with me," Condor's hollow voice said. "Sooner or later."

"I wouldn't live in your nest," Coyote said, "with everyone dead and complaining about it."

"The dead ones don't complain."

"They do if they belong to me," Coyote said.

"The very ones that make trouble," Condor said ominously.

"You should be grateful for them. Without them nothing would happen among the living."

"They make a mess. They are jealous and leave old love affairs all over the place."

"You don't know art when you see it," Coyote said. "Old Duster." He jumped up and bit the end off Condor's beak and then fell back into the dry oak leaves, laughing.

Others' Child watched with horror. Something blotted out the branches and the moon, and she heard Great Condor raise his dark wings and rattle his feathers. She ran away through the trees. The night got as dark as if a hand had closed around it, but she could still hear Coyote howling and laughing and rolling on the ground behind her.

* * *

Others' Child woke under the blanket with Sea Otter and Brother, and no matter how she tried, she couldn't remember coming back. She remembered it getting dark and the wings beating around her.

"I saw my old husband yesterday," she said as soon as Sea Otter woke up, so that she wouldn't be dishonorable. "He wants to see Little Brother."

Sea Otter yawned. "That is reasonable."

It didn't seem reasonable to Others' Child. She thought about it uneasily while she made his breakfast.

"Take him to the Manzanita Clan's camp for a while this morning." Sea Otter stretched and poked the embers of the fire. He seemed to know where Night Hawk was living.

"I don't want to," Others' Child said dubiously.

"Do it anyway."

Others' Child gave him a dark glance. They didn't often argue—it was hard to argue with Sea Otter—but she didn't see why he should be solicitous about Night Hawk. She knew what Coyote would think of that. She could still hear Coyote's voice in the breeze, creaking in the journey hut, like little strings of laughter.

"I want to see Father," Little Brother said, waking up. He looked uncertainly at Sea Otter. "My other father."

"Of course," Sea Otter said. He looked at Others' Child, who shrugged and gave up.

She scooped acorn mush from a basket sealed with tar and gave him a bone spoon. "Eat, then. Likely he won't have anything to feed you."

Sea Otter sat across the fire from her and smiled gently. "Why don't you want to see this man?"

Others' Child looked at him from under knitted black brows. "You are not stupid."

"I would rather you saw him than thought about him," said Sea Otter.

"How do you know I think about him?"

He grinned. "You grind your teeth."

Others' Child unclenched her jaw. When Little

Brother had eaten, she took him by the hand, and they went to the Manzanita Clan.

She thought Night Hawk was surprised when she got there. He was sitting at the fire, drinking water from a shell, and when her shadow fell over him, he looked up, his eyes wide, the water running over his chin.

"I have brought Brother."

Brother sat down in his lap.

"You are big," Night Hawk said. He looked as if he were wondering what else to say.

"I can swim."

"Very good."

"Mother can swim, too."

Half his words belonged to the Channel Clan now, Night Hawk saw. After a while Brother wouldn't speak the language of the Kindred unless Others' Child spoke it to him, and why should she? It wasn't hers. He stood up with Brother clinging to him.

"Let's go to the stream. You can show me."

"That isn't deep enough to swim in," Brother said scornfully.

"It isn't deep enough to drown in, either," Night Hawk said, "if I don't watch you. I want to talk to your mother."

What if I don't want to talk to you? Others' Child thought rebelliously. "I brought him because Sea Otter said to."

"You are learning to obey your husband," Night Hawk said, apparently impressed.

She glared at him. "He says he would rather have me see you than think about you," she added pointedly.

"Were you thinking about me?"

"No."

They walked side by side down the dusty path that led to the stream. Already it had been trampled out by hundreds of feet. She looked to see if there was anything in the trees (it had been about here, hadn't it?), but nothing moved. Her eyes slid to Night Hawk. It was hot, and he wore nothing but a breechclout, like Sea Otter and all the men who weren't so old that their bones were cold all the time, even in summer. Little Brother wore nothing but a blue bead on a thong around his neck. Their red-brown skin blended with the warm shadows of the live oaks and the rustling grass.

Her skin hummed in the summer heat. She looked at herself. She was still good to look at. Sea Otter had thought so; it wasn't only the picture magic, wasn't only his wanting a woman who was different from the Channel Clan, he who was so of them himself. She hadn't grown bony, and her breasts didn't turn down yet, even after feeding two babies. She looked at them to make sure.

"What are you watching?" Night Hawk asked. "Is there a bug on them?"

Others' Child jerked her head up.

"You will fall down."

She stubbed her toe on a rock in the trail because she was looking at him. "I wasn't watching anything!"

Night Hawk gave a faint chuckle. "Don't worry. They are still nice. I am sure that New Husband likes them."

"He has a name!"

"That is a name."

"If he likes them, that is good, then, since you don't," Others' Child said angrily. Her voice quavered on the last word, and she felt like crying again. She blinked furiously.

"I liked them. But they are yours, and you were mad at me. They aren't stones on your front, or cactus blossoms." Night Hawk leered at her. "I'll show you mine. It hasn't changed, either. It's still attached to me." He reached under his breechclout and waggled it at her as if he were holding the shaman's seashell stick.

Others' Child looked away, flushing. Up ahead of them Little Brother had reached the stream and was walking along the round rocks that crossed it where it met the trail. Below the rocks was a pool, not as deep as his waist, with tiny fish like small shiny fingers.

Night Hawk sat down on one of the stones, his feet in the water. Others' Child sat beside him while Brother squatted in the pool trying to catch the fish with his hands. The moss on the rocks floated in the current like green hair and brushed against her ankles. The water was clear and cold, snowmelt from the mountains.

"Where will you go next?" she asked him. He had his hands in his lap now. "After the Trade Moon?"

"Anywhere," he said. "Maybe north."

"Not home to the Kindred?" She spoke carefully, a polite conversation with an old acquaintance, not one who had waggled his cock at her.

"Why should I?"

"I don't know. Because it is a long time since then," Others' Child said.

"Then maybe I'll go." He watched the water·ripple past his ankles, moving downhill. The mountain's breath, always going toward the sea. What did it want in the sea? The same thing he wanted on the next trail? "If I went home to the Kindred, would you come?"

"I brought Brother because it is right he shouldn't forget you," Others' Child said. "But I won't cross the desert again." The skin on the back of her neck crawled. "I am afraid of it. And as you say, I have another husband."

"Which is more important, the desert or the husband?"

She thought of the dark shapes soaring over the desolate land, dead land, not wild but only dead. What had they been saying to her in the sky? *Come here no more,* she thought, but it might have been a different language altogether. It didn't matter. She was still afraid.

"The desert," she said and knew that was true. "But my husband matters also."

"I will tell him," Night Hawk said solemnly. "He will be glad."

"Why was I always the one to have to change?" Others' Child demanded.

"You changed. You changed into Person Always Living at the Coast," Night Hawk said grimly. He shook his head. "Maybe you started out as too many different things. Your father's people and your mother's people and my people. There are too many of you. Maybe you will always go on changing, like Sky Woman.''

They turned and looked silently at the water running away under their feet. Little Brother pounced suddenly at the stream, and it rose over him in a great spray like a waterfall running upward. He stood up, dripping, with a fish in his hand, the only one of them who had caught anything.

VII

Why There Is Sex

The Manzanita Clan's village was inland, at the end of a narrow canyon choked with the twisting red branches of manzanita bushes and white-flowering anise and the oily gleam of poison oak. The Manzanita Clan chopped the last out where it grew along the trail, but it clung to the canyon walls, its trifoliate leaves shining faintly red like the rash it raised. Night Hawk had learned to be wary of it since coming here, but he had found that most of the Manzanita Clan were immune to it. They lived among it, they said, and so it didn't harm them. Night Hawk wondered if he might get used to his discontent if he lived among it long enough. The Manzanita woman might help. She brought him food and had seemed willing to warm his bed since he had come here after the Trade Moon, when its round shell had shrunk again to a thin white hook and Others' Child and his son had gone away with her new husband.

Night Hawk nuzzled the Manzanita woman's neck. Her name was Walks Loudly. She smelled like woodsmoke and anise, and her hands were large and flat with short fingers. She made him think of a badger. She had large dark eyes and a round head with a white streak through her dark hair. She put more food in front of him, a greasy mass of deer meat and roasted soaproot. He ate most of it and put his hands on her breasts again. She smiled.

"You should make up your mind what it is you want to do," she said in mock reproof.

"I want to go foot-on-trail," Night Hawk said experimentally. "Will you come?"

She looked at him in horror and shook her head. "Out there?" She nodded toward the dark beyond the fire. "No."

They never went with him. He had tried another woman before the Trade Moon, a small thin girl of the Falling Water Clan. Now he would move on and try a woman of the Split Rock Clan and then a woman of the Tarpool Clan, and all of them would like his bed and his stories of adventures, and none of them would come with him when he left. He could see how it would be, as if someone had shaken time out for him and showed him things that were tomorrow's.

In the fall when the People Who Lived at the Coast went to the oak forests to gather acorns, Night Hawk went to the Hot Springs Clan to trade.

The women there were putting up the acorns in basket granaries, big woven hampers on stilts that kept the damp out. When he came down the trail, they gathered around him, chattering like soft birds, to see what he had brought.

Night Hawk unrolled the packs from the dogs' travois while the men stood back watching. They would look at the spearheads and knife blanks and the pile of red fox skins and make offers later, after the women had bought.

Night Hawk had bone combs and spoons, deer-leg flutes, and shell jewelry: necklaces and bracelets and anklets and ear ornaments to poke through the holes that

these people made in their ears. (He wondered if Others'
Child had holes in her ears now.) A woman with a fall
of black hair that covered her like a cloak came up and
picked up a long necklace of shell beads, smiling.

"I could give you the finest ground acorn flour for
this."

Night Hawk furrowed his brow, considering.

"I could even cook it for you."

"How would your husband like that?" he asked.

"I don't have one." She laughed, a ripple of water
going downstream.

"No one wants her." Someone else laughed. "That
one is too bossy."

The woman made a face at him.

"Her husband died," the plump woman next to Night
Hawk said, squinting her eyes at a long-handled spoon.
"Rattlesnake got him, and she says now she is his. There
is a crack in this spoon."

"There isn't," Night Hawk said.

Rattlesnake's Woman twined the shell beads around
her neck. They stood out like surf on dark sand. She
took the spoon from the other woman and tapped it on
her hand. "There is no crack."

"Well, I see it," the plump woman said.

"You see ghosts, too," Rattlesnake's Woman said.

"I will give you a good berry basket for this," another woman said. "Tar-lined, as smooth as skin inside.
I'll show you."

She fetched it, and Night Hawk inspected the basket
while she tried on bracelets. The men were beginning to
finger the spearpoints. The chieftain peered at the un-
derside of the fox skins.

Night Hawk turned to Rattlesnake's Woman. "This
much acorn flour," he said, holding out his hands to
show her. "I will give you another necklace, too, if you
will cook for me."

"No, these." The woman held up rings for her ears,
spiraled pink curls of shell.

Night Hawk grinned. "All right."

She put them in her ears. Her ears were little and

graceful, like dark shells themselves. She shook her head, and the shells danced. Her rabbit-skin skirt was sewn with heavier shells along the hem so that it swayed and clicked when she moved.

At night she moved into the house that the Hot Springs Clan had given Night Hawk. These inland houses were half buried in the ground and stayed cool even when the air was hot. The woman seemed matter-of-fact about her moving in. She built a fire and cooked acorn mush in a basket, and fried pieces of baked yucca root on a flat rock. The Hot Springs Clan had given her a goose to cook for him—he was a guest—and it had been roasting all afternoon on a stick. She took it down, set a bowl of dried summer berries in front of him, and watched him while he ate.

"You have to eat, too," Night Hawk said. Others' Child wouldn't have waited.

And why did he want another wife like Others' Child? He hadn't wanted a wife at all until she came along, but now he was used to the curve of a warm back against him at night, and someone to talk to on the trail.

The woman put a berry in her mouth and smiled. She wore a short fox-skin cape over her shoulders, and the fur looked like sunset against her hair. The curve of her breasts showed at the opening. The dogs looked at the new woman without interest. She wouldn't be permanent, and she was afraid of them.

"They look like coyotes," she said. She pulled a piece off the goose and ate it warily, as if she thought they might take it away from her. (If Night Hawk hadn't been there, they might have.) Thief yawned, showing the zigzag of his teeth.

"Their mother was half-coyote," Night Hawk said. "These are three-parts, but they have dog ways. For instance, they bark. And they wag their tails."

Gray Daughter fanned hers gently on the floor to be polite.

"Well, that is all right." Rattlesnake's Woman relaxed and turned chattily to Night Hawk. "What do you do when the female is in season?"

Night Hawk shrugged. "She can pull a travois big-bellied as well as not. When the pups are born, we put them in the travois, but mostly they run off as soon as they are weaned. Mostly they are coyotes."

"We?"

"The dogs and I," Night Hawk said, but he had meant Others' Child. She had had her babies the same way. Small wonder she hadn't liked it, not being a dog. He still didn't know what to do about it, though. This was how he lived. When he was in a village he could feel the houses getting closer together and would wake thinking that they had moved in the night. But it was very lonely now, when it hadn't been before Others' Child.

"I get lonely," he said. This woman looked very beautiful under the fox-skin cape; he wanted to put his hands under it and touch her.

"Rattlesnake ate my husband," she said. "I didn't like him, so now I tell the men I am Rattlesnake's, but it's not true." She looked at him happily.

"I will be leaving soon," he said to see what would happen. "Mostly women are afraid of the wild lands."

Rattlesnake's Woman smiled agreeably. "I wouldn't be. Not with a husband. Did you beat your other wife?"

"Certainly not," Night Hawk said disapprovingly (And she would have hit him back; he knew that.)

"That is very important," Rattlesnake's Woman said. "I have had one of those. I will go to the wild lands with you."

Night Hawk lay wrapped in a pile of fur blankets with her and realized he had got another wife. She seemed to be very adaptable. Her breathing was slow and shallow, her black hair spread on the hide pillow like charcoal, her lips a little parted. She was very pretty, prettier than Others' Child. And since she was a widow, he hadn't had to pay a bride-price. Maybe he would stop one more time among the Channel Clan. He would see how New Husband and Old Wife liked that.

* * *

They left a quarter-moon later with all her goods tied on the travois. The shaman, an old woman with wild gray hair, gave them her blessing, and a short broad man with a nose that someone had broken glared at them until they were past the village, but he didn't say anything.

"Who was that?" Night Hawk asked.

"My old husband's brother," Rattlesnake's Woman said. "He smells like rancid fat, and I do not like him."

Night Hawk chuckled. "He looked like a bear in a temper."

"He wanted to marry me. Because he is my old husband's brother. That is how the Hot Springs Clan do, mostly."

"Oh." Night Hawk wondered if Bear in a Temper would come after him. The shaman hadn't said anything about that.

Rattlesnake's Woman laughed. It burbled like the stream. Night Hawk had never seen someone so cheerful. "He was very angry. He will probably put a curse on us."

"I do not need a curse," Night Hawk said uneasily.

"It won't matter." She displayed a small black stone on a thong around her neck. "This will send it back to him. I got it from my grandmother, who was a chieftain's sister. She found it inside a fish. It will make his curse turn back on him, and perhaps he will die. I would like that."

She seemed to be fearless. She kept up with Night Hawk easily on the trail, her bare feet kicking up little brown puffs of dust like clouds above a miniature terrain. A beetle scuttled across her path, a tiny buffalo running from the rainstorm. She swiveled her head, eyes excited, looking around her at the unfamiliar canyon walls. Coast women didn't travel much. If there was hunting to be done, the men did it, traveling in a group and leaving their women behind.

"When will we see the desert?" she asked him, over and over.

Imagine a woman eager to see the desert, Night Hawk thought. "No," he said, "we'll stay along the coast a little while. Then you will see all the desert you want.''

"And buffalo?''

"Yes.''

"And stone trees, and the bones of Great Cat?''

Night Hawk wondered if he had elaborated too greatly. These things might be disappointing. "They are very far away,'' he said. "We won't see them tomorrow.''

"Oh.'' She did sound disappointed.

They stopped at late afternoon beside a pool where the stream spread out under a tall overhanging rock shelf. Night Hawk tied some line—braided from Rattlesnake's Woman's long black hair—to his fishing pole, while Rattlesnake's Woman climbed the rocks to look around her. Night Hawk couldn't help thinking of snakes—those were snake rocks if he'd ever seen any, tumbled and honeycombed with crevices—but she insisted that because Rattlesnake had eaten her first husband, he wouldn't take anyone else from her family. Night Hawk thought apprehensively that Rattlesnake might have acquired a taste for them.

He caught two fish while Rattlesnake's Woman was standing on the tall rock, and when he whistled and waved at her, she came down to cook them.

"You can see all the way back to our village,'' she told him. "And as far as where we picked acorns last moon. Is it even farther than that to the buffalo?''

Night Hawk decided not to answer. Her cheerful assumptions that the world was small disquieted him, like Bear in a Temper's curse.

Rattlesnake's Woman gutted the fish and threw the heads and offal to the dogs, who swallowed them in one gulp. Their jaws made a sound like cupped hands clapping, with the click of teeth at the end. She threaded the fish onto sticks and propped them over the fire, cuffing the dogs away. They lay down and sulked, watching the fire.

When the fish were done, the skin crisp and blackened and peeling off, Rattlesnake's Woman and Night Hawk shared the biggest and divided the other between the dogs. Then they splashed into the river to wash, muddying the clear current that ran along the edges, roiling up dark clouds above the smooth pebble bottom.

The water ran green-brown and mysterious over the surface of the pool, opaque as polished stone. Rattlesnake's Woman swam out into it and splashed armfuls back toward Night Hawk. He dove after her, the stone opening to its liquid center. He caught her around the knees and pulled her under, and they twisted like fish under the surface, her skin glowing as iridescent as scales in the green light. They came up spluttering, spitting water and laughing, and he grabbed her so that they floundered together toward the shore. She stuck her hand between his legs, and they coupled in the muddy shallows while the dogs watched them from the bank. What did dogs think when people did that? Night Hawk wondered.

Afterward while they lay and let the water wash them, dusk thickened the sky like someone churning the shallows of the air. The heart of the cook fire on the bank glowed red, and they got up and wrapped themselves in blankets beside its comforting warmth. The dogs tried to get between them, but Night Hawk pushed them away and they retreated, growling, and lay down, one on either side. He drowsed between the dog smell on one side of him and the woman smell on the other, the warmth of the fire like a skin over all four of them. Sleep came quickly, the deep, unaware sleep of contentment.

Rattlesnake's Woman felt Thief's hairy body against her back. She could smell him, too, a hot thick smell of coyote and raw fish that seemed to get stronger as it got darker. She buried her nose in Night Hawk's river-smelling shoulder, and knew with a growing certainty that she shouldn't look up.

His sleep shattered like layers of shale, cut by Rattlesnake's Woman's scream.

Night Hawk sat up, his heart pounding, reaching for his knife, spear, and spear-thrower. Rattlesnake's Woman sat with the blanket clutched to her chest, her head thrown back and eyes looking wildly around her at the sky.

Night Hawk thought he saw a shadow of wings. He twisted his head to look behind him and saw that the dogs were nose on paws, indifferent. Slowly he lowered his knife.

Rattlesnake's Woman shrieked again and tried to bury her head in the blanket, but she was sitting on it, and it tangled itself around her legs as she tugged at it.

"Be quiet!" Night Hawk grabbed her by the shoulder. "What is it?"

Rattlesnake's Woman hiccuped, gulping air down as she pointed at the sky.

Night Hawk tipped his head back again. The stars spun above them, so many, like pinpoints of ice wheeling in the vastness, the black endless star road. He saw it for an instant with Rattlesnake's Woman's eyes, saw the stars revolve, faster and faster, spinning off souls like chaff in a threshing basket. The silver abalone moon had dark patches on it, skeleton eyes, Old Death watching to see who was next, who might be caught out alone in the awful night.

Night Hawk jerked his eyes away, pulled them down from the endless star road that Rattlesnake's Woman was watching. He shook her. "Be quiet. You are making me see things, too."

Her mouth was an egg-shaped black O. "There is too much of it here. You didn't tell me there was so much of it," she whimpered, trying to close her mouth. She looked at the dogs and began to wail again. "And the dogs look like coyotes at night."

"They look like coyotes in the daytime," Night Hawk said.

"Not this way."

He looked at them and saw what she meant. They stood side by side now, watching the woman. He tried to make them look like dogs, but they stayed silver-gray in the moonlight, tails tipped with black, and they smelled like Coyote.

"Go in the river and wash, Piss Breath," he said to

both of them, but they didn't move. He wondered if they were what was making the sky spin around, flattening the constellations against its black roof.

Rattlesnake's Woman stood up, floundering in the fur blankets. "I am going home!" she whimpered.

Night Hawk grabbed her. "Not now," he told her. He held on to her wrist.

"I don't want to be here!" she wailed. "There is too much of it here!"

"Too much of what?" Night Hawk asked her, but he knew. Too much of the world, too much of the night. She hadn't known what it would be like.

"Too much," she said. She looked around them, frightened, staring into the darkness beyond the thin skin of the dying fire.

"I will make more fire," Night Hawk said. "You can't go anywhere now. Something will eat you."

He wondered if it was Bear in a Temper's curse that was making her see all the ghosts in the night. Ordinarily people couldn't see those. Night Hawk knew they were there, but he was used to them. They seemed comforting to him, spirits that didn't need to be enclosed in houses. But he could see how they would frighten Rattlesnake's Woman if something showed them to her. She had a charm to send anything that Bear in a Temper sent to her back to him. He looked at the dogs again. "Did *you* do this?"

An owl went by on silent wings, its feathers nearly brushing their heads. Rattlesnake's Woman shrieked again, stifling it into a hiccup with her fist. Her eyes were as round as the owl's. In a moment there was another shriek, but this one was not human, was thinner, and cut off short. Rattlesnake's Woman flung her arms wide, fingers convulsed as if she had been the mouse, pierced and lifted in thorny talons.

"That's owl business," Night Hawk said, hanging on to her wrist. "You don't have to listen to it." But he didn't like it. An owl was bad luck any way you looked at it. If you heard one say your name, you knew you were already dead. He built up the fire and got Rattle-

snake's Woman to sit down beside it, never letting go
of her wrist. He thought she would run into the night
and get eaten by Puma if he did. Owl would say her
name.

She didn't go to sleep again. When the sun came up
and he let go of her wrist, she pulled her belongings off
the travois and tied them into a deer-hide pack. It was
Night Hawk's deer hide, but he didn't try to stop her.
He watched morosely instead while she ate a handful of
dried berries and the little that was left of last night's
fish, and picked up her bundle.

"You didn't tell me there was so much of it," she
said accusingly.

"I told you."

"Then there is more of it at night." She slung the
bundle over her back. "You will never find a woman
who will sleep in that with you," she told him.

He watched her walk off up the trail toward her village. He thought she could find her way. Her back was
resentful. Adventure hadn't been the way she had imagined it would be, and she would go back and marry Bear
in a Temper, he thought.

Night Hawk sat down, stiff with having sat up all
night, and stared at what was left of the fire. Gray
Daughter stuck her smelly muzzle in his face.

"Go away," he said angrily. "You drove her off."

Gray Daughter looked offended. Night Hawk pushed
her away anyway. He yawned, staring into the embers.
They looked back at him like sullen red eyes.

"You are untidy," a sepulchral voice said from above
him.

He looked up. A bald red face with a collar of dark
feathers loomed over him. Night Hawk flung himself
backwards, skating along the ground away from the fire.
He hadn't remembered a branch overhanging the fire
like that, or he wouldn't have built it there. The branch
was undeniably there. The dark figure that perched on it
dipped its beak lower as its neck lengthened startlingly.

"You are making a great deal of extra work for me."
The voice was low and deep, as if it came from inside

something. It made the skin on Night Hawk's neck prickle.

"With respect, Uncle," Night Hawk said, "I don't know what you mean." It seemed better to answer it. If he was polite, maybe it would go away. *Please go away.*

"The woman is leaving a mess, too," Condor said gloomily.

Night Hawk looked up the trail the way Rattlesnake's Woman had gone. The canyon looked different than it had before.

"Not that one. The one you left with the Channel Clan. She is not proving satisfactory. I am certain it is because of you."

"She sent me away," Night Hawk said politely but stubbornly. He thought it might not pay to let Condor have his way in an argument, that it might be construed as acquiescence. Then he might find himself disposed of like other rubbish, cleaned up in the Great Efficient Beak.

"Look at what you've left behind you," Condor said reproachfully. "Bits of old lovemaking, pieces of anger, bones that make music." He hunched his shoulders and pointed with a dark feather.

Night Hawk could see a valley now where the fire pit had been. The valley ran between two mountains with a dark stream in the center, and all along the edges of the stream were pieces of pale people that he couldn't quite see through and piles of smoke and stones that he knew were things he had done or words he had said. They littered the banks as far as he could see, and talked in low, indecipherable voices.

"Everyone leaves things," he said to Condor. "That is the way life is." He stared curiously at his leavings. Sometimes he thought he could see himself with Others' Child, and sometimes he heard Little Brother's voice among the stones. He saw a hand that was Old Auntie Leaf Fall's, and a breast that he thought belonged to Rattlesnake's Woman. There was an ear that might be Old Tidepool's.

"Most people don't leave so much," Condor said.

"They are tidier. Their things fade when they aren't used anymore."

Night Hawk wondered if it was the music that made things stay.

"This is all rubbish you are keeping, you and the woman between you, and I haven't the time for it." Condor looked reproachful. "There is too much other cleaning to do."

He sounded like an aggrieved wife, and Night Hawk folded his arms across his chest. "Then leave it alone," he said. He was sure Others' Child's pictures made things stay. "Ignore it. I'm not asking you to clean it."

"It's my job," said Condor. He shook his head and hunched his shoulders, his massive beak swaying from side to side. "You will see."

Condor spread his wings, blotting out the sun. Night Hawk cringed backwards, wishing he hadn't been so disrespectful. Condor lifted from his branch, rising into the sky, and the valley below them began to rise, too, drooping like folds of a hide, as if it were being lifted in Condor's talons. Night Hawk thought of the owl's last-night mouse. Then the valley fell back down with a thud, crumpled into new ridges, with the river flowing the other way, but still there, weighty and unwieldy, as if Condor had lost hold of it.

Night Hawk heard a dark angry mutter above him, and a shadow banked overhead, riding the thermals. The splayed shadow feathers of its wing tips brushed his skin, and he twitched. Then it moved away, flapping ponderously to a higher current, a different airstream, and diminished in the distance. The sun poured through the trees, which had gone back to their proper places. The dark valley had vanished, too, and the fire in the fire pit had gone out.

Night Hawk shook himself, examining his skin for signs of decay in the thin sunlight.

"You need to dance faster before Old Feather Broom sweeps you up," a seductive voice said behind him. "You aren't dead yet."

Night Hawk turned to look. "No," he said, disquieted. "Go away."

Coyote shrugged. She leaned against the tree where he had seen Gray Daughter standing. He didn't know how he knew she was female, under the fur, but he did. She smelled female. It was musky and not unpleasant, and he felt his cock stiffen. With a *dog*? he thought.

"I could put you in there." Coyote pointed at Thief, who was watching her with interest. "I've done it before. I tried once with that woman of yours, but it didn't work very well. You might be different."

Night Hawk eyed her suspiciously. The idea made him feel outraged, even if it could change sexes. It seemed disreputable. Also, he was jealous. "Did you do it with my wife?"

"She wouldn't stay," Coyote said. "She kept trying to be a human person inside, and she didn't fit."

"Then you *didn't* do it?"

"It's all in how you look at things," Coyote said airily. "Is she doing it with New Husband if she's thinking about you while she does it?"

"Is she?"

"Some of the time. She's trying to make a baby, too, so maybe she isn't concentrating."

"I don't want to know all this. I don't care what she's trying to make. Maybe she'll have coyotes," Night Hawk said nastily. "A whole litter."

"It's happened before," Coyote said. She smiled maternally. "I have a lot of children."

"How do you tell if you're their mother or their father?" Night Hawk asked. He glared at her.

"It doesn't matter. I'm both." She chuckled. "That's why it's so easy to be my lover."

Night Hawk suspected it might be dangerous, too. His cock shrank, informing him of its agreement with that. He might stick it in something he couldn't get it out of.

Coyote came out from under the shadow of the tree, padding on gray paws and somehow walking on bare brown feet at the same time. Her hair was gray, like an old woman's, but her face was young and hungry. Coy-

ote was always hungry. Hunger was what kept Great
Condor from sweeping up the earth until he had rolled
it into a ball and eaten it. Hunger kept new things being
born, faster than he could sweep. Suddenly Night Hawk
could see how it would be to mate with her, to push
himself into that soft gray fur, smell the thick coyote
scent, salty as blood.

Coyote's eyes were like yellow pools, like the hot
springs that went to the core of the earth. Night Hawk's
skin prickled and melted, and he felt himself growing
smaller, whirling in that yellow water until he fit inside
Thief. He was aware of the two of them in there, Thief
like a lupine undercurrent to his own awareness. The
gray skin flowed over his bones, and he heard deer in
the underbrush across the valley and smelled their dusty,
grassy smell.

Coyote stood on her hind legs and began to climb the
sky—there were steps cut in the air—and Night Hawk
and Thief followed her, seeing the pale stars like translucent fires against the blueness. The sun was a river of
yellow light, as if someone had broken open a honey-
comb. They loped beside it. "Be careful," Coyote said
over her shoulder. "You'll burn your feet."

Night Hawk ran after her, skirting the fiery river. The
muscles in his shoulders bunched and stretched, leaping
across the firmament, gaining on her now. His tongue
lolled over his teeth, and the cock that he and Thief
shared stuck out whether he wanted it to or not. He
thought fleetingly of dogs enticed from the Kindred's
fires by a coyote in heat and found the next morning
eaten. The thought flew away, whipped out of reach on
the solar wind. He caught Coyote and sank his teeth into
the back of her neck.

Her haunches bunched under him, waiting, and he
could hear the singsong growl in her throat, like the fires
that drove the stars. He plunged it into her, and it was
like sticking it in the fire, but it didn't matter. As long
as he could feel the flames, he was alive, too hot for
Great Condor to pick up.

Night Hawk shuddered and felt his seed planted in the

universe, and then he was falling backwards, down past the translucent stars, revolving nose over tail, the gray fur flying away from him. He dropped like a stone out of Thief, naked in the air in his own skin.

Night Hawk woke facedown in the dirt beside the fire. He sat up gingerly, but there was no one else there with him. He bent his head to see if he was burned, but he wasn't. He could still feel Coyote's warmth around him, and he looked suspiciously at Thief and Gray Daughter sleeping nose to tail on the other side of the dying fire. Gray Daughter opened one yellow eye and looked at him. For a moment he saw the hot yellow water of the pools that went to the core of the earth, and then it was gone. She yawned and closed her eyes. Thief was snoring.

Night Hawk got up and began to string more fishing line from his pole. The fishing line was all that was left of Rattlesnake's Woman. He wondered what was left of Others' Child and whom he had coupled with in his head last night. If it had been in his head.

He glanced over his shoulder uneasily. The more fool he, then, for falling in love, he decided. It did things to your head. Love was for stories around the fire, people in legend. Not for human people, who were trying to keep Great Condor at bay. It was plain that he needed a woman, but he didn't need love. Night Hawk looked at the sun. Winter was coming on, but that didn't matter much in this country. There would be snow out in the desert, so he supposed he would have to stay here until spring. He supposed Coyote had known that.

He would build a better fire and see that Coyote didn't get into his camp again.

VIII

Death and Power

Others' Child peered at herself in the shallow water where the green stream slid around a string of rocks and was caught, spread thin as light over the shiny stones and the little darting fish on the bottom. If she tilted her head just the right way, she could see her reflection in the water, her dark hair tied into a knot on her head—it was hot inland—and stuck with a spray of spotted turkey feathers like an outstretched hand.

Crescents of pink shell poked through the holes in her ears, luminous as fish against her dark skin. It had hurt to have the holes made. The Channel Clan had it done when they were babies and didn't have anticipation to contend with as well as the pain. Others' Child had nearly bitten through Sea Otter's hand when he had given it to her to hold, but she was determined to be a Channel woman, and so she had asked Old Tidepool to put holes in her ears.

Now she rather liked the effect. She turned her head this way and that, preening, while Little Brother tried to skip a rock across the water. It bounced, bumpy as hope, and disappeared with a *plorp!* like a diving fish. The Channel Clan were spread out along the riverbanks on either side, bathing and eating a midday meal. By tonight they would come to the oak forests, where they collected acorns every fall. The forests belonged to the Split Rock Clan, but the Channel Clan and the Knifenose Fish Clan gathered acorns there, and in return the Split Rock Clan were allowed to fish on the coast. That was how it worked. If you owned too much of something, you traded it for fish or acorns.

The Manzanita Clan owned acorn forests of their own. But Night Hawk likely wasn't with them anymore anyway, and besides, he didn't matter. Others' Child smacked her hand down flat on the water because she thought she had seen his reflection deep in the pool beneath her own.

"Do you think he is the reason I can't have babies?" she asked Blue Butterfly later, while Blue Butterfly trudged through the dry grass beside her and Sea Otter was out of earshot. "Do you think he has cursed me?"

"No," Blue Butterfly said, considering. "A man would think of something else. He would make it hurt when you coupled with your husband, for instance. Or give you boils down there. He wouldn't think about babies."

"Maybe the last baby damaged me, when she died," Others' Child said dolefully. She still imagined her daughter floating among the icy desert stars. "We let her die. Who could blame her, if she was angry?"

"My son is not worried," Blue Butterfly said. Sea Otter was ahead of them, with Brother on his shoulders. "But maybe you should talk to the shaman."

Others' Child suspected that her husband and his mother worried more than they were telling her. What if something *was* wrong with her? Foam didn't have children, either, since she never stayed with her husband long enough. If no one had children, who was going to take care of them all when they were old?

Now that Others' Child had brought up the subject,

Blue Butterfly's soft wrinkled face was pursed into a knot of distress, but she didn't say anything more about it. "While we are picking acorns," Blue Butterfly said philosophically, attacking the problem she had had the longest, "it will be a fine chance for you to talk some sense into Foam."

Others' Child thought she could as easily talk sense into the real foam on the ocean, but she didn't say so. Old Tidepool had already said so, and so had the woman who was shaman of the Knifenose Fish Clan.

When they came to the oak forests and found the Knifenose Fish Clan, Foam said so, too.

"You are supposed to tell me to behave," said Foam expectantly.

"Your family wishes that you would," said Others' Child.

"I wish my family would fly up into the trees and lay eggs in nests," Foam said. "Which of us do you think will get their wish?" She stuck her stubborn jaw out at Others' Child, and Others' Child laughed.

"They only want babies," Others' Child said. "I would give them babies if I could. I would lay eggs in a nest if it would work." She looked wistfully at the children spilling through the oak forest, like brown acorns themselves, poured out of a basket. Everyone who could walk and carry a basket was picking acorns. The men climbed the trees and shook out the ones that had not fallen.

Foam looked at Others' Child sympathetically. "I want babies, too, just not with that man. If I have a baby with him, I may have to stay. The children will belong to him if my parents won't give back the bride-price."

They found a tree with acorns thick beneath it. The branches made a roof over them, like laced fingers. The oak forests covered the low rolling foothills and the narrow valleys that wound between them, most with a trickle of a stream in the middle. The deer came here in autumn to eat the acorns, too, and this was when the Channel Clan and their kin hunted meat on the deer trails and sometimes killed ducks and geese as they flew over

the coastal marshes. Others' Child had not thought she
would tire of fish and the snail things, but she had. She
made deer, many deer, in the dirt for the hunters, and
gorged herself when they came back with a kill. It was
odd, she decided, how when there was plenty of food,
one grew capricious and demanding, and wanted deer
instead of snail things.

The trees were a constant source of mystery and
magic to Others' Child, who came from a land where
trees were few, except for the stands of piñon pines on
the high slopes. Her father had told her of the wet jun-
gles to the south, where there was nothing but trees, tall
as the sky, entwined with creepers, with red and blue
birds and monkey people living in them. But Others'
Child had not seen them. Those trees were as foreign to
her as the idea of the Endless Water had once been,
beyond her imagining. These trees were real, their con-
voluted branches laced together like lovers, their dark
green spiny leaves scratching her hands and pricking her
toes through her yucca sandals. Their shade turned the
waving foxtail grass dark gray-brown, and their dusty
leaves whispered things to each other that she couldn't
hear. Of the coming of the deer, maybe, to browse on
their nuts; of the squirrels who lived in holes in the gray
trunks. Brown cocoons, split open, clung to the serrated
leaves of a bush that grew between the oaks, whoever
had been in them carried on the wind to some other
place. Would they come back to the oak forest on powdery brown wings to lay eggs there again before the
winter killed them?

The forest seemed to Others' Child to be what she
had been trying to draw when she was learning that she
wanted to stay here—concentric rings of belonging, deer
inside the forest, squirrels inside the trees, moths coming
back forever to lay eggs on the same bush—she and
Brother inside the house of Sea Otter and Blue Butterfly
and Condor Dancer. Foam was out of step with the pattern, one foot outside the circle, balanced precariously
on its edge. No wonder she ran away. No wonder she
didn't want to make babies who would stay, like the

squirrels, in the tree where they had been born. She had come to the wrong tree and been caught in its branches.

"Why did you marry him?" Others' Child asked Foam, scooping up nuts in cupped hands, putting them in her basket. The basket was deep and conical and hung from a sling that went around her forehead when she walked. She had woven it herself, a thing that she could do properly and so was proud of. She cocked an eye at Foam, who wasn't picking acorns but was swinging by her arms from a low branch instead.

"He seemed all right then," Foam said darkly.

"Does he beat you?" Others' Child couldn't remember hearing him accused of that.

"He is boring," Foam said. "I go to sleep when he talks."

Others' Child grinned. A lot of women would consider that a good point—you didn't have to listen, and he entertained himself—but she felt her sympathies leaning toward Foam. Sea Otter wasn't boring, but he wasn't Night Hawk, either. Others' Child glared at the acorns as if Night Hawk might be in them. He had no business coming into her head that way.

"If I were you," Foam said, "I would have stayed with the trader." She swung from the branch, trailing her toes in the oak leaf prickles.

"You aren't me," Others' Child said shortly. "You don't know what trouble is until you marry a man who wants to keep moving." She rubbed an acorn between her palms. It was smooth and red-brown, the color of skin, and came to a point at the bottom. On the top it had a cap of bark where the stem grew. If you put it in the ground, it would grow a whole oak tree. "What will you do if you make your parents give back the brideprice?"

"Marry another man," Foam said. "But I will be more careful."

Others' Child considered. "You are troublesome. How do you know another man will want you?"

Foam chuckled. She dropped from her branch. "That's how I will find one who is not boring."

Night Hawk, Others' Child thought, but she didn't say it. Foam might like to be foot-on-trail always. Others' Child compressed her lips in a tight line and put her head in her acorn basket to see how full it was.

That night, when the Split Rock Clan and the Knifenose Fish Clan and the Channel Clan made fires together, Others' Child pointed out to Foam the men she saw who might make good husbands. Foam's real husband was at a fire with Abalone Catcher and Condor Dancer and the chieftain of the Knifenose Fish Clan, telling them how long the walk had been from the Knifenose Fish Clan's camp and what journey food he had brought on the way, and how he had decided on it, and how many quail he had killed with his throwing-stick on the ridge just over there.

The valley was dotted with fires, the way it had been at the Trade Moon, and the voices carried in the clear night on waves of shouting and laughter. There were skins and tar-lined baskets of fermented cactus and berry juice at every fire. The coyotes were meeting, too. All around them in the hills she could hear their warbling howls.

"That one!" Others' Child pointed at a Split Rock man lurching by, his hair half unbraided and a skin of berry juice in his hand.

Foam considered him. "Too thin," she decided.

"This one, then." They both guffawed as an enormous man of the Knifenose Fish Clan lumbered up to their fire and sat down with a thump. They could feel the ground shake.

"What is your wife laughing about?" he demanded of Sea Otter.

Sea Otter shook his head. "Women are very mysterious."

Foam and Others' Child buried their faces in their hands. Others' Child elbowed Foam. She pointed at Old Tidepool with his nest of wild hair, as if a bird lived on his head. Foam whooped with laughter.

Sea Otter shook his head affectionately. "They are drunk," he told the large man.

Others' Child dipped a clam shell in the basket of cactus juice and drank. If she was drunk, would Night Hawk be more or less likely to appear in the bottom of her clam shell?

"It would be different if I were you," Foam said, slurring it into Others' Child's ear and having a little trouble with the "f" sound. "You are a magic woman, and everyone gives you great respect." She waved her arms to show how big the respect was and bumped Others' Child in the nose.

"I am only a magic woman here," Others' Child said dolefully. "Not where *my* people live. My sister is holy there, but I am not."

"Why is she holy there if you make the pictures?"

"Because she is the Maize Girl. My father brought it from the south to the Yellow Grass People, and my sister brought it to the Kindred. It is complicated, but it is as if someone had brought you the oak trees, when you hadn't had any before."

Foam thought about that. "No oak trees?"

"None." Others' Child shook her head solemnly.

"There have always been oak trees."

Others' Child sighed. Foam couldn't imagine it. How could you imagine there not being something you had always had? Foam could not see the brown-furred hills rolling inland forever, treeless like the haunches of sleeping lions, shorn of the twisting branches of the live oaks, as if they had never been. She could not see as Others' Child could see. "Well, my people do not have oak trees," Others' Child said. "Not enough to feed us, anyway, so my sister is holy for being Maize Girl, and I am not."

"But you make pictures of things and they come!"

"Therefore my people do not trust me. If I make them, maybe I will stop. If I can make things come, maybe I can make things go away." Others' Child scooped up some more cactus juice and grinned unsteadily. "I can put things in places sometimes. Once I put scorpions in the old Grannies' beds."

"I would like to be able to do that," Foam said.

"No." Even drunk, Others' Child had more sense than that. Old Tidepool had managed to draw a fish even though his skill was unreliable, because he was so full of power otherwise. Foam might be good at it, and that would be even worse.

"Maybe one who is truly powerful is never respected at home," Foam said, thinking hard. "Your father came from the south with whatever it is. The food. Your sister had to go to the Kindred from the Yellow Grass People. You had to come to us. Here you are . . . are . . . with honor. No one makes you marry men you do not like."

"No one made you marry your husband," Others' Child pointed out.

Foam glared at her.

Others' Child sniffled. The cactus juice was making her cry. "I only wanted to belong somewhere, to have a place. You do not know what it is like, never having a place, belonging to nobody."

"You belonged to your husband. He belonged to you. He did not talk about fish all day."

Others' Child scrubbed her eyes with the back of her hand. She could feel Sea Otter watching her. "It wasn't enough. He belonged somewhere else, too, but I didn't. I was born to the Kindred, but I lived with the Yellow Grass People because I got left behind when they had a war. It didn't matter what I did, because no matter who I was with, it was wrong because it came from the other people, the ones who were different. They were too close together. They were old enemies."

"Didn't you have any Shell Men to make peace? To tell you whose fault it was and how much comp . . . compensation should be?"

"No. No Shell Men." Shell Men made everything sound easy.

"You just fought each other?" Foam looked shocked.

"How can you talk like an old granny when you don't

listen to anyone yourself?'' Others' Child wanted to know.

"That is different." Foam sucked the cactus juice off her fingers. "I am going to sleep," she added, standing up with difficulty. She steadied herself with a hand on Sea Otter's shoulder and shook her head. "I don't understand any of what we have been talking about."

Others' Child watched her weave toward the Knifenose Fish Clan's camp. Foam would have a headache in the morning that probably wouldn't clarify matters. Others' Child wondered if she understood things any better than Foam.

Foam skirted around the far side of the camp, away from where her husband was talking to Abalone Catcher. Abalone Catcher looked as if he was asleep. Foam stumbled on what must have been a rock in her path and righted herself, walking carefully as if she were balancing her head on her shoulders like a basket. The things that Others' Child had said swirled around in her head like soup, and she thought that if she didn't walk very carefully, she might spill them out, and she wanted to take them home to think about.

When she got to her journey hut, Foam lay down in the bed she shared with Not in a Hurry and watched the pattern that the breeze made in the leaves of the roof. It was the kind of crisp fall night that was like cutting open a green plum. She thought she could smell some new way to be on the tart, woodsmoke-tipped air.

Others' Child had done as she pleased, and everyone gave her much honor for it, even though they were beginning to suspect now that she couldn't have any more babies. Foam thought hard. Surely it was only a matter of figuring out how to have a magic that they wanted, and then everyone would let you alone. Foam wrestled with where to find a magic as her eyes closed.

In the morning, when Not in a Hurry was lying snoring beside her and Foam had a headache, it still seemed like the right idea. She was sure she had understood that much. She looked at her hands, trying to will magic into them. How did you become magical? Shamans had visions, but Others' Child had never had a vision. Her mother had taught her the pictures, she had said. That was a new idea, that magic was teachable.

Foam sat up carefully, trying not to disturb Not in a Hurry, and looked for some willow bark for her headache. Could you teach someone magic and not know you were doing it? she wondered as she chewed the bark and made faces. She dug the dried grass out of a piece of the journey hut's dirt floor with a rock, and smoothed the place with her hand, crumbling the little clods of dirt between her fingers and looking furtively over her shoulder. Not in a Hurry flung an arm wide and snorted, but he didn't wake up.

Foam stared at the patch of dirt. What should she make? What did she want? She didn't know how to make a not-husband, so she tried to think of something she did want. She wanted a new otter-skin cape, she thought, so she took the rock and tried to make it, but it looked like a journey hut with the top cut off. She tried to make the otter instead, but there was something wrong with its legs.

Foam banged the rock on the dirt, scrubbing out her cape and her otter. They had looked to her like a centipede crawling into her journey hut, and it made her nervous. She could feel its many legs like whispers on her bare back.

I know what I can make, she thought, and she started to make it. Anyone could make a trail; it was just lines. Lines going away from here, going away from Not in a Hurry, not coming back. Foam drew them slowly, as if they were a spell, curving lines for trails around the rocks on the shore and the place where the tumbled boulders were that gave the Split Rock Clan their name, straight lines for the spear-shaft road that led away from here in her head, the spear-thrower that would throw her back where she came from. She could feel the road open up under her hand, feel the tingle in her skin. If she touched Not in a Hurry now, she could burn him with a little piece of that tingle the way it happened when you rubbed your hand on a fox skin in dry weather.

As if the thought had arced from her to him, Not in a Hurry mumbled and turned over. He patted the bed beside him. When his hand didn't find her, he sat up.

Not in a Hurry scratched his head. "Are you fixing my breakfast?"

"No." Foam rubbed out the road in the dirt. She thought it had been there long enough, and she didn't want him to see it.

"Then what are you doing? Why are you awake if you are not fixing my breakfast?"

"I am awake." Foam smiled a small, secretive smile to herself.

Not in a Hurry looked at her suspiciously. "Then you should be fixing my breakfast. I am hungry. I talked about many important things last night with the chieftain of your father's people, and it has given me a headache."

"That is the cactus juice."

Not in a Hurry looked affronted. "When men talk together, they get headaches from serious talk. Women get headaches from cactus juice."

"Oh," Foam said as if she had never thought of that before. She tightened the laces on her hide skirt and crawled through the journey hut door into a thin mist to get kindling. The fire still had a few red embers in the ashes, and she blew on them and dropped sticks in until the kindling caught. "I am glad you explained it to me," she said earnestly.

Something is wrong, Not in a Hurry thought.

Foam built up the fire, stirred acorn meal into a basket of water, and put hot rocks in it. She made it a ritual, like Old Tidepool making a spell, slow and elaborate and satisfying. She could hear Not in a Hurry's stomach growling. While the mash bubbled, she cut some late onions into it and some sage for flavor. She felt as if she were another person, Dutiful Wife, come to live with Not in a Hurry while her road practiced being. When she thought it was solid, she could leave Dutiful Wife there with Not in a Hurry, like a butterfly's empty shell. He might not know the difference.

Foam spooned out the mush into a turtle-shell bowl and gave it to Not in a Hurry. She could feel the road bump under the dirt under the grass that was the journey hut's floor.

Someone was shouting in another camp. Not loudly, but it made an important sound, like rain beating on a hide. Foam lifted her head, listening. Not in a Hurry put his bowl and bone spoon down.

The sound was louder now, a lot of voices together, and bare feet smacked the paths that had been worn through the grass in the camps. The earth hummed. Foam crawled out of the journey hut before Not in a Hurry could tell her to stay inside.

Catches Crows, the old woman who was shaman of the Knifenose Fish Clan, walked past Foam's nose with her staff in her hand. Foam could see that it was her most powerful staff, with the knifenose fish head on the end. She goggled in the doorway, and Not in a Hurry bumped into her backside trying to get out.

"What is it, Auntie?" Foam said, not moving while Not in a Hurry pushed at her bottom.

Catches Crows stopped long enough to look at them solemnly. "The chieftain of the Channel Clan is dead," she said.

Foam could hear the news humming through the earth like a taut string. "I saw him last night, talking with my husband." That a chieftain could suddenly be dead was frightening. That Foam's husband had been there just before it happened was somehow ominous. All things were connected. Catches Crows knew that.

The shaman stroked her chin, which was covered with fine soft wrinkles that clung like a loose hide to her jawbone. "Something that was inside him killed him, I think. That is what Old Tidepool thinks. It was something he could not suck out, and very powerful."

Not in a Hurry shoved Foam aside and crawled out past her. His eyes were uneasy. "We spoke last night about important things. But he was tired. He said that. And he drank much cactus juice.''

"For the pain, I think," Catches Crows said. "Old Tidepool was with him all night. But this is dangerous. It may be something that will spread. It is not good for a death like this to happen at acorn-picking." She stumped on down the trail, her black hair flapping behind her.

Not in a Hurry scrambled back into the hut and pulled his leggings on. It was cold, and one shouldn't take a chill even in emergencies. Foam pulled a coyote-fur cape around her and followed him out, not listening while he told her this was man's business. The Knifenose Fish chieftain's wife and aunts were already hurrying through the mist down the trail that led to the Channel Clan's camp, with most of the rest of the Knifenose Fish Clan behind them. The chieftain would be in the Channel camp already, consulting with the shamans and other chieftains. Foam trotted along behind them, excited now.

"This is a dangerous matter," Not in a Hurry said severely.

"I know." Foam hung her head, for once willing to listen to him. It was exciting. The whole camp was shifting, like an anthill turned over. The air crackled with it. Foam could almost feel the magic road under her feet twist like a snake and wriggle in its scales.

The Channel women had laid Abalone Catcher on a bier of young oak branches and grass bound into shocks, in front of his journey hut, where he had died. They had bent his arms and legs so he looked as if he were sleeping. Old Tidepool knelt on his haunches beside him, eyes closed, lips moving silently. The shaman's wild hair stuck out like someone who had been hit by lightning, and his bony, gnarled hands were splayed like starfish on Abalone Catcher's bare chest, as if he might still call him back into his body.

Others' Child wondered if the Shell Men on their islands would see the chieftain's spirit go by, trailing clouds of blue light, the red fire of his disease rolling along beside him. And if they did, could they shout and call him back? Or had the door into the Otherworld already rolled shut behind him, its closing booming across the water like stones banged together? Everyone knew that he had not been well, and everyone had pretended not to see that, because Abalone Catcher had been young and it made them afraid.

The young shaman of the Split Rock Clan stood uneasily over the head of Abalone Catcher's bier. He had three missing teeth, which people said had been knocked out when he had wrestled the spirits in his vision dream, and his tongue darted nervously between them. This death would make anyone afraid, Others' Child thought. So much pain in that still face, the skin gray as old ashes, the mouth still twisted as if whatever had tried to claw out his belly still had it twisted in its talons. The tame eagle shrieked from its perch inside the hut.

When someone died like this, people said that Coyote had eaten him. Others' Child knew that was true, but she also knew Coyote didn't choose. He threw names in the air the way he had thrown the stars, and when they fell down, he ate the one that landed in his mouth. One day he might eat her. It wouldn't matter that he had been fond of her until then.

Cannot Be Told stood at the other end of her brother's bier and bit her lip to keep from crying, which did not befit her status as leader of the Channel Clan until they could choose a new chieftain. The man she was to marry, Fisher Skunk, stood beside her. He was stocky and had a silky mane of hair with a white streak down the middle that had given him his name, but he wasn't very old. Not old enough for white hair. The joke among the Channel Clan was that Cannot Be Told had given it to him. Fisher Skunk didn't seem to mind that. He put a wide hand on Cannot Be Told's shoulders, and she leaned back against him for a moment.

Then she said, "We will make a mourning for my brother. We will wait here until it is time, and then we will bury him at the heart of the oak grove."

Old Tidepool and Catches Crows looked at each other

solemnly, before they raised their eyes to the shaman of the Split Rock Clan. A little murmur ran through the people peering over each other's shoulders at the bier. If they buried Abalone Catcher here, he would live here for a while. The spirit could be in two places at once. Everyone knew that. Spirits did what they felt like. What if he kept his disease spirit with him? That was why they had to ask the shaman of the Split Rock Clan, who owned the oak grove.

The young shaman of the Split Rock Clan looked thoughtfully at Cannot Be Told and at the uncertain face of the Split Rock chieftain and made up his mind. "Abalone Catcher will make the oak trees grow if his bones are here." He nodded to himself. "He was a great man. It would not be good to carry his body so far back to the coast." Not with the disease maybe running loose beside it.

"My brother's grave will bring much good to the Split Rock Clan," Cannot Be Told said, to make it clear that she was doing them a favor and not the other way around. Others' Child could tell from the way everyone looked at Cannot Be Told that she was understood to be a woman of power now. Until the Channel Clan chose a new chieftain, Cannot Be Told was chief. It wouldn't have mattered if Abalone Catcher had been married. The sister, not the wife, had power. If there had been a son, Cannot Be Told would have been chief until he grew up.

Old Tidepool and Catches Crows had begun to chant, and the shaman of the Split Rock Clan added a high quavering note that rose above theirs, like a scrap of smoke hung in the air.

The mist had cleared into thin sunlight, and the air hummed with the rattle of autumn insects as the shamans circled the bier, chanting their incomprehensible plea to the dead chieftain. It was hard to tell their voices from the bugs. They were saying, *Go away*, Others' Child suspected. No one wanted dead spirits to linger, even if they had once been friends. They were too likely to be jealous of the living and want to take the living with them on their dark road.

Others' Child knew that these people buried their dead, unlike the Yellow Grass People and the Kindred, who burned theirs. Her father had come from a people who didn't burn bodies; he had made her mother promise to bury him when he was dead, because otherwise he would have no body in the Otherworld. As it turned out, his children had done it, and he was part of the Yellow Grass People's maize field now, but the idea still made Others' Child's skin crawl. To be trapped in the earth like that. When she thought of it, she thought of her baby buried in the rain, water filling up the hole. She wondered if she could persuade Sea Otter to burn her if she died first, to let her loose on the wind.

"How can a chieftain just die?" Others' Child whispered to Sea Otter, because she needed to speak, to talk.

"There was something wrong in his belly. I saw it. You saw it. No one talked of it, but we all saw it. He had to be carried most of the way here."

"That is not the same as dying." She felt stubborn, the way Little Brother did when he kicked his heels and didn't want to sleep. "I don't see why Old Tidepool couldn't have sucked it out of him. Why do we have healers?"

"He tried. Do you think it is as easy as that?"

"No." Others' Child looked shamefaced. "I just want it to be."

Sea Otter rubbed his face against her hair. "No harm in that."

"I can't have babies, maybe." The words came out as if they had been pressing against her lips. "If Old Tidepool can't keep Abalone Catcher from dying, maybe I can't have babies."

Sea Otter looked at her solemnly. "You had babies before. Is this my fault, do you think?"

"No!" Others' Child leaned her head against his chest, butting into the otter-skin shirt he wore. "No. Some moons I think I am going to have one, and then it goes away and I bleed. A lot. I think I am damaged inside. I asked Old Tidepool, and he said he will try to see, if I will let him.'' She kept her face buried in his chest, with the musky otter smell in her nose.

"You have never talked of this," Sea Otter said.

"I talked about it with your mother. It is not a man thing."

He scratched his head. "Are you afraid I will take another wife?"

Others' Child jerked her head back and glared at him.

"See?" he murmured. "I would be afraid to."

But he might. In a few more months, Blue Butterfly might tell him to. Others' Child felt like a bird that had been caught in the rain, flapping wet feathers, drowned and miserable, her home place vanished.

"Stop it," Sea Otter said. "You will make yourself sick. I am not going to take another wife."

Not now. Others' Child trudged behind him as they went back to their own hut to get ready for the mourning. But in another moon? Another six moons? She watched Blue Butterfly and was relieved to see her preoccupied with the death and burial. Death ritual was elaborate here, a matter given much thought and preparation. No one who died among the Channel Clan would be bones on a fire. He would live, forever rotting, in a hollow in the ground, with his prized possessions hung on a stick above his grave. The other possessions would go on the fire, but never the body itself.

The Channel Clan came back to Abalone Catcher's bier, their faces blackened with ash and ashes on their feet. Others' Child felt its powdery darkness sinking into her skin. At midday the shamans drank datura and went into a trance while the Channel Clan circled endlessly around them. At nightfall the shamans staggered to their feet, weaving, and the Knifenose Fish Clan fed them acorn mash. Then they danced around the bier, eyes glazed with having spoken to Death.

The shamans wove their ritual around the corpse all night, drawing in the important people of the clan, including, to her surprise, Others' Child, with Sea Otter, Condor Dancer, and Blue Butterfly. She watched their

feet for the pattern of the dance, and wove it around the
bier. Like making a basket, she thought, a basket to hold
the soul in.

At dawn, when the sky spilled over the mountains like
blood, they set fire to a stack of Abalone Catcher's possessions, his knife and hunting spears, his fox- and otter-
skin blankets, his pouch of magic things, and his
necklaces of shell beads. The eagle screamed and
thrashed on Cannot Be Told's arm, but she had tethered
it to its leather perch and paid no mind to its flapping.
She would feed it fish later, and it would decide to stay
with her, Others' Child thought. It was only a bird, even
though it was a sacred one.

The sun climbed over the tangled trees, and the light
outside the grove was suddenly golden. Inside, the air
was dappled gray and green. The fluttering shade covered Abalone Catcher like a blanket. The young men of
all three clans had been digging a pit all night under the
largest of the oaks, whose ponderous trunk was so thick
it took three men with outstretched arms to ring it. Now,
dirt-smeared and panting, they lowered Abalone Catcher's bier into the pit with ropes, tipped head-down, and
pushed the dirt back in. The eagle shrieked again, and
Cannot Be Told fed it some meat from a pouch at her
waist. The shamans chanted, arms upraised, their eyes
still blank with datura, and then it was done.

The silence fell into the grove like a pebble into water,
and Others' Child thought, *Is that all there is?* What
more she might have wanted, she couldn't say.

The next morning they began the long walk back to
the coast. Any child old enough to walk carried a basket
of acorns in a sling around its head. Some had baskets
nearly as big as they were, bumping along behind them.
The grown men and women carried two and three, and
the Channel Clan's dogs pulled travois of hide and sticks
that thumped on the trail, snagging on brush and stones,
and had to be untangled.

The Channel men had killed three deer as well and
given the Split Rock Clan a bag of shell beads for them.

Women were not allowed to hunt, or to catch most fish. Woman magic was too powerful—it might infect the game and make it powerful and wily, too, or dampen the hunter's magic. It might do anything.

Cannot Be Told walked at the front of the band, with a basket of acorns slung from her forehead, but with the eagle on her arm, too. Fisher Skunk walked with her, keeping up a solid, rolling gait. The eagle glared at him, and he looked back at it stolidly until it turned its head away and ruffled its feathers.

As they neared the coast, their trail parted from the Knifenose Fish Clan who had walked with them partway. Others' Child said good-bye to Foam while Not in a Hurry watched them suspiciously, but Foam dutifully pattered after him when he called her, and walked away toward the Knifenose Fish Clan's camps to the north.

"Maybe she will stay now," Sea Otter said hopefully.

"Maybe we will be too interesting now, and she won't," Others' Child said. There would be an election as soon as Cannot Be Told found an auspicious day for it. The next chief might be any man of substance in the clan or of relationship to Abalone Catcher on his mother's side. A man would be chieftain, but it was the matrilineal relationship that counted if the old chief had no sons. Until it was decided, every man with a claim to be chief would do his best to convince the clan of his worth. That usually meant feasts. Followed by long, boring speeches, Sea Otter said.

"Will you be chief?" Others' Child hadn't thought of that before.

"No." Sea Otter smiled and shook his head. "Father maybe."

And then you, Others' Child thought. She wondered what it would be like to be a chieftain's wife and felt a swift surge of pleasure at the notion.

"More likely it will be Sand Owl," Sea Otter said, spoiling her daydream. "His mother was the old chief's mother's sister. Or Hawk Feet. He is very rich."

"Oh," Others' Child said. She watched her feet making little puffs of dust on the trail. Just as well not to be a chieftain's wife anyway. It only made other women jealous.

When the Channel Clan came to their home camp, Others' Child had ample time to observe the effects of someone's possible elevation. Bone, Sand Owl's wife, was giving herself airs already, until Tern slapped her. Blue Butterfly regarded Bone with massive silent dignity which proclaimed, to anyone who was interested, her own greater fitness for the honor. Sand Owl and Condor Dancer and three other candidates gave feasts at which they made speeches that were as boring as Sea Otter had promised.

Others' Child watched Sea Otter sneak away into the darkness from Condor Dancer's speech with a skinful of berry juice.

Brother tugged Blue Butterfly's arm. "New Father went that way." He pointed.

"Hush." Others' Child laughed. "He is very undutiful."

Condor Dancer's speech rolled over them like the breakers on the shore, booming and important, but endless. Others' Child yawned. She wished she could sneak off after Sea Otter. She wouldn't be able to vote for a new chieftain anyway. That was for the men, although the women's opinion would carry weight. But not even Cannot Be Told, sitting erect at the top of the circle around Condor Dancer's fire, could vote. She could name the day for the election but not vote. So far she had found the days inauspicious.

It was not good manners to ask when the election would be, but Others' Child thought the men were getting impatient. Sea Otter and Condor Dancer talked about it the next morning, shaking their heads over their fishing nets, pulling their questions through with the knotted black thread.

"It will be winter soon," Condor Dancer grumbled. "It will not be good not to have a chief at the solstice."

Sea Otter looked grave, despite his desertion of the night before, and his normal good nature was wearing

thin with irritation. Or maybe with the big head left from
the skinful of berry juice. "Old Tidepool just laughed
and sat there sticking crow's feathers in his hair when I
asked him. He looked like a bird a coyote had got."

"He is getting old," Condor Dancer said.

"He should talk sense to her!" Blue Butterfly said
behind them with a little click of her tongue. She slapped
a handful of acorn mush down on her cooking stone for
emphasis. "That girl was always willful." She smacked
the mush into a flat pancake with her spoon.

Others' Child's lip twitched. She rather admired Cannot Be Told for holding out against the men like that.
As soon as there was a new chief, the old one's sister
would have no power left at all.

"Hawk Feet has gone to talk to her," Condor Dancer
said. "He is tactful." As opposed to Sand Owl, who
was not, and who had drunk too much last night and
made that clear.

Tact appeared to accomplish little. Hawk Feet came
scowling and sulking to Condor Dancer's house and said
that Cannot Be Told had told him that all the days were
unlucky.

Blue Butterfly sucked her tongue to say that she had
told them so.

"We will all go to her at once," Condor Dancer said.
He got his condor mask from the woven chest in his
house where he kept it, and put it on, to be sure that
Cannot Be Told listened to him.

The mask unnerved Others' Child. She was half-afraid
it might speak to her. But she followed the men anyway
out of curiosity. Something was bound to happen.

Condor Dancer, Sea Otter, and Hawk Feet went to
Sand Owl's house and hustled him away from his breakfast. Then they stood and shouted outside Old Tidepool's house until he came out. Others' Child peered
inside curiously. Lizard skins and a dried toad hung from
the roof amid bunches of herbs, their gray-green leaves
and stiff flowers dry and powdery. If you stood on your
head, she thought, it would look as if your feet were on
the ground. An upside-down world, where the sky was

on the floor. She bent over and then turned her head upward, trying to see what it would be like.

"I was talking with a fish," Old Tidepool said irritably. "What do you want?"

"We want you to talk to Cannot Be Told and tell her to tell us when a chief will be chosen," Sand Owl said.

"A woman with a name like that," Old Tidepool said, "has a name like that for a reason. She will have to come to it her own way."

"She is taking too long," Hawk Feet said. "It is nearly winter."

"Come with us." They hustled him along. When Others' Child straightened up, they were halfway across the camp. She ran after them. Blue Butterfly and Tern and Bone were following them, too, and a gaggle of children trailed behind. Fisher Skunk came out of his house at the noise, and Condor Dancer pulled him along with them.

"She will listen to *you*," they told Fisher Skunk.

"It is time you married that woman and made her behave."

"Have you finished paying the bride-price?"

"Haw! We'll help you pay it. She needs a husband!"

Fisher Skunk didn't answer them. Others' Child wondered what he was thinking. She felt as if she were looking at these adopted people through a hole in a rock, which made each separate one very clear but kept her from seeing them as a whole. Collectively, they were mysterious to her. Women had great power here—they could be shamans or chieftains' sisters—but when they stepped outside their boundaries, everyone spoke of making them behave. Their boundaries were merely a little wider than those of the Kindred. Night Hawk had probably tried to tell her that.

The men stopped in front of the chieftain's house, where Cannot Be Told lived now. The eagle sat sleepily on a wooden perch outside the door. It opened its beak and beat its wings at them when they came close.

"Peace, Uncle," Old Tidepool said. He took a dried fish from the pouch at his waist (Others' Child had come to believe that anything might be in there—once she had seen him take out a live dragonfly) and fed it to the eagle. He was careful of his fingers.

"Come out, Chieftain's Sister," Old Tidepool said. His voice jerked the day into a bright focus. He looked so comical that it frightened Others' Child when he suddenly became serious. When he used his shaman's voice, everything he said floated over his head in the air, limned in bright yellow, as if it sat against the sun. She could see the words. They looked like round blue stones.

Cannot Be Told could see them, too. She came out and looked right at them, compressing her mouth into a stubborn line.

"It is time for a new chieftain," Old Tidepool said gently. The words bumped against Cannot Be Told's forehead.

She straightened her shoulders and ignored the words butting at her face. "A favorable day has not come."

"There are many favorable days," Old Tidepool said. "Days of clear light, days of big catches, days of the flight of birds. We had one two days before the new moon and one three days after. I saw them go by."

"No," Cannot Be Told said. "He was *my* brother. Can anyone else choose the day?"

"No," Old Tidepool admitted.

"Then I will choose it when I am ready."

"Now!" Sand Owl roared, losing his temper. "Choose it now!"

Cannot Be Told snapped her head around at him, and Others' Child heard her teeth come together the way the eagle had clicked its beak closed around the fish. "If I choose it now," she said between the teeth, "it will be very unlucky. It will be an election you will not want to win. You will die of what my brother died of!"

There were howls of outrage from the men at that. Cannot Be Told looked satisfied.

"She'll curse us! It isn't right!"

"You tell her." They pushed Fisher Skunk forward.

"It is not right for a woman to be chief," he said.

"A woman may be chief until there is an election," Cannot Be Told said.

Fisher Skunk looked over his shoulder at the men. That was true. The question had never come up of how you made the woman have an election. Other women knew what they should do and did it.

"We'll be a laughingstock," Bone said angrily. "Someone should make her behave. They should ask the Shell Men."

"And what can they do?" Tern asked. Others' Child thought she looked secretly amused. Tern's husband was not likely to be chieftain.

Condor Dancer shouldered his way forward. His condor mask swayed heavily from side to side on his shoulders, the bald head and dark eyes ominous. The feathers around his neck ruffled in the salt wind. The eagle screeched at it and shuffled back and forth on its perch, the leather thong around its foot holding it there.

"It is bad for the Channel Clan when they do not do things properly," Condor Dancer said, his voice low and booming inside the mask. Others' Child remembered Great Condor and looked for him involuntarily in the sky.

Cannot Be Told folded her arms across her chest. She was wearing a fox-fur cape over her broad shoulders and big breasts, and many strings of beads. Her long black hair was tied up on her head with some of the eagle's feathers in it. She was tall enough to look Condor Dancer in the eye, and did.

"Who may choose the day of the election for a chieftain?" she asked him.

"That is already known," Condor Dancer said. "It only remains for the chieftain's sister to do it."

"Who may choose?" she demanded.

Condor Dancer made an angry noise in his throat. Others' Child thought she heard a faint answering cough from the trees, but when she looked to see if anything was perching in the shadows, she couldn't be sure. She edged a little closer to Sea Otter and hoped that Great

Condor hadn't heard her approving of Cannot Be Told in her head.

"You may choose," Condor Dancer said angrily. He didn't like being forced to say it.

"Is this true, Old Uncle?" Cannot Be Told looked at Old Tidepool.

"The chieftain's sister is making a grave mistake," Old Tidepool said, "but yes."

"And no one else may choose?" she prodded him insistently.

"No. No one else."

Cannot Be Told untied the eagle's lead from its perch. It sidled onto her arm, where the leather pad was. She wore it all the time now. She looked defiantly at the men, first at Condor Dancer and then at Fisher Skunk. Her eyes settled on each one in turn. "Then I will choose when I am old," she said.

IX

The War Between
Men and Women

Such a thing had never happened among the Channel
Clan before. Old Tidepool said so, even while he told
them there was nothing he could do about it.

Cannot Be Told sat at the head of the Council Fire
listening, as was her privilege as chieftain. The men
could not make her go away, so they chose to ignore
her. The sky around them was dark, pricked with stars,
and there was a cold wind off the shore. The fire outlined
the bones in her face, unyielding as rock, mysterious as
a fish.

"It isn't right," Sand Owl said sullenly.

"It is not right or wrong, it simply *is*," Old Tidepool
said. He was weary with trying to explain that to them.
"You cannot change the way things are. If you change
the way things are, you will unstitch the Universe, and
things will fall out of it."

Sand Owl stuck his chin out. "*Women* are not supposed to keep the chieftainship. They are for deciding what *man* will have it next."

Old Tidepool looked thoughtfully at Cannot Be Told. She sat very straight-backed, with the eagle on her shoulder, claws digging into the fox-fur cape. She had so many shell necklaces around her neck that she looked like a waterfall.

"If the woman does not see that," the shaman said, "it cannot be forced. I have told you that." His hair stuck straight out as though he had run his hands through it thinking.

Cannot Be Told lifted her eyebrows. "It is the law. You can ask the Shell Men."

They glared at her for speaking.

"And have them think we are fools because we have a woman who will not let go of the chieftainship." Hawk Feet spat into the fire and glared at it when it hissed at him. The wind whipped the flames sideways, spread thin on the air, and the smoke billowed into the faces of those downwind.

"Are we concerned with being fools or looking like fools?" Sea Otter inquired, coughing. He cast a quick glance over his shoulder. The women were sitting at their own fire, and the sound of their voices carried like gulls on the wind. He thought they were arguing, too, but every so often a burst of laughter ran through them, like surf over sand, before it ebbed into solemn murmuring again.

"What is the difference?" Sand Owl demanded. "Between being and looking?"

"We look like fools to our wives," someone else said. "That is bad enough."

"It is not right that this should happen to us!"

They nodded at each other, affirming that. They had said it; thus it was so.

Old Tidepool's black eyes gleamed with exasperation, with not being able to explain it to them. They were not stupid men, but they were stupider than he was. That was why he was shaman. When a thing like this happened, it had meaning. Everything had meaning, just as everything had power. You had to know how to recognize it. Old Tidepool recognized that he was living in a story, a story that would be told around fires long after he was bones in the ground, of how a woman was chieftain in the days of Old Tidepool the shaman. He had suspected that a story had begun to tell itself when the woman who could make pictures had come to them, and now he was sure of it. They would all live forever in this story. He could feel its power in his fingertips whenever he looked at Cannot Be Told. But in the meantime they couldn't stop the story. Stories had to finish telling themselves.

"How will we eat?" Sand Owl demanded, practical. "The chieftain leads us to hunt and fish."

"The chieftain will lead you," Cannot Be Told said, speaking for the second time.

Sand Owl jumped up from his seat by the fire. "Women do not hunt," he shouted at her. "Women do not fish."

The rest of them murmured uneasy agreement. Woman magic was frightening. Only women could make new people. Only women bled every moon from wounds that did not kill them. Against woman magic, a hunter's strength would wither. The woman did not even have to intend harm. Her presence on the hunt would drain his strength without her wanting it to. Women knew this and kept themselves away from the hunt, and did not fish lest the fishermen grow weak. Only women were strong enough to lay out the dead.

"It is not right!" Sand Owl howled. "We will starve!"

"Hunt without her," Hawk Feet snapped, and they all stared at him. It seemed a very daring thing.

Condor Dancer scratched his head. "If the chief does not hunt, the game will think we do not consider them important. They will be insulted."

"The fish will go into deep waters and sulk," Sea Otter said. "I myself have seen it, when a clan took too many and left the extra to rot on the beach. They know when they are insulted.''

''The chief will lead you,'' Cannot Be Told snapped back at Hawk Feet. ''I will lead you. I am not ignorant.'' She slid her eyes sideways toward the shaman. ''Old Tidepool knows the way it is done.''

Old Tidepool shrugged. The story would tell itself. No one promised it would have a happy ending.

The women were watching, as if the story were already unfolding around the men's fire. They saw the men as tellers of the story, although the men did not see themselves that way. What would happen depended on what the men did, as almost all things depended. But there was that strange thread running through this story, like a stick woven by mistake into a sandal, poking through the sole. Cannot Be Told poked through the order of the men's decisions, as hard and uncomfortable for them as a stick in their shoe. The women wondered if they were going to be blamed for that; they would be blamed for the shoe.

But we didn't weave Cannot Be Told, they thought. *She isn't ours, even if she is a woman.*

Tern and Bone were annoyed with her for upsetting the balance and making things unpredictable. But Tern admired her a little, also. That came of being friends with Strangers' Daughter, Bone said. Strangers' Daughter was a kind of shaman woman; she could do things others couldn't. That didn't mean you had to go and imitate her, Bone said with a sniff.

''Also, *you* want to be chief's wife,'' Tern said with a chuckle.

''So does Strangers' Daughter,'' Bone said acutely. She looked at Others' Child. ''Don't you?''

Others' Child grinned. ''Find me a woman who doesn't.'' She was rubbing a piece of blue stone, brought from the Kindred's land, in a scrap of coyote fur, polishing it. The men talked about starving, but there was plenty of food here. Others' Child still wasn't used to it. There was time to not work, to sit polishing a stone between your fingers. "But I think that life is easy here, whether you are a chief's wife or not."

"It will not be if that one drives the fish away," an old grandmother said. "In my day, girls knew how to be." She scowled at the younger ones as if she, too, thought they were responsible for the chieftain's sister.

"It isn't to be easy that a woman wants to be chief's wife," Tern said. "It is to be important." She bowed to Bone. "May I continue to be your sister, Most Powerful, when you are chief's wife?"

Bone gave her a push and laughed. "Only if you are respectful."

"Cannot Be Told is making it very confusing," Laurel Tree said. "How are we to talk to her, if she is chief *and* a woman?"

"She is not chief!"

"She is until there is an election."

"What will the men do if they can't make her hold an election?"

"Burst into flames." Others' Child giggled. "Did you see Sand Owl?"

Tern hooted, and Others' Child glanced at Bone. "It will be good for him. He will learn to respect women this way."

"Men respect women who behave as women," the old grandmother said. She sucked on one of her remaining teeth and squinted her eyes at Cannot Be Told sitting at the men's fire.

"Har!" Old Seagull said. "Men only listen to women who take them by the balls and say, 'I will pull these off if you do not pay attention.' Men's attention is very hard to get. I have found it to be so."

"If you treat them that way, they do not feel that they are men," a young wife said seriously. "And they sulk."

Laughter rippled through the voices around the women's fire again. Here and there a giggle was left, like bubbles on the wet sand. The men turned suspiciously from their fire. The women's fire fell silent. The men turned away.

"Nothing good will come of it," the grandmother said.

Sea Otter said the same to Others' Child, lying snuggled close against her back under the furs. Brother was asleep, rolled in his blankets like a cocoon. He would hatch in the morning with first light, but for now he was elsewhere, in the oblivious metamorphosis of childhood. Others' Child and her husband had waited for him to close his eyes before they began to whisper. There were very few things that the children of the Channel Clan didn't know, but this was a solemn matter, for adults.

"Old Tidepool says if we take the chieftainship away from her before she is ready to give it, we will tear holes in the Universe. But I think that what she is doing is making holes, too." Sea Otter spoke quietly in his wife's ear. "Something bad will come of it. Can you not talk to her?"

Others' Child turned toward him so that their noses bumped. "Why do you think she will listen to me? Foam didn't listen to me; Cannot Be Told is even stronger. *Why* should she listen to me?"

"Because you are different." Sea Otter ran his hand down her bare back, warm under the furs, and counted her vertebrae with his fingers, as if there might be extra ones. "People always listen to people who come from somewhere else, because they think they know more, the way they listen to people who are crazy, or blessed, or can't tell their dreams from their waking. They know things no one else does."

"I don't," Others' Child said. "Maybe I am just crazy."

"Of course you are crazy. Otherwise you wouldn't have walked all that way with that other man, just to get to me." He tightened his arms, protective.

Would I? Others' Child wondered. She counted up Sea Otter's virtues in her head, where he couldn't see. He was kind, and he laughed at things, and he loved Little Brother. He was a good hunter. He was handsome. Not in the reckless way that Night Hawk was handsome, but in a sensible way, as if he were handsome because he was so sensible. "I don't know why I walked all that way," she said, putting her head down against his shoulder.

"To get to me, of course," Sea Otter said complacently.

He was certain of it. As certain as he was that she was magic and could talk sense into Foam and Cannot Be Told, even though nothing like that had happened yet. Others' Child closed her eyes and fell asleep listening to all that certainty breathing in his chest.

When the sun was just dripping pink streaks over the hills to the east, Cannot Be Told stood in the center of the Channel Clan's dance ground and shouted at the men to come out. They emerged from their houses, blinking and staring, and the women scrambled out behind them on the sound of a long indrawn breath.

Cannot Be Told had cut off her hair below her shoulders and tied it back with a thong the way the men wore it. She was bare-breasted, a short hide breechclout tied around her waist. Her face was daubed with the mud markings that the men put on before they hunted. She carried her brother's spear.

None of the others seemed able to find their voices, so Others' Child whispered, "How are we to call you?" because she was the different one, the odd one, the one from far away. Cannot Be Told's heavy breasts jutted out from her chest, negating the breechclout and the spear.

"I am Man Who Hunts." Cannot Be Told stared at them, challenging them to say otherwise.

Old Tidepool nodded his head at the gaping Channel Clan several times, as if he had thought of this already. "Man Who Hunts," he said, acknowledging her.

The men looked at each other. If a woman dressed as a man, then she was a man. It was the same way with soft men who dressed as women. But a woman hunter was a man and could not be married to a man, and they were all thinking of Fisher Skunk.

"Man Who Hunts will lead you to kill the deer today," Cannot Be Told said. "As we agreed with the Manzanita Clan at the Trade Moon that we should hunt on their hills, in exchange for the dried fish we brought them."

"The deer will be angry." Hawk Feet folded his arms across his chest. He had a reputation as a man who stood for no nonsense.

Fisher Skunk didn't say anything. His cheeks were flushed red so that his brown skin glowed.

Others' Child snuck a look at Sea Otter. He was staring at Man Who Hunts' breasts. She put a hand over her mouth so she wouldn't giggle.

"This is not right!" Sand Owl braced his feet wide apart as if he thought someone, Man Who Hunts maybe, was going to try to push him over.

Old Tidepool came to the center of the dance ground on bowed legs that Others' Child thought looked like the willow poles they bent for their house frames. He stuck his neck out like a sandpiper stalking its food and looked at them all in turn. "If a woman wishes to be a man, a woman may be a man," he said. "The gods have always known this, and told us that such people are holy. And may be chieftains."

"Women who have always wanted to be men!" Sand Owl yelped. "Not women who are betrothed to marry hunters, and who have never wanted to be men before now!"

Fisher Skunk's mouth compressed into a tight line, and he glowered at Sand Owl and Cannot Be Told.

Others' Child watched to see what they were going to do. It was the same among the Channel Clan as among her own kind—people of one sex who wanted to be another could do it. A man in a woman's body or a woman in a man's body was considered sacred, made that way by the gods to be the gateway between, the one who was both and neither. But such people as that knew it when they were young, and spent their life that way. Others' Child had never heard of anyone doing it so she could be chieftain. Or doing it just while she hunted.

But there didn't seem to be a law against it. Maybe because no one had thought of it.

Old Tidepool stood balancing on the balls of his feet, rising up and down, his wild hair sticking out like yucca leaves. "I will speak to Man Who Hunts," he pronounced. "We will speak to the gods together and hear what Great Condor and Knifenose Fish wish to tell us. We will tell you what they have said."

They stood around him muttering until he ran at them and flapped his hands. Then they retreated, taking up a grudging stance on the edge of the dance ground.

Old Tidepool stumped across the cleared space to his house, leaving Man Who Hunts alone. She folded her arms the way Hawk Feet had done. When Old Tidepool came back with his sky mask and his sea mask, she didn't unfold them. She stood stiffly while he put the sky mask on and talked to the blue air.

The sky mask was covered with blue stones that traders such as Night Hawk had brought from the eastern deserts. Rays of plaited grass stood out from the sides like the sun's rays, and it had white hair made from the fluff of cattails. When he wore it, Old Tidepool could talk to Sky God and Great Condor, and they would tell him what Great Condor's eyes saw on the earth.

After a while, when Condor had seen all that he could see, Old Tidepool put on the sea mask and talked to Sea God, while Sea God sent Knifenose Fish out to look at things for him. The sea mask had a face of tiny spiral shells and big abalone shells for ears. Old Tidepool cocked his head toward the ocean beyond the ridge, as if the abalone ears could hear its voice.

Others' Child thought she could hear it, too, just for a moment, the low murmur of the breakers and a high thin song among them that must be Knifenose Fish telling what the fish people thought of it all. Old Tidepool pulled the mask off and turned to the Channel Clan.

"Knifenose Fish has spoken to the tuna, and Great Condor has heard the deer. This is how it is to be, as Man Who Hunts has said."

Sand Owl kicked a stone against the dance ground

fire pit, and Hawk Feet swore under his breath.

"Peace!" Condor Dancer shouted. It was the first word he had spoken, and they jumped. "Go and get your spears."

Sea Otter smacked Others' Child's backside affectionately. She could feel his relief. "I will bring back a deer hide for you." She thought he was eager to be moving, to have the argument stopped. He disliked quarrels and had told her once that he thought the gods did, too. They spoiled the taste of the air, he said.

"Are you going to follow her? Him?" Sand Owl demanded. He stumbled over what words to call Cannot Be Told by.

"I do not care whether Man Who Hunts is a woman." Sea Otter grinned. "I do not have to marry her."

Fisher Skunk flushed darker red and stalked off toward his house. He came out with three spears and his spear-thrower. He grasped the spears as if someone were attacking him, and he walked at the end of the hunting party as they left, well away from the woman who had suddenly decided to be a man.

The deer were in the oak forests, the higher ones where people had not stolen all the acorn nuts. Sea Otter couldn't see them, but he could feel them, feel their furred warmth, the delicate steps of their graceful legs, their dark sharp hooves picking their way through the stones that tilted through the ground on the high slope. The oaks here did not bear as many acorns as those lower down, and the deer browsed on dry grasses and bark and withered winter berries as well. The Channel men tracked them by the signs of their browse and their trampled beds, as well as by the faint prints of their hooves.

Sea Otter knelt on the deer trail, his nose to the dirt, squinting at a blurred track. Man Who Hunts stood beside him but made no offer to help. There had been another woman/man once among the Channel Clan. Sea Otter's grandfather had been able to remember and had told Sea Otter of her. She had been a famous hunter;

she could see deer in far valleys. But she had been a man since she was young, and she had *not* been a chieftain.

This woman/man here had never learned to track or to use a spear, either. Sea Otter hoped she wouldn't try. It would be too easy for her to get hurt, and then they would have to wonder whether it had been through someone's intent. Sea Otter didn't want to wonder that. His conservative soul did not approve of Cannot Be Told in either of her incarnations, but he didn't want to think about the Channel Clan being cursed for killing a chieftain, either.

He stood up and motioned the hunters forward, wondering what it would be like to be a woman. To bleed once a moon and have to stuff cattail fluff between your legs and go and live in the women's house that they kept for that purpose, away from the rest of the camp. But you would know that you had such power. You could grow babies inside you. And no matter what a man did to you, he could never have that power, he could never make you give it to him. No wonder some men grew sour and angry and beat their wives, Sea Otter thought. They could kill, but women could make life. If your wife angered you, it would be hard to forgive that. He looked at Man Who Hunts and wondered if she understood that. He thought about telling her, but then he thought of his wife and his expression turned rueful. He had expounded this theory to Others' Child once, and she had said, "Yah bah, men have every other power. I never knew they were longing to waddle like a duck for ten moons. You tell us you envy us so we will be content with our lot. Go away and tell it to the other men." Ordinarily she was not a sharp-tongued woman. Sea Otter scratched his head and decided to think about the deer instead.

The deer were browsing in a thicket of manzanita bushes, eating the ripe, rotting fruit from its red-brown stems. They had begun to drop their antlers, and the bucks looked oddly bald, like a chieftain at a Council Fire without his hat of feathers and grass. Sea Otter wondered if Man Who Hunts would wear the chieftain's hat, which was also a thing that women could not touch for fear of harming the chief.

The deer in the bushes lifted their heads, noses twitching in the wind. Sea Otter crouched, spear in hand in case he got a good shot, although it wasn't likely. More likely was that they would have to drive the deer through the scrub into the dry wash that lay beyond, where they would be hemmed in on both sides, and where the rest of the hunters waited for them.

The buck raised his head and snorted.

The deer were running, the hunters running behind them like stars spread out across the pale sky chasing the two bears into dawn. The Channel Clan's gray-brown dogs followed at their heels. The world was made of gray and brown, the tawny deer, the red-brown men with pale mud daubed on their faces, the gray stone, the gray dogs. The deer leaped nimbly, their delicate legs like spiders scrambling among the stones.

The wash narrowed, and the deer hurtled wild-eyed toward the end of it, a buck and three does, haunches bunched and then exploding into flight again, skittering on the stones in the riverbed.

Beyond them, in a tangle of dead grass and bent trees, a stone cliff rose up, where the water, when it flowed in a rainy spring, would pour over the stone lip, cascading down into a pool at the bottom. Now there was only a trickle wetting the pink rocks, and a shallow pool waiting for the rains. From behind the fallen stones at the bottom, men leaped up, spears notched into spear-throwers, shouting, their arms spread wide.

The deer skittered away from them, legs churning, trying to run back the other way against the pursuing hunters, trying to scale the rock walls. The spears whistled from their throwers, a sound like birds, and the largest of the does, her mouth foaming, thundered past Sea Otter.

Sea Otter spun, letting loose his spear. Man Who Hunts, spear raised to throw, stood beside him, hesitating. A man in the rocks shouted, and Sea Otter looked back and saw the buck coming. He could see the dark wide eyes, the tongue in the open mouth, the foam on the forequarters. Dark sharp hooves pounded over the stones.

Man Who Hunts still stood with her spear raised, and now she leveled it at the buck. She held it with both hands, not in a thrower, and braced her feet against the ground.

Sea Otter saw what would happen. The buck would slam into her, impale itself on the spear, bear her down onto the rocks under the tearing, flailing hooves. In an instant's waking dream, he saw the hunters lift the buck's bloody body by the antlerless head and stare down at the crushed woman beneath it. He looked past the plunging buck at Hawk Feet and saw that he had seen it, too.

For a moment they stood immobile, Sea Otter and Hawk Feet, staring at each other, while the buck chose its own auspicious day. Then Sea Otter lunged at Man Who Hunts, grabbed her by the arm, flung her away from him, leaving her ignominiously scrabbling among the rocks, spear shaft snapped off as her weight came down on it, while the buck thundered past, bearing down on Fisher Skunk at the mouth of the wash.

Fisher Skunk got out of the way, flinging himself behind a pine tree, his arm back to send the spear flying from the thrower, landing solidly in the buck's breast. It leaped like a bird, hooves beating the air, as if it would take to the sky, climbing up and up past their reach. Then it came down, staggering, head flung back, foam flying from the open mouth, and ran down the wash while the spear shaft tangled in the brush and pushed deeper. Fisher Skunk trotted after it.

The other men had killed a second doe outright, and in the sudden stillness left in the wash they sat down around her body in the tumbled stones and panted hard. Condor Dancer came up, puffing, from the rock fall. The dogs stuck their noses against the dead doe's belly, waiting for the hunters to cut it open and give them the offal.

After a moment Sand Owl got up and trotted after Fisher Skunk to bring back the buck. The buck had a deep wound and was unlikely to get far. The doe that Sea Otter had hit they would look for later. If they chased her now she could just run farther. Left alone, she might lie down and die somewhere close by. The men around the dead doe in the wash examined themselves for cuts and scrapes, their breath slowing gradually. Sea Otter said the thanking-the-deer prayer.

Hawk Feet took his belt knife and slit the doe's belly open. The dogs crowded around him, and he cuffed them away.

"Go and be still or I'll cut your nose off." He kicked at a big dog, and it retreated. Hawk Feet sliced the liver out of the deer and cut it into pieces. The men ate it greedily, greedy as the dogs, the blood running down their chins.

Three deer, Sea Otter thought. That was a good kill. Only the littlest of the does had got away.

Man Who Hunts got to her feet and limped over the stones in the riverbed. They paid no attention to her, and she seemed not to know how to come into their circle. She stood behind Sea Otter's shoulder.

"It was not right that you pulled me away."

Sea Otter looked up. He wiped his chin with his dirty hand. "Deer are heavy," he said. "Heavier than you."

"It is not right that you pulled me away. It is right for the chieftain to make his kill."

"You do not stand still and let a deer run over you," Sea Otter said.

"Not more than one time," someone added. There was a stifled snort of laughter from around the dead doe.

Man Who Hunts snapped her head around looking for it. "It is not right that the hunters disrespect the chieftain." She narrowed her eyes. "It may be time for new hunters to come to Council and dance the dances if the old ones grow disrespectful."

Sea Otter stood up. He took a piece of the doe's liver and gave it to her. Man Who Hunts ate it defiantly, tearing at it with her teeth. Her lip was bleeding. Her face and breasts were scratched with brambles and bruised where she had fallen in the rocks.

"With respect, we have been hunting since we could walk, we men." Sea Otter looked at her angry face. "It is not a thing that can be learned in a day, just from the wanting to."

"The chieftain hunts," she said stiffly. "That is how it is."

"That is why a man is chieftain," Sea Otter said, exasperated. He could feel her stubbornness. It was easy to understand it, but some things couldn't be. You couldn't make a deer out of an owl.

Man Who Hunts stalked past him into the center of the men around the dead doe. She sat down, and they made way for her. When Fisher Skunk and Sand Owl came back with the buck, they gutted it without looking at her. Then they slung both deer on poles, feet tied together with yucca rope, and hefted them onto four men's shoulders: Fisher Skunk, Sand Owl, Hawk Feet, and a man named Bear Paws who was short-legged but enormously broad in the shoulders. Sea Otter would trail his wounded doe with Young Clam Catcher, whom he was teaching to track.

Man Who Hunts took her place at the head of the hunters on the trail. Fisher Skunk pretended not to see her. When she stopped, he walked onto her heels as if she were invisible and he were surprised to find an obstacle in his way.

It took that day and another to get home again. They waited at night for Sea Otter and Young Clam Catcher to come up with them, and made a fire and had a big feast with meat from one of the deer. Man Who Hunts sat around the fire and slept on the ground like the rest of them, but no one knew what she was, and so everyone tried not to see her.

When they came into the Channel Clan's camp with the deer, all the women and children ran out to see. Brother flung his arms around Sea Otter's knees and hung on until Others' Child pulled him loose.

"New Father brought us a deer!" he said, dancing

around it. He saw Blue Butterfly watching him. "New Father will teach me to hunt," he informed her.

"No doubt," Blue Butterfly said.

Fisher Skunk dropped the end of the deer he was carrying with a thud that nearly pulled Sand Owl nose into the dirt.

"I have paid a bride-price for a woman named Cannot Be Told," he said. "This woman should now give me my bride-price back."

Others' Child grabbed Little Brother, cavorting under the hunters' feet, and pulled him away while everyone stared at Fisher Skunk.

His face was blazing, and he folded his arms stubbornly, still not looking at Cannot Be Told. "A man should have sons to teach to hunt. I will not have sons with a woman who thinks she is a man. Let this woman give me back my bride-price."

"Wait." Cannot Be Told went into her house while Fisher Skunk stood with his chin up, glaring ferociously at the sky. She came out again empty-handed with a hide skirt wrapped around her hips. She had scrubbed the hunting signs off her face and untied her hair so that it fanned out just over her shoulders. "Fisher Skunk paid his bride-price to my brother, the chieftain," she said, carefully not looking at him, either. "It is not mine to give back." Others' Child thought Cannot Be Told felt insulted.

"This woman's brother is dead," Fisher Skunk told the sky. "She thinks she can take his place. Then she can give me back my bride-price."

Cannot Be Told lost her temper and marched up to him, nose to nose. "A bride-price is given back when a woman is a bad wife. I have not married you yet, so I cannot be a bad wife, so I cannot give back your bride-price!"

"A woman who thinks she is a man is not a good wife." Fisher Skunk backed away from her.

The Channel Clan were beginning to be interested in the problem. A woman as chieftain was a serious matter. The bride-price part of it was funny. It was a relief.

"Isn't she a man when she hunts?" Bear Paws asked.

"But that is not in the house, where a man is married to a woman."

"If she's a man at all, I wouldn't marry her!"

"It might be handy. You could make her do your hunting. And your fishing, too. Lie around all day and talk."

There were guffaws from the men.

"You do that anyway!" a woman shouted, and the men slapped each other on the back again and chortled.

"This is not a matter for being funny," Condor Dancer said. He could see Fisher Skunk's angry red face, cheeks puffing out like a fish breathing.

"She looks like a woman to me," Young Clam Catcher snickered, and Condor Dancer glared at him. Young Clam Catcher held his hands in front of his chest, as if he were holding up breasts. He jiggled them.

"Bah, you are a baby. Go and be ashamed of yourself," Condor Dancer said.

Young Clam Catcher looked abashed.

"It is an important matter," Condor Dancer said. "A man may ask for his bride-price back if the woman is infirm."

"Then he ought to be able to get it back if she's a man!" someone shouted.

They began to argue again.

"She's not a man."

"Just sometimes."

"Sometimes would be enough for me. How's that for a surprise in your bed?"

"SILENCE!" Condor Dancer roared at them, but they were not inclined to be quiet. "This is a matter for the chieftain to decide, but the chieftain is part of the dispute. Therefore—"

"Ask the shaman. Where is Old Tidepool?"

"In his house," Others' Child said. "In a trance."

"Therefore—" Condor Dancer said.

The argument went on around him, no one listening.

The women pressed around Others' Child. "Can't you wake him up?"

"I don't think so."

The shaman had been drawing fish under her instruction, and had almost made Knifenose Fish look like himself and not like a belt knife stuck in an owl, when the hunters had come back. That was when the trance had come on him. It had been very quick. One moment he had been drawing Knifenose Fish's tail and the next he had been flat on his back with his eyes closed. She had shaken him to see if he was dead, and he had opened one eye and told her he was in a trance. Others' Child supposed he was there yet. She wondered if he had known what Fisher Skunk was going to do. He might be asking the gods for an answer. She cast a suspicious glance at Old Tidepool's house. Or he might be making certain that he didn't have to give one. *I wouldn't want to decide that,* she thought. *Someone is bound to be angry.*

"Well, it isn't right to ask for it back," a young woman said to Condor Dancer. "She hasn't even married him. What would happen if men could ask for it back like that?"

"We will ask the Shell Men," Condor Dancer said, trying to make them pay attention.

"No!" Fisher Skunk shouted at him. "I will not be made a fool to the Shell Men. This woman who thinks she is a man will give back my bride-price or I will come and get it."

"If this man comes into my house, I will take his bride-price, which he gave my brother, which is now *mine*, and push it down his throat." Cannot Be Told shook her skinning knife at him. "Then I will cut him open to get it out. Even a *woman* may carry a knife!"

"Silence!" Condor Dancer stamped his foot again.

"She ought to give it back," the men grumbled.

"What is he afraid of? That she is a better man than he is?" the women hissed.

"Har! Women are lazy. They don't have to hunt or catch fish. They sit and their backsides grow large while the men bring the food! Therefore they should do as they're told!"

"Har, it is the men who are lazy! Who has the babies? And cooks the food, and finds the berries and grinds the acorns, and makes the clothes so that *your* backside does not freeze and fall off in the winter? When men do all that, they may call women lazy." The women glared across the dead deer at their husbands.

They were in two groups now: the men on one side of their kill, the women, a number of them armed with skinning knives, on the other. Even the women who had criticized Cannot Be Told for wanting to be chieftain had arrayed themselves beside her now. The men looked at them uneasily.

"This is not right," Sand Owl said to Condor Dancer.

Others' Child saw Sea Otter standing with the men, his arm on Fisher Skunk's shoulder. She glared at him, and he pretended not to notice. Others' Child turned on her heel and pushed her way through the crowd of women around Cannot Be Told. She crawled through the doorway into Old Tidepool's house and shook him.

"Wake up. They are going to fight with each other."

Old Tidepool's eyes closed more firmly.

"They have skinning knives," Others' Child said.

Old Tidepool sat up. "Go away. I am talking to the gods."

"Ask them whether to make Cannot Be Told give Fisher Skunk's bride-price back," Others' Child said.

"The gods aren't in charge of things like bride-prices. The gods are in charge of holding the Universe together."

"He is threatening to take it back by force, and she is threatening to kill him if he does. I expect one of them will kill the other."

"Bah!" Old Tidepool said. "Bah." He got up, creakily, shifting the otter-fur blankets off his thin legs. He stuck his head through his door.

"You see," Others' Child said.

The men and women had moved farther apart. They scowled at each other, ignoring the children, who were separating themselves, too, not knowing why, boys with their fathers, girls with their mothers. Brother was clinging to Sea Otter's breechclout.

Old Tidepool snatched up his shell staff and crawled through the door. "You are all fools," he said. He shook the staff at them, and the shells rattled. "And you have woken me up. Give him back his bride-price when you are a man. When you are a woman, he has to give it back to you. Now leave me alone."

"That won't work!" the men and women both howled. Cannot Be Told and Fisher Skunk stamped their feet.

"Har! You shouldn't have asked me, then." Old Tidepool jumped up and down, pounding the staff on the ground. They backed up. "Sit down," he shouted at them. "I will tell you something more important than that. I will tell you about men and women."

The Channel Clan sat, men on one side of the dance ground, women on the other, while Old Tidepool stomped back and forth and looked at them very fiercely until they settled down. Then he began.

Once, when the world was very new, there were not very many people in it. In fact, Coyote had just made people, and the people had just come from the north to live at the coast. It was very good eating at the coast. There were fish in the sea and many whales, and on the land there were many deer for the people to kill, as well as berries and fruit and acorns to gather.

First Man and First Woman built a house near the shore, and every day First Man went hunting or fishing and First Woman went to gather acorns from the many oak trees there and ripe berries. It was easy to get fat in those days.

It was easy to get fat, and there was nothing to do but hunt and gather food and eat and make love. First Woman ate the fat meats that her husband brought home and got bigger and bigger. First Man ate his wife's fine cooking and got bigger, too. Then they got big in the head and decided that they didn't need each other.

First Woman started it. After dinner one night, a fine

dinner of venison stew and mussels and rockfish and acorn bread, she leaned back against the wall and belched loudly and slapped her stomach. Then she slapped herself between the legs and said, "That's where dinner comes from."

"What do you mean?" First Man asked, shocked. He looked at his wife disapprovingly. "That's dirty talk."

"You don't think it's dirty under the blanket," First Woman said. "If you didn't get that from me, you wouldn't bring home food. I work hard all day grinding meal and cooking for you, and you wouldn't even bring me food if you didn't get that at night."

"That isn't true!" First Man said indignantly. "You think that's all we are interested in!"

"It is," First Woman said. She was surly because he had woken her up in the morning wanting it, too, and then had come nuzzling her neck while she was trying to cook. "Name three other things you are interested in."

"There are lots of things," First Man said, but he couldn't think of them at the time.

"And then when we are tired from working, you complain that we don't want to do it. Women would want to do it more if you would leave them alone for a few days at a time."

"We men work harder than you do," First Man said. "And furthermore, we can take it or leave it."

"Ha! You would be running after us if we were separated for a day!"

"I personally would not run after you if we were separated for ten days. But you women would want it. You are the ones who are always after us."

"Har!" First Woman said. "That is funny. When do you ever leave us alone long enough for us to chase you? I wouldn't mind if we were apart for two moons."

"We men," said First Man with dignity, "wouldn't care if we were apart for six moons. Anything you do for us we can easily do for ourselves."

"Ha!" First Woman said. "We women could do your work and ours if we didn't have you to bother us. We *wouldn't mind being apart for eight moons."*

They argued back and forth, saying ten moons, a year, two years, and that each could do the other's work, until First Woman went and lay down under the blanket with her back to First Man and went to sleep.

First Man tried to go to sleep, but he couldn't. So he lay awake getting madder and madder, thinking about what his wife had said, and what he should have said to her. By morning he was in such a rage that he got up at dawn and went and woke up all the other men.

"Listen to what my wife said," he told them.

The other men listened, and they were so shocked that they went right home and woke up their wives with the story, so that they could come back and tell the other husbands that they didn't have that problem. But the wives, pushing the men away sleepily in the gray dawn, said that they agreed with First Woman. And please, leave them alone, they were sleepy.

The men were even more shocked at that, and their feelings were hurt, so they clustered around First Man while he stamped and raved.

"I'm not going to stand for it!" First Man shouted. "I am going to go and live across the river, and then she will be sorry, and we will see who can do without whom."

He waded into the river, taking his hunting spears and his fishing hooks and line. The other men, who were feeling very insulted, followed him.

The women woke up again at all the commotion, and when they looked out the doors of their houses and saw what the men were doing, they said, "Fine, then. That is fine. Let them go. We will see how long they can do without us. They do not even know how to cook."

The river was only a little stream that flowed from the hills down to the shore, but when First Man and the other men had waded across it, a big wall of water roared down it and cut the channel wide and deep, so that no one could cross. The women could only stand on the bank looking down at the furious water, and across it at their mates. The men could not cross, either,

*but they turned their backs so that the women would see
that they did not want to.*

*For a while everything was all right. The men built
themselves houses on their bank and went hunting. The
women gathered acorns and berries and fruit. Every so
often, a woman would call across the river, "How are
you getting along?"*

*The men would answer, "Just fine. We don't miss you
at all."*

*"We don't miss you, either," the women would shout.
"Now we sleep in the morning, and no one bothers us."*

*But secretly the women did miss the men, and they
missed making love, too, just as First Man had said they
would.*

*For their part, the men sat around their fires at night
and told stories about how they didn't miss women. It
kept them from thinking about how much nicer their
houses had been on the other side of the river when the
women had kept them clean.*

*It went on like this for a year, and by that time the
men were still fat but the women were thin because they
didn't have any animal food. The game didn't come to
them, and the fish swam away from their hooks, and they
came home empty-handed and tired no matter how hard
they tried.*

*The men had plenty of food, but it didn't taste the way
it had when the women had cooked it. The men never
learned to cook properly, and the food was always
burned or half raw, and when they tried to make stew,
it tasted like mud. So First Man stayed fat, but it was
no pleasure. And there wasn't much pleasure at night,
either, with nothing to make love to but his hand.*

*Finally, one of the young men, who hadn't been mar-
ried but a moon when the men and women separated,
said to First Man, "It has been two years now. Do you
think they have learned their lesson by this time?"*

*First Man knew he was homesick. "I think we have
punished them enough," he said. "Maybe now we
should go back and take care of them."*

"Go back and take care of them!" the other men said.

"Yes! It is our duty to take care of them, the poor things."

"Well, you can see how thin they are," First Man said.

The women were all thin as reeds, no flesh on them, and they were starving with loneliness, too. When the men said, shouting across the river, *"Have you learned your lesson now?"* the women were silent for a moment.

"We have learned ours," First Woman said finally. *"Have you learned yours?"*

First Man thought about how to answer. *"We know that it is not good for men and women to be apart,"* he said.

"That is not admitting they were wrong," a young girl said.

"It is as close as they will get," First Woman said tiredly. *"And I am hungry, and I miss my husband even if he is the way he is."*

So First Man spoke to the river, and the channel shrank back to the way it had been, and the men waded across with their spears and their fishing lines. And they dried off and went to their old houses, to their wives. And the women grew fat again, and men and women once again spent their time eating and making love, and both were a pleasure again.

But they never forgot what had happened when they had tried to live separately, because each year in flood time, the river came up again and filled the channel to remind them.

And that is what happened when men and women could not get along, and thought that they could do each other's work.

The Channel Clan all nodded at each other. They looked accusingly at Cannot Be Told and Fisher Skunk, who had almost led them into the same mistake. Old Tidepool looked satisfied.

"I told you that story," Others' Child said indignantly. "It happened in my people's country, and it was River Old Man that separated them."

"It doesn't matter," Old Tidepool said. "It is a true story everywhere."

X

Ax and Oyster Shell

Night Hawk the Trader was now well known among the People Who Lived at the Coast. Never had he stayed so long among them, more than a year while the sun turned around into a second spring. There were reasons why he could not go, he said, but when he tried to explain them to the People Who Lived at the Coast, they didn't care; they were just glad to have him. He had a wealth of stories to tell about his adventures, and of places they had never seen, where strange animals lived like songs in the water and the rock.

That he traveled with two of Coyote's children (although they were mannerly) made him seem dangerous and exciting to the younger folk. The older ones were prepared to overlook that. What the coastal people thought about Coyote was very much the same way that the Kindred saw him. Coyote was old, oldest of the gods. He was there at the beginning, and he always would be there, a fact of life like death and fleas. He was powerful, and it didn't pay to offend him, although you wanted to be careful if he gave you presents. You couldn't get rid of him.

Thief and Gray Daughter allowed the coastal people's children to pat them and the wives to bring them bones. The village dogs slunk out of view to commune resentfully with one another over the interlopers, but that was to be expected. No dog ever tried to fight them. Gray Daughter had another litter of puppies, and this time Night Hawk gave them to a chieftain of the Tarpool Clan in exchange for a bag of shell beads and another of dried venison, enough to feed them all season.

"Hah, maybe you are worth something after all," he told Gray Daughter on the trail. Gray Daughter didn't look upset. She yawned and laid her gray nose on her paws in front of the fire. In another moon she would be in heat again.

"Yah, you are a dog. You don't care who raises your children," Night Hawk said. The idea of another man teaching his son to hunt, to grow into a man, gnawed at him.

He got up to get more wood for the fire—as soon as the sun fell it was cold in the coastal valleys in spring. It was the rainbow season here. The hills were green from the late winter rains and flooded with yellow mustard flowers and sun-colored poppies. The stream was edged with cress and skittering with water striders. The trees were grass green with new leaves. The sun went down over the western ridge in a cloud of pink like the inside of a shell, bright against the turquoise sky. When the color faded, the cold would come.

Night Hawk gathered an armload of downed wood and dragged a dead trunk behind him to the fire with his other hand. He put the wood beside the fire and got his ax from his pack on the dogs' travois. It was a very fine ax. He had spent much time chipping its blade and fitting it to a wooden handle, lashing it with sinew. He had been offered a pair of good obsidian belt knives for it, but he wouldn't trade. He had worked on the ax after he had left Others' Child, to give him something to hold in his hands and shape the way he wanted it. All his

furious concentration had been given to the ax and not
to the woman who wasn't there anymore.

Night Hawk lifted the ax above the dead tree trunk.
It felt powerful enough in his hands to bite through anything, like a tooth in the great cat's jaw. It came down
in a whack that sent bark flying; he lifted up, and it bit
again. Night Hawk braced the trunk with his foot. This
time when he raised the ax, it came down across his toe.

The ax handle went flying wide as Night Hawk bent
over, howling, his hands covered with the blood that
poured out of his woven yucca sandal. He was afraid to
look, but the blood kept coming and he made himself
pull the sandal away. The end of the sandal was cut
clean through, and he howled again as it came off. There
was no one to hear him but the dogs, who came and
stuck their noses in his face. He pushed them away and
wiped the blood with a handful of grass. The toe was
still there, not cut through as he had been afraid, but
with a deep slice into the end so that a thick flap of
ragged skin hung loose.

Now that he knew it wasn't cut off, Night Hawk gritted his teeth against the pain and hobbled to the travois
to get a length of fishing line. He wrapped it tight around
the toe and held his breath to see if the bleeding stopped.
The blood slowed. He hopped to the stream bank and
stuck his foot in the cold water among the cress. Blood
rippled away from it on the current, eddying in little red
circles, fainter and fainter on the water's surface.

Night Hawk hobbled back to the travois and rooted
through his medicine bag. Traveling alone, he was as
well equipped as a healer and could do what any healer
could, though Others' Child had never understood that.
But there were some things even a healer shaman
couldn't cure, and talking to the gods about them was a
waste of your breath. Nor would they converse about
something as mundane as his big toe.

Night Hawk got a skin sack of cattail fluff out of the
medicine bag and a salve of greasewood leaves and fat
that he carried in a tar-lined basket. He sat down cross-
legged by the flickering fire, trying to see what he was

doing in the falling dusk. He closed the flap of skin and
held it down with his thumb while he rubbed the toe
with salve, wincing. He stuck a wad of cattail fluff on
top of it, wrapped a soft piece of rabbit skin around it,
and tied the whole thing with a length of string. The toe
looked as if wasps had built a hive around it. It hurt with
a dull throbbing ache now, and Night Hawk pulled some
hot stones out of the fire to boil water for willow tea.
He put his head on his knees, feeling sorry for himself
with his great lumpy toe. While the water boiled, he
thought that this should not have happened to him. He
should not have been alone in this strange wood nearly
cutting off his toe.

"What were you expecting?" a sultry voice said, and
Night Hawk lifted his head to see Coyote standing on
the other side of the fire, next to the dogs. She wore a
dress that looked as if it had been made out of badly
tanned rabbit skins, and smelled like it, and her mane of
yellow-gray hair fell over her shoulders in a tangle of
oak leaves and thornbush twigs. The dogs were licking
her bare toes.

Night Hawk narrowed his eyes at her, to see if she
would go away again. "I wasn't expecting anything,"
he said. "I was just thinking."

Coyote sat down across the fire from him, teeth bared.
The remains of a rabbit, his dinner, lay beside her on a
stone, and she picked a bone up and gnawed it, cracking
it in her back teeth. Her front teeth looked very white
and sharp. "Something always comes when you think
about it," she told him.

"I wasn't thinking about *you*," he said.

"Everyone is always thinking about me," Coyote
said. She scratched her side, reaching one hand through
the furs of her dress. "Is this all you have to eat?"

"You can hunt better than I can," Night Hawk said.
He stuck his toe out at her. "Look what I have done."

"You're out of balance with the world," Coyote said.
"That's why these things happen to you. You are falling
over one of your other selves." The bone in her teeth
made a sharp crack as it split open. She sucked the mar-

row out of the middle, working the last bits out with her tongue. "Or maybe you are just clumsy."

"What other selves?" Night Hawk said. "And I didn't ask for your advice." He wasn't afraid of her tonight. His toe hurt too much. And she didn't make his cock stand up, either. After the last time, he would just as soon stick it in a bees' nest.

"There are lots of selves," Coyote said. "You, me, we all have lots. It's which one you decide to be that matters."

"Very good. Now that you have told me, you can go away," he said, sulky.

Coyote shifted blurrily in front of the fire and tucked her black-tipped tail around her paws. She had paws now. In the twilit, foxy light he couldn't be sure if she was a dog or a woman. She seemed to be both. "I think I'll stay here," she said.

"Why?"

"Your woman isn't interesting anymore. There is no point in visiting someone who has dug into the sand like a clam."

"Well, I won't be interesting for you," Night Hawk said. He was determined not to be.

"I'll stay anyway," Coyote said. "You might get interesting."

"I won't." The wind blew the smoke in a swirl over the fire pit, billowing out gray clouds. Night Hawk could smell her sharp, musty, salty smell behind the smoke.

"Your woman is trying to have more babies," Coyote said chattily.

"You told me that."

"It's not working, though. Maybe she is falling over her extra selves, too, but it is hard to tell."

"Good!" Let Others' Child cut her toes open, too.

"Yah bah, you are stupid," Coyote said. For a moment her face looked like his wife's. Night Hawk stared at it through the swirl of smoke, and then the resemblance flickered away.

"Did you do that on purpose?" he said.

"Do what?" Her face was the way he had seen it

before, long-nosed with hairy, arched brows and gray, coyote-colored hair.

"Look like my wife?"

"Only if you want me to," she said suggestively.

"No!"

Coyote stretched. It was hard to tell what was fur and what was the rabbit-skin dress. Her tongue lolled out. "I told your woman, if you come into the wild lands, then you have to make love to me, some way or another."

"I have been in the wild lands all my life," Night Hawk said. "Since I could travel. Since I was a man. I never made love to you."

"You just didn't know it," Coyote said.

"Well, I don't want to now. I have had bad luck with women."

"Old Feather Broom will sweep you up. He'll smell that toe. But it's no concern of mine," Coyote said airily. "If you aren't going to make things happen, I'll find someone else. But I had hopes for you. I even bet old Feathers Behind that I could make things happen faster than he could sweep them up. If we let *him* tidy up, the world will stay the same, and then people will start to die. Change is what keeps you alive. You have to move faster than old Feathers. If he had his way the world would be clean, but it would be dead. He wouldn't know the difference."

"He would when he didn't have anything to eat," Night Hawk said thoughtfully.

"He eats what's dead."

"So do you."

"I kill mine."

"I meant," Night Hawk said, "that he would notice when there were no more dead things. When he had eaten them all."

"He wouldn't notice until it was too late," Coyote said. "People like that don't."

"Well, why is it up to me to make things change? I don't like it. It's unsettling. My wife left me. Is that change?"

"That's because old Feathers On It got hold of her. We have to shake her out. Otherwise art won't happen."

"What is art?" Night Hawk peered through the smoke at her. It was getting thicker. And he didn't know what she was talking about.

"Art is change," Coyote said. "It's beauty with teeth in it." Her jaws closed over her own teeth, and with their white points gone, Night Hawk couldn't see anything of her in the smoke.

He fanned a dry branch at the thick clouds, coughing, his nose burning, and when it cleared, she was gone. His back ached from sleeping hunched over, and he could see the imprint of the thongs of his winter leggings on his forearm where he had slept with it pressed into them.

I will not stay in this place any longer, he thought. *I will go back to people, and she will not come after me there.* He wasn't sure about that. Coyote came when she felt like it. But the woods seemed bigger now, and the solitude that he had always liked seemed too full of presences he couldn't see. He heard the dry rustling of feathers in the dark oaks. Was that what had frightened Rattlesnake's Woman? Was he going to end up like her now, afraid to venture out of the skin of his own village? That thought frightened him even more. *I will just go until my toe is healed,* he thought. *That must be what is letting all these things in.*

In the morning he set out, limping behind the travois and finally sitting on it, which the dogs resented fiercely. But he was determined to be out of that woods, and could feel the presence behind him of something watching his progress. At noon, maneuvering the travois down a steep slope of scattered rock and ground squirrel burrows, he caught his heel in a hole and pitched face forward down the trail, bloodying his nose and scraping the skin off his left arm. He stubbed his bad toe, and it began to bleed again.

Night Hawk's head swam. He sat on the trail and watched the dark shapes circling in the fierce blue sky overhead. He shook his fist at them. "I am not dead yet! I am not going to be dead. Go away."

They lifted on a rising thermal and were gone, diminishing into specks, like black stars.

Night Hawk felt a warm, slightly fetid breath on the back of his neck. "Everyone comes to me when they start to fall downhill of their own accord. A little accident with the skinning knife, with the ax. Unexpected deep water." Great Condor was perched on a dead branch just above the trail.

Night Hawk's head spun. Great Condor vanished. Night Hawk sat up groggily, spitting dirt out of his mouth. One of his teeth came with it. He limped to the travois and untangled it from the underbrush. A little pile of bones whitened beside the trail with a handful of spotted feathers clinging to it. Someone's lunch, Night Hawk thought. He envisioned what would be left of him: bones and a mat of black hair. Indigestible tools: a belt knife and his cooking spoon. He righted the travois and limped on.

The next day he caught a quail in a snare, and when he was cutting it open, his belt knife slipped, and he gouged a long furrow between his left thumb and forefinger. Dark feathers rustled behind him in the manzanita.

Night Hawk swore and sucked the blood off his thumb. His injured toe still throbbed, all the pieces of his body telling him he was off-balance. More and more the world seemed skewed, its normal arrangements shifted as if they had been tossed up in a hide. Night Hawk had no sense of knowing the trail. The next day a piece of the dogs' harness came loose, flew back, and caught him in the eye. He walked on unfamiliar ground, squinting, while a padding of interested paws and a dark rustle of wings followed him. He could have done without the company. Maybe a shaman *could* tell him how to make them go away, he thought, when he caught himself looking over his shoulder at dusk. He could hear the dull boom of the ocean to the west now. Maybe the water would wash them clear.

* * *

The Knifenose Fish Clan were happy to have him back. Night Hawk arrived on a soft spring night, the kind when it is neither hot nor cold and the air is imperceptible to the touch, yet still smells of flowers and salt and warm skin. The stars were out, strung across the sky, and the Knifenose Fish Clan were getting ready to dance.

Night Hawk looked nervously for Condor, until he saw that this was the Fish Dance. He let out a sigh of relief, sank onto the piled hides that they put out for him, and watched the dancers eddy through the water. The men swam by him, waving their fins, and the women followed, grass tails rippling the invisible air. He recognized Sea Otter's sister, Foam, swaying among the women fish. A flight of gulls wheeled overhead, gold and white against the darkening sky. The last watery rays of the sun glowed on their wings.

Below them the village shell mound gleamed white in the dusk. It was taller than two houses, the bones of all the food the Knifenose Fish Clan took from the sea. No wonder they praised it.

Knifenose Fish led the dancers, swimming in a spiral toward the center of the dance ground. Foam's husband, Not in a Hurry, was Octopus, and another man was Whale, lumbering, menacing, driven onto the shore by Knifenose Fish. Whale leaped first one way and then another, holding his arms wide, while Knifenose Fish prodded him along. A high roaring whistle came from a piece of wood on a thong that Catches Crows, the shaman, whirled above her head. The other fish dancers ran behind, stamping, leaping, while the men along the edge of the dance ground sang to them through flutes of elder wood and bone.

Night Hawk took his flute out of his belt and sang with them, swaying into the music. It was water music, long waves rolling in to shore, slow lifting of the swells beyond the breakwater. Fish music, in which you could swim endlessly in the Endless Water. Another world to live in, where Coyote and even Great Condor would drown if they followed.

"You can't go there," Catches Crows said, sitting down beside him, and he realized that the whistle of the wood she swung above her head had stopped. The dancers had stopped, and the elder-wood flutes had stopped. Only he was still playing.

"You have two legs," Catches Crows said. "The fish people cannot take you in."

Night Hawk sighed. "Why did you think I wanted to go?"

Catches Crows laughed. The sound jiggled the loose skin on her neck. "When I see a man with a bandage on his toe, and on his hand, and another around his arm, I think he is trying to go somewhere."

"I only want things to be the way they were before," Night Hawk said angrily.

"Well, you can't have that," the shaman said, as if she was talking to a child. "Why do you keep injuring yourself?"

"I don't know. I see visions." Night Hawk told her about them. He left out parts about Coyote, but from the smile that twitched her lips he thought she could tell.

"That is good. Something is trying to keep you alive." Catches Crows nodded. "It may be that Condor is telling you to come to him. But it may also be that you are attracting his notice. If that is the case, you must find out why and stop doing it."

"How do I do that?"

"Tell me what has happened."

"My weapons have turned against me," Night Hawk said angrily.

Catches Crows scratched her chin. She didn't say anything for a long time. Night Hawk watched her uneasily. Her black hair fell about her shoulders, eagle feathers and shells braided into it here and there like hunting signs on a landscape. It should have been gray, judging by her wrinkled face, but it wasn't. A young boy, just past his initiation, trotted by, and she snapped her fingers at him. "Bring me something to drink."

"Yes, Aunt."

"And a fish to eat," she added thoughtfully when he had brought the drink, carried carefully in a turtle shell. When he came back with the fish, she ate it pensively, from the tail end up.

Night Hawk wondered if a hot stone from the fire would cure his headache, and if it would be rude to go get one. And maybe a fish of his own. The other Knifenose Fish people were crowding around the fire pits, digging fish out of the hot ashes. He started to get up, but Catches Crows put her hand on his arm to make him stay there while she thought.

Her wrinkled hands were clawlike, with long thick nails and big joints and three black hairs on each finger. Night Hawk stared at them while she thought, wondering if she could transmit wisdom through them, from her to him, magic to set his world right.

"In the morning I will tell you what to do," she said finally. "I have to see about why you are making Great Condor watch you." She stumped away, leaving Night Hawk uncomforted. He went to eat and found that the fish were gone.

"Poor man." A wiry woman with a jutting chin came up and gave him a shell bowl full of oysters. He recognized Foam, sister of Sea Otter. "It isn't right for you to be hungry among us." She smiled at him, and he saw her husband watching them. "No one is hungry among the Knifenose Fish Clan."

"You are kind," Night Hawk said with a wary eye on the husband.

"Will you be long among us?" She sat down on a stone beside the banked fire and patted another seat beside her. "We will have a big time at the Moon When Children Come of Age," she said. "You should stay here until then." She cocked her head at him curiously, taking in his hawk nose and cropped hair.

"I don't know," Night Hawk said. He could see Not in a Hurry lurking at the edge of the shell mound, its white slope rising behind him like a huge moon anchored on the beach. He envisioned his own bones put there by Not in a Hurry.

"I would like to go foot-on-trail," Foam said.

"It's very dangerous."

"Three times I have walked home to the Channel Clan by myself." She looked over her shoulder at Not in a Hurry. "When I have been tired of my husband."

"A wife shouldn't get tired of her husband," Night Hawk said severely. He hoped Not in a Hurry could hear him.

"It is very easy to get tired of a husband," Foam said with a sniff. "When all he talks about is himself."

"What else is there to talk about?" Night Hawk asked, but he knew: the world, the cat bones, the stars, why there is salt in the ocean. Others' Child had talked about those things with him.

"He could talk about what I do all day," Foam said sulkily. "No one cares what *I* do. When I ask him what it is that he thinks makes the acorns bitter before you wash them, he looks at me as if a rock had talked, and says, 'Why do you want to know?'"

"I don't know, either," Night Hawk said. He stood up and threw his oyster shells onto the shell mound, being careful not to hit Not in a Hurry, who was still lurking in its shadow. He had one wife he didn't understand. He didn't want Not in a Hurry's. He walked toward the house the Knifenose Fish Clan had given him, stubbing his toe on a stone he didn't see.

Foam looked after him consideringly, tapping her small hand against her hip. Not in a Hurry came away from the shell mound and took her by the arm.

"Tell her why the sky is blue, Not in a Hurry!" someone who had overheard them shouted. "Let her tell you what she does all day! Ask her how to cook! Har!"

Not in a Hurry flashed a furious glare over his shoulder and dragged Foam away.

In the morning the sun came through the thatch of the Knifenose Fish Clan's guesthouse and shook Night Hawk awake with little trouble. He had been half drowsing for most of the night, trying to hear who was talking to Catches Crows in her house. The voice was low, deep, and rumbling like the ocean, and he couldn't make out the words. Just as he thought he understood, he would drift into sleep, or wake with a start, cold, his blanket balled up at his feet where Thief and Gray Daughter had trampled it into a nest.

He sat up and snatched it out from under them, shoving them off with his foot. There was no sound from Catches Crows' house now, just the soft rush of the surf and the wind and the shriek of children cavorting between the houses, first awake as always.

He went behind the house to piss and cut his foot on an oyster shell. Night Hawk leaned on the house and made water and saw Catches Crows behind hers doing the same thing. They politely pretended not to see each other. That was manners. Night Hawk went around to the front of her house and waited until she went in and then came back out again, acknowledging his presence.

"Have you thought what is troubling me?" he demanded.

Catches Crows scratched her head. Something fell out of her hair, and Night Hawk jumped because he thought it was alive. The breeze blew it past him before he could tell.

"You have broken a taboo," she said. "Come inside." She disappeared into the house on hands and knees through the low door.

Night Hawk followed her apprehensively. The house smelled like mice, and there were several dried ones hanging from a stick propped against the wall. Catches Crows' bed was a jumble of sealskins and clamshells. An old dog was sleeping in the middle of it.

Catches Crows sat down cross-legged on a mat by the fire, which she had been poking up. Night Hawk put more wood on it for her. "What taboo?" he asked her when she didn't say anything else.

Catches Crows put on a feathered mask and retreated behind it. He wondered if she was going to stay there, but she came out again. "I don't know," she said. "You need to find out, because it is a big one, or you wouldn't have things looking over your shoulder.''

''Who were you talking to last night?''

She cocked her head at him like a gull. ''I was never sure, but I didn't like it. Pah! I smelled rotten eggs all night.''

''How can I find out what it is?'' he asked, feeling exasperated and uneasy. Someone should have told him these things. Taboos were the things that each individual must or must not do. If you went against them, you upset everything.

''You were not told when you were a boy?'' The shaman clucked her tongue as if that had been careless of someone.

Night Hawk thought of the Three Old Men of the Kindred. If they had set a taboo on him, they would have said so. Taboos were powerful. And they conferred power on the people who carried them. The Three Old Men would have told him.

''Well, it is yours,'' Catches Crows said. ''It is not of this place. I can see it around you.''

''What does it look like?''

''Like power. What do you expect it to look like, a fish with an elk's head? Things aren't that easy.''

''No one has given me any taboos.''

''It is possible to have a taboo that no one has given you. One that has just come. I have seen them. Particularly when a man travels with Coyote.''

''Those are just dogs,'' Night Hawk said. He didn't want to mention Coyote's other apparitions.

''Those are Coyote's children. *That* is a dog.'' Catches Crows pointed at the old bitch asleep on the bed. ''So maybe it is something Coyote has given you.''

''What?''

''That is hard to tell.''

''Can you undo it?''

''Can I untie a knot I can't see? And anyway you cannot undo a taboo. You can only stop breaking it. Stop straining against the harness and go where you are told. That is life.''

"*I* am not a dog."

The shaman hooted with laughter. "We are all somebody's dog."

"Well, no one is telling me where to go." Except for Great Condor, and Night Hawk didn't want to listen to him yet.

Catches Crows held up her hand. "How do you know when you are doing the wrong thing?"

Night Hawk held out his bandaged thumb. The skin around it was soaked through. It wasn't healing. His toe opened up again every time he touched it. Now the oyster shell cut hurt.

"Those are signs that any fool can read," Catches Crows said. "What else does Coyote tell you?"

"Nothing." Since the night he had cut his toe, Coyote hadn't been back. Night Hawk had finally tried calling her, when he had cut his thumb and nearly put his eye out with the snapped harness, but she wouldn't come. She was just a presence behind him on the trail, watching through yellow eyes behind a sage bush, saying nothing.

"The dogs belong to Coyote," Catches Crows suggested. "Maybe they know."

The dogs belong to my wife, who left me, Night Hawk thought irritably.

Catches Crows shrugged. "You will have to go back to the place where you broke the taboo to find out what it is. Maybe the dogs know where."

"Is that all you can tell me?" Night Hawk looked at her pleadingly.

"I am not buying sealskins from you so you cannot criticize my offer," she said indignantly. "I told you what I know. If you want to know more, ask your dogs."

Night Hawk made a gesture of respect and laid a string of shell beads on the stones by her hearth. He backed out of the shaman's house, wincing as he put weight on his thumb. The dogs were waiting for him outside.

XI

Another Crazy Woman

Night Hawk was following the dogs, hobbling with his walking stick. The dogs were a gray streak on the land, like a path marked out, an old trail through the scrub. The dogs flowed along it, making the path, being the path. Night Hawk followed them resentfully. The gray coastal sky, thickened with sea mist, watched them go.

He clung stubbornly to the idea that the dogs didn't know where they were going, that they were following whatever rabbit scent brushed past their noses on the wind. But Catches Crows had told him to follow them, and so he would, and then he would prove that shamans knew no more than ordinary humans.

As if something heard him, the sky, which was often gray in this moon, darkened and spat water at him, an unexpected late spring rain that felt like ice. Night Hawk swore, dirty words concerning other people's excrement, and looked for some place to get out of the wet. The dogs stopped, water dripping from their noses, and watched him peer through the rain.

They had been moving along a low ridge of sagebrush and scrub oak, nothing thick enough to keep out water. Whatever road the dogs had been on, they seemed uninterested now. They sat down in the mud and waited for him to think of something.

"Move, Worthless. It won't get dry by sitting down." He shouted at them and shoved the travois into their backsides, and they got up reluctantly with baleful wet-dog stares.

Night Hawk headed them down the ridge, looking for an overhang of rock, a small cave, anything with a roof. It was raining harder now, and below them in a low valley he could see a dry wash filling up with water, muddy froth roaring between its banks. His feet slipped in the mud, and the travois threatened to slide away, taking the dogs with it. Below him he could see the rounded backs of boulders riding on the hillside. Maybe under them there would be a hole to crawl into.

They slithered down the hillside, roadless, floundering in the brush, while rivulets of water raced downhill past them. When they got to the rocks, Night Hawk maneuvered the travois fearfully down the side while the dogs backed off and kept the lines taut. At least they were well trained. At the bottom there was a small opening in the piled stones, most of which were bigger than the Channel Clan's houses. Night Hawk peered in to make sure that no one else, like Puma, had decided to live in it first. The dogs sniffed suspiciously. When they didn't smell anything, he followed them in.

The cave wasn't very deep, which must be why no one else wanted it. There were bones at the back and someone's droppings, but they were old. Night Hawk pulled the ropes off the travois and spread their belongings out.

The clamshell that held his fire starter was full of water. He spread the slow-burner of rotten wood and shredded sage bark out to be sure, but there was no warmth left in it. Whatever had left its droppings in the cave had done them a favor, Night Hawk thought. He unpacked his fire drill—a flat piece of wood and a stick nearly as long as his arm—and crumbled a handful of dry dung into the hole in the piece of wood, the hearth piece.

And of course there was nothing to burn, no wood for the fire.

Night Hawk sat back on his heels, wondering why he had been going to start a spark. And how much crazier he was likely to get on this journey.

The dogs didn't seem to have an answer to that. Night Hawk set a water basket outside the shelter to catch rain, and dug his sack of dried meat out of its pack. At least they had food. The dogs eyed the meat hungrily. Night Hawk's thumb throbbed, but he ignored it, biting into the dried meat, tearing it with his back teeth.

"Where are we going?" he asked the dogs, just to have someone to talk to.

The dogs yawned and curled into balls, conserving dog warmth.

The rain sheeted down outside like a hide. Night Hawk stared into it. He knew where they had been going. They had been going toward the Channel Clan, toward his wife, ever since he had let the dogs have their heads. *Not tomorrow,* he thought. *Tomorrow I will decide which way we take, and they will like it just as well.* He sniffled, shivering. His head and thumb were hot, but the rest of him felt as if he had doused himself in the cold surf. He sneezed, and pulled a blanket out of the travois and crawled under it, wedging himself between the dogs.

In the morning, all his deer-hide clothes were stiff from having been wet, and his sandals were shredded and waterlogged. But the sky was blue again and the air balmy. A white butterfly drifted past him on its currents. Night Hawk took the stiffened leggings and shirt off, and tied a breechclout around his waist. His second-best pair of sandals was in the pack on the travois, but it felt fine to go barefoot on the damp ground. The dogs were trying to dig a ground squirrel out of its hole, sending sprays of wet dirt up behind them.

Night Hawk whistled to them, and they gave up and

let him hitch them to the travois. His hand was better.
They turned their heads southeast, and he tugged on the
harness leads. He could see the road the way he had
seen it yesterday, a gray dog road going where he didn't
want to go.

"No. It is a fine time to visit the Manzanita Clan."
Night Hawk swung the travois until they were heading
northeast.

The dogs didn't seem to mind. They picked their way
along the slope until they came to a ridge and scrambled
to the top of it. It was easy traveling along a ridgetop,
and you could see what was coming, but this one ran
only a little way before it butted its back against a larger
ridge that cut across it. The mountains here ran north-
west to southeast. If you wanted to go against them, it
was hard traveling. You hit your head against the mountains the way the little ridge had.

The trail from the Knifenose Fish Clan to the Manzanita Clan began in the Knifenose Fish Clan's camp.
To cut across country was harder than it looked. Night
Hawk would have to go back and start again properly,
he thought. The dogs sat down and looked at him, twin
pairs of eyes the color of the pale mud on the trail. The
way to the Channel Clan was easy from here, they said
clearly.

"No." Night Hawk turned them around again. "We
will go back to the Knifenose Fish camp first. Besides,
I want some slow-burner that is not wet, and I will pack
it better this time."

And maybe he would tell the shaman of the Knifenose
Fish Clan that he had tried her advice and got wet and
therefore the road must be the wrong one, and she would
change her mind.

They backtracked through the drying brush under a
blue sky that danced with careening birds and scraps of
windblown butterflies. The wet earth was soft and
springy. Night Hawk's mood lightened as the gray dog
road turned into hillsides of blowing poppies blazing like
the sun. They made good time even though at midafter-

noon he realized that his head still ached and his cut thumb had hurt steadily more all day.

I will stop early tonight, he thought, *and put a poultice on it.* He looked at the thumb dubiously. It hurt now if he even touched it, worse than it had when he had talked to the shaman. Worse than before he had turned back. He looked over his shoulder to see if anything was following him. *I am seeing things that aren't there*, he thought. *Next I will be seeing the Rolling Head.*

"I am hungry," he told the dogs. "Also my thumb hurts. We will stop here."

The dogs sat down and waited for Night Hawk to make a fire in the little space he had cleared in the scrub in a spot they had passed yesterday going south. The brush was easy to chop away, but it was hard to do with one hand.

"Yah, you are no use," he said angrily to them. "If you had hands, then you would be useful."

If we had hands, their eyes said to him, *we would be people and not dogs, and we would not work for you.*

Night Hawk didn't answer them. He pulled the brush he had cut into a pile and got out his fire starter again. The hearth piece—the flat piece of wood—had a deep notch cut into one side, and at the innermost point of the notch was a shallow, bowl-like depression. The rounded end of the drill stick fit into the bowl. But it was more than that, in the way that an acorn is more. The relationship of stick to bowl to notch was crucial; they were linked shapes that might as well have stood for the geometry of the Universe, so vital was fire. It was a gift, a craft, to make a good one, to grow fire.

Night Hawk set the hearth piece on the ground and took out the dried dung he had brought with him from the cave. He dropped some of the dung into the notch and a few grains of sand and charcoal into the bowl. Then he put his knee on the hearth to hold it down and turned the end of the stick in the bowl, spinning it fast between his palms, spinning up fire. This was magic he knew, the familiar magic of practical things.

Black dust began to fall onto the tinder in the notch,

a thin spiderweb drift of smoke rising from it. Night
Hawk turned the drill faster, bearing down, trying not to
touch it with his inflamed thumb. Slowly the smoke
grew thicker, rising now not from the friction of the drill
but from the hot black dust and tinder in the notch in
the hearth. Night Hawk stopped drilling and blew on it.
A lick of flame came from the tinder, tasting the air. He
lifted it with bone tongs and set it on dry grass under a
propped cone of kindling. The kindling caught, and he
added more, cautiously, larger and larger sticks. Too
many too fast, and the flame would go out.

When it was burning well, he sat back and stared at
it. His thumb felt as if the flame were in it, too. *Is it
because I turned back?* There was a low hollow cough
in the trees. He thought it might be Condor. *You
wouldn't care if I turned back. If I die of this, I will be
easy to clean up.*

There was water nearby. Night Hawk remembered it
from the day before. If he was still, he could hear it in
the bright air, smell it on the sinuous wind. When the
fire was burning well, he took a water basket toward the
sound of the stream.

The stream was snowmelt from the mountains. He
knelt beside it and put his face to the cold water, drinking deeply, breathing the sharp green scent of the cress
that grew at its edges. Then he stuck his thumb in and
let the coldness bathe it. He slipped the old bandages
off and looked at it under water. An angry red gash ran
the length of the thumb like a streak of red lightning.
The wound hadn't closed properly—the edges gaped
wide, and blood and pus flowed out into the water. Night
Hawk unbandaged his toe and the oyster shell cut on his
other foot. They were not as bad, but the toe was not
good, either. He soaked all of them, letting the stream
wash them clean, and hobbled back to camp with his
basket of water.

"Go to the stream and drink," he told the dogs when
they tried to stick their noses in the basket. "This is for
cooking."

They trotted off, and he set the basket near the fire

and began putting rocks in the fire to heat. They were easy to find here, smooth stones that must have been washed by water in the early times. The dogs came back with their muzzles dripping and sat and watched him while he boiled dried meat with sage leaves and a handful of onions found on the trail. They drooled.

Night Hawk chuckled, cheerful in spite of his throbbing hand. "Greedy coyotes," he told them affectionately. "Go and catch mice."

They lay down with their noses on their paws and watched the cooking basket.

When it was done, Night Hawk threw in a handful of acorn meal to thicken it and spooned the dogs' share out of the basket onto a flat stone. They gobbled it, swallowing the meat whole, and licked the stone while Night Hawk was still settling to eat his.

Gray Daughter lifted her muzzle and growled. Night Hawk set the basket down. Someone was coming along the trail from the north. A human someone. No animal made that much noise. Night Hawk got his spear and stood up. The crackling in the scrub was coming from just over a little rise, where the trail wound around another spill of old rock. Night Hawk had been told that First Man had made it by throwing rocks at the Great Game, the legendary prey that had been taller than a mountain. He could almost believe it. It would take a stone that big to kill Old Great Cat, whose bones he had seen, who was two times the size of New Great Cat who wandered the mountains now.

Night Hawk gripped his spear tightly in his good hand. Whatever was coming wasn't a hunting party or a hunting animal. It was making too much noise. Maybe that meant it didn't want to kill him. He relaxed his grip on the spear a little so that his knuckles didn't hurt.

Or maybe it was the Rolling Head. Night Hawk had heard that story in every camp of the coastal people. He didn't believe a word of it, but the hair went up on the back of his neck. It was something that didn't care how much noise it made.

Thief growled, too, a low grumble in his throat. He

usually waited for his sister to tell him that something should be growled at, and then he did. The crashing in the brush grew louder, and a woman's head appeared over the top of the rise. The dogs growled louder, a singsong snarl that stopped her when they could only see her from the neck up, a disembodied head. The eyes in the head widened.

Night Hawk snapped his fingers at the dogs to be quiet. They sat down with the canine equivalent of a shrug. If he wanted to let dangerous women into his camp, that was his business. They would bite her if he needed them to. When they sat down, the woman came a little closer. It was Foam, a walking stick in one hand and a fur blanket trailing from the other, carrying over her shoulder a skin pack so badly tied that it slipped around and bumped her hip as she walked. She was flushed and out of breath, and she kept pushing her damp hair out of her face with the back of one arm.

"Ho," she said, panting. "I thought you would be farther along than this." She dropped her pack on the ground by his fire and sat down.

"I turned back," Night Hawk said. "What are you doing here?"

"Why did you turn back?" Foam demanded.

"No reason. I just did."

"You were going toward my brother's village," Foam said.

"I am going where I want to go. Did you follow me?" he asked her suspiciously.

"I am going south, too," Foam said. "I would have come sooner, but my husband stayed home all day yesterday. He kept watching me. I don't know why he thought he had to do that."

"Maybe because you keep running away," Night Hawk said.

"He is a very suspicious man," Foam said. "When he went fishing this morning he told his mother to watch me. So I put cascara in her mush, and when she was busy with the runs I came away. Do you have any water?"

Night Hawk thought about saying that the stream was that way, but he gave her the last of the water from his waterskin. "Why are you following me?"

"Because you are going back to my mother's village. I will go with you. If I tell my father that you will marry me and pay him a bride-price, he will give Not in a Hurry's back to him."

"Who said I wanted to marry you?" Night Hawk demanded. "Go away before your husband follows me, too." He took the waterskin back.

"You need a wife." Foam peered into the cooking basket. "Although that smells good. I heard about that Hot Springs woman. *I* wouldn't be scared. *I* have run away five times."

"What would I want with a wife who runs away?" Night Hawk inquired. "Anyway, I already have one of those."

"Your old wife will be a very important woman once my father is chieftain," Foam said. "She won't want to leave my brother. I will be a very important woman, too."

"Why is your father going to be chieftain?" Night Hawk asked, diverted.

"Because the old chieftain died at the acorn gathering last fall, and there will be a new chieftain as soon as Cannot Be Told picks a day to choose one. Only *I* heard that she won't pick a day and wants to be chieftain herself. Can I have some of that? I am very hungry."

"I thought I needed a wife," Night Hawk said, amused. "If you will eat my cooking, maybe I don't."

"I can cook," Foam said. "I was just afraid to stop to."

"Are they chasing you?"

"They will be."

Night Hawk imagined so if she had put cascara in her mother-in-law's mush. Once the runs stopped, anyway. But by that time Foam would probably be too far away to make it worth their while. This time Not in a Hurry might ask for her bride-price back if his mother had anything to say about it. Night Hawk spooned some of the stew into a bowl from his pack for her and sat down to eat the rest from his basket. "Can a woman really be chieftain?"

"That is what they are arguing over," Foam said, eating. "There is a woman from my people called Diver, who just married a man in my husband's village, and she told us all about it. She says that Old Tidepool, the shaman, says that the old chieftain's sister can be chieftain until there is an election, and nobody can name the day for an election but the old chieftain's sister. Also, she says that Fisher Skunk wants *his* bride-price back."

"He doesn't want to be married to a chieftain?"

"He doesn't want to be married to a man. The chieftain has to lead the hunters, and so Cannot Be Told has to be a man because women can't hunt."

"Is it that easy to be a man?" Night Hawk inquired.

"Well, a man can be a woman. He just has to wear women's clothes and do woman things."

"A man like that can hunt, though," Night Hawk said.

Foam cocked her head, thinking. "That is true. Well, then, I don't see why Cannot Be Told can't get married anyway if she is that kind of man."

"You would if you were Fisher Skunk," Night Hawk said. "Would you marry a man who was a woman?"

"I might. He couldn't be worse than Not in a Hurry. He might even listen to me talk. But those men don't marry women. I think this is different."

"So do I," Night Hawk said. "I think this is going to make trouble." And see how Old Wife liked that when her new people were a laughingstock. "Why is my old wife's father-in-law going to be chieftain?" he asked Foam. "If there hasn't been any election?"

"Because he is the most important man in the clan," Foam said loftily. "You don't think *Sand Owl* or *Hawk Feet* is more important than my father?" She scooped the last of the stew out of the bowl with her fingers, eating greedily. "I will be a chieftain's daughter and after that a chieftain's sister. It would be very good for you to be married to me."

"Not if I don't stay here," Night Hawk said shortly. "And I am not going to."

"You won't go very far if you don't fix that foot," Foam said. She had been eyeing his bare toe while she ate. "And your thumb looks like wood rats ate it. Do you want to die of that? Are you crazy? Come here and let me treat it for you."

She rummaged in her pack, holding it very close to her chest so that only she could see into it. Finally she pulled out a medicine bag.

"I have medicine," Night Hawk said. "But it doesn't heal."

Foam considered that. "Maybe there is a curse on you."

Night Hawk didn't want to tell her what Catches Crows had said. "Then you had better not marry me."

Foam came over to him with her medicine bag. It was made of otter skin with round slices of shell sewn on it like eyes. The eyes watched him while she got out a salve pot, made from a hollowed-out hipbone. She dipped out a scoop of salve on the end of her finger and worked it into his toe while he winced. She put some on the cut on the other foot and bound them both up in soft pieces of skin, shaking her head disapprovingly.

"You are very clumsy. How did you do this?"

"With an ax," Night Hawk said shortly. "It slipped."

"And cut both your feet?"

"No. I cut the other on an oyster shell. In your camp," he added accusingly.

"The whole world is covered with oyster shells," Foam said. "First Man threw his leavings all over it. In the days of the great water, he waded through it, eating oysters and throwing out the shells. You will just have to be more careful."

"I am not careless," Night Hawk said.

"Then something is after you," Foam said. She took his hand and looked at the thumb. "This is very bad. How did you do this?"

"With my belt knife."

"On purpose?" She looked at him uneasily.

"No. Cutting up a quail. It slipped."

Foam rubbed some salve into the cut, and Night Hawk howled. He clamped his lips together. Men did not make a fuss over having a wound dressed.

"I would talk to Old Tidepool about this if I were you," Foam said. "When we get to my village. Maybe it is because you need a wife."

"I am not going to your village," Night Hawk said again, but he knew he would go where the dogs wanted to now. The thumb was dangerous. He had seen men die from wounds like that. The red streak would go from the wound up the arm or the leg, and then the skin turned green and black and stank, and then it fell off. If the person was lucky, he died before that happened. "*Maybe* we will go there," Night Hawk conceded.

In the morning Foam was awake before he was, putting wood in the fire and humming a little song under her breath. She had drawn a strange series of lines in the dirt by the fire.

Night Hawk peered at them groggily. "What are those?"

"That is my road," Foam said. "Your old wife taught me how to make one. That is my road to walk on to where I want to go."

"My wife taught you that?" When had Others' Child ever wanted a road, these last few years, anyway?

"Not exactly," Foam admitted.

"Then she has not gone completely mad since she left me," Night Hawk said. Imagine teaching someone like Foam to call what she wanted.

"But I have watched her make things from the dirt, so I tried it myself. I couldn't make an otter-skin cape, but I found out I could make a road. I could feel it under the dirt. I only had to draw on top of it. A road is just lines. Anyone can make lines, make a line that goes from here to there."

"Maybe you should make me a road," Night Hawk said. "I have just been following the dogs."

"Well, that is what I said to you," Foam said. "My

road goes back to my mother's village, and you can follow it, too, and marry me. I don't know why you don't want to do that.''

"While my old wife is married to your brother?'' Night Hawk scratched his head. "My old wife left me because I wouldn't stay in one place. You would just do the same thing.''

"I might not,'' Foam said.

He sat down gingerly, being careful of his thumb and feet. He felt as if pieces of him were being broken off. Was this what it was like when Great Condor ate somebody, cleaned him up piece by piece? Night Hawk made a crossed-fingers sign to keep away whatever that thought might have called up. Foam was putting dried fish and little dried salted squids into a pot. Their tentacles unfolded and waved gently in the hot water.

"Did you bring those?'' he asked, thinking at least he wouldn't have to hunt to feed her. Or give her his meat. He felt disinclined to do either. She might take it as a proposal of marriage.

"I took a lot of them when my husband's mother was busy.'' She stirred the pot with a long spoon.

"What else did you steal?''

She gave him a quick glance and looked back at the cooking basket. She reached out an arm for her pack and pulled it closer to her while she stirred. She had stolen something, he thought, but she wasn't going to tell him. That was fine. They could use more food.

When they set out, Night Hawk tied Foam's blanket and pack on the travois with his belongings. She didn't want to let go of the pack at first, but he said, "Do you want to carry it all the way? It is heavy, and you already have blisters. I saw them.'' She let go, and he lashed it down. "I don't want to look in it,'' he said.

He gave the dogs their heads, refusing to go anywhere until the dogs chose. They turned their noses southeast again, toward Foam's village. Night Hawk shrugged. He had expected that. Had Coyote sent this woman to put him on the right road? He could easily believe that she was Coyote's; certainly she caused chaos. She was beautiful, too. Not like Others' Child—rounder in the face and wiry where Others' Child was angular—but her breasts were pretty, and her bottom was round. Night Hawk could see it bounce under her short hide skirt as she walked.

With her pack on the travois, Foam trotted briskly, chatting about the state of things among the Channel Clan and stopping impatiently to wait for Night Hawk when he fell behind.

"Diver says Old Tidepool says things just have to happen. My father wanted to go to the Shell Men for advice, but Fisher Skunk wouldn't let them because he was embarrassed. Come *on*."

Night Hawk chuckled, happy enough that someone else besides himself was having woman trouble.

"Your old wife made Old Tidepool come out of his house when Fisher Skunk was asking Cannot Be Told for his bride-price back and they had knives in their hands," Foam said. "Diver said Cannot Be Told told Fisher Skunk that she would stuff it down his throat and then cut him open to get it back out. That was when your old wife went for the shaman."

"Stop calling her that." Foam had gotten farther ahead of him on the trail, and Night Hawk shouted it after her.

She turned around, eyes wide. "Well, she can't be your now-wife while she's married to my brother. Women can't have two husbands. Men, yes, if they are very important, but not women. I don't see why not," she added. "It isn't fair."

"I don't want to marry you if you want two husbands," Night Hawk said, grinning. He was beginning to think that maybe . . .

Foam danced down the trail ahead of him. "Hurry up!" she called back over her shoulder, disappearing among the trees.

When dusk fell, they were near the Channel Clan's village. It would have been faster to go along the coast by boat, but Night Hawk didn't have one, and besides, he couldn't have followed the dogs in a boat. He was, however, mildly surprised that Foam hadn't stolen one.

At night when they went to sleep, he rolled himself into his blanket beside Foam in hers. He didn't reach for her, but he thought about it. She was thinking about it, too, he suspected. In the middle of the night, when the nocturnal world was about its business, he felt her snuggle closer and tuck her hand under his blanket. *Well,* he thought, *why not?*

There was just enough moon to reflect in her eyes, twin crescents of light like slivers of shell. She butted her head against his chest, and her hand crept lower. Night Hawk smiled. She hadn't wakened in fear of the vastness of the night, but because she wanted his own fine self. That felt good. He could almost ignore the fire in his thumb for the one in his groin.

In the morning she was singing again, the same little unintelligible song under her breath, and there were the same lines in the ground by the fire. Maybe he would marry this one, he thought, and take her foot-on-trail, and Old Wife could sit by her house and get fat and see what she thought of that! Maybe Coyote wouldn't show up in his camp wearing Old Wife's face then.

Night Hawk began to pack the travois while Foam cooked breakfast. He hefted her pack back onto it. It didn't weigh as much as he would have expected, if it was full of food, and he was feeling inquisitive. "What have you got in here? I thought you brought food."

"Mostly," Foam said. A secretive look crossed her face. She grinned, the naughty, anticipatory grin of a bad child.

Night Hawk looked at her with mock suspicion. "What else?"

"Things," Foam said. "Never mind." She gave him a dignified look and set the pack beside her.

Night Hawk grinned back. She *was* very pretty, and he liked that stubborn chin. It might be a good chin to travel with. He sidled up to her, looking away at the dogs, who were catching grasshoppers in the sage. "We will be there tonight," he said. "If it wasn't for my foot, we would have made better time." On the last word, he snatched the pack away and ran, prancing on his sore feet, pulling the top open.

Foam leaped up and ran after him, yanking at his arms while he lifted a bundle wrapped in fox skin from the pack. He held it playfully above his head while the fox skin fell off.

"Give it back!" Foam jumped for it.

Night Hawk's eyes widened. It was a mask, with strange curving tentacles like a squid's on the sides and huge round eyes that stared back at him unnervingly. The head wasn't pointed like a squid; it was bulbous, and the tentacles hung like snakes from the bottom of it.

"Hoo," Night Hawk said, "that is ugly. What is it?"

"Put it back!" Foam hissed, jumping at it again. "That is Octopus, and it is my husband's. If it sees us, it will tell him where we are."

Night Hawk narrowed his eyes at her. He had seen Octopus before, but it had been dark. "This is magic. You stole *this*?"

"I am bringing it to my father," Foam said. "So *he* will have the magic, and he will be willing to give my bride-price back."

"He will beat you, more likely. Your husband will come after this."

"I told you that." Foam sounded exasperated.

"You didn't tell me you stole sacred masks."

"Just this one."

"This one is enough." Night Hawk stuffed it back in its fox skin. "You are crazy, and I am crazy to think that I might want to marry you. Go away with this." He shoved it at her.

Foam looked hurt. "We are nearly there."

"I have trouble enough already. I am not going to be caught with your husband's Octopus mask. He might send Octopus after me the next time I am in the water." Night Hawk had seen a real one, nearly as big as he was, with baleful eyes and thrashing tentacles. The men had dragged it from the ocean near the Channel Clan's village, and Night Hawk had wanted it to dry and take home to give the Three Old Men something to think about, but the Channel Clan had eaten it instead.

"No, he won't," Foam said.

"He will do something. I don't want to think about what it will be. You can't keep that thing here."

Foam shrugged. "The Knifenose Fish men will raid my father's village and take something of ours, and then the Shell Men will say who is to pay recompense. That is all."

"War isn't a game," Night Hawk said. "I am not going to get into your war."

"There are rules." She stamped her foot and tried to explain them to the stranger. "If I took the Octopus mask, then they are entitled to take something. But you didn't take anything."

"Take it *away*," Night Hawk said, looking over his shoulder. "This isn't a basket of meal or a stolen fish. This is sacred. You are a fool! Your husband will come after this, and I want no part of it."

Foam snatched her blanket from the travois. She stuffed the mask back in her pack and hefted them both.

"Leave it here on the ground, and I will go with you," Night Hawk said.

Foam shook her head and wrapped her arms around the pack. "No."

Night Hawk folded his arms. "Then I'm not coming."

"It is hard country between here and there," Foam said plaintively. "Likely I shall get eaten by Cat without you."

"You ran away before, and Cat didn't eat you."

Foam sniffled. "I thought you were going to marry me."

"I am not going to marry Octopus." Night Hawk thought about being embraced by cold tentacles, pulled deep, made devouring love to in the wet dark. His skin twitched.

"Well, I should have known one man wasn't any better than another," Foam said. "I shall sooner go into the desert and marry a snake like Blue Racer's wife did, before I marry another man.'' She slung the pack over her shoulder and stalked into the brush with it bumping her backside as she went.

Night Hawk sat down beside the fire. *Hoo,* he thought, *that is a dangerous woman.* He picked gingerly at the hot mush she had been frying on a thin stone, trying to get a piece without burning himself. He singed the end of one finger and sucked on it morosely while he looked for the shoulder blade she had been turning the mush with. She had taken it with her.

Night Hawk pushed the frying stone off the fire and sat down to wait while it cooled. He thought wistfully of last night. His thumb was throbbing, and his head felt hot. Where was he going now? he wondered. With or without Foam he didn't want to go back to the Channel Clan's village, but particularly not without her. What would he say to Others' Child, hobbling into camp with his sore feet and his burning thumb—*I am here so you can laugh at me because something has cursed me?* He looked at the woods. ''I am not going any farther,'' he said. ''That is the second crazy woman you have sent me. Now you come and tell me what I have done wrong, and I will undo it.''

It didn't seem strange at all to be talking to the trees. He was almost sure he could hear them answer.

XII

Ghosts

Not in a Hurry crept along the edge of a dry wash with the men of the Knifenose Fish Clan behind him. They had paddled south for two days and were coming back north on foot along the coast where the Channel Clan's lookouts wouldn't expect them. Not in a Hurry was very proud of that idea. He had thought of it himself. Some of their band would bring the canoes up the coast and would be waiting for them south of the Channel Clan's village. Not in a Hurry had thought of that, too.

He had thought of all these things the night he had come home and found Foam and his mask and most of his dried fish gone, and his mother lying weakly on a bed in her house with an expression like a fish herself.

When Not in a Hurry had finished shouting at his mother and blaming it on her, and had begun to think what to do about it, he said to the other men, "That woman they gave me has taken the Octopus mask and food from my house and made my mother sick." Then he called all the men of the Knifenose Fish Clan to a council, and they all thought, too, some of them more respectfully than others.

"Har, maybe you should have told her why the sky is blue!" hooted a young man who had heard Not in a Hurry's wife talking to Night Hawk at the Fish Dance. "Ooh, sweet thing, tell me what you think about it all!" Everybody knew that Not in a Hurry's wife kept leaving him, and some of them were beginning to think there must be a reason. But they were divided about whose fault it was.

"Be silent," an older man said. "You yawp like a coyote. The woman has done something wicked this time."

"I said she was a bad one," Not in a Hurry's mother commented. She sighed weakly. "Sons never listen to their mothers in these days. It is not like it was when I was young." The women sat just behind the men, away from the fire and ostensibly not part of the council, but close enough to make their opinions known.

"Nothing is like it was when you were young," a girl said behind her hand to the girl next to her. "It must have been a fine world when everyone was dutiful and the sky so much bluer."

"And the deer so much tastier," the other girl whispered.

"And the children respectful and not giving you cascara." They giggled, and the Knifenose Fish chieftain's wife, who was the authority concerning mannerless girls, glared at them sharply. (The Knifenose Fish chieftain didn't have a sister, to the wife's immense satisfaction.)

Not in a Hurry's mother sniffed and looked at her son reproachfully. No one knew what her trials had been.

"It is Not in a Hurry's business what he wishes to do about his wife," the chieftain said. Not in a Hurry's mother sniffed again. "But she has stolen a sacred thing and it is necessary that we raid the Channel Clan and take it back or Octopus will think we are disrespectful and he will spoil our catch."

"This is true," Catches Crows said. She sat apart from both groups, barred from the men by her sex and from the women by her position, on a pile of soft deer hides with an otter-skin cover. A young girl brought her a bowl of cactus juice. Catches Crows had had two husbands and had outlived them both. Her daughters were married to men in the Split Rock Clan. "Since I have been old enough to see what happens," she said, "I have not seen a woman so willful or so likely to make trouble. It means something, and more than just that Not in a Hurry has picked a wrong bride."

"It means the women are getting lofty," a man grumbled. "The Channel Clan have a woman chieftain now. It's enough to make a dog laugh." He glared around him at the women sitting behind.

"It means there is change coming," Catches Crows snapped. "Without a woman you would not be here."

He ducked his head away from her eye and muttered. She looked at him again, and he crossed two fingers.

Catches Crows gave the rest of the men a glance that made them uneasy. "Do you want to raid the Channel Clan for our belongings, or do you want to insult the mothers who bore you?"

They hunched their shoulders, shamefaced, and the girls looked smug.

"What will we take?" a young man asked them. He was newly initiated, and his eyes were excited, dark and anticipatory. He had never been to war.

"Our Octopus mask back again," they answered him.

"Food to make up what she stole."

"Something of theirs. That is honorable. What do they have that we want?"

"Girls!" someone shouted.

"Not Channel girls!" The men all guffawed, their spirits revived. "We don't want wives like Not in a Hurry's."

"We should take his back for him, though."

"He doesn't want her!" his mother snapped.

"Her father has a Condor mask."

"That would be a mistake," Catches Crows said.

"Shells, then!"

"Shells are the proper thing to take." Shells bought everything else.

"Shells!"

Foam and Others' Child were tanning a deer hide. They had been sitting all day with it between them, rubbing and kneading it soft in the patch of sun between the family's houses. The rain had scented the air with the pungent oil of sage and spring pine sap. Now the sky had turned as blue as a robin's egg, puffed with small white clouds that faded into thin spiderwebs in the breeze.

Others' Child lifted her face to it while she worked, bored with the pulling and kneading. Yesterday they had cooked the deer's brains and rubbed them into the hide with a round stone. Today when it was soft, they would smoke it over green wood. Little Brother was engaged in finding chips of bark and rotten wood to add to the smoke, and complaining that when he was a man he would not do women's work.

"When you are a man," Others' Child said, "I will not have the chance to keep you by me all day. So I will keep you now while I can." She reached out as he went by and caught him for a kiss.

"I am not going to have children," Foam said darkly. "They grow up and leave you. Or grow up to be men." She cast a resentful glance over her shoulder at her father's house, where Condor Dancer had smacked her three times hard on the bottom for stealing the Octopus mask, instead of being glad to have it.

"I would kill any woman who stole my Condor mask!" he had roared. "You are an ignorant and disobedient daughter!"

"That is what that other one you were married to said, also," Foam said sullenly to Others' Child, kneading the hide as if it had had her father inside it. "I don't know what you wanted with him."

Others' Child was torn between questioning Foam further (he had hurt himself, Foam said) and pretending that she didn't care that Foam had met Night Hawk on the trail and slept with him. (He was fun at night, Foam said. Others' Child knew that.)

"I *didn't* want him," Others' Child said shortly. "That is why I am here."

"I don't know what you want with my brother, either," Foam added, continuing her grievances. "I told him that if he and Father didn't want the Octopus mask I took such trouble to bring them, they could send it back. He said they wouldn't because it is very powerful. But he still blames me for bringing it."

Others' Child stretched the end of the hide between her hands, inspecting it. "This is ready."

"He was going to marry me," Foam said, aggrieved. "Until he saw the mask. I wanted to marry him. He is much more interesting than my husband."

"Get the needles!" Others' Child snapped. She began rolling the hide into a cone with a small hole open at the little end. She glared at it while she waited impatiently for Foam.

Foam brought two needles threaded with thin sinew and jabbed one of them through the edges of the hide. "He said I had eyes like stars," she said chattily.

"He says that to the old Grandmothers, too." Others' Child snatched up the other needle and began work on the wide end. Her face flaming, she stitched it together while Foam, undaunted, described the finer points of their lovemaking.

"He's very big, isn't he?" Foam said. "And he likes to kiss ears. Not in a Hurry never did that."

"Will you shut your mouth?" Others' Child shrieked at her. She dragged the conical hide to the smoking fire and began to hoist it onto the framework of sticks that stood over the fire. "Help me with this!" she demanded, coughing.

"Well, you don't want him," Foam said, heaving the other side of the hide up and flopping it over the framework. "Why shouldn't I have him?"

They bent down to lay a collar of wet thatch against the bottom of the hide, which hung a forearm's length off the ground so it wouldn't singe. Doubled over on hands and knees, they glared at each other through the smoke.

"Because you will make trouble for him," Others' Child said.

"You *do* still want him!" Foam said.

"I don't."

"You do. You want both. You want my brother, but you don't want anyone to have Old Husband. You are just greedy."

"I am not!" Others' Child slapped thatch against the framework and tried to lash it down, her eyes stinging. "You already have a husband, too. You can't have another one until your father gives the bride-price back. And he won't," she said, goaded, "because you are too much trouble to have at home!"

"Huh!" Foam said. "I don't think he ever said *your* eyes were like stars."

"He said so all the time," Others' Child said grimly. Her eyes were streaming, and she stood up, rubbing them, backing away from the fire. The smoke was billowing through the little hole at the top of the hide now. "He said yours were like a squid's," she added.

"He did not!" Foam darted around the hide. "You are jealous," she said, hands on hips. She leaned into Others' Child's face. "He told me that. He told me you were jealous all the time because you are old!"

"I'll show you how old I am!" Others' Child smacked Foam in the jaw with her fist. She kicked her shins. "Call me old and see what happens!"

Little Brother stared openmouthed. Aunt Foam stuck her foot between his mother's legs, and they both dropped to the ground, rolling beside the fire pit. Mother had her hand in Aunt Foam's hair.

Little Brother began to cry. Mothers didn't fight. When he fought, Mother made him sit alone in the house. If adults fought, the world might be ending. Little Brother looked anxiously for Sea Otter and didn't see him. He began to howl. He turned on his heels and ran for his grandmother's house. Surely Grandmother could make them stop. She could stop anything.

Foam and Others' Child rolled in the ashes, clawing at each other. "Dirty bitch!" Others' Child screamed. "Lying in the dirt with any man who comes along! He doesn't need you! And he said you were stupid!"

"You are jealous he doesn't want *you* anymore!" Foam said, panting. She managed to pin Others' Child beneath her and dug her elbows into her ribs. Others' Child kneed her in the belly. They thrashed, clawing at each other.

Before anyone else in the camp could see what was happening, Blue Butterfly darted from her house with fire in her eye. She kicked them both. "Get up! Get up, you sluts! Who told daughters of mine to roll in the dirt?" She kicked them again.

Others' Child and Foam let go of each other reluctantly. They crouched where they had fought, disheveled and dirty, looking up at her.

Blue Butterfly started to berate them further, and then her mouth opened wide. She stared past them. "Get in the house!" she snapped.

Foam and Others' Child looked at her, puzzled.

"Move!" Blue Butterfly shrieked.

They spun around to look behind them. The men of the Knifenose Fish Clan were streaming through the camp from the opposite end, hacking the houses down.

One of the Knifenose Fish men had grabbed a girl by the arm, and she screamed and pulled away from him, diving between two houses with him after her. The few Channel men in the camp were pouring from their own houses to fight, but most were at the coast, fishing. The Knifenose Fish men must have come from inland.

Blue Butterfly gave Foam a shove. "Run! Out of the camp. Hide in the rocks or they'll find you. This is your doing!" She pushed her again, and Foam took to her heels.

"Get your husband's spear," Blue Butterfly said to Others' Child. "No Knifenose Fish man is going to steal my things!"

Others' Child got to her feet and ran to her house.

Sea Otter's spears leaned against the wall. She grabbed the lightest one and stood in her doorway, waiting.

Not in a Hurry hacked with his ax at the willow-pole frames of houses as he passed them, leaving them tilted and askew. Another man behind him stuck a spear through the thatch to drive the occupants out. When they ran, the Knifenose Fish men let the old women and children go but tried to grab the girls. Men of both clans circled each other warily, looking for an opening. The chieftain would stop the battle when the first man was wounded, and if it was someone on the Knifenose Fish side, that would be shameful. If the wounded man was from the Channel Clan, then they had won. Mostly the Knifenose Fish men grabbed the outnumbered Channel men and tied them up.

Several houses stood untouched in the middle of the wreckage, houses where sisters or in-laws of Knifenose Fish people lived. That was understood. Also understood was that Not in a Hurry would take back his mask and anything else he could find, including his wife, because everyone was laughing at him.

Blue Butterfly stood guard at her threshold with Little Brother whimpering behind her. She took a quick glance at the approaching melee and said to him, "Quick! Go hide with your aunt and keep her safe. Run now!" Little Brother darted from the hut into the bushes.

She could see Not in a Hurry heading for her. A spiteful man, who didn't deserve her daughter, Blue Butterfly thought now.

There were three men behind Not in a Hurry. Catching Not in a Hurry's wife was a game. Other girls might be captured and returned unharmed when the Shell Men told them to, but Not in a Hurry's wife was a fair target. They weren't even very concerned over what Not in a Hurry would like, especially when they saw Blue Butterfly waiting for them with a spear. Women were not supposed to fight for the same reason they were not sup-

posed to hunt. These women didn't care if their woman
magic weakened the Knifenose Fish men. The men were
outraged.

Others' Child braced the butt of Sea Otter's spear in
the crook of her arm and watched the men come. They
seemed to be coming for a very long time, pounding
across the dirt yard where foot traffic had worn away
the spring grass, their legs making slow sweeping arcs
like the leaps of deer, as if they were running in water.
And then in an instant they were there, on top of her,
their spears pointed in her face, and she was jabbing her
spear back at them while they danced out of the way,
still surprised.

They pushed against Others' Child. One of them, a
stocky, square man, grabbed her spear by the shaft just
past the point and tugged on it. Others' Child pulled
back, her teeth bared. He was trying to pull her out of
the doorway. She yanked back harder and then suddenly
drove the spear forward. It sliced open a cut on the top
of his shoulder, and she jerked it out of his grip while
he was still surprised.

"Where is Not in a Hurry's wife?" Square Man
growled at her. A spray of spittle from his angry mouth
hit her face. "Where is Not in a Hurry's Octopus
mask?"

Others' Child stabbed the spear at him again. A man
with a white scar on his lip was hacking the willow-pole
supports of the house apart so that it began to lean. Three
others were attacking Blue Butterfly's house, while she
ran around inside it, stabbing her spear through the
thatch at them.

"Go away! Leave our houses alone! Dirty men with
sand fleas!" Others' Child screamed.

Not in a Hurry pursued Blue Butterfly inside. Others'
Child heard a frantic thrashing, and Not in a Hurry
emerged with the mask in one hand and a sealskin blanket in the other. Blue Butterfly limped after him, beating
at him with the broken shaft of her spear. Others' Child
abandoned her house and ran at Not in a Hurry. She

leveled her spear at him, and three other men caught her from behind, pinning her arms back. She thrashed in their grip, turning her head like an owl to bite Square Man on the forearm.

Square Man howled and let her go, giving her a kick that sent her flying. Not in a Hurry went back in Blue Butterfly's house and came out with the basket that held her jewelry. Two more came from Others' Child's house with a pile of skins and Sea Otter's spears, strings of shell beads hanging from their arms. One wore her best cooking basket on his head.

They whooped and pranced, kicking Others' Child and Blue Butterfly out of the way. Others' Child crouched on her hands and knees in the dirt, growling at them. She drew a big snake in the dirt, and someone's bed over it, with her fingernail, and Square Man scraped it out again with his sandal.

"Where is my wife?" Not in a Hurry demanded.

All over the camp, Others' Child could hear women screaming. Mostly they were screaming curses, she noted with satisfaction. "We are not afraid of Knifenose Fish men," she spat at them. "Knifenose Fish men have no balls and have to come and steal them. Your wife said so," she added to Not in a Hurry, who was wearing Blue Butterfly's beads around his neck.

Square Man glowered at her. "That is not respectful. Tell us where Not in a Hurry's wife is, or we will kick you again."

"Something worse than snakes will come in your bed if you kick me again," Others' Child said.

Square Man started to do it anyway until Scar on His Mouth caught him by the shoulder and pointed. While Square Man was looking, Others' Child scuttled away and hid behind a bush. She saw a growing battle at the other end of the village. The men had come home.

Not in a Hurry ran for the other end of the camp, with Square Man and Scar on his Mouth behind him. They were carrying their stolen goods under one arm, spears in the other hand. Now that the Channel men were back, someone would get wounded—small scratches didn't count—and the battle would be over. They wanted to be sure they were part of it first.

Sea Otter and Condor Dancer had heard the fighting before they were in sight of the village. They laid their catch down and ran, clutching belt knives and fishing spears and roaring with anger. Cannot Be Told—who was Man Who Fishes today—ran ahead of them like a chieftain, brandishing a bone fish spear. They poured into the camp amid the rampaging Knifenose Fish men.

The Knifenose Fish men were better armed but hampered by their booty. The two sides flung themselves at each other in a melee, while the women shouted triumphant invective.

Sea Otter roared at the sight of his sealskins under Square Man's arm. He lunged at him with his fish spear and stabbed him between the ribs. Square Man grunted and dropped the skins. He staggered backwards as Sea Otter pulled the spear out. Blood poured from his chest.

The Knifenose Fish chieftain shouted angrily at his men. The Channel men had scored the first blood. A young man from the Channel Clan leaped in the air, yipping in triumph. Scar on His Mouth spun around and ran his spear through him. It came out the boy's back, and the boy crumpled over it.

"Home!" the Knifenose Fish chieftain roared. Scar on His Mouth jerked his spear loose, his eyes wide. The Knifenose Fish men fled for the coast, their arms full of loot, the Channel girls abandoned.

The air between them shimmered with something bright, as if there were specks of mica in a veil of blood. Slowly the Knifenose Fish men disappeared into it, running for their boats, running again as if in water while the Channel Clan stared after them.

Cannot Be Told laid down her spear and took off her man's clothes, in front of them all. When she was a woman again, she cradled the dead boy in her arms.

It was Young Clam Catcher, who had made fun of her once. That didn't matter. Cannot Be Told stroked his face and watched his eyes glaze, as if someone had pulled a cloud across them.

The boy's mother and aunts were howling and pulling at their hair, and Old Clammer, his father, shook his fist in Cannot Be Told's face. "This is not the way it is done! We will make the Knifenose Fish Clan pay for this!" Old Clammer whirled on Condor Dancer. "This is your daughter's fault! This is the fault of women!"

Others' Child pushed her way through the shouting, weeping people. Sea Otter saw her and caught her by the shoulders, checking her dirty face for injuries. Blue Butterfly was limping behind her.

"It was *men*!" Others' Child said. "Men who did this." She pointed at Young Clam Catcher's body. And because she was holy to them, because she came from elsewhere, this one last time they closed their mouths in tight lines and listened to her.

"*Men* killed him. They came while you were fishing. And they have taken my mother-in-law's things, and *we* fought them while you were not here. They were going to take Light Fish and Turtle Girl, but we made them afraid, and they left them." She pointed to two sobbing girls, who were clinging to each other and weeping muddy tears.

"The men coming home made them afraid," Sea Otter said.

Others' Child decided to concede that. "All the same, it was not women who killed a boy. And it does not matter what Foam did. That does not give some man rights to do as he pleases and then blame her."

"That is right!" The rest of the women pushed forward. They had been slapped and kicked around by the Knifenose Fish men, and they were angry. Even the ones who were kin to the Knifenose Fish Clan, whose houses had been spared, felt sick when they looked at Young Clam Catcher and saw their world, their rules, turned over. If people didn't follow rules, there was no way to keep you from spinning off the earth into the dark empty sky, falling forever into nothing. Only rules could hold you to the ground.

"It is the Knifenose Fish men who have broken the law," Bone shouted.

"It is time to call the Shell Men," Blue Butterfly said to Condor Dancer. "And to do as they say. We should have called them long ago."

"Yes," Others' Child said.

"No!" Onion Woman, Young Clam Catcher's mother, stood up shrieking.

"No!" Old Clammer grabbed her by the hand, but he stuck his chin out. "The Knifenose Fish Clan have killed my son. Now we will kill them. This is not business for the Shell Men."

Cannot Be Told stood up, too, leaving the dead boy to his aunts. "This old man is right. This is war business," she said.

"War business!" They echoed her, shouting it louder. The sound ran down the ridge like waves.

Foam crept out of the bushes holding Little Brother by the hand. She stopped at the wreckage of her mother's house and listened to the shouting.

"War!"

"We will take *their* women and cut down *their* houses!"

"Now we will kill them! Now we will kill *their* boys!"

Foam sat down in the dirt and buried her face between her knees. Little Brother tugged at her arm, and she looked up, her teeth chattering. She reached for him and pulled him into her lap. They rocked that way, back and forth, her arms cradled around him.

The men were making a canoe. The Channel Clan already had enough canoes to carry all their men to the Knifenose Fish Clan's village, but Others' Child thought that it was the making that was important. Some of their canoes were made by hollowing a log with fire and axes, and some, the lightweight ones, by tying bundles of tule stalks together. This one was a war canoe, made of planks shaped with bone and stone knives and smoothed with sharkskin and then sewn end to end. It was very beautiful, like a dolphin taking shape on the beach, Others' Child thought.

The men were very serious about it. Old Clammer directed the building, and Old Tidepool sat on the sand and watched it grow. At the right time he burned pine sap and waved the smoke over the canoe, chanting.

The village had purpose now. Even Foam had been taken back into its good graces. The people could not blame her and the Knifenose Fish Clan at the same time, and had made their choice. It would have been different if Scar on His Mouth had not killed Young Clam Catcher, but there could be no going back from that. The idea of it hung over them like a veil of dark, dry rain, smelling of rot and mice.

The rules that had seemed so civilized to Others' Child began now to look inexplicable, as if the shaman had announced that every person should order his feet to turn green and his head to sprout poppies. They were to raid the Knifenose Fish Clan and kill *two* men, just two. How did you do that? How did you not do that? She and Night Hawk had stopped a war one time between their two people, but Night Hawk wasn't here, and if he were, he wouldn't care if the Channel Clan and the Knifenose Fish Clan killed each other.

On the beach Condor Dancer and Sea Otter were building the canoe. Sometimes the women crept down to watch them, but the men rarely noticed. The men sat with the boards in their laps, smoothing them painstakingly with a bone plane and rubbing them soft with sharkskin, their hands moving back and forth, back and forth to some inner chant that sang of spilling blood and getting vengeance. Beside the boat a basket of hot tar streaked the air with its scent, and two boys were tying brushes for it. Long ago, Others' Child had watched her brother, Mocking Bird, getting ready to kill Night Hawk's people with the same stolid concentration.

She sat down cross-legged in the sea grass on the dunes above the beach, knowing she should be cooking dinner, grinding meal, making a rabbit-skin blanket for the cold nights to replace the sealskins Square Man had taken; all the things that women did, those were what she should be doing. *Yah,* she thought, *Great Condor take all the things that women should be doing.*

Others' Child cupped her chin in her hand and watched Little Brother stirring the hot tar with an older boy to watch him. Maybe she was glad she didn't have to watch her girl baby be told all the things she couldn't do—didn't have to watch her swallow a war, as if she were eating poison, but not be allowed to fight it. Others' Child's eyes filled with tears the way they always did when she thought of the girl baby. Everything seemed to make her cry now, it seemed, salt water welling up in her eyes like the sea coming up in holes in the sand. She even cried when she thought about her brother, who was as arrogant as all males and had thought he owned their sister Maize Came and herself. She had walked to the Endless Water with Night Hawk to prove he didn't.

Others' Child smoothed the sand on top of the dune and drew in it idly with one finger, a woman with wings, herself floating in the sky like Condor, above her brother and sister and all, wingspan stretching from one mountain to the next, able to see across the world. Then she would know why things were. The sunlight on the white sand dazzled her eyes as it bounced from the bright water. She squeezed them closed, trying to shut it out. The sounds of the men making the canoe grew fainter and far away like the yapping of gulls.

"I'm always glad when a two-legged person wants to see things properly," Condor said. "It doesn't happen often."

Others' Child stretched her arms in delight and caught the air current on stiff feathers. She swooped, laughing, while Condor regarded her with a fatherly eye. He chuckled deep in his throat.

Others' Child smiled at him. Down below she *could* see Maize Came and Mocking Bird like dots. "I didn't know you ever laughed," she said.

"Oh, not down there," Condor said. "That wouldn't be polite. Only up here."

From here she could also see the Knifenose Fish vil-

lage and her Channel Clan's camp and what she thought
might be Night Hawk and the dogs on the trail. She
hadn't asked to see him. "My new people are going to
fight the Knifenose Fish Clan," she said. She swooped
over Condor on her new wings.

Condor shook his head. "They always do that. It isn't
necessary. They'll die soon enough anyway."

"I don't think they do it as a favor to you," Others'
Child said. She put a wing out, feeling for the thermals,
riding them like an otter sliding down a bank.

"No, that is the way two-legged people are. Why do
you want to be different from them?"

"I don't *want* to be different. I just am." She soared
above tiny blue mountains, fist-sized deserts. A spiral of
gulls flew up around her as if blown on the wind.

"Don't be prideful about it."

"Everyone tells me I am. When I was little they all
spanked me for it."

"Well, what else do you want?"

Others' Child slowed her careening to Condor's
stately glide. Up here he seemed not very frightening,
avuncular almost. His dark eye watched her encourag-
ingly. "I wanted to get to where I was going," she said.
"I wanted to belong somewhere."

"And do you?"

"I don't understand them." Below them the canoe
makers were tiny dark dots like ants, making their ant
canoe.

"That is because it isn't the getting there that's important, it's the journey," Condor said. "When you get
to some place, you never understand it."

"That is what Coyote said," Others' Child said accusingly.

"Old Egg Stealer knows what he is talking about
most of the time." Condor nodded his head solemnly.
"He is very old, as old as I am, even if he has no manners."

Others' Child flapped her wings, startled, and tumbled
over Condor. "I thought you wanted me to stay with

these people. I thought that was what I was supposed to do.''

''It was what you wanted to do. Sometimes that amounts to the same thing.''

''I did want it,'' Others' Child said stubbornly.

''You have given these people something they needed. Something they were waiting for.'' Condor floated complacently on a thermal and tipped a dark eye at her. ''Now what happens to you doesn't matter. You have already fulfilled your purpose in the plan.''

''What purpose?''

''Progress,'' Condor said. ''I don't make up the plan,'' he added testily.

Well, *that* wasn't what Coyote had said to her. Not exactly. ''I am not through!'' Others' Child said indignantly.

''Perhaps not,'' Condor said. ''But they don't need you.''

''My husband needs me!''

''Which one?''

Others' Child rolled in the sky again, bottom downward, feet reaching for the air. She beat her wings and climbed onto the thermal like a child climbing onto a rock in the river. ''I have to pay attention,'' she told Condor. She tilted one wing, banked, practicing. A pair of coyotes in the ravine below were eating a woodchuck. Her shadow passed over them, and they looked up at her with teeth bared.

Others' Child soared, climbing toward the sun, its light hot on her back. If she stayed up here, she wouldn't have to think about husbands. She swooped, sailing down the currents like a boat, scattering the coyotes; rose again with a flap of wings past the cool shade of the pines. She would just stay here.

''Your husband needs you,'' Condor said. He nudged her out of the sky.

Others' Child sat down with a bump on the dunes. A dark shape floated above her, ominous again. It soared toward the ravine where she had seen the woodchuck and began to descend.

Others' Child beat her fists on her knees. She lifted her arms to the sky again, but the air didn't take her.

Night Hawk watched the Channel men rowing up the coast. The new canoe was painted a rust color with red earth, and it took eight men to row it. There were shells stuck to its bow with tar. Smaller canoes followed behind and ahead like ducklings around a duck. Night Hawk lay flat on the ridge above the coastline and tried to count the canoes, but his head was swimming, bobbing like the ducks, even though he tried to keep it still. His hand throbbed, and he had got a basket of cold water to soak it in, but it didn't help. When he took it out of the water, Gray Daughter licked it, and that helped some.

He had hidden while the Knifenose Fish men went south to raid the Channel Clan, just as he had thought they would. He had seen them paddle by again with their canoes full of loot. Now he supposed the Channel men would do the same. He should go to the Channel Clan and get his hand seen to; whatever was trying to tell him that had convinced him. But when he stood up, his legs shook, and then he fell down again. It had happened twice. His skin burned when he touched it, too, but he was cold. He wrapped himself in his furs and watched the canoes, the way he had watched a trail of red ants earlier—distantly, as if he were seeing them through something else's eyes and someone had borrowed his own.

While he watched, Knifenose Fish canoes came down the shore from the north, and spears flew over the water. The canoes were beached, and Night Hawk couldn't tell which men were which; they blurred in and out of each other like ghosts. How could he go to their shaman when they were fighting? They might as easily kill him, either side might, for coming from or going to the other side. He didn't trust their rules. Rules were slippery. Others' Child would find that out.

The sand was red when he focused his eyes again. Men were dragging bodies across it, leaving red tracks like snail trails. One man lay facedown in the surf, the foam bubbling around his ears, lifting his hair like kelp as the waves ran up the beach and down again. Blood ran away with the water.

Night Hawk could hear a high thin keening coming from the red canoe. It put out into the surf again, wailing as if it were something alive. Night Hawk was puzzled until he decided it must be the men inside it who were keening. He seemed to hear them in the hills behind him, too. The sunset dazzled the water, pieces of fire going out in it. A man from the Knifenose Fish Clan pulled the dead man from the sand, heaved him over his shoulder, and dropped him into a dugout canoe that bounced on the sea. Night Hawk could see the spirits of the dead men standing on the water, dripping fiery blood. The canoes paddled through them.

Night Hawk got to his feet. The water moved until it was on the other side of the ridge. He could see it shining in the valley where he had slept last night. He tried to walk the other way, toward the sea, where water was supposed to be, but the dogs barked at him. Gray Daughter tugged at his wrist with her teeth. Thief butted him from behind. *You are a fool,* their eyes said to him, but he didn't understand them. He fell, and rolled down the ridge away from the sea.

XIII

The Red Boat

The war with the Knifenose Fish Clan burned in the air like a fire. Others' Child thought she could see it. When she would get up in the morning, she would smell something on the wind that no one else could smell. *Maybe it is because I don't belong to them,* she would think. Then she would remind herself that she did belong, that this was where she had been going, and now she was here. She would try to smell other things in the air, salt fish and sage and clover honey, but the smell of the war was still there, like the faint first taste of food going rancid, smoky and sweet.

The Channel men came back from their raid on the Knifenose Fish Clan bringing another body with them, and being dark and sullen about it. They had killed *two* of the Knifenose Fish men, they said, and wouldn't say more. Then their boats and the Knifenose Fish boats met partway up the coast, and they fought again, and two more men were killed and one drowned when a Knifenose Fish man's spear hit him and he fell out of the boat. The air around the Channel Clan's village was sharp with wailing, and there were new graves on the hillside above, with spears stuck in them to show everyone that warriors had died.

Sea Otter didn't talk to Others' Child anymore. Cannot Be Told didn't talk to anyone; only her male half, Man Who Fights, spoke to the village.

The Knifenose Fish men attacked again and stole a girl. They stuck torches in the thatch of the Channel Clan's houses. Sea Otter's dark eyes watched all this, but he kept silent unless he was fighting. To Others' Child he seemed to be fighting all the time, even when the Knifenose Fish men had been driven off or the Channel men had come home. His face was marked with it, as if someone had drawn war on his cheeks.

"Why can't we send for the Shell Men?" Others' Child asked Blue Butterfly. "My husband has bad dreams every night."

Blue Butterfly patted freshly ground soaproot into a ball. They were going to wash themselves and Little Brother this morning. Some things did not stop because the rest of the world had grown fearsome. Those were the things you held on to.

"It has gone too far," Blue Butterfly said. "No one will admit fault."

"Bone and Tern say it is the fault of Cannot Be Told," Others' Child said, "of having a woman for chieftain. I don't know. I am afraid every time my husband leaves my house, and every time I see men coming up the track until I know they are our men."

"There are six of our men dead," Blue Butterfly said bitterly. "How can anyone ask the Shell Men to say what that is worth? The Knifenose Fish Clan are evil."

"You married your daughter to one."

"I would not marry her there now!" Blue Butterfly spat at the fire. She threw dirt in it and crossed her fingers. "My daughter was right to run away, no matter what is said. I hear the talk, spiteful old witches," she added. She spat at the fire again. "And I will not give back his bride-price now. He owes it me for the grief he's made." She vibrated with anger; anger at the Knife-nose Fish men, anger at her kin, anger at whoever was responsible.

Sea Otter did not speak, but Others' Child heard the rest of the village talk, even when their voices were silent. When their mouths kept still, their true voices hummed in the trees.

"The Knifenose Fish Clan are the enemy now."

"Whatever the Shell Men say will be unfair now. The Knifenose Fish men all lie."

"The Knifenose Fish men will be shamed to be beaten by a woman chieftain. That will make them fight us harder."

"It is all because of the woman who won't give over the chieftainship."

"And the woman who ran away from her husband and stole."

"It is the women who fought when they came to our camp. That has made a bad magic."

"It was the trader's woman who taught them that."

Sea Otter thought about it as he paddled the new red war canoe. He had wanted a woman who was different from the other Channel women, but now all the women seemed to be different. He couldn't see how that was Others' Child's fault, but it *had* happened since she had come. The wonderful pictures had happened, too, of course, the magic likenesses she could pull out of the ground—even Old Tidepool had almost learned to draw a fish. But Sea Otter felt as if he had somehow been too close to the heart of the fire.

A woman cooked and made your clothes and gathered food. She tended your babies and brought them up to be honorable people. That was what his mother had done. A woman did not dress as a man and be chieftain, and Sea Otter harbored the secret fear that this had somehow come about because he had married the magic woman the trader had brought. They were living in a time of legend, Old Tidepool had said to Sea Otter's father; they were living in a story that would be told and told. Sea

Otter was not sure he cared for that. In stories people often died and came to life again, but Sea Otter thought the coming-to-life-again part must have been added later. In the story of the war with the Knifenose Fish Clan, no one had come alive again.

Old Tidepool sat in the next canoe, a lightweight one of tule stalks, dipping his paddle on one side and then the other, looking like a bird on a nest. His eyes were bright with the knowledge that he was living in the time of legend.

Cannot Be Told sat straight as a tree in the bow of the red war canoe, her brown arms dipping the paddle swiftly in the cold gray water. She wore a man's breech-clout and carried her spear-thrower stuck through the lacing of it. Her war spears lay bundled in the bottom of the canoe. Her breasts were painted with red earth, just as the canoe and the men's bare chests were, and the effect was one of looking at two things that occupied the same space at once.

The blue sky overhead shimmered like a hot stone. It was the dry season now, when chia seeds and manzanita berries ripened. The women had harvested the hillsides with gathering baskets, and it was time for the summer burning. Someone—they all claimed credit—had said they should raid the Knifenose Fish Clan while the Knifenose people were out burning their hills. The enemy couldn't leave a fire alone to come and defend their houses, someone had said.

Sea Otter could see the smoke on the horizon inland, where the Knifenose Fish Clan's land met the Channel Clan's. His muscles twitched with the thought of fighting them, of taking back the things that were his, of killing the man who had called his sister a slut while he was cutting down her mother's house. His stomach felt sick when his mind thought these things. It was as if there were two men living inside him, one who liked to fight and one who didn't.

They paddled past the smoke and beached their canoes near the Knifenose Fish Clan's village. The enemy had probably seen them coming, but it didn't matter. The

Channel men would get there first. They slunk up the
trail from the beach in deathly silence. Sea Otter gripped
his spear so tightly his knuckles showed white through
the skin. He thought about the bones underneath and
how easily they could be excised by sharp stone. It was
his last true thought before the fighting.

Only a few old men were left in the Knifenose Fish
camp. The Channel men ran at them, whooping and
howling, letting them know that War was here. The
fighting caught in Sea Otter's throat like a fish bone.
The dust and salt burned his nose, and he choked on
sand kicked up by thrashing feet. Even Cannot Be
Told's tame eagle screamed and flapped in a tree overhead, shrieking for her to hold her arm out for it.

Condor Dancer and Hawk Feet fought methodically,
grunting and stabbing, pushing their way into the camp.
Old Tidepool jumped up and down, yowling, stabbing
his spear at anything that came close. Mostly the Knifenose Fish defenders were too afraid of the shaman to
fight him. They left that to Catches Crows, and so the
two of them stood throwing spells at each other while
the war raged around them.

The old men who were in the camp fought viciously,
and so did the women—all rules were gone, and women
clawed and stabbed with spears. Sea Otter saw one kill
Old Clammer. A death didn't stop the fighting now. No
number of deaths would stop it until the raiders had
taken what they wanted or been driven back. There were
no rules, and so the world tipped, getting ready to slide
people off into darkness.

Sea Otter stabbed his spear at a Knifenose Fish
man's chest, grunting, bracing the shaft with both
hands, wondering why this man had stayed at home.
Maybe he was here to guard the camp. Man Who
Stayed at Home was older than Sea Otter, but he was
not old. His face was barely lined until he twisted it
into a snarl and thrust the shaft of his spear against Sea
Otter's, pushing it out of the way. Sea Otter staggered
aside. He could feel the battle tipping him over. He
caught his balance and lunged again, pushing Man Who

Stayed at Home backwards this time. Everyone around them was fighting except the two shamans, who stood in a cup of red-gold light roaring at each other, their splayed fingers crooked like lightning forks.

The ground was slippery with blood. Sea Otter pushed Man Who Stayed at Home onto it, and he fell. Sea Otter jumped, stabbing his spear down into the bared throat. It went in and stuck in the sand. Sea Otter pulled it out and stared at the red end of it.

The noise was deafening, seagulls screaming, Knifenose Fish women screaming, dogs barking. Sea Otter thought that even the blood made noise. The men's furious shouts hurtled through the air, telling the Knifenose Fish Clan who had won, bragging, *Ha, we have taken your things!*

Condor Dancer grabbed a piece of dry wood and thrust it in someone's fire. He whirled it around his head to fan the flame and stuck it in the nearest roof thatch. The roof exploded in flame.

"Home!" Cannot Be Told roared, and they turned and raced for the canoes. The smoke from the thatch rose to meet the smoke from the burning hills on the horizon. Sea Otter vaulted into the red war canoe, the satisfaction at that so tight in his chest that he thought it would hammer through the ribs. His heart pounded, and his blood sang a vicious little triumph song to the blood on the end of his spear.

They began to row, putting the fury that had fueled the battle into the stroke of the oars. The canoe was piled with shells and hides and whatever else the Channel men had come near. A coil of yucca rope, a child's shirt, a basket of sea grass only half tarred, lay among the jumbled spoils. The shouts and wails behind them intensified. The Knifenose Fish men came running and panting from the hills, their faces and hands blackened with the fire. They poured down the shore toward their own canoes, and the Channel men laughed because they had knocked holes in them as they fled.

"Yah hah, we are warriors!" they shouted as they paddled.

* * *

They were three parts of the way home to their own camp when Cannot Be Told saw flames on their own hillside along the shore. She waved her arms from the bow, shouting to turn, as the others saw it, too. Sea Otter swung his paddle sideways, and Hawk Feet's came up and knocked him in the teeth. They stared at the shore while it exploded in a wall of flame, as if the sun had gone the wrong way and set the edge of the earth on fire. Dark figures ran back and forth in front of the flames waving their arms, still trying to beat them out.

The men swung their canoes into the rolling breakers, bellowing with fury. They beached them on the sand, not even stopping to drag them beyond the high tide line, and scrambled up the cliffs. They scrabbled among the dried kelp and broken shells while the gulls, hysterical with the fire, swirled out to sea.

Sea Otter raced inland behind Cannot Be Told, pushing his way into a wall of heat. Ashes flew in the air, swirling like dust devils, stinging red-rimmed eyes, settling in throats already parched from shouting. The whole unharvested hillside along the coast was in flames.

The women ran along the edges, flailing at it, forced farther and farther back toward the water, their black ghosts edged with red. The air around them shimmered with heat, like ripples on a sheet of water, and cinders rained down angrily. Sea Otter brushed one from his shoulder when he felt it bite into his skin, and Others' Child, face blackened with soot, ran toward him, dragging the hide with which she had been trying to beat out the fire.

"We were cutting the grass," she gasped, "when the Knifenose Fish men were burning their hill. They saw us and came and burned ours. We almost had it out, and then the wind changed." The last words were a wail of despair.

The women kept beating at the fire, crying, dancing around its edges. "Stop!" Cannot Be Told shouted at them. "Get back! You cannot put it out!"

Sea Otter watched a gathering basket, left in the flames, blacken and shrivel. "Where is Brother?" he demanded.

"In the camp," Others' Child said. "With Foam. I nearly brought him, but none of the women will speak to Foam, so she stayed. They are angry with her again because Sand Owl was killed. Everyone is angry at someone else." Her mouth trembled, and tears of exhaustion slid down her sooty face. She looked as if she might lie down there in the tinder-dry grass and give up.

Sea Otter pulled her toward the beach. He saw Blue Butterfly limping ahead of them. No one could walk through the fire. The only way down the coast was to go by water and try to outrun it, stop it with a backfire before it got to the village.

"Run!" Cannot be Told was screaming. "Get in the boats!" The eagle flew above the women, beating them with its wings as if she had sent it to drive them. They staggered down the cliff again, limping and sliding in the loose sand. Most of the boats would hold more than they had been carrying. The cliff above them was on fire now, the dry grass and oily bushes going up like tinder.

Cannot Be Told divided them as they reached the beach: the strongest women and the unwounded men in the red war canoe and the fastest of the dugout boats; the wounded and the old women in the tule boats. Others' Child settled into the canoe against Sea Otter's knees and wrapped her hands around the paddle just below his own. They pulled it together. Behind them six other women were helping paddle. Fisher Skunk paddled behind Cannot Be Told to give Bone and Tern his place. The fire raced them down the shoreline.

This piece of the coast was too close to their home to let it burn; that was why the Channel Clan never burned that field, and why it was choked with dead brush and stunted trees so that now it burned like hatred. The Knifenose Fish men had known that.

They were lucky. The wind died, and they beached the first canoes ahead of the fire. Fisher Skunk and Cannot Be Told stepped apart like two halves of a clamshell.

Only the fire had made them paddle together, because they had learned to do that a long time ago and you didn't forget it no matter how angry you got. Cannot Be Told marched to the fire line without another look at Fisher Skunk and without taking off her men's clothes. The fire was already drifting ash into the village and the people there had set a frantic backfire, to burn off the land in the fire's path and leave it nothing to eat, wetting down the ground behind it with water from the river. Foam was flinging a wet hide over the roof of her mother's house when Others' Child and Sea Otter ran up the trail.

"Where is Brother?" Others' Child shrieked.

"Taking water to the fire line," Foam shouted.

Sea Otter and Others' Child snatched up hides to soak in the river, and more baskets to carry water, and ran toward the flames. They could see the fire now, coming over the mountain like red teeth. The air here was thick with ash. Beyond the first foothills the old men and the children were setting the backfire, and Others' Child could hear it roaring and crackling, as if a piece of the real fire had been unreliably tamed.

They poured their water along the line of the backfire, beating it out with wet hides when it walked the wrong way. It talked to them as they worked, soot and sweat caking their faces, smoke seizing their lungs. *I am hungry,* it said. *I hunger. I eat. I will eat you.*

No, you won't, Others' Child thought, beating it back. Smoke roiled above them in a cloud like a sign, a monstrous signal from the backfire's hunger to that of the wildfire. Slowly the backfire crept toward the wildfire, while behind its line the Channel Clan stamped out embers as they fell in the last dry grass left between the village and the burning hills. The fires met and ate each other up.

The Channel Clan counted their dead and burned, numbly, then buried them and set about thinking how next to harm the enemy. Cannot Be Told held angry councils over it, shouting at Fisher Skunk and Hawk

Feet while they shouted back. One night they went north and set fire to a meadow near the Knifenose Fish Clan's camp, watching with satisfaction as it burned its red way through the dark, and the Knifenose Fish Clan could see how it liked that.

The Knifenose Fish men burned an oak forest that belonged to the Channel Clan, and a Channel man died putting it out. The men came home cursing and somehow bewildered, as if not only the fire had got away from them. *How had this happened?* their faces said while they planned their next raid on the Knifenose Fish Clan.

Others' Child, who had lived among the warlike Kindred as well as the Yellow Grass People—who didn't fight unless they had to, but then fought viciously—thought uneasily that if the People Who Lived at the Coast didn't understand war, if it was a game to them, then this real war would have them looking for someone to blame. And she knew that the someone to be blamed was the women, who had not behaved as women should, and so had tipped the Universe.

She had heard the grumblings about Cannot Be Told and Foam, and also knew that she was credited with having taught them unsuitable ways. Once she had been the shaman who was to teach the Channel women to behave properly. That had been in good times.

Sea Otter took her part defensively, and no one wished to go against him, so there were murmurings rather than shouts. Others' Child felt as if she were a badger being dug from its hole by hundreds of mice rather than one determined coyote. The end effect was the same. Only Old Tidepool seemed to find her presence among them stimulating.

When she heard even the women whispering and asked him what she should do, he only cocked his bright eyes at her and said, "Stories have to tell themselves."

"I am not a story!"

"Yes, you are. I know a story." He seemed pleased. "Everyone will remember me because I was here when this one was told. It began when you came to us. I thought it had.''

The war didn't seem to distress him. He went on all the raids and flung magic at Catches Crows. At home he thought of new spells and made amulets to ward off hers.

''Waxing Moon's baby died,'' Bone spat at Others' Child as they were washing cooking things in the stream. She slapped her basket down hard and sent a spray of dirty water into Others' Child's face.

''Babies die,'' Others' Child said shortly. She wiped a piece of greasy fat from her face. ''I know.''

''Then you shouldn't have given it to her. My husband is dead, too. You shouldn't have come here.''

Others' Child hunched her shoulder away from her.

''Why don't you go to the Shell Men?'' Others' Child pleaded with Sea Otter at night, but Sea Otter was also stubborn.

''No.'' His lips compressed in a firm line. ''You don't understand. The Knifenose Fish Clan has done us evil after evil. We will not forgive them.''

''But they are kin to you!'' And how could he blame the Knifenose Fish Clan and the women at the same time? But he did. Not herself, she thought, but Foam and Cannot Be Told. Maybe herself.

Sea Otter watched her uneasily, not even listening to her argument. ''We never had a war like this before,'' he said. ''I don't know why it has come upon us.'' He seemed to feel it was unstoppable, as if some giant thing had been set in motion and must go on forever of its own momentum, eating everything in its path like the Rolling Head. The Rolling Head was really war, Others' Child thought, endlessly hungry.

She shivered. Since the fire, she was always cold, as if the great heat had sucked all her warmth out with it. *Had* she done this to these people? She didn't know how. *I hurt everything I touch*, she thought miserably.

Sea Otter saw her face and sidled over to her, beside the fire, to put his arm around her. Brother climbed in her lap.

"It is all right," he said, not sounding convinced.

Others' Child kept shivering. There was something in the air tonight, she could smell it, like the old fire waking. It tasted like stones on her tongue. She watched the hairs on Sea Otter's arm lift themselves. He looked puzzled.

Others' Child sat up straight. "Storm," she whispered.

It was the wrong time of year for a storm. In the dry season no one along the coast thought of rain, much less the kind of storm that flared and raged over the red mountains where Others' Child had come from. But there it was, Others' Child peered through the door of their house. It was only afternoon, but the air was growing thick and blackish-gray, and the trees bent in the wind. It was not a right storm for this place, Others' Child thought as lightning flared, burning its snake shape into her eyes. Had she brought it with her?

Thunder boomed behind the lightning like stones grinding together. Others' Child buried her face in Sea Otter's chest. The storm felt personal, as if it had come for her, to root her out of this place where she had only caused trouble.

The wind whipped the trees, but no rain came with it to wash away the sharp scent of lightning. The clouds crackled again and loosed the water that was in them over the far mountains. Only the lightning came down the coast, fiery fingers burning their way to the ground. They sank into the dry hills, the ones the Channel Clan had saved, and burned straight through the earth.

The wind whipped the air through the dry grass and the brush that had never been burned away. The lightning opened its mouth and ate it, belching out flame. New fire grew, walking through the hills on red legs, roaring up and down the canyons.

Night Hawk fled ahead of it. When he looked at the trees, they turned slowly end over end, so he quit looking and put one foot in front of the other, methodically, eyes closed, with the heat of the fire on his back to tell him he was going the right way. His hand, tied up in a thong sling, bumped his chest with every step, and the waves of pain seemed to meet the heat of the fire and melt into it.

The travois bumped along the ground behind the dogs, things falling off it. Thief and Gray Daughter sat down and chewed through the traces while Night Hawk reeled among the trees. When they caught up with him, he was standing with his face in a pine's trunk, as if he had stopped walking when he encountered its barrier and nothing in his head seemed able to remember how to go around it. They nudged him on, pushing him past the tree.

Night Hawk stared blindly at the weaving, undulating air that pulsed in time to the pain in his hand. Since he had watched the Channel men fight the Knifenose Fish men, he had lived in a cave that Thief and Gray Daughter had shown him. His head had been clearer then, and he had come on a jumble of red sandstone rocks jutting out from the hill, with enough overhang to sleep under and build a fire that would keep Puma out. Night Hawk had crawled under the rocks and dosed his thumb with remedies the old Grannies had taught him, because he was too sick to walk anywhere else. Mostly he slept or had fever dreams about looking for things he couldn't find.

He had smelled the smoke from the fire the Knifenose Fish men had set and watched it lick up the hillside, getting ready to run if he had to. When it stopped, he went to sleep again, exhausted, and dreamed that he watched Condor sweeping the ashes away with a rush broom. Where they had been, new little people came up in tidy rows. Once he thought he smelled Coyote in the smoke, but she never said anything to him.

Now there was fire again, and it was on his heels. Night Hawk stood weaving and cursed the Knifenose Fish Clan who had played with fire and so called this one up. He looked over his shoulder and suddenly saw it coming after him. The dogs had run ahead, and he couldn't see them. The air was getting thick with smoke, and his lungs burned in his chest. The infected hand throbbed as if he held a piece of the fire in it.

Night Hawk lurched through the dry foxtail grass and oak leaves, looking for the dogs. Jumping mice and grasshoppers skittered under his feet, and a fox went by with her kits after her, diving frantically through the grass. Crows clouded the sky overhead, screaming *Fire!*

The voice of the fire roared back to them, and he heard a tree crash behind him. He floundered on through the smoke. Thief and Gray Daughter were shadows he couldn't find, sucked up by the smoke.

The new fire roared down the canyons faster than the lightning had gone up them, spreading its ravenous mouth and licking up the brush. Blocked by the charred hillsides of the old fire, it turned toward the coast and came down on the village like a vengeful ghost, a flaming revenant eternally hungry. Before the Channel Clan could fight it, it had swept nearly to the village, driven by the capricious winds that lifted burning debris and sent it soaring into new tinder. Another fire grew from this one's seed between the village and the shore, and the people were driven back toward the first fire. Only a narrow gap lay open to the sea.

"Leave it!" Cannot Be Told bellowed into the wind and the roar of the flames. She knocked an armload of baskets and a fur cape from Tern's arms. "You can't carry anything!" She shoved at Tern and then ran to drag Blue Butterfly forward. Others' Child pushed her mother-in-law from behind.

"My spoons," Blue Butterfly wailed.

Sea Otter picked up Brother, and they went, pushing Blue Butterfly ahead of them. Condor Dancer was somewhere ahead, trying to beat out the flames along the trail.

"Where is Foam?" Blue Butterfly screamed.

"I saw her," Others' Child screamed back over the flames. "She went already." She hoped she had.

They could hear the fire behind them before they got to the water. It raged on their heels, hurling shards of flaming debris. The dry sea grass on the beach was burning in patches as they clambered down to it, and the air was thick with vicious ash. The tule canoes caught fire and went up in a single moment like roof thatch.

Cannot Be Told was pushing children into the red war canoe and telling the oldest ones to paddle it. They screamed and clung to their mothers, and the mothers fought to get in the canoe with them. Others' Child dragged Little Brother toward the canoe, but it was full. Cannot Be Told was driving mothers away, pushing the canoe out into the breakers. The clan retreated back up the beach to squabble over the dugout canoes while Cannot Be Told and Old Tidepool shouted at them.

"Follow me!" Old Tidepool bellowed, jumping up and down, and finally some of them did, stringing out in a line along the beach, going north to get ahead of the fire. If they could get far enough, they would come to the shoreline that had burned less than a moon ago, where this fire would find nothing to eat.

Sea Otter gave a look of disgust at the ones who were fighting over the canoes. He took Others' Child's hand and pulled Little Brother along with his left. They staggered up the beach, feet sinking in dry sand, legs aching. It was almost high tide, and the water lapped among jagged black rocks that sprouted from the shore. Burning debris sizzled at their feet, hissing at them as it went out, little vicious curses. The air was choked with ash, and Others' Child's lungs ached. She could hear Little Brother gasping.

The rocks, slimy with kelp, grew thicker and harder to climb over. Others' Child knew that the rocks ahead rose straight up in bluffs that hung over the ocean and that at high tide the water beneath them was too deep to stand in. She tried to run faster, floundering in loose sand between the outcroppings.

"Where is Foam?" Blue Butterfly shrieked again. Condor Dancer dragged her on. Bone trudged behind them in silence, tears streaming down her blackened face. When Blue Butterfly wailed again for Foam, Bone threw sand at her, a mean, impotent gesture. The sand fell unnoticed behind her.

It was hard to see for the ash in the air. Others' Child's eyes stung. The cliffs were creeping out into the water, and they skirted them, plunging through knee-deep surf, battered by the waves. The grass above was burning in crackling patches, and cinders and sparks floated from it, falling like fierce stars.

"Hurry!" Condor Dancer shouted. "We can climb up if we can get there before the fire." He pointed at the place where the cliffs rose sharply, but where the Channel Clan had cut a path to hunt for birds' eggs.

They all began to run, floundering in the surf. A wave knocked Little Brother down, and Sea Otter grabbed for him desperately as the retreating undertow pulled him away. Others' Child let go of Sea Otter and dived through the cold water, kicking and sputtering, until she caught Little Brother by the ankle. She and Sea Otter fought the water for him. As the breakers sucked back again, he surfaced, floating limply facedown, a piece of seaweed borne on the surface. They pulled him to them, and Sea Otter put the child over his shoulder. Others' Child pounded Brother's back, frantically beating her fists on his wet skin as the waves roared around them. Little Brother coughed and threw up water and began to thrash, terrified, on Sea Otter's shoulder. Others' Child held out her arms for him, and he clung to her, wrapping his legs around her waist, coughing and sobbing. In a few more steps, the water was waist-high.

Ahead of them, Cannot Be Told raced for the path up the cliffs, waving at them to follow her. The wind had changed, and the fire was slowing. Sea Otter and Others' Child plunged through the water again, their sandals sliced to ribbons on the rocks. Sea Otter could see blood dripping pinkly from Little Brother's feet whenever they lifted above the water. The waves battered the base of the cliff while they watched the fire move along the top.

"Climb!" Cannot Be Told shouted. She pushed Old Tidepool ahead of her. He scrambled up, and she began pushing the next one after him. The Channel Clan milled in the water, watching the fire. Only one person could go up the path at a time, and it wasn't easy. Hawk Feet splashed past it suddenly and began to climb alone, farther along the cliff base, clinging precariously to the wet rock. Two men and a woman ran after him.

Sea Otter watched Old Tidepool scramble to the top and fall, his legs sticking half over the cliff. Someone shoved him from behind, and the legs disappeared. The fire roared closer as the wind whipped around from the south again. There were too many people ahead of them. Sea Otter pulled Others' Child away, toward the ocean.

"We have to go up!" she shouted at him.

"No! The fire is coming too fast and the water will get too deep. And Brother can't climb that." Sea Otter's soot-smeared face was adamant. He grabbed Others' Child and dragged her into deeper water. While she floundered, crying, over the sharp stones, he put Little Brother on his shoulders again.

Cannot Be Told was climbing, pushing the last straggler ahead of her. Burning grass blew around her head like feathers. Overhead she could hear the eagle shrieking, afraid of the flames and afraid to fly away. That was what happened when you tamed something, she thought. It couldn't go back and it burned up. Was that what had happened with her? She knew she couldn't go back now, not from being chieftain. It was the chieftain's job to see to the clan. If the gods wanted her before they would stop the fire, then that was chieftain's work, too.

The fire was almost to the head of the path, but there was no use going back down. She climbed into the face of it. The tide was all the way in, banging against the rocks, smashing anybody left at the bottom. Rocks tumbled down on her head from above, and someone screamed. Cannot Be Told heard fingers clawing at air— they made a sound inside her head like the eagle's screams—and saw Bone fall. Cannot Be Told flattened herself against the cliff face and tried to catch her. Her hand reached out to Bone's flying hair and the flames that licked the hem of Bone's skirt, but she hurtled past Cannot Be Told's grip like a falcon falling.

More screams came from the top of the cliff. Cannot

Be Told clawed her way up into what the world might look like from the center of a burning fire pit. The air was black and thick with smoke and smoldering ash. The ground was covered with patches of flames. The only thing she could hear was the voice of the fire. Hot ash burned through what was left of her sandals, and she danced frenziedly, looking for cool ground, but there was none. She ran away from the fire with the rest, burned feet sending pain up her legs with every step.

The Channel Clan fled coughing through the smoke, running up-coast along the bluffs, trying to outrace the fire. Cannot Be Told saw a child with its hair on fire, and wrapped her arms around its head to smother the flames. The child looked at her with a ghastly blistered face and ran on. Cannot Be Told felt the burns sizzle into her arms, but they didn't hurt more than her feet. Her breasts were splotched with blisters from falling cinders, and she could see the raw flesh bubble under the ash. "Run!" she shouted to the fleeing clan as they wavered, wandering in the heat, bearings lost. "Stay ahead of it. Run!"

The fire roared along the coast, its hands reaching ahead, picking up people on the bluffs. Most who fell died of the smoke before the flames reached them. Some panicked and blundered back off the cliffs again to smash on the rocks below as Bone had. Most outran the fire to the end of the bluffs and climbed back down into shallow water again, where a wide sandy beach had nothing to burn. They stumbled into the water, screaming as the salt ate at their burns.

Cannot Be Told pushed the burned child ahead of her. She saw its mother lying in the sea grass and picked the woman up. Together they staggered down the trail to the beach, where she handed the burned mother to Fisher Skunk. She turned back to the cliffs.

Fisher Skunk watched her climb up them. He could have shouted at her to come back, but he didn't. There were still people on top of the cliffs. Burned people, probably dead people, but they were still the chieftain's business until they were all dead. Cannot Be Told's broad-shouldered form moved up through the smoke away from him. She didn't come down again.

Others' Child floundered in the cold sea, trying not to cling too hard to Sea Otter, who was holding up Little Brother. The shore was a billow of black smoke and red flame, looking as if some huge and angry fire animal were raging along it. Even this far out in the cold water the smoke was like breathing knives. At first they could see dark figures running past the flames, but soon there was no movement but the fire.

Sea Otter looked north, and Others' Child knew he was trying to decide if they should swim or wait and hope the fire burned itself out. Her legs ached unbearably. Where had the red war canoe gone with the other children? she wondered. Where had Condor Dancer and Blue Butterfly gone? And Foam? She never had seen Foam. She had lied to Blue Butterfly to get her moving.

A shriek cut through the smoke over their heads. Others' Child looked up. Cannot Be Told's eagle flew past, banked, and turned to circle them again. It screamed in bewildered fury and flew away, this time straight out toward the horizon. Maybe it would fly to the Shell Men and tell them, Others' Child thought. Maybe it would just keep flying.

The fire had started as a wildfire, lightning-sparked, but now it was following a path carved out for it by the Knifenose Fish Clan and the Channel Clan, a path of thick brush and dry summer growth that led between the blackened hills. Everywhere that the Channel men or the Knifenose Fish men had saved the land from the others' burning, the new fire went. It roared up the coast like a snake, twisting through the dry brush.

The Knifenose Fish Clan ran to fight it, but it was no use. It ate the bluffs by their village in one gulp, and they fled inland, pursued by its hot breath.

Staggering a few steps ahead of the flames, his face blistered and eyebrows singed, Night Hawk blundered along a canyon wall until he found a hole in it. He went in and the dogs followed, their eyes gleaming with terror. They had not gone far from him. He had expected them to leave him and run, but they were dogs and had no idea of how to run. He was their human; he would know what to do, they thought.

The cave was deep, a narrow passage going into the hillside, at times so close that Night Hawk had to turn sideways to fit through. The dogs started to growl, but he pushed his way along. If there was something living in here already, it couldn't be worse than fire. Bear probably wouldn't fit, he thought, and then fell over something furry in his path. Night Hawk leaped up, scrambling away from it, and fell on skin.

"Who is it?" a voice snapped. Hands pushed him away and felt along his arms and legs.

"It's only the trader," someone else said before Night Hawk could answer. He thought he had fallen into a bigger room at the end of the passage. "Old Hunter here can smell those coyote dogs of his."

The dog he had tripped over was growling, and Thief and Gray Daughter snarled back. Night Hawk cuffed at all of them blindly. "Peace be with the house," he said, a ritual formula that covered any entrance into someone else's territory. He heard a scraping on stone as an arm reached out and grabbed Old Hunter by the scruff of the neck. He wondered if they were Channel men or Knifenose Fish men, and if they would have killed him if he had been one of the enemy kind.

"How many are here?" Night Hawk asked.

"Five of us."

The air smelled smoky, and he wondered if they were going to suffocate when the fire burned past. He coughed.

"Over here," someone said. Hands pushed him toward the back of the cave. A faint breath of cool air brushed his face.

"This is a sacred cave," the voice said sternly, as if the speaker thought he might defile it. "There is air through this crack. Sit still so you don't use up too much of it.''

"Don't cough," the other voice instructed him.

Night Hawk lay down on the cool stone of the cave floor. He knew he must be burned, but it was hard to tell in the dark. His whole body felt as hot as his injured hand, and when he touched the skin on his legs, it felt sticky. He thought about asking these people who they were, and if they had a torch, but it was too much trouble. What was burned was burned. Maybe he was dead already and underground in the Skeleton House, and these were his own people. He felt his leg again to see if it was bones, but there was still skin on it. The skin hurt. And the dogs were not bones. He felt Gray Daughter's singed fur. It was brittle, frayed on the ends, and one patch of it near her tail seemed to be gone altogether. She snapped at him when he touched it.

Night Hawk could hear the fire roaring outside the cave, and the air inside grew thicker with smoke. He breathed shallowly and closed his eyes. If he was dead, he might see Others' Child and Little Brother. Maybe they had been burned, too. He felt ashamed of the hope that they could all be dead together, ashamed of wanting them that badly.

XIV

What Bat Said

Night Hawk woke because the people in the cave were pushing him, poking him in the ribs with their fingers.

"Are you dead, Trader?"

"He is breathing. I can feel it."

A palm pressed flat against his chest, and Thief began to growl at the liberty taken. Night Hawk batted at the growl to quiet him. "I am not dead," he whispered.

"Good. We thought you might be."

"Get up, then." Hands grabbed him under the arms.

They stumbled single file through the passage, half dragging Night Hawk along. At the cave mouth he bumped into the ones in the front, who had stopped and stood blinking in the sun, staring at the wasteland that smoldered outside. One of them began to sob.

Night Hawk saw that these were Knifenose Fish people. He remembered Not in a Hurry, Foam's husband. Not in a Hurry had been holding him up. Now he stepped back and let Night Hawk prop himself against the blackened stone of the cave mouth. The dogs peered out from behind his legs and whined.

The land was blasted, as if rot had passed over it. Black and desolate, with the charred shards of trees sticking up from still-glowing embers. Even the red stones of the canyon were as smoke-darkened as a fire pit. The smell of charred flesh hung in the air, and Night Hawk saw the corpse of a bear, twisted and smoking, splayed out in the dry wash that ran along the canyon bottom. Its teeth showed white in the blackened skull, biting on nothing.

He looked down at his legs. They were blistered and weeping under the soot, and the skin on his feet had cracked open. The bandage on his hand was gone, and his hand was so black he couldn't see the wound.

The hills around them were blacker, ravaged and brittle like burned bones as far as they could see.

A woman took Night Hawk under the arm. "We have to leave this place," she said gently. He saw that her lips were blistered and her eyes ringed with soot. "We have to find water."

They began to walk, putting bare feet down gingerly. The ashes were still warm, and here and there a live coal lay buried in them. In the center of a split tree, Night Hawk could see the red, glowing eye of the fire.

Not in a Hurry went ahead. His sandals were not quite burned off, despite the cracks that went clear to raw flesh. While the rest picked their way whimpering through the coals, he climbed slowly to the canyon's rim.

He came back down shaking his head. "All burned." He spread wide his dirty, blistered hands. "Maybe inland, where the Manzanita Clan are. Maybe the Channel Clan still has living land. I don't know."

"Where is the closest water?" the woman asked, practical.

"Below White Rock," Not in a Hurry said. "It may be burned, too."

"Water doesn't burn." She looked at him fiercely from reddened eyes. Night Hawk remembered her now.

She was Grass Laughs, the chieftain's wife. There were three other men, but he didn't see the Knifenose Fish chief among them.

Night Hawk tried to speak. His mouth was full of ashes. He pried it open. "We have to have water," he said. It was the first coherent statement he had made, and they looked at him as if that conferred upon it incontrovertible, perhaps holy meaning.

Night Hawk moved his tongue inside his parched mouth. He stared at them glassily and toppled over.

Not in a Hurry and another man picked him up. They turned east toward the pool by White Rock, three humans and three dogs, with two more humans carrying the sixth. The sun was low, and they cast elongated shadows across the burned ground, a dark multilegged shape that scuttled on the ground like a spider.

Others' Child crawled from the surf, her head bent nearly to the wet sand. Above her the hills were black and silent, only ash drifting like feathers on the air. Sea Otter came behind her, carrying Little Brother. Even the ocean seemed quieter. The tide was going out, and they could see Bone's body at the foot of the bluffs, wedged between two rocks, her long hair splayed out like a sea anemone. There would be other bodies in the water. They would wash up, bloated and unrecognizable, to break the hearts of the ones who hadn't died.

Others' Child rocked back and forth on the sand, her arms around her rib cage, retching.

Sea Otter was swaying on his feet, clutching Little Brother. "Get up," he said to her. "We have to find water."

The water that flowed a day downstream from White Rock was foul with ash and dead fish. But it still flowed, and the grass around it was unburned, a miraculous small stripe of green and yellow at the bottom of the charred hills, a straggling of white poppies clinging to its upper edges, sooty and battered as if they alone had held off the fire.

Maybe they had, Others' Child thought, limping down the black hill, her mouth yearning for the stream. They looked like sentinel gods, unexpected in the desolation. She licked her lips, thinking about the water. She and Sea Otter had had to fight Little Brother to keep him from drinking sea water. He had cried all the way from the shore, until he had gone to sleep on Sea Otter's shoulder.

There were already people at the stream: Fisher Skunk and Tern, Old Tidepool tending everyone's burns, and Foam, sitting sullenly by the water, staring at the black land beyond the white poppies as if she thought the fire might still come for her. Some of the men were scooping up the dead fish with a net so they could be eaten before they rotted. Others' Child saw a trout float by, white-eyed, its gills clogged with ash. She knelt on the bank, holding Little Brother while he drank first, trying not to think about the trout.

Sea Otter drank and sat down beside Foam. He touched her singed face. "We were afraid you were burned."

"No." Foam sniffled. "I was on the beach when I saw the fire. I took a tule boat out and sat in it."

"What were you doing on the beach?"

"I was going to run away. Somewhere else. It doesn't matter now. Father took my tule boat to the Shell Men, and we will all have to do what *they* say."

"Father is all right?"

"And Mother. I found them on the beach. But she went with him to the Shell Men, without even finding any water first. She said that if she didn't go with him the fire would still get him. Mother is getting old and crazy."

"She has a right to," Sea Otter said.

Foam hung her head. "I have been bad. I wanted a man I would feel that way about, the way Mother feels about Father. Now I have made this happen."

"No, you haven't." Others' Child lifted her head abruptly. "You didn't burn those meadows. And you can't make your heart want a man it doesn't want. Or stay someplace it doesn't want to be.''

"That doesn't make it not her fault," Sea Otter said. He took Others' Child by the elbow. "Now we have to get in the water and wash, and see what is burned."

Others' Child flinched. It would hurt. Sea Otter pushed her in, step by step. Foam picked up Little Brother, walked out into the stream with him, and sat down in the water with him in her lap. Others' Child clenched her teeth and followed them. The cold bit into her blistered skin like teeth.

More people came at dusk, stumbling up the stream-bank, and slowly the Channel Clan took stock of its survivors. Most of them were burned, more or less badly. Some who had been carried here by the rest would not live, and everyone knew it. Others' Child listened to their moans and tried to close her ears while she pounded salve in a shallow stone under Old Tide-pool's direction. To make medicine, they had only what they could find along the stream. He made a wash of elder leaves and a salve of oil from the dead fish to keep the skin supple. Hawk Feet's hands were badly burned, and he cursed Others' Child while she dosed them. Old Clammer's wife, Onion Woman, was burned over nearly all her body. Others' Child washed her with elder leaves and gave her willow tea and waited for her to die. Onion Woman didn't want to live anyway, with her son and her husband dead, but she was taking a very long time to die, and she moaned incessantly, a thin whimper that set everyone's teeth on edge because they couldn't stop it, had no way to make her stop hurting.

They had no chieftain now. Everyone had seen Cannot Be Told go back up the cliffs. Sea Otter began to tell them what to do, and no one argued with him.

Old Tidepool, still half covered with ashes, looked like a black crow who had been mauled by a coyote. Tending to everyone who was burned, he hadn't slept in two days, and had no time for things like how to hunt or who should dig a cook pit, except to tell them to clear the dead fish from the water. The men straggled out to hunt and came back with very little: a singed rabbit and a burrow dog dug from its hole.

"Tomorrow we will move," Sea Otter announced.

"You will kill that one." Others' Child pointed at Onion Woman.

"She will die anyway," Sea Otter snarled. He turned away from her. Everyone's nerves were raw with listening to Onion Woman scream. He clenched and unclenched his fists slowly. "There is unburned land farther upstream at White Rock, where the pool is. We have seen where the burned land stops, but it is too far to come and go from here. There will be something to eat there."

"Yes. All right." Others' Child touched his arm gently. "All right."

They put Onion Woman on a travois made of brushwood and pulled her along, closing their ears to the sound. Halfway to White Rock, Old Tidepool gave her another drink of willow tea, and she died. They carried the body more easily now, relief running down their skin like sweat.

Others' Child didn't ask Old Tidepool what had been in the willow tea.

At White Rock the stream spread out into a wide pool ringed with willows, deep enough to bathe in and soak the burned skin loose. As Sea Otter had said, the land around it was still golden, thick with summer grass and dotted with oak trees. Here, too, white poppies stood like guardians. Higher up, there were pines in the steep rocks, and pine nuts to eat. It was far from the coast, but they would have something to keep them alive here until the burned hills sprouted again.

The land would sprout. Others' Child knew that. She had watched the hillsides that they burned away on purpose and had seen them turn green again. But the people wouldn't sprout, not the burned ones. There were more besides Onion Woman who were just waiting to die, and more yet among the ones who straggled in each day.

The women tended the burned, and the men sharpened digging sticks in the fire to cut graves into the dry hillside.

The morning after the day after they came to the pool, three Knifenose Fish people walked into the camp. One was the shaman, Catches Crows, leaning on her walking stick, her black eyes like shiny stones in her sooty face. She and Old Tidepool stood and looked at each other for a long time, while the Channel Clan waited to see what he would do.

Finally Old Tidepool sighed. "We are ashamed of ourselves."

The two shamans, the old man and the old woman, went away together to talk of medicine, and the Knifenose Fish people came into the camp.

The next day five more came, with three dogs at their heels and another man between them, barely walking, his arms supported on two men's shoulders.

Foam looked once and then pretended that she couldn't see Not in a Hurry.

"Your old husband is here, too," Tern said to Others' Child.

Others' Child looked up from her mortar. "My old husband has gone home," she said, shaking her head. "Why would he stay for a war? He is not stupid."

"I don't know, but he's here. He looks like Onion Woman. He is all burned."

Others' Child stood up. Why should she have to see him that way? Why should she have to see him die? That wasn't fair of someone. She walked over to the little group by the pool, and the dogs came up to her. Thief butted his head into her knees. Night Hawk was lying on the ground where they had put him, looking at the sky.

"We have to wash you," Others' Child said to him.

He blinked his eyes at her, squinted them shut hard, and opened them again. She wasn't sure what he was seeing.

"Take him down to the water," she said. She looked

for Little Brother. Sea Otter had scooped Brother up in his arms. Good.

They carried Night Hawk to the pond and waded in with him. He screamed when the water hit his burns. Others' Child gritted her teeth and washed him, running her hands down his flanks, scrubbing gently with the yucca soap she had made that morning, remembering the angle of his bones.

"Hold him still," she said between her teeth when he tried to fling himself away from her. She pretended he was Tern or Hawk Feet or anyone else whose burns she had washed. His injured hand was black and crusted with soot and dirt. When she began to clean it, he slumped suddenly between the two men holding him.

Others' Child washed away the dried blood and pus, and hoped he wouldn't wake up until she was through. This wasn't a burn, she saw. The infected flesh went nearly to the bone. But there were burns, too, crusted blisters on his legs and face and back. When they dragged him out of the water, she found the cut on his foot, still unhealed.

Foam and Tern had cut a bed of grass without being asked, and Others' Child had them put Night Hawk on it, wishing for a hide to keep the grass out of his burns. Everyone in the camp was nearly naked, and a blanket was beyond even wishing for. She knelt beside him, listening to his breath, wondering how that breathing could be so familiar, how it could make a sound that she would have known anywhere in a dark cave of sleeping men. She put her knuckles between her teeth so she wouldn't say anything. Who knew who was listening to her?

She snuck a look at the sky, but Condor wasn't there waiting for Night Hawk. Condor's children floated in the blue above the burned land, but not over the pool. Maybe he wasn't going to die. And if he didn't die, what was she going to do with him?

She stared at the yucca soap in her hand. She had boiled it herself from one of the spiky plants she found growing in the rocks. Tern had sniffed at it because it wasn't what the Channel Clan washed with, but Old

Tidepool had been interested. Others' Child put the soap away in the ragged grass basket she had made in a hurry to hold it. It wouldn't wash some things away, she knew that.

The next day Condor Dancer came with five of the Shell Men, with Blue Butterfly still walking just behind him, hands outstretched as if she would catch him if he fell, or snatch him from flames that might leap up at his feet. The Shell Men wore strings of shells like skirts around their middles that clicked when they walked. The Channel people and the Knifenose Fish people looked shamefaced, as if they had been caught stealing something. Old Tidepool and Catches Crows talked for a long time with the chief of the Shell Men, and the chief nodded solemnly. In his lifetime he had seen nearly everything that human people could think of to do. When it was over, Old Tidepool and Catches Crows began to look less hunched over, straightening themselves in their skins. They had used power badly, for the sake of being in a story, and now nobody could think how that had happened. They scratched their heads, and said that Coyote must have got into somebody's brain.

The Shell Men had brought medicine for burns, and a stack of blankets, and a big basket of acorn meal. Sea Otter told Others' Child to take charge of them, as if it were natural that he should give the orders. Others' Child made beds for the burned ones out of the blankets, while she tried to listen to what the Shell Men were saying. For the rest of the day they conferred with Sea Otter and Condor Dancer and the chief of the Knifenose Fish Clan, who had come into the camp yesterday, their voices murmuring on like the surf, authoritative. They would sort everything out now and make order, Others' Child supposed.

She sat among the burned, staring at the landscape of Night Hawk's body, the scarred, red rolling hills of his hip and ribs, the dark, ragged sea of his singed hair, the charred branches of his fingers. Thief and Gray Daughter lay on either side of him. Gray Daughter stuck her nose in Others' Child's hand.

Night Hawk opened his eyes. "Are you dead?" he asked her wistfully, but his blistered lips had trouble making the words.

It felt like lightning in her hair to feel him seeing her and to hear his voice. "No," she said carefully, arranging her words in a neat row like small stones, so that they didn't tumble away, saying things she hadn't told them to. She didn't say, *You may be.* "What have you done to your hand?"

He looked at it curiously, lifting his head. There was a dressing of cattail fluff and salve on it. "It won't heal," he said.

Others' Child bit her lip. "You are burned, too," she told him.

"Are you the one who washes me?" he asked.

"It has been me. I can ask Old Tidepool, if you—"

"No." He reached a hand out to her. His blistered fingers closed on hers. "I want you. I saw Coyote," he went on conversationally, but he was looking over her shoulder. "She—"

"*She?*" Others' Child said. But he had let the words drift off. He was still looking over her shoulder, but Others' Child didn't think he could really see anything now. Slowly his eyes closed again. Others' Child put a hand flat on his chest. His heart thumped under it. So close to the skin, she thought. *Everything inside us is so close to the skin.* If the skin was burned away, it was so easy for life to spill out.

Others' Child was praying. She put three pieces of elder bark and three white poppy heads and a green stone she had found in the stream on a flat leaf. She sprinkled a pinch of acorn meal over it. "It's all I have," she said. "All our masks and magic capes are burned up. If you will take this and make him not die, I will give you great honor when we go back to the coast, when our people are well enough to dance for you. All of you," she added, not really sure to how many of them she was talking: surely to Coyote, who always ate things that were injured; and Great Condor, for whose black wings she watched fearfully every evening, neck craned to the sky; but also to Grandmother Spider, who wove everything in her web; and to Knifenose Fish, who might have some influence here; and the Fire God; and the two War Gods of Night Hawk's Kindred, in case they had followed him here and done this. She tried to think of others. If she had had some maize she would have given it to her father's restless spirit. She went and got Night Hawk's flute instead, and sat and played it over her collection of offerings. She played badly, not like Father had, or Night Hawk or Mocking Bird. It sounded like something crying. She flung it in her lap and stared fiercely at it. "Just don't let him die," she told it.

When she came back, she found that the Shell Men had ordered the world again. They stood in a row and spoke in unison, while the Channel Clan and the Knifenose Fish Clan listened. Condor Dancer and Blue Butterfly were to give Foam's bride-price back, but they did not have to do it until the next year, when the Channel Clan would be rich once more. Foam looked at her toes while Not in a Hurry listed what she had been worth to him.

"Three deer hides and four fox skins and five good baskets of abalones," he said. Not in a Hurry looked at the Shell Men. "That is a long time to wait for them back. I do not want to wait that long."

"You are lucky that you have not had them back already," the Shell Men said. "Then they would be burned. We saw the spirits of your dead and the Channel Clan's dead, going across the water, carrying all their hides and boats."

"If they would be burned anyway, then my father should not have to pay," Foam said.

"Be quiet," Condor Dancer and Sea Otter and the Shell Men said together.

"We will talk of injuries now," the Shell Men said. The two clans nodded solemnly, and the Shell Men pronounced compensation: For every man dead from the fighting, the other clan would pay a deer hide. If there were any stolen girls, they would be returned now.

"And if any man has taken liberties with one, he will marry her and pay her father," the Shell Men added, looking sternly at the young men.

The young men shook their heads earnestly.

"One sealskin for each burned house."

Condor Dancer and the Knifenose Fish chieftain began to count.

"Three sealskins for the stolen mask. Also, the woman who stole it must cut off her hair and give it to Octopus."

Foam howled, but Blue Butterfly took a skinning knife and hacked it off then and there, jerking Foam into submission by the ear. "It will grow. Be glad they do not want me to give *you* to Octopus," she said. She handed the shock of black hair to the oldest of the Shell Men, who stuffed it in a sharkskin pouch, patting it down as if it had been alive.

Foam pulled at the ragged ends of her hair.

"She is not so beautiful as I thought," Not in a Hurry said to Grass Laughs. He shook his head. "I was deceived."

"Furthermore." The Shell Men coughed and waited until everyone paid attention. "If each village owes the other the same number of hides, you will still pay them. This is to make you remember that war is not a good business and can never be made even, despite our best advice."

Everyone looked ashamed again. The chieftain of the Knifenose Fish Clan said, "We will go back to our own place now and find a new camp." No one wanted to fight, but no one wanted to live together, either.

The Channel Clan nodded. There was too much to remember and be ashamed of.

"What about him?" Sea Otter pointed at Night Hawk. He made it sound as if he had just thought of it.

The Knifenose Fish chieftain shook his head. "We will leave the trader because he is not ours. He cannot

be moved, anyway. Our shaman says he is to stay here.''
He looked with dislike at Thief and Gray Daughter.
''His dogs do not want to go.''

Sea Otter compressed his lips. It would be a wicked
thing to tell your wife not to tend a man who was so
badly burned, a man who might die. But when that man
was her first husband and you watched her eyes mem-
orizing the lines in his face and the little bones of his
spine . . . well, then you might find yourself hoping that
he did die, and that was not good for your own soul.

Night Hawk did not die, not yet. The burns healed,
making thick, tight, ridged pink scars, one of which
pulled his left eyebrow up so that the two halves of his
face didn't match. But the injured hand still gave him
feverish dreams, and his skin was hot to the touch. Little
Brother brought things he thought Night Hawk would
like—gifts of a white stone, a green worm, a small sil-
very fish in a basket of water—and sat with him most
of the day, cuddled between the dogs. Sea Otter tried
not to be jealous of that, too, since Night Hawk could
only see them sometimes, and sometimes he couldn't.
Sometimes he saw things that weren't there.

Around him, some of the other burned ones died, and
some got well. The Channel Clan soaked willow poles
for new houses, and put up brush huts to live in for the
meantime, and walked to the marsh to cut thatch and
reeds for baskets, and otherwise became civilized people
again, while Night Hawk hovered in a world between
earth and the Skeleton House, his spirit sometimes in his
head and sometimes roaming, across the water maybe,
where Others' Child thought that the Shell Men might
see it wandering.

Finally, one morning when three parts of a green
moon had gone by, Old Tidepool went to look at him
and came in a hurry to get Others' Child.

''This hand has to be burned.'' Old Tidepool lifted
Night Hawk's arm for Others' Child to see. ''Otherwise
we will have to cut it off.''

Others' Child's breath hissed. The skin along the

edges of the wound was turning black, and it smelled, the unmistakable, fetid odor of death.

Night Hawk opened his eyes. "I'll put a knife'n you if you do it," he said. The words were slurred, but his other hand fumbled, looking for one.

Others' Child stood inert, solidified with fear; she could see the thing coiled inside Night Hawk's hand like a dark snake. Old Tidepool pressed the hand, and dark pus ran out. Night Hawk screamed, and his eyes rolled back in his head.

The dogs had been watching, and now the newly grown fur on Thief's back lifted. He lowered his head with a rattling snarl. Gray Daughter closed her jaws around Old Tidepool's wrist, not breaking the flesh but tight enough to say what she wanted to. Others' Child pried the jaws open, digging her fingers into Gray Daughter's gums.

"Heat a knife," Old Tidepool said. He ignored the dogs. "And get some men to hold him down."

Others' Child's fear snapped like a branch breaking, or ice on a river, as if Old Tidepool had put the hot knife in it. What had to be, had to be. He would die otherwise. She could see that. She turned to Sea Otter and said calmly, the way she would have asked him for help to carry something heavy, "Have Little Brother tie the dogs up. They will fight us."

Little Brother stared at Night Hawk and put his thumb in his mouth. (He had never sucked his thumb before, Sea Otter thought, irritated.) The child put an arm around each dog, hugging them to him. Thief licked his face. Gray Daughter lifted her lips enough to show her teeth and growled at Sea Otter.

"Take them away from here," Sea Otter said. He found the shreds of the dogs' harness and gave it to Brother.

Little Brother wrestled them into it and looped a piece of rope through. He tugged on it. "We have to go somewhere," he said, pulling them along. He headed into the pine trees, looking for a sturdy one, giving the task all his concentration so he wouldn't have to think of what they were going to do to Father. Behind him the Channel Clan women shook their heads in mild disapproval. It couldn't be right for those coyotes to follow a child like that. He might get who knew what kind of ideas.

Condor Dancer and Bear Paws came to hold Night Hawk down. Bear Paws was short and broad with hands as big as his feet. He knelt across Night Hawk and put his hands on Night Hawk's shoulders. "You don't want to move now," he said. Night Hawk's eyes were still closed, but Others' Child could see the pulse racing in his throat. She thought he was trying not to wake up.

She brought Old Tidepool the obsidian knife that she had heated in the cook fire, and he took Night Hawk's hand and showed Others' Child and Blue Butterfly how to hold it flat with the fingers splayed out. Others' Child felt Night Hawk's fingers try to close around hers, and she forced them open again.

Old Tidepool cut the rotting flesh out while Bear Paws sat on Night Hawk's chest and Condor Dancer leaned his whole weight on Night Hawk's arm to hold it down. Night Hawk writhed and twisted; he screamed, his lips pulled back from his teeth.

In the trees, Little Brother smacked Thief on the nose with a stick to make him stop trying to bite through the rope. He had to take his fingers out of his ears to do it, and the scream came in when he did. Little Brother felt sick to his stomach, but he stood over Thief with the stick and called him curse words that he had learned from older boys to shut the sound out.

Old Tidepool handed Others' Child the knife. "Heat it again."

She took it to the fire and held the blade in the flame, watching the blood and pus and shreds of skin shrivel and hiss, and then blacken. Her arms were shaking, and her knees felt as if there were water inside them. Bear Paws was still holding Night Hawk down, but he wasn't struggling now. His head was thrown back, and his breathing rattled in his chest. The knife quivered in her hand. Smoke lifted off the blade, a quick dark sibilance like Death going out of it into the air.

Others' Child took the knife back to Old Tidepool and spread Night Hawk's fingers again so that Old Tidepool could lay the blade against the raw skin and hold it there. Night Hawk thrashed, screaming, while the smoke rose from his hand.

When he was through, Old Tidepool stepped back and signaled them to let go. He wiped his forehead with the back of his hand and gave the knife to Condor Dancer. "Hoo, that was hard," he said. "Something was fighting me. Something was living in that hand."

Blue Butterfly knelt beside Night Hawk. She looked over her shoulder at Others' Child. "I will sit with him," she said pointedly.

At evening Night Hawk woke to find himself staring at stars through the leafy roof of a brush hut. The dogs were at his feet, growling at anyone who passed. There had been a woman there earlier, he thought. He had had a vague sense of someone female. Not Others' Child. She had held his hand while they burned it, but she was gone now. He struggled up onto his elbows, holding the hand carefully. Someone had tied a basket over it, probably to keep the dogs from licking it. A deerskin was spread over him, and there was one under him, and they were both drenched with his sweat. He wondered how long he had been there. It was dark outside, with the moon like a thin thorn pinned above the hills, but it could have been days.

Something rustled outside the hut, and a figure slipped through the door. "Ssshhh," it said.

Night Hawk swallowed. "New Husband won't like this." His mouth was dry, and it was hard to talk.

"Yah, I have been tending you since you came here," Others' Child said. The shell beads in her hair rattled. "It was only yesterday my mother-in-law decided I should not." She put a bowl of broth down on the ground beside him and dipped a bone spoon in it. "My husband killed a deer," she said. "I made them give me some of the liver."

"New Husband won't like that, either," Night Hawk said. He opened his mouth as she spooned broth up to his face. It was hot and flavored with sage. He slurped it greedily out of the spoon.

Others' Child didn't answer him.

"Does my son like this New Husband?" Night Hawk thought of Sea Otter, who had been a friend once, as someone else entirely, not the man who now slept with Others' Child.

"He is very kind to Little Brother."

Night Hawk closed his eyes. "I want to take him with me," he said without opening them.

"Where?" Others' Child was indignant.

"Wherever I go."

"You can't go. You are sick."

He opened his eyes. "You could come."

Others' Child dipped more broth. "I can't," she said, but she had known when she saw Death leaving the knife that this was going to happen.

Night Hawk put his good hand on her arm. He felt the skin twitch, and she sucked her breath in hard. He touched his fingers to her throat and felt the pulse under the skin. There was gray in her hair now, he saw. It didn't really matter. Always the body he saw was over-laid with the body he had first seen, young, the color of the russet mountains of home. His hand slid down her throat to her breast.

"I will do that," Blue Butterfly said briskly. She ducked through the door and took the spoon from Others' Child's hand.

Sea Otter watched his wife walking back from Night Hawk's hut. Since the trader had come back, when Sea Otter put his arms around her in bed at night, she was somewhere else. Foot-on-trail, maybe, wandering through the night with *him*, out among the stars. Maybe all women were crazy. Maybe Sea Otter shouldn't have asked the gods for a woman who was different. He felt bewildered, as if his wife had turned suddenly to something other than human, like the Deer Wife in the story. Different had proved dangerous before now.

She came to the door of their willow-pole house, newly built yesterday, and he said to her, "You won't be happy anywhere if you don't know who you are," to see what she would do.

She didn't spin into smoke, or grow a new coat of tawny fur over her rufous skin. She only went past without speaking to him and bent over Little Brother, sleeping by the fire. She sat down and put a hand on his head and stayed there.

Sea Otter stood up. It was beneath his dignity to talk to a woman who wouldn't talk to him. He thought she wouldn't talk to the trader, either, which didn't make him feel any better. He left his new willow-pole house and went to Old Tidepool's.

"The trader is better," Sea Otter said to Old Tidepool. "Now my wife is still going to his house."

"That is true," Old Tidepool said, as if Sea Otter had somehow doubted it.

"I want to know why this is," Sea Otter said, exasperated.

Old Tidepool closed his eyes. When he opened them, he said, "This story is not over. Before dawn I can still feel it in the air. Perhaps someone must ask for a vision to show us the end of it."

"That is an excellent idea," Sea Otter said. "Let the trader have a vision."

Old Tidepool cocked an eye at him. "The trader is not of us."

"That is no reason why a vision cannot come to him," Sea Otter said with satisfaction. Sea Otter had had his vision when he became a man. It was a very holy experience, but it was not something that most people were eager to do twice. "He told me that the shaman of the Knifenose Fish Clan said he had broken a taboo," he added cagily. "When he had the fever and was raving, he told me this. That shaman sent him here to find out what the taboo is. Maybe we should be generous and give him a vision to find out how he has offended the spirits.''

"But *you* are the one who wants to know why your wife still looks at him.''

"Maybe he wants to know, too,'' Sea Otter said. "Maybe that is part of the taboo. Also,'' he added, "my father will be the next chieftain. Sand Owl is dead, and Hawk Feet's hands are twisted; for him to be chieftain would be bad luck. So it is not proper that my wife be looking at other men, particularly not at that one. If he has a vision, he will see this.''

"He may see other things, too,'' Old Tidepool said. Sea Otter looked argumentative. Sea Otter was always sure that things would turn out the way he wanted them to. "I will think about it,'' Old Tidepool said. He closed his eyes and kept them that way until Sea Otter went away.

While they were closed, he thought. Old Tidepool had already let himself be caught up in the story of war. He did not want to make the same mistake again. But it was true that he could smell change in the thin light before the sun came up. Something coming, something that the trader's woman had brought, something that she had to leave here before he took her away again, if he was going to. The birds talked to him about it in the dusty leaves of the live oaks. When he went to the coast, the seagulls screamed it back and forth above the breakers. Even Bat had come out in the daytime to tell him.

"What?'' Old Tidepool had asked. "What?''

"Eeeeee,'' said Bat.

It was hard to tell who was supposed to have the vision. Datura brought strange dreams, colored with sharp sound, and sometimes madness. It was even possible to die of it, if you took too much or your body did not open its house to the datura. But if it did, the spirits might speak to you out of it, radiant faces in the air. They came from the sun, or sometimes the dark ground at your feet, wild hair billowing like the sea, to tell you secrets.

Old Tidepool had become a shaman when he had seen

his first vision, and he had had many since. But most men, unwilling to set themselves adrift again on its furious current, only took datura once. Would Sea Otter be willing to do it again, to find out his wife's fate?

And what of the trader? Might the story actually be his and not the woman's at all? Old Tidepool was willing to contemplate that idea, because he was, after all, a man. But he knew it wasn't true. The trader might have his own story, but it was the woman's that Old Tidepool heard the bat telling the magpie at dawn. It was the woman who had the picture magic, who had been sent here to teach Old Tidepool to make the likeness of Knifenose Fish in the dirt. Old Tidepool frowned. When he made Knifenose Fish, he still looked like Rattlesnake with flippers. That was what old Laurel Tree had said, snorting and guffawing as she passed by. Old Tidepool decided not to think about Laurel Tree, who had been impertinent ever since she was a girl.

Of course it might be the shaman who was supposed to have the vision, but Old Tidepool didn't think so. He had seen the misty outlines of it caught in the trees, and it was waiting for someone else. Old Tidepool sat back in his new willow-pole house and waited for the trader to come to him.

Night Hawk slept again after Blue Butterfly fed him, and then woke and slept again, and woke and slept. Others' Child didn't come back, but he could see her across the communal cook pit, watching him.

Little Brother brought him a piece of deer bone that he had found in the woods. It was white and had been eaten clean by ants. "I want you to make me a flute." He balanced it carefully on Night Hawk's knees so the music wouldn't run out. Little Brother knew there was music in it because he had heard it when he put his ear to the bone.

"When my hand heals." Night Hawk smiled at his son. He would bet New Husband couldn't make as good a flute. To make a flute you had to know how the deer bone would sing before you drilled it. Others' Child's brother, Mocking Bird, had taught him that. "What is your mother doing?" he asked Brother.

"Arguing with New Father." Brother sat down beside Night Hawk. "And with Grandfather and Grandmother. About you. Also, Thief came in the house and ate a rabbit."

"And what do they say about me?"

"They said you are dangerous. That the fire wanted you and didn't get you and that maybe it will come back. Mother said they were stupid."

Night Hawk thought that the fire he could feel on his skin lately wasn't the one that had burned the Channel Clan's hunting runs. It had a fiercer light. He set the deer bone aside and stood up, lifting himself carefully on his good hand. He brushed Little Brother's head with the back of his healing one. "I will make you a flute soon. Now I have to talk with someone."

Night Hawk walked across the open circle between the houses, feeling the Channel Clan's eyes on him. The village still made him feel that the houses were closing in on him, that he should take Others' Child and Brother and run. Laurel Tree gave him a toothless smile as he passed, and her fat old husband lifted his hand in greeting. Not everyone thought he was dangerous. Of course, Fat Old Husband hardly moved anyhow these days. He had burned his foot and taken that as his message to relax.

Old Tidepool was waiting for him when Night Hawk came to his house. The shaman crooked a finger to beckon him inside. "Peace be with the house," Night Hawk said. It already smelled medicinal, thick with the laurel leaves and sage that hung in the roof. Old Tidepool's eyes looked like shiny bugs in the smoke from his fire, strange luminous dragonflies hovering, peering at him intently, maybe to see if he was edible.

"The shaman of the Knifenose Fish Clan says that I have broken a taboo," Night Hawk said.

"Very likely." The beady eyes rose up and down. "You have been among many magical things in your travels. Magic may rub off on a person, like pollen."

"I want to know what the taboo is," Night Hawk said.

"What did Catches Crows tell you?"

"She said the dogs might know."

"And what did they tell you?"

"They brought me here. And when I tried to turn back, my hand got worse. Also, I have seen Coyote, who came to me as a woman."

Old Tidepool's hovering eyes widened. "Are you sure?"

"Positive," Night Hawk said shortly.

Old Tidepool scratched his nose. He had a passing acquaintance with Coyote and knew that Coyote was not above jokes. They often left their victim missing teeth or other vital parts, however.

"I don't know what Coyote wants with me, and I don't know what taboo I have broken," Night Hawk said. "And she kept looking like my wife."

"Then no doubt your taboo has something to do with this woman who seems to be married to two men at once," Old Tidepool said. That was a situation of which only Coyote would approve.

"I didn't make her do it, so what can I do about that?" Night Hawk demanded. "She isn't married to me now."

"That is the trouble. She thinks she is. You are like a tar pit. She had one foot in you, and then she tried to pull away and put the other foot in someone else's house. It is a very irregular situation and may be disturbing the Universe. I wish the two of you would settle down."

"Men have two wives," Night Hawk said because he was feeling argumentative. But he didn't like sharing his with another man.

"Men, not women," Old Tidepool said with authority. "And only if they are very important, such as chieftains or shamans. It is not proper or even lucky for a woman to have two husbands. This is why Sea Otter is being made crazy, and it will not do for the chieftain's son to be crazy, so she must decide. Unless you are going to go away?''

"No," Night Hawk said, deciding that he didn't care if Sea Otter was crazy or the village was closing in on him.

"Then a decision must be made." Old Tidepool held up one finger to convey the import of this. "The woman is not capable of making the decision, and therefore it is up to the men, which is the proper way of making a decision, anyway. But it would not be right for Condor Dancer to make it, even though he will be the chieftain."

"No," Night Hawk conceded. Not unless Condor Dancer was tired of having his son married to Others' Child.

"Perhaps you will drink sacred datura and a vision will come to one of you," Old Tidepool said, as if he had just thought of that.

Night Hawk's heart thudded uncomfortably behind his ribs. He felt as if he were standing on the edge of a precipice, face to the long drop. He thought he could feel his fingers close around the magic bowl, and he shivered. Occasionally datura gave people visions that they didn't come back from. Old Tidepool's eyes grew lighter and his ears longer. Night Hawk caught a whiff of scent that wasn't mice and seaweed.

"Do it," something said above his head, a tiny bat voice flittering just beneath the roof of the house. Old Tidepool stood up and snapped at it, and it vanished in a quick flurry like a blown leaf, skittering on the wind. "Datura visions are *my* business." The irritated voice came from Old Tidepool's gray throat.

Night Hawk scooted backwards on the mats, away from him. He could see Others' Child's face in the smoke now, with Little Brother behind her, and the dead babies like mist behind him. The thin voice of Bat chittered at him just outside the door, while inside, Coyote's eyes burned through the smoke, boring holes in his skin. The dead babies began to talk to him, too, crying in Bat's voice. Night Hawk had never had visions, but he could see without datura what his life would be like if he stayed foot-on-trail any longer without the other half of himself. He would be mist in the air like those babies.

"All right," he said. "I will do it." He leaned forward, looking over the precipice, watching himself fall into datura. "All right."

The yellow eyes faded. Old Tidepool wore his own ears, and he shook his bird's nest of hair and spat on the floor. "Hoo," he said. "I didn't like that. He takes up too much room."

XV

The Wind Between the Stars

Sea Otter came to the journey hut that the Channel Clan had built for Night Hawk. It was not a proper house because everyone hoped he was going to go away.

"Old Tidepool says that you are going to have a vision," Sea Otter said.

Night Hawk smiled. The scar that lifted his left eyebrow gave the smile an unsettling tilt. "*We* are going to have a vision. You will teach me."

"I am not the one who does not know where to go."

"You are the one who is married to my wife."

Sea Otter thought. It was not right to be dishonorable just because you would like someone to drink poison and die. "This is because the woman can't decide," he said.

Night Hawk leaned forward. "Has she said so?"

"No. But I can tell," Sea Otter said angrily. "Her eyes see things that I did not put there. If the vision spirits tell us that she should stay with me, will you leave?"

"If the vision spirits tell us that she should go with me, will you make her?"

How did you make a woman like Others' Child do anything? They looked at each other for a long time, Sea Otter standing because he had not been asked to sit, Night Hawk sitting because he refused to get up. Sea Otter shrugged. "I will try," he said. "If the spirits say it is so, then she may not stay here. My father will order that."

"Then if the spirits say I am to leave, I will leave." Night Hawk touched his healing hand with one finger. How did you know what the spirits might say? Could you find out how to pray to them?

"Sea Otter and your old husband are going to drink datura," Laurel Tree said. She plumped herself down beside Others' Child and looked at the picture Others' Child was making for the rabbit hunters.

"What?" Others' Child stopped with her drawing stick in the air over Rabbit's hindquarters.

"Old Tidepool told them that the vision spirits might say who you should be married to, so they are going to drink datura and find out."

Others' Child's jaw hung open until she snapped it shut. Old Laurel Tree smiled and nodded, fingers laced over her stomach. She studied Others' Child's rabbit. The head and ears seemed to leap from the dirt, although she thought the ears were too short. Better not to say that. The hindquarters must only be buried beneath the surface, waiting to come out. "Is it the picture that makes him come when you hunt him?" Laurel Tree asked.

"Sometimes." Others' Child put down the drawing stick.

"There are no words to say? I thought there would be a spell."

"The picture is the spell," Others' Child said, but she left that one unfinished, half a spell with no back end.

Laurel Tree watched her stamping across the village toward the trader's journey hut. There was no point in getting upset with men, Laurel Tree thought. They were always like that. Useless to expect them to ask you what *you* wanted. She returned her attention to the rabbit. Carefully she picked up the drawing stick, as if it might be alive. Someone had said it was really a frozen snake, but Laurel Tree saw that it was only a stick.

She touched it to the soft ground where Others' Child had been working. It made a smooth line. Slowly Laurel Tree drew the rabbit's back half, her tongue in her teeth. It had a round haunch and strong legs ready to leap. She gave it a flag of a tail and sat back and inspected the work. She made the ears a little longer.

Others' Child put her face up to Night Hawk's. She hadn't scratched on the post outside the journey hut or asked if she could come in, she had just come. Now she crouched on the floor, hands braced in front of her, and glared at him. "Who gave you the right to drink datura and talk to spirits about me?"

"Keep your temper, Porcupine," Night Hawk said. "Who has a better right?"

The shell beads in her hair quivered, and the pink circles of shell that hung from her ears jiggled as she clenched her jaw. "This is for me to decide. If it takes datura to do so, then *I* will drink it. And who said I couldn't decide?"

"New Husband. He should know."

Others' Child looked down. Her expression grew less fierce. "Maybe so."

"You have put holes in your ears," Night Hawk said, looking at them. "They are interesting, but maybe all your good sense has run out through them. You can't drink datura."

Others' Child snapped her head up to him, eyeball to eyeball. "Ha! That is all you know. Shaman women drink datura." Was she actually going to do that? The idea had come to her in a furious surge as soon as she heard about Night Hawk and Sea Otter making her decisions for her. Now it beckoned, like a little voice in her ear, though she knew at the same time she was as afraid of it as she was of crossing the desert again.

"You aren't a shaman woman," Night Hawk said. "But I don't care if you drink datura." He thought it would take more than datura to kill Others' Child. Maybe they would see each other in the dream. "Condor Dancer won't let you, though."

Condor Dancer disapproved of the idea most thoroughly. Women who drank datura were chancy after that, flighty and unstable and prone to strange urges. Such behavior was all very well in a shaman, but you didn't want it in your son's wife.

Sea Otter told Others' Child she was forbidden to do it; datura was business for men.

Others' Child, stubborn, stuck her lip out. "You told everyone that I don't know what I want. So why do you think men can tell me?" She crawled out the door.

"Where are you going?"

"To talk with Old Tidepool." She skirted around the side of their house toward the shaman's and stopped short, puzzled. Someone had finished her rabbit.

"Old Tidepool will tell you the same thing I have told you," Sea Otter said, following her.

"We will see." Others' Child abandoned the rabbit, marching, *thump, thump*, to the shaman's house. Her bare feet made round prints in the dust when she slammed her heels down.

The rest of the Channel Clan followed her. They had heard about Sea Otter and the trader taking datura together to see who would get Sea Otter's wife. If the wife did it, too, it would be more interesting yet, but some of them didn't approve.

"She will be like Wander," old Seagull said to Laurel Tree. They both remembered Wander, a strange, moony girl who was the chieftain's daughter of the Abalone Clan and had married a Channel man. She was said to have drunk datura in her youth, and not been right in the head since. Finally she had fallen off the seal rocks.

"An ordinary woman cannot take datura," Fisher Skunk said. He had had his fill of women who considered themselves not to be ordinary. Old Tidepool would tell this one to behave.

Laurel Tree thought about Fat Old Husband as she pattered after Seagull and Fisher Skunk. He wasn't as beautiful as Sea Otter or as dangerous-looking as Night Hawk (and Laurel Tree knew what an attractant danger was in a man, just like a fine set of feathers on a turkey cock), but he didn't tell her what to do like Fisher Skunk, except a little when the other men were watching, and he wasn't prideful the way that Sand Owl had been. He had been happy to play pat-a-cake with their children and help her tan the skins of the animals he caught. Now he sat in the sun and played shells with Old Seal Barking, Tern's husband. It must be uncomfortable to have two men want you. Laurel Tree was glad it had never happened to her. How would you make up your mind?

They all stopped in front of Old Tidepool's house, and Others' Child went inside. It was no good telling them to go away; she knew they wouldn't. She could hear them shuffling their feet and breathing outside.

Old Tidepool nodded at Others' Child through the dried things that hung from his ceiling. He was burning sage leaves in his fire. Now that she was here, she couldn't think what to say to him and stood biting her lip. "I don't know what I want," she blurted.

"You want the end of the story, but the story is you and you are still being told."

"My husbands think they can see the end," she said. "Without me."

"Ah." Old Tidepool chuckled. "That is insulting."

"They want to drink datura and tell me what they have seen on the journey. I do not entirely believe them, so I wish to go along."

"And see for yourself? How do you know you will take the same journey?"

"I will take *my* journey. And they will not be able to tell me about it as if I had not been there."

"And what does the chieftain say about this?"

"He says not to."

Old Tidepool pursed his lips. He could hear the people shifting their feet outside. They all moved closer when he appeared in the doorway, their faces full of opinions. Condor Dancer stood in the front, beside Sea Otter.

"With respect," Old Tidepool said to Condor Dancer, "this woman has caused a great deal of trouble."

"Indeed."

Everyone nodded and murmured their agreement, and Sea Otter looked abashed.

"Therefore she is very powerful. Therefore she can wrestle with the vision spirits and not die. Therefore she should drink sacred datura and see them, too. I say this because I see things that the chieftain cannot," he added to mollify Condor Dancer. *And because I want to see the end of the story.*

It took much preparation to get ready to drink datura. You did not just grind up datura root, or eat its knife-edged leaves or moon-white flowers. That was how people went mad and fell off the seal rocks, Old Tidepool said. Magic was magic, and was treated with respect. The root was soaked in hot water, and then the water was drunk, in a sacred place. Old Tidepool decided that their sacred place would be the cave that was hidden in the cliffs above the pool.

"It is very dark in there," Night Hawk said. He had seen it once before, hunting birds' eggs. It had a long narrow passage like the cave where he had hidden from the fire, and a cold wind seemed to blow out of the earth through it. "It might make our wife afraid." Night Hawk looked at Sea Otter and thought he saw Sea Otter suppressing a grin, but the thought of another cave made Night Hawk's skin crawl.

"You do not need light to see visions," Old Tidepool said. "Now come."

They were elaborately dressed, Old Tidepool in a skirt of eagle feathers, Night Hawk and Sea Otter and Others' Child in their skins, painted with lines of red earth. Like the war canoe, Others' Child thought, uneasy about this voyage, now that she had launched herself on it. They

followed Old Tidepool along a trail that he seemed sure
of but which none of them could see. Behind them came
Condor Dancer with a tar-lined basket and Fisher Skunk
with a digging stick.

The datura grew on rocky slopes, tenacious as magic
and taller than their heads. Long-throated milky flowers
protruded from the branch forks like white hands. They
waited while Old Tidepool spoke to it, and then Fisher
Skunk set the digging stick against the roots and worked
it into the dry ground. The datura rustled, flowers brushing against his hair. Fisher Skunk dug faster, sweating,
while the flowers caressed him. When the root was
loose, he grasped the stem with both hands and pulled,
leaning backwards. The datura held on to the ground
with knotted fingers. Fisher Skunk pulled harder. The
root let go, and he staggered backwards, flower hands
pushing against his chest. He sat down hard in the
stones.

Old Tidepool took a cutting knife and sliced the root
away, and they left the cut stem on the ground. Others'
Child would not have been surprised to see the other
plants bend toward it, lily hands outstretched. She eyed
the root with respect as Old Tidepool put it in his pouch.

They continued along a circuitous route of Old Tidepool's devising and came out on a ledge above the cave.
Others' Child could see the village and its inhabitants
below her. If she were Hawk, she could swoop down
and carry them off. Old Tidepool produced a ladder of
knotted rope, and they let themselves down on it, swaying above the village until Others' Child felt like ripe
fruit that the wind might take. When she put her feet
down on solid stone, she crouched at the cave mouth,
breathing hard.

Fisher Skunk and Condor Dancer took a slow-burner
and lit torches that they set in piles of stone at the entrance. Beyond their light, the passageway was dark and
mysterious, like crawling to the center of the earth. Others' Child felt Sea Otter ahead of her and Night Hawk
behind. It gave her a certain satisfaction to smell that
they were afraid, too. The scent was acrid on their skin.

At the end of the passage, the cave widened until five people could just sit. There was almost no light left, just the faintest flicker of red on the walls, moving like the datura flowers when the wind danced outside the cave. Condor Dancer and Fisher Skunk sat down to watch them while Old Tidepool boiled water with a fire he had lit from the torches. Others' Child knew he would soak the root in the hot water, but for some reason they were forbidden to watch him. Making datura drink was sacred. No one could watch. She looked at Night Hawk. She could barely see his hawk-faced profile staring at the cave walls. She willed him to look at her, but he wouldn't. Neither would Sea Otter, she saw. She was the object of their dispute and still an interloper here. Fisher Skunk and Condor Dancer regarded her with stolid disapproval. Only Old Tidepool acknowledged her existence.

The shaman came back with the basket between his hands, three shell bowls floating in it. He spoke to the spirits who might be there, riding in the shells like people in a canoe, waiting to be swallowed, before he dipped the bowls full.

Night Hawk felt the bitter liquid slide past his tongue as if a snake had got in his mouth somehow. He felt it settle in his belly, coiled and waiting.

Sea Otter's eyes widened. Something no one else could see was talking to him. It had gold snakes for hair and eyes that had been stars once. He could still see Night Hawk beside him. The trader's black shadow glowed green, but Sea Otter didn't want to kill him anymore. Datura sometimes made men reasonable, the way death did. He could feel it making him so, sucking the wicked parts away. Sea Otter watched them go with a feeling of relief, and saw that now he could lift himself off the ground, while the bad parts went winging out through the narrow passage, careening in a black flutter of wings.

There were monsters flapping in the air. Night Hawk

saw them fluttering around his head. He began to run
from them, and they chased him.

Others' Child felt the ground move under her as if the
Great Cat was waking and shifting the rocks that were
its bones. She clung to its flanks, and the wind rushed
by her. Voices chattered in her ear. She heard Great
Condor's lugubrious tones, and the implacable voice of
Grandmother Spider. Knifenose Fish and Octopus spoke
in bubbly words. Even the cat hissed a message to her.
"You cannot stay," they all said, and she thrashed her
heels against the cat's sides and beat its shoulders with
her fists.

"Where is Coyote?" she asked them all. This was his
doing. But none of them spoke of Coyote.

The cat leaped high, and Others' Child could see a
long way away, to the desert where Baby Daughter was
buried. A basket cactus grew out of the grave, covered
in sun-colored flowers, and Baby Daughter played
among them with a horned lizard in her hand. Others'
Child reached for her, and she smiled and shook her
head.

Others' Child clung tightly to the cat's back as it
bunched its muscles under her legs. It leaped across the
sky, touching the moon with its dusty paws and leaving
its prints.

Then Others' Child was alone in the sky, shivering
among the stars, abandoned, wailing for Baby Daughter
to come back, for Night Hawk, for Sea Otter, for the
cat. A dark cyclone wind began to blow, sweeping the
sky clean. It sucked every other thing into its mouth,
and the stars winked out. There was nothing in the Universe but Others' Child and the black wind.

It roared like the pounding of the sea, like the wildfire
in the hills. Its voice was blackness and terror, and anything might fall into it. Others' Child shivered, staring
down that mouth, and knew where the voice of Coyote
lived.

The yellow-gray skin he put on, the tricks he played
on humans, the clown, the thief, all were disguises so

that human people might see him without running mad. Here, in the darkness, she looked into the true face of Coyote.

Others' Child braced herself against the force that sucked her toward his mouth. Now that she had seen him, that was the only way for her to be, braced between ignorance and madness, pulled both ways always.

"That is what makes art," a more familiar voice said in her ear, but she knew that the true words had come from the heart of the cyclone wind.

Night Hawk was running from the winged things. Sea Otter was trying to beat them away from him, but they kept coming out of Sea Otter's mouth anyway.

"Don't help me!" Night Hawk gasped. He saw Thief and Gray Daughter waiting for him. When he got close, he saw that it was only their skins, and he put Thief's on. The winged things swirled around him in a cloud, pulling at the other skin. It leaped up suddenly, teeth bared, and the wings retreated, shrieking. He saw them coalesce into a green-black cloud and vanish. Others' Child's eyes looked at him out of Gray Daughter's skin. Her fur trailed lights. Then the skins were empty again, and she was gone.

The winged things came back and beat around his head, and he ran after her.

Others' Child woke with her face on the cool damp stone of the cave floor, with Night Hawk's arm flung across her legs. Bursts of light still came and went in front of her eyes. She struggled up and saw Old Tidepool watching her by torchlight. The cave was smoky with it.

"Did you see the end of the story?" he asked her. His eyes glowed.

"It was too dark," Others' Child said. She didn't want to tell him.

Night Hawk woke and looked wildly around him. He pulled his hands away from Others' Child's legs, embarrassed. "Something was chasing me," he mumbled.

Sea Otter was sitting cross-legged, his face bent to his knees. He lifted his head. "Are you alive, brother?"

Night Hawk licked his lips. He wondered if they had had the same dream. He thought they had. "Barely," he whispered.

"What do the vision spirits say?" Condor Dancer demanded.

"We don't know," Sea Otter said. He put a hand out toward Night Hawk. It flopped to the ground, weighted like stone. "But we are brothers."

"Tchah!" Condor Dancer said. "That is no answer."

"Some things an ordinary man cannot have," Sea Otter said carefully. He eyed Others' Child with respect and a certain wariness.

Others' Child stood up on watery knees and waited a moment to be sure they weren't going to give way. "I will tell you what they have said to me," she told Old Tidepool. "They have said that I will have no more children and therefore I must take the one I have back to his father's people to be raised by them. They have said that I may not stay here. That I have brought what I was intended to, and now I must go. So I must go with this man, because they gave him to me." Night Hawk didn't say anything. She could feel him watching her.

"What were you supposed to bring us?" Condor Dancer demanded.

"I don't know," Others' Child said. She rubbed her head. She knew she was not afraid of the desert anymore. She knew she would leave with Night Hawk because they were two halves of the same thing. But she didn't know what.

"I will make something for you instead," she said, hoping that would do. "Give me your knife, Uncle."

Old Tidepool handed it to her, and she walked unsteadily to the far wall of the cave and began digging out the soft sandstone with the tip. Old Tidepool watched with interest as Others' Child showed them Coyote dancing among the stars. She couldn't make him as she had truly seen him—they did not want to know him that way—so instead she ringed him with concentric circles of light, which was how datura made you see things.

Others' Child saw that Sea Otter had come up to her elbow and was watching her. She looked at him apologetically. "I was wrong," she said. "I thought I could belong."

"I was wrong," he said. "I thought I wanted a woman who was different."

Others' Child smiled. She dug at the soft sandstone again until Sea Otter stood there on the wall, in front of the Channel Clan's round houses, his hands full of fish. "See," she said. "There you are. Where you belong."

Sea Otter stared at his picture. He would catch many fish now, there was no doubt about it. He would be First Fisherman when his father was chieftain, and he would live forever in this cave.

That was immortality, Others' Child thought, seeing that he was pleased. She felt less wicked now that she had given him that. Now they had to take Little Brother back to the Kindred to learn from the Three Old Men before it was too late and he was not Kindred anymore. She and Night Hawk could stay half the year among the Kindred, and trade the other half. Night Hawk would agree to that now, she could see it in his face. When Brother was grown and didn't need her, maybe they would even come back to the Endless Water and see what it was that Coyote told her she had brought them.

She took Night Hawk's hand and felt his fingers dig into hers. She led him through the narrow passage to the front of the cave and stood blinking in the morning sun.

"It will all be different when you come back," Sea Otter said, stretching. "I can see that now. So I will stay here and watch it change. That will be good for me."

"Now is the time to go," Old Tidepool said. "Before anyone changes his mind."

Others' Child nodded. She climbed down the rocks into the village and went to Sea Otter's house for her things. She put on a hide skirt and an otter-skin cape that she thought it would be all right to keep. Night Hawk and Little Brother and the dogs were waiting for her when she came out. They started along the trail that was beginning to be worn between the White Rock camp and the coast. From there, they could go inland again, across the desert that didn't frighten Others' Child anymore, where Baby Daughter was playing with the cactus bloom.

Behind them the village of the Channel Clan murmured in the pine trees, thin voices rising and falling. The men came back from the rabbit drive, shouting their prowess to the women, dancing their good fortune on the ground. The rabbits drawn in mud on stones at the head of the hunting trail danced, too.

When they got to Laurel Tree's house, they stopped, and Bear Paws knelt and gave three fat rabbits to Laurel Tree, while Fat Old Husband watched happily.

Tomorrow, Laurel Tree thought, she would draw a deer.

Epilogue

*Others' Child and Night Hawk are a spark over the fire.
The grandmother finishes her tea and her story. "So the
People Who Lived at the Coast began to make great art,
on stones and in their secret caves, and they do so to
this day, and it is all because a woman of our fore-
mothers went and taught it to them."*

*"I have met a trader from the coast," a young man
says. "And he told me that it was they who taught us."*

*The grandmother smiles. "They are ignorant. Every-
one knows that all art began with the People." And if
the Grandmothers of the coast know another story, well,
there are many truths. Every people has their own.*

*"What happened to them after that?" a girl child
asks her. "The trader and his woman. Is their story
over?"*

*"Stories are never over. That is what Coyote taught
the woman. Only pieces of stories. Their piece is over,
but who they are is not over, and never will be."*

"Who are they?"

306

"*They are the ones who must be thrown out of a place before they are appreciated.*" *She bends her gaze on the young man who knows the trader from the coast.* "*Likely someone here may have the same problem,*" *she adds, and the rest guffaw.*

"*But who are they?*"

"*Look outside.*"

The girl child goes to the window and peers into the swirling snow. She leans way out, with her anxious mother holding on to her jacket. In a recess in the cliffs below and to the right of them, she can see the figure cut into the rocks: a dancing person with a pack on his back and a flute to his lips. The woman who follows him you cannot see, but she is there. She is the hand who made him visible.

Author's Note

The humpbacked flute player is a figure you may see carved in the rocks all over the American Southwest. In some versions he is said to have a bag of songs on his back, in others a bag of corn. In many he is embarrassingly phallic. He is known as Kokopelli, and he is so old that no one knows where he came from. In nearly every guise he is associated with corn and fertility, although in some incarnations he looks startlingly like a beetle or a turtle. Every person has his own truth, as Grandmother said. Most people have several.

Stories change, are added to for dramatic purposes or to teach a certain lesson, or just because the storyteller likes it better that way. The story of Bear Woman and Owl Boy is my retelling of two myths that appear in *Tunkashila* by Gerald Hausman. The Rolling Head story appears in numerous works on California Indian mythology. Mine is very loosely derived from the version in *American Indian Myths and Legends*, edited by Richard Erdoes and Alfonso Ortiz. "Men and Women Try

Living Apart" is also a ubiquitous story. Mine is based on two versions, one in *American Indian Myths and Legends* and one in *American Indian Mythology* by Alice Marriott and Carol K. Rachlin. I owe each of them a debt of gratitude.

I also owe thanks to Pamela Lappies and Elizabeth Tinsley of Book Creations and to Ellen Edwards of Avon, as always. I would also like to acknowledge the indefatigable efforts of the staff at the Raleigh Court Branch of the Roanoke, Virginia, Public Library, Jay Stephens, Joan Kastner, and Gail Krieg, for ferreting out weird information and putting up with innumerable overdue books and interlibrary loan searches.

#1 BESTSELLING AUTHOR OF
THE THORN BIRDS

Enter ancient Rome
in her critically acclaimed
epic tales of tragedy and triumph

THE FIRST MAN IN ROME
71081-1/ $7.99 US/ $9.99 Can
"A truly astonishing work...Fiction at its best"
Time

THE GRASS CROWN
71082-X/ $6.99 US/ $7.99 Can
"Incomparable...engrossing...McCullough has
triumphed again"
Chicago Tribune

FORTUNE'S FAVORITES
71083-8/ $6.99 US/ $7.99 Can
"Epic...commanding...irresistible"
San Francisco Chronicle

SUE HARRISON

"A remarkable storyteller...
one wants to stand up and cheer."
Detroit Free Press

"Sue Harrison outdoes Jean Auel"
Milwaukee Journal

MOTHER EARTH FATHER SKY
71592-9/$6.50 US/ $8.50 Can

In a frozen time before history, in a harsh and beautiful
land near the top of the world, womanhood comes
cruelly and suddenly to beautiful, young Chagak.

MY SISTER THE MOON
71836-7/ $5.99 US/ $7.99 Can

An abused and unwanted daughter of the First Men
tribe, young Kiin knows that her destiny is tied to the
brave sons of orphaned Chagak and her chieftan mate
Kayugh—one to whom Kiin is promised, the other for
whom she yearns.

BROTHER WIND
72178-3/ $6.50 US/ $8.50 Can

HISTORY-MAKING BESTSELLERS FROM

"A master storyteller"
Los Angeles Times

THE THORN BIRDS
01817-9/ $6.99 US/ $8.99 Can

THE LADIES OF MISSALONGHI
70458-7/ $4.99 US only

A CREED FOR THE THIRD MILLENNIUM
70134-0/ $5.99 US/ $6.99 Can

AN INDECENT OBSESSION
60376-4/ $5.99 US/ $6.99 Can

TIM
71196-6/ $4.99 US/ $5.99 Can